My mind is shattered glass,

Here are the pieces.

E.M.

DAYWALKERS

Emilia Mondragón

ISBN: 979-8-218-60144-7

Cover Illustration & Design by Aude Ziegelmeyer

Second edition, 2024

To my 13-year-old self. You created these characters so they could hold you when you needed them most, and now we finally get to share them with the world.
And to the people who believed in me as well as those who never did. Without any of you, this story wouldn't have become what it did.
Enjoy this labor of love and rage.

Content Warning:

This story has mature content. If you are not comfortable with blood, violence, blasphemy, cursing, or mild spice, read at your own risk.

Daywalkers also had descriptions of panic attacks and nightmares as well as situations involving PTSD, child abuse, implied sexual assault, machismo, family trauma, and homophobia. Most are brief and not described on the page, but again, proceed with caution.

Finally, this story is a work of *fiction* and the characters within are not real. Use critical thinking and treat it as such.

Listen to the Daywalkers
playlist as you read along!

DAYWALKERS

Prologue

"I... I can't do it."[1]

Eric's trembling voice matched the shaking of his small hands as he gripped the dagger for dear life. The stone hilt bit into his skin, as did the frigid air of December. He kept his eyes on the forest floor, where once pristine white snow was now sullied by dirty footprints. His brown curls obscured his face as he desperately tried to hide the tears welling up in his hazel eyes. He kept his back turned, away from the task the commander was asking him to complete.

"What did you say?" Michael's deep voice rumbled.

Without looking up, Eric held the dagger out towards him. Despite the boy's efforts to hide his emotions, the quivering voice of the 11-year-old was hard to miss.

"T-take it back. I can't do it. I'm not ready."

Michael sighed and crouched to look him in the face. His steel-gray eyes shone like the blade in Eric's hands, yet they struck a different kind

---

[1] Goldwing - Billie Eilish

of fear in him. The jagged scars on the left side of his face accentuated the cold ferocity he was still unaccustomed to.

"Are you crying?" the hunter asked. He did not bellow or raise his voice, but the accusation was there.

Eric averted his gaze and wiped away a stray tear.

"No," he uttered.

"Hey, kid." Michael put a large hand on his shoulder, speaking in a more soothing, paternal tone. "I know this is scary. We've all been there. Hell, even I've been there."

"You have?"

"Yeah." The man nodded, a wolfish smirk pulling at his lips. "But I'll tell you right now, tears won't get you very far in life, E. Especially in the hunt. You know what does? Fighting. So, you better shed them all now because they're only going to get in your way in the long run. What's the most important rule about being a hunter?"

Eric sniffled, and in his small voice, he answered, "Don't make things personal."

"Exactly." Michael inclined his head to catch his eye. "E, we talked about this. This is part of the deal, remember? This is part of the job you said you would do. We all went through it, your mom went through it, and now so do you."

The boy shook his head. "Maybe if I train a little longer or wait until I'm older like the other kids—"

"But you're not like the other kids, E. You're special. You and your brother can do stuff they can't, which means you have the potential to do amazing things. You've got a wolf inside you, E. Just like me."

Eric perked up at that. "I do?"

"I know it. You can be better than all of them. You just need a little push in the right direction."

The commander stood upright and put both hands on Eric's shoulders. With little effort, he spun him around, and before the boy could protest, he was met face-to-face with the most nightmarish thing he had seen in his life. He bit back a gasp, creating a squeak at the back of his throat.

A few feet before them was a man—a vampire with sallow skin that was tinted purple. He bled from various gunshot wounds and was bound in silver chains. Duct tape wrapped the lower half of his face. Two hunters flanked him, keeping him on his knees, but all Eric could focus on were his glowing, pale blue eyes.

The boy stared at the vampire, petrified. His body trembled once more, and he could feel his heartbeat pounding hard in his rib cage.

"Come on, E. You know what to do. Make it quick, and it'll be over," Michael encouraged.

The commander gave Eric a small shove, and the little boy stumbled forward. He squeezed the hilt of the dagger as he tried mustering up the courage to use it, to do as Michael asked, and to make him proud. So, with a rush of bravery and his eyes forward, Eric stepped toward the monster before him.

I'm a wolf, he said to himself. I am a wolf.

He wanted to be. At that moment, he wanted to be like Michael and like his brother. He wanted to be special, to be better, and to prove everyone wrong. So, he convinced himself that maybe if he got it over with this one time, it wouldn't be so hard after all.

But sometimes "special" isn't enough.

Before Eric could close the distance, the vampire lunged. Even though he was bound and could do nothing to him, it was enough to send Eric floundering backward with a yell, falling to the ground. The dagger flew out of his hand, and he stared wide-eyed as the vampire's muffled laugh echoed through the trees.

Behind him, Michael let out a disgruntled sigh. "Damn it, kid."

"I-I'm sorry," Eric stuttered.

The commander walked past him and plucked the blade from the ground. Then, the boy watched in shock as the old hunter marched towards the vampire and, without an ounce of hesitation, sliced his throat before his very eyes. The monster choked and writhed as thick blood oozed out of the wound.

All the child could do was gape in horror.

"Finish him off," Michael ordered the others before looking at Eric and saying, "Better luck next time, kid."

†††

Eric winced as he adjusted the sling on his left arm. It was a reaction to the sharp pain at the crook of his neck and the sudden unwanted flashback. The physical ache brought him out of the memory, only to remind him of his unfortunate reality as he walked into the familiar Brasov cathedral known as The Black Church.

He hadn't been to Romania in years or the Transylvanian city he once called home. It had been nearly half a decade since he packed his bags and left The Colectiv behind. It was a choice he made for his own sanity, but recent events brought him back to this place of bitterness. The root of all his nightmares. A choice he *didn't* make, and yet...

He stopped in the middle of the red-carpeted aisle to admire the architecture of the Gothic structure. Eric had to admit that it was breathtaking. Churches and cathedrals of the same kind were often so intricately made that he couldn't help but admire them and bask in their beauty. Unfortunately, it did nothing for the huge discomfort he harbored over places like this. It was somewhat due to a feeling of not being allowed inside, and in part due to the weight of memories linked to them.

Eric and his twin brother James had been forced to go to church plenty of times in Romania, but even before then, they went with their mother, Anya. She took the church less seriously than The Colectiv or the Commander ever has, but she believed in a higher power, and when she died, her funeral was in a place much like this. And now that Eric was here, gazing up at the interior of The Black Church, he couldn't help but wonder if Anya had been here all those years before. He wondered if she had thought it was beautiful too when she lived in the city.

Did she find faith here, unlike her bastard son?

All at once, he was 11 years old again, in a room full of faces he didn't recognize, friends of hers he never saw again, all to mourn a life that never should have ended so soon. It made him well aware of a hole in his heart that never went away, even with time. He often contemplated if eternity would fix that or make it worse.

Why do bad things happen to good people?

Eric asked himself that question a lot, but he couldn't answer it honestly without getting theological. He couldn't even count the number of times people would tell him and James that "things happen for a reason" or that it was all part of "God's plan" that their mother suffered and died so young from a horrible disease. Some even called it karma. It only made it more unjust—it only made him *angrier*. And no matter how many religions he studied over his university career, no matter what he was taught growing up, he found no home or solace in any of them. His feelings always remained the same.

Who was God but a man with too much power to decide who lives and dies based not on true goodness...but on the plot of some fucked-up story in his head?

Eric bore his eyes into the giant cross on the wall.

Even now, life has managed to tear everything down and bring him back to the place he swore he would never return. Was that fate? Was that bad luck? Was that "God's plan"? Or was that just Eric's fault?

He had a hard time believing anything meant anything anymore.

"Keep staring like that, and you might burst into flames."

Eric sighed to himself, not remotely fazed by the sudden sound of his adoptive father's voice. He had already anticipated him and heard him lingering on the sides of the church. Although his heartbeat was steady, it was loud in a place like this. The young man's eyes flitted to him as he came out of the shadows.

The Silver Wolf of Romania.

Commander Mihail Andrei Iovaneau, a.k.a. Michael.

The tall man walked languidly, like a tiger coming out of the green. He took Eric in as he placed himself in front of the altar, facing his old student—his prodigal son.

The graying hair at the top of his head was slicked back, now matching his steel-gray eyes and contrasting with the black coat that fell to his thighs. Stubble peppered his jaw and there were noticeable wrinkles at the corners of his eyes. Even though he looked older, his presence was as powerful as ever, and the fire in his eyes seemed to intensify with the years. White jagged lines scarred the left side of his face—claw marks that stretched across from ear to chin.

Michael chuckled at Eric's unamused expression, his eyes sparkling. "Don't look so serious, E. It's just a joke."

Eric hummed, "Right. Ha."

The young man walked closer to the altar so that he was finally face-to-face with the commander. He made a questioning motion toward the entire building.

"Did we really have to meet here?"

"What can I say? I'm a religious man. Churches are private, and, you know, it keeps the vampires away."

"Not all of them," the boy said dryly. It was a fact, but also a mild, threatening joke.

The commander's grin was filled with challenging mirth. "You plan on doin' something, kid? Because you're out of practice, and I wouldn't recommend it with that injury of yours."

Eric rolled his eyes. "Don't worry, Mike. I'm not here for you."

"Then, pray tell, why *are* you here, E? This doesn't have anything to do with your incident, does it?"

"I mean, what else would it be about?"

He wasn't particularly eager to make small talk with Michael Iovaneau.

"You know you're lucky to be alive, right? I had to pull a lot of strings to get you here. You scared the shit out of Jimmy, which isn't easy to do. Hell, you even scared the shit out of *me*."

"I know," Eric rumbled.

The guilt rattled him still. The image of his brother looking haunted by his hospital bed was still fresh and hard to shake. After 22 years of living in blissful and arrogant oblivion, everything changed when Eric nearly lost his life *that night*. And it worsened his preexisting rage and self-hatred.

"Twice, E." Michael raised two fingers. "Twice I had to pull you from the grave. Once because of that injury, and the second time because of what you did."

Eric immediately became defensive. "Me? What the fuck did *I* do?"

"You know why. Getting personal with a vampire is a punishable offense under The Colectiv's laws. You, of all people, should know that."

The old hunter's charming demeanor fell for a moment, revealing the authoritative steel underneath. Eric glared at him, the final statement cutting deep.

"I didn't know they were vampires, alright?"

The commander clicked his tongue. "Bullshit," he sang, elongating the vowels.

Eric didn't let him continue.

"Believe me, or don't, I don't give a shit. But I left The Colectiv years ago anyway, which means your law technically doesn't apply to me."

"And that's precisely why you're still alive," Michael said with a nod. "That, and the fact that your brother is my sergeant, and he argues for you pretty well. Not to mention, both of you are the best The Colectiv has ever seen."

Eric snorted. "Gee, I wonder why that is."

Daywalkers or *Dhampir*, that's what Eric and James were, otherwise known as a half-vampire. They were a rarity, and some would say an abomination, but the twins were valuable. After all, what makes a better hunter—a better *soldier*—for an organization of monster hunters than the spawn of a *monster itself*? Two were worth more than their weight in gold.

Michael fixed him with a stern, paternal look. "You are more than just your blood, E. I've told you that time and time again."

"Sure. Amongst other things."

"You act as if I don't care about you, E," the commander hissed. "I've always treated you and your brother as if you were my blood. I'm the one who took you in, remember? If it wasn't for me, God knows what The Colectiv would have done to you."

I know.

Michael exhaled his tiredness the same as any exasperated parent would.

"*Why are you here?*" he repeated. "As you said, you left. You made it pretty clear you never wanted to come back. I'm surprised you haven't run back to America already. So... why did *you* specifically request to see *me?*"

Eric took a pause and let his gaze sweep across the church to gather his words.

As a child, he used to dream about what he wanted his life to be like, and he'd pray to God, asking him why things didn't turn out better. But he didn't do either of those things anymore. It was useless because now he knew his options were always going to be death or "*this.*" Death or running. Death or loneliness. Death or fighting. Death or killing. Death or betrayal. Death or grief.

Now, it was death...or *rage.*

He at last locked eyes with the commander, who was expectantly watching him. Never in a million years would he have asked to see Michael privately, but today was different.

In a level tone that defied his burning feelings underneath, Eric said, "I want revenge."

A bewildered grin spread across Michael's face. "Revenge?"

"Yeah," Eric confirmed. "I wanna get back at the asshole who did this to me."

He lifted his injured arm slightly, his mind going to the healing injury. As if the memories weren't enough, every day the skin around his scar pulled with every movement, no matter how careful he was— a constant reminder of his mistakes.

Michael narrowed his eyes, surveying the young daywalker with piercing curiosity. He ran a scarred hand over his beard in contemplation.

"I've never known you to be vengeful, kid. Angry, yeah. Spiteful, maybe, but not vengeful."

Eric shrugged. "A lot can change when shit goes wrong. There's a lot you don't know about me."

"Or maybe I always knew." The boy clenched his jaw as Michael went on, "And I can help you with that, how?"

The next words were agonizing to say, but necessary.

"I wanna come back to The Colectiv."

For the first time in years, Michael looked genuinely taken aback, but Eric kept going before he could start cheering in victory and popping metaphorical champagne.

"I wanna come back to The Colectiv. I wanna train, hunt, and use everything at your disposal to find him myself and kill him when I'm ready. And I don't want you or anyone else getting in my way."

"Woah, kid," Michael chuckled, raising his hands to interrupt him. "I respect the ambition, but you're acting an awful lot like you run the place. Need I remind you of the dangers of making hunts personal?"

"Yeah, well, considering everything is still fresh, it's gonna feel a little *personal*. But I think you should be happy, considering I want to come back at all. I'll do anything and everything. I want to 'reach my full potential'. Isn't this what you wanted?" he asked with a cold smile that didn't reach his eyes.

The commander scoffed, "With that attitude? You could at least pretend to be happy about it."

"You know, I was." The words tasted bitter in his mouth. "I just can't pretend when I'm not anymore."

"And look where that got you, kid. Sometimes what we think we want isn't what's best for us."

Even if he didn't say it out loud, he could hear Michael distinctly saying, *"I told you so."* Loud and clear.

"Do we have a deal or not?" Eric asked banally.

Michael regarded him for a long, tense moment. The commander made a show of thinking long and hard about Eric's request, but the young man knew better than that. He knew that internally, Michael was leaping with joy at the idea of Eric coming back within his reach, but chose to toy with him for a while longer.

Finally, with a wolfish grin, the older man extended his hand to him. "Deal."

With his uninjured hand, Eric clasped Michael's callused one, and the two hunters shook hands before God in the middle of the Black Church.

"Welcome home, MacNamara," the commander said.

Eric grimaced at the use of the infamous name.

MacNamara, the name he'd been called for half of his life and the one that belonged to a dead father he'd never met. He hadn't used that name in years, but now, he supposed, was as good a time as any to use it once more.

"Good to be back, I guess."[2]

---

[2] The Foundations of Decay - My Chemical Romance

1

Sons of the Silver Wolf

Eric

Romania – Three Years Later

[3]The Jeep's engine roared as it sailed through the streets like a cheetah in the savanna, hot on the heels of a white vehicle up ahead. At the wheel was none other than Eric MacNamara, his intense gaze locked on the car like a predator trained on his prey. Tonight, it was a pack of three vampires—nothing too challenging. The group had been desperately trying to evade the hunter for a few miles but to no avail. Even when the vampires ran, Eric was relentless, and with his equally merciless twin at his side, nobody was ever truly safe from their clutches or their wrath.

The cars soared through the streets of a small city at the edge of the forest. The night sky was an inky black curtain against the snow-

---

[3] Party Poison - My Chemical Romance

covered town, illuminated by golden lamp posts. On the passenger's side, James MacNamara reached over his shoulder and casually brought out a crossbow and a few bolts from the backseat. Loud, fast-paced music blared from the speakers, matching the adrenaline of the high-speed chase. Hardly anyone was out on the streets this far past midnight, save for the occasional car or pedestrian. If they were speeding, no one ever reported it, but even if they did, they were never caught.

Suddenly, their target took a sharp left turn into a small alleyway, too small for them to fit.

Bitch.

Luckily, Eric was clever.

"Hold on," he muttered.

Eric pressed down on the gas pedal, going faster until he came upon a large street. He then switched gears and with a sharp turn of the wheel, their bodies moved with the momentum, the snow making them glide. James braced himself, mildly cursing with a bolt between his teeth. Eric then righted the vehicle and bounded up the street as James preoccupied himself with loading his weapon.

Car chases weren't particularly common in hunts, but they weren't rare, at least not with Eric and James involved. They liked the thrill, and with Eric as the driver, things hardly ever went wrong. He had been a getaway man since they were rebellious teenagers, and it was sheer dumb luck that it became useful in adulthood. He was just proud to be good at something so exhilarating, and James had a much better time planning a mode of attack in the meantime.

At that moment, Eric's twin scowled in confusion, having now realized their target was missing.

"Where the fuck did they go?"

"Hold on," Eric repeated.

He stared through the windshield, his gaze fixed on the intersection in front of him as they approached it ever closer. Then, just as expected, he caught sight of a white bumper coming from the right. Eric smirked devilishly and went at full speed. James, catching on to his brother's tactics, lowered his window and braced himself again. Seconds before contact, there was a flash of panic in the other passenger's eyes, and before they knew it, the Jeep collided with the nose of the vehicle and sent it flying sideways. Their bodies lurched forward, and they groaned, but the shock was brief.

In the moments of recovery, James took immediate action. He stuck half his body out of the window, aimed his crossbow, and fired a bolt at the passenger window. It shot through the air with a faint whistle before breaking the glass and sinking right into the man's skull with deadly precision. A panicked yell came from the remaining vampires, just as James fired two more in succession. At the same time, the driver booked it, making him miss the driver's head by inches and leaving a hole in the back window.

"Shit."

"They're going to the forest!" Eric told him, his eyes following their path.

"Perfect."

James tapped the roof of the car and pulled himself back inside as Eric punched the gas. They trailed behind their victims and, before they knew it, they left the town behind as the road gave way to the thick woods of Codrii Seculari Sinca. Eric weaved through the forest, managing the rough, uneven terrain, and in the safety of the trees, the brothers kicked into high gear.

Eric took out a silver 1911 pistol from his chest holster and cocked the barrel over the steering wheel as his brother loaded his crossbow yet again. He lowered his window, the wind sweeping up his hair. The twins shared a look and, in unison, stuck their heads out and fired at the tires of the white car. Their shots landed perfectly, causing the driver to lose control and then flip as it hit a large boulder. It rolled multiple times until it came to a full stop, teetering upside down.

The twins parked the car, and like soldiers preparing for battle, they grabbed their respective weaponry—steel swords and silver pistols, as well as James' crossbow and Eric's daggers. They secured their hunting jackets, concealing the lower halves of their faces with masks. Though they were certain no one else would be coming through these woods any time soon, it was still precautionary.

Snow began to slowly fall as the boys flanked either side of the overturned car, weapons at the ready. Two vampires crept out of the battered vehicle, while another lay unconscious with a bolt protruding from his head in the passenger seat. The one from the back ran, playing right into James' hands.

"I got him," he muttered, followed by a whistle.

[4]The driver, however, was left to Eric and Eric alone. He got to his feet—bleeding, bruised, and clutching the shoulder where James' shot had landed. He tried making a run for it, but the hunter was faster. Without breaking his stride, Eric raised his pistol and shot two silver bullets into the vampire's back. The man let out a cry of pain, stumbling to his knees. They wouldn't kill him, but between that and the bolt, he was already getting weaker.

The vampire whipped his head around, his eyes glowing pale blue as he bared his fangs in a hiss. In a futile act of bravery, he lunged at Eric with a growl. The hunter drew a dagger from his hip, and with fluid motion, he sidestepped the vampire's attack and slashed at his face. When he tried again, Eric punched him in the nose with a hit that

---

[4] The Wolf - Fever Ray

was hard enough to knock a human out but was enough to knock an undead man to the ground so he'd stop fighting.

With swift and nimble movements, Eric put his gun and his dagger away, only to then reach behind him and wrap his hand around the sword that was strapped to his back. He unsheathed it, the sound of scratching metal echoing through the clearing. A silver solar eclipse glinted on the crossguard as he closed the distance between him and his victim.

The vampire's demeanor instantly shifted, and he raised his hands in an attempt to surrender. Eric ignored his pleas and kicked him square in the face. He fell back against the white snowcapped earth, now splattered with crimson blood. As the man groaned, the young hunter put his boot on his sternum to hold him down and put the tip of his sword to his throat. With his dark-vision, he could see his skin was starting to take on a purple tint—a clear sign of a weakened vampire.

Aside from the terror, there was a clear sign of hatred in his expression. It was a look Eric was all too familiar with.

"Paraziţi," the vampire hissed.

Vermin.

"Sentimentul este reciproc," Eric replied in Romanian.

The feeling is mutual.

Eric pressed the blade a little deeper into his throat, and the vampire grunted in pain. The hunter let his eyes brighten and glow like two suns, the golden counterpart to the pureblood's icy blues. The vampire's loathing doubled.

"*Dhampir.* I've heard of you. You're the one who kills his own kind. You disgust me," he spat.

While Eric's expression never gave anything away, a twinge of rage flared through him. But it wasn't the blatant insult that made him feel that way.

"I don't have a kind," he said. "Especially not one like you."

Without another word, he raised his sword with both hands on the hilt and turned it downward. The vampire begged for his life once more.

"Te rog, aşteaptă-te rog nu mă ucide. Îmi pare rău, voi face orice!"

Please, wait—please don't kill me. I'm sorry. I'll do anything!

Eric scowled and, with all his strength, drove the blade down into the vampire's neck. He then adjusted his grip on the handle and sliced the sword sideways, severing the head clean off. Silence fell until the only significant sound was a heartbeat a few feet away. The smell of motor oil and blood filled his nostrils, intermingled with the cool, forest air as snowflakes continued to trickle down. There was a dragging noise and Eric looked up to see his brother pulling the unconscious body of the other vampire behind him.

James looked him up and down. "You know, shooting them in the face usually shuts them up."

He put the body down by the car and then severed its head with his sword to finish the job. It was a casual, necessary step that every hunter took and got used to.

Eric scoffed. The rage and adrenaline were already subsiding. "I know that."

His twin kicked the head away and wiped the blood off the blade on the sleeve of his leather hunting jacket.

"Oh, so you *do* like being a melodramatic asshole."

"Says you," Eric shot back as he cleaned his sword on the dead vampire's clothes.

"Yeah, but I like getting straight to the point."

Eric raised an eyebrow at him. "Are you saying I should be nicer?"

James snorted. "Fuck no."

"Well, Michael *has* said, 'There can be a lot of value in a vampire's dying words. You never know what they'll say to save their heads.'"

"Look at you, quoting Mike himself," James teased. His eyes flashed over his mask.

Eric rolled his eyes. "Shut the fuck up."

A sharp breeze flew by, biting at his skin and sending the snowflakes sideways. Eric shivered and an uncomfortable grimace pulled at his face. Winter was his least favorite season, and he hated the snow even more. For a moment, he even swore he could feel frostbite creeping up into his fingers and started clenching and unclenching his hand until the horrifyingly familiar sensation went away.

Too many bad memories.

"Let's call the cleanup crew and get the fuck out of here."

†††

Brasov, Romania—The Iovaneau Estate

The twins stepped back into their Romanian home, reeking of blood and sweat, their gear in hand. Eric pushed back his hood, his mask already gone, and ran his fingers through his thick, shaggy hair. James pushed his chin-length hair behind his ears, his piercings glittering in the light. They made their way out of the checkerboard foyer and up the mahogany steps. With a sigh, Eric took out his phone to make a quick, dreaded call.

"Corporal," Michael answered.

"Commander," he greeted in the same tone, all business. "We're back. It's done."

"Good. Any hassle? I heard the clean-up crew was called."

James made a noise between a cough and a laugh. Eric threw him a glare.

"Yeah, in the middle of the forest," he contested coolly. "There were three of them in a car, and we had to chase them down, but no one saw anything."

"They said it was pretty banged up on the side."

The brothers shared a knowing, vexed look. *Snitches.*

"Well, you can partially blame physics for that...and a large rock. I made a decision, and the decision was to make sure they didn't get away at any cost. They did enough damage as is."

"Hey, it's not a judgment," the commander chuckled. "As long as no one saw you, and you got the job done, I'd say you did a good job. Just don't let it get too far, alright?"

Eric raised his eyebrows at the praise, but he didn't get too excited about it.

"Yeah... Thanks."

"Rest up, boys. Oh, and E?"

"Yeah?"

"I appreciate the phone call."

Eric couldn't help but feel a twinge of discomfort in his chest. "Yeah. Goodnight."

"Goodnight."

With that, Eric hung up and stuffed the phone into his pocket. They reached his bedroom door, and James leaned against the wall, arms crossed.

"See? That wasn't so bad," he said. "One fucking phone call every once in a while. It's just a mission report."

"Yeah, yeah."

Eric had been deliberately avoiding phone calls and conversations with Michael for as long as he could remember. It was a habit he acquired as a teenager, but if he wanted to stay in his good graces and gain more power, one of the habits he had to adopt was communication. It was simple. A phone call was nothing compared to taking someone's life, yet...

He was working on it.

†††

Since joining The Colectiv, the MacNamara twins were raised in the confines of what is known as the Iovaneau Estate. It was where every hunter was trained, learned various non-combat lessons, ate, slept, and then repeated. For as long as Eric could remember, the estate reminded him of a small castle, with its gothic revival architecture—the mahogany and patterned walls, stained-glass windows, pointed arches, and box-beamed ceilings. While it wasn't a *real* castle, it was still very large and spectacular. Eric spent most of his life admiring it and exploring its many hiding places, and when he wasn't required to be a hunter, he exhausted the library, which is where he acquired most of his knowledge, as well as anything to do with the history of the estate itself.

It was built in the 1800s, deep in the woods of Brasov. Although The Colectiv existed before that, Michael's ancestor, Alexandru Iovaneau, built the estate just over 150 years ago. For decades, it was an above-ground building with little protection or subterranean use until after World War II, following the Soviet Union's invasion. The Iovaneau's then decided to add underground levels to protect their remaining hunters who had not been drafted into the war, using the manor only as a front.

Following two communist dictators up until 1989, it served its purpose well. During that time, the estate appeared to be silent and disbanded, when, in reality, it was still operating in secret in spite of the government. However, following the rise of The Silver Wolf, Mihail Iovaneau, alongside his father, Constantin, the estate was restored to its former glory. Now, it was in full operation, just in time for James and Eric MacNamara to join the fray.

At present, the manor was protected by a giant iron-wrought fence and surveillance technology, and it was even registered under the guise of a military facility and dubbed a no-fly zone. It was home to members of The Colectiv who needed it and included not only sleeping quarters but also training grounds, an armory, interrogation rooms, a dungeon, a giant library, and a greenhouse.

The bedrooms were not exempt from the beauty of the estate's architecture and were far superior to anything two poor little orphan boys could have hoped for. Even before Michael took them in, the boys always shared a room, and when they first got to Brasov, it was the same. Of course, now that Eric was back and they were both adults, they were finally given a decent space just for themselves: mahogany walls with gold detailing, arched windows, a four-poster bed, a large red rug, and a private bathroom. Compared to how he grew up as a child and where he was three years ago, he now practically lives like a prince, which in a lot of ways was a bit jarring.

Of course, Eric, being Eric, had to leave pieces of himself throughout the room and modernize it in his own way. He had a TV with speakers and in a corner by the window was a desk with a laptop and books scattered all over it. In fact, books were stacked everywhere, whether on the bookcase, his bedside table, or the dresser. Hanging on the wall above the desk were charcoal sketches. In another corner hung a punching bag next to a mat and a rack of weights. And beside that was a mini fridge containing bags of blood acquired from The Colectiv's physician. Around the room, there were small gashes in the wall, some noticeable and some not, from all the knives Eric had thrown either out of fury or boredom. There was, of course, a rack of swords and a shelf for his guns and daggers. And here and there he had posters of movies, TV shows, and musicians he liked. It was the perfect safe space for himself, or as safe as it could get in a vampire-hunting institution.

Later that night, in the bathroom adjacent to his organized chaos, Eric rid himself of the blood and grime in the shower with haste. When he was all done, he stood before the sink with a towel wrapped around his waist, staring into the mirror before him.

[5]He didn't want to be dramatic, but sometimes he wished the lore about vampires not having reflections was true. Not because he didn't like what he looked like, but because sometimes he didn't like what he saw when he looked in the mirror. There was a disconnect in those hazel eyes that gazed right back. He didn't know who he was seeing sometimes. He lived and interacted with a walking, talking reflection of himself all the time, but James was more familiar than *this*. Half of the time, Eric didn't know if he was seeing his twin, his mother, his long-dead father, Michael, or even himself.

Physically, he looked more and more like his father every day. Not his adoptive father, but his biological one, Wade MacNamara—the vampire that made him what he is. Even the name didn't sound real anymore. Neither he nor James ever came to know him, as he had gotten himself killed long ago, but they were familiar with what he looked like. They had seen his face in a picture their mother had kept

---

[5] Me, I'm Not - Nine Inch Nails

in a golden locket around her neck, and even now, the image is ingrained in Eric's memory.

It was a small portrait taken in the 90s of a man who didn't look older than his late twenties. He wore a white t-shirt and a motor jacket, and a single earring dangled from his earlobe. Stubble peppered his jaw, and his long, brown curls were pushed back, out of his face. His bright blue eyes were alight, grinning past the camera at the person who took it.

Growing up, their mother had always told the twins that they resembled their father, but Eric never saw it. After all, how could he, a *child*, ever look like a *man* like that? But, now, almost 25 years into his life, it was there every time he looked in the mirror, especially these last three years. It felt strange and wrong, knowing what he knew about him.

Eric pushed his damp hair back, which fell just past his ears. He had changed a bit since coming back to the estate. Before then, he had spent the better part of four years in an American university, and he remembered a time when he thought 18 was so grown up until he looked back and realized how small he was. Now, his features had sharpened and the intense training made him broader and more muscular. A patchwork tattoo sleeve went up his right arm, adorning his bronze skin with several blackwork pieces. A butterfly, Frankenstein's monster, a viper, a skeleton hand, a marble design that bled onto his chest, to name a few. The most important one was that of a solar eclipse on the side of his neck.

He looked just like Wade, except not. The rest was that undeniable edge from his mother's side, and that, at the very least, gave him solace, knowing he was her son too.

His gaze hovered over to the other side of his neck, at the crook, where a large scar stood against his tattoos. He had come a long way from not being able to look at it. The first year, he refused to take his shirt off outside of his room, and when he did, it was wrapped in bandages. Now he had long accepted it as a part of himself and made the deliberate choice to not cover it up. The mark itself was a mangled circle made up of small, jagged lines and indents, resembling a shark bite. However, it wasn't a shark or any smaller animal that tried to take a chunk out of Eric. No, it wasn't some*thing*, but some*one* that did the deed, and it was the most damning change of all.

He ran his fingers over it, the bright scar stark against his skin. It was bumpy and uneven in some places, and even now there was a vague numbness as if some nerves had been damaged.

Although daywalkers could instantly heal, even Eric's vampire blood could not get rid of this one, leaving him the one and only immortal being with a scar. It was a reminder that he had survived something brutal, and it was a reminder of what had happened to him *that day*.

One step closer, asshole.

Eric might not know where *he* is yet, but he hoped that the perpetrator could feel his wrath from a distance even now.

But of course, trailing right behind was always the thought of *her*. Because he couldn't think of *that night* without memories of *her* rushing in, and any anger turned into sorrow and betrayal. It was brief, but it was enough.

It all began with her.

Emilia.

Traitor, a voice whispered in the back of his mind. *Her* voice. Rather, the voice in his mind dressed up like her. He returned his gaze to the mirror, half expecting to see Emilia standing there like a ghost, but all he saw was himself and himself alone.

A whisper of his own followed:

Daywalkers

You don't know anything.

Daywalkers

You don't know anything.

2

Prodigal Son

Eric

[6]Eric and James MacNamara were born on February 13th, 1997, to a woman named Anya Isabella Mészáros. Anya was a Romanian-American woman from a colorful family of hunters, and eventually, she met Wade MacNamara, an alleged 150-year-old Irishman with a bad reputation. They were people from two completely different worlds, destined to kill each other, yet, like a Shakespearean tragedy, they fell in love. Thus, creating the biggest scandal in vampire-hunter history.

The Colectiv is an organization with religious roots and a government that works with its own set of independent laws and regulations. One of those laws makes it forbidden for a hunter to have a romantic affair with a vampire. It is an offense punishable by exile or,

---

[6] Typical Story - Hobo Johnson

worse, death, but to bear a vampire's child was a crime against God. Daywalkers were seldom heard of, partially due to biology, but partially because they were often seen as abominations in the eyes of anyone undead or not, and were often killed by any means necessary. Anya managed to break every law under the eyes of God and The Colectiv, so in the end, she had no choice but to flee for the safety of her small family, leaving everything that she knew behind.

Much to her detriment, Anya was cursed with not *one* daywalker child but with *two*, and with The Colectiv at her back and Wade MacNamara having been slain, Anya was left to bear the weight of her world in full. As her boys grew, she and the twins moved across the United States, never sticking to one place for too long while working multiple jobs to keep them afloat. Yet, amidst the chaos and instability, she raised Eric and James with every ounce of love and passion that she had to give.

To the twins, Anya was an angel, a goddess, and their whole world, and she was the only person who never compared them, even when others did. Even when the boys started to stand out and exhibit qualities and abilities that the other children did not, Anya never treated them any differently and did her best to provide for their needs, no matter the costs. She also taught them that, above all else, they should protect each other no matter what.

For a long time, the twins weren't entirely aware of what they were and what that meant. They didn't know why everything was so overwhelming all the time. They didn't know why they could hear a heartbeat from the next room or how they could see in the dark so well. They didn't know why they were so fast and strong that "mommy" had to urge them to hold back so they didn't hurt the other kids. Of course, like any child obsessed with media, they ultimately started putting the puzzle pieces together. After all, "normal kids" didn't drink blood from a bag. Still, Anya did her best to protect them from the truth. The one answer she ever gave them was that they were different and "special like daddy," but they had to keep it all a secret to stay safe from "villains." She also told them that "daddy" died fighting in a war. A war for what, she didn't say, despite their biting curiosity. But to her last, dying breath, she maintained her story.

When the twins were about 10 years old, their mother was diagnosed with late-stage breast cancer. At that point, the running had stopped, and they had been living in Queens, New York for a few years. She underwent chemotherapy and multiple surgeries and spent time in and out of the hospital, which Eric remembered with painful vividness. At a certain point, there were a few babysitters, some were her work friends, and others he didn't quite know. But by the time the boys turned 11, Anya Isabella Mészáros succumbed to her illness and passed away.

In her last days, Anya had told the boys that a friend of hers was going to take care of them in the event of her death. According to her, they had never met this person, but she trusted him with her life, and they would be safe with him. At the time, they didn't want to accept the idea, but when the inevitable came, it was all they could do to hope that she was right. And, of course, just as she promised, someone *did* come, and his name was Michael Iovaneau.

Mihail Andrei Ioveanu arrived at Anya's funeral and introduced himself to the twins as an old friend of their mother. With the scar on his face, Eric didn't know whether to be in awe or fear of him, but the smile he flashed made him lean toward the former. He pulled them aside and, in private, told them to call him "Michael." And what Michael did was tell them the truth. He talked about The Colectiv, about who their parents truly were, and he told the boys that they were what was called "dhampirs" or "daywalkers." He told them that he made a promise to their mother to protect them from "bad people" and to take them in the event of her death. In his arms, they would be safe, and if they agreed, they would be trained to fight just as he and Anya were, because Michael was the commander—a *king*—and under him, nobody could touch them.

In their 11-year-old minds, it was a dream come true. After having lost the most important person in their lives, what child *wouldn't* take the offer? So, of course, the boys agreed, and with a smile, the old hunter took them in, and they spent the following years training under his wing.

Upon being released into society, it seemed that the twins were doomed to be hated by the entire world. Humans and vampires alike loathed them for what they were, and anyone who knew about their family history saw them as unworthy of having a place in The Colectiv at all. Even those who respected Michael Iovaneau's authority questioned his adoption of these little abominations, but obviously, none of them did anything about it. Whatever strings he pulled behind the scenes did more than enough, though it didn't keep the others from making their hatred for them known.

"Walker," they'd call them. A shortened version of "daywalker" that was used as a label and derogatory term. As well as *half-breed*, *leech*, *freak*, and many other slurs alike. When it came to the adults, they could hardly do anything about it, but if it was someone their age, it often ended in a physical fight. It was reminiscent of their time in grade school when they had to deal with bullies, but just like those times, Michael urged them to hold back lest they take it too far. The last thing they should want is to prove everyone right. It caused problems for the commander, but at the very least, he always made sure the culprits were punished.

In the end, Michael was the sole person who believed in them and became a surrogate father for the twins. Considering they never had one to begin with, and the commander didn't have any biological children of his own, they all seamlessly fell into those roles. And those first six months of training and learning at his side had been enthralling and somehow comforting after losing their mother, but as time passed, things changed.

[7]Eric and James were "naturals" in the hunt and it brought a lot of joy to the commander, but perhaps *too* much. The twins had remarkable inhuman abilities, which gave them advantages no other hunter possessed. In the beginning, it was fun and games. They trained with swords, guns, and various weapons they had only ever dreamed of wielding and surpassed humans in physical training with flying colors. It was easy to get caught up in real-life fantasy for a while, but the further they improved, the more their commander pushed them past their limits and demanded more.

Michael had no problem throwing two daywalkers into the metaphorical fire, despite how young they were compared to everyone else. Most hunters started with the fundamentals at the age of 14, but Eric and James were doing things at 11 that others weren't allowed to. James, despite a few angry complaints, managed to pull off what he was told because he was competitive and liked the challenge. Eric, however, abhorred it. He hated the pressure, and he hated that something he once enjoyed became an expectation put upon him. And there came a point where it was too difficult to keep up as Michael continued to advance him forward. Even if his body could heal from the physical wounds of it all, it began to take a mental and emotional toll on him. The gravity of what he was being asked to do as a hunter became

---

[7] Heathens - Twenty One Pilots

increasingly apparent, and it put him in a constant state of anxiety and dread. In turn, it affected his performance, which gave the other hunters more fodder for bullying and torment and even incentivized Michael to find creative ways to get Eric to improve.

The fact of the matter was that the boy's heart lay in things that had nothing to do with violence at all. Eric found most of his joy in reading, learning, exploring, and perusing the internet. He adored horror movies, kept a stack of books on his desk at all times, and listened to music every chance he could get. He loved his academic lessons and liked to learn how the weapons were forged as well as wield them. He also liked sneaking off to the library and learning about everything and anything that had to do with society, hunters, vampires, and where he came from. He was observant and absorbed most information like a sponge. It made him a walking, talking encyclopedia that both impressed and irritated those around him, but above all else, he learned more about the world outside the walls of the estate.

Although there wasn't too much information written about daywalkers, Eric read the few books he found over and over. Considering what they used to do to half-vampires, most of it wasn't positive, but he did his best to take what was useful. Everyone knew that purebloods were immortal from the moment they were turned, but according to "legend," daywalkers aged until they turned 25 (something to do with the development of the brain). This meant that for Eric and James, immortality was on the horizon. Even Michael told them to keep it in the back of their minds, but while the commander always had his ideas, Eric had his own, and the boy wondered what he would do with eternity. It wasn't a hard thing to do, considering how much time he had to himself once James advanced farther than him.

From a young age, Eric could see that his brother's place in The Colectiv was solidified, whereas Eric's mind was straying. Instead, he fantasized about the "real world." He dreamed about going to school, traveling, making friends—normal friends—and participating in everything that children his age did. He wanted to change the world because he was "special" and anything was possible, and he wanted to do it all before he grew up and became immortal forever.

So, with perfect trust, Eric made the decision to voice this to Michael and even practiced what he would say in the mirror. After all, he was like a father to him, and the commander himself told him time and time again that he had the potential to do anything. However, when he got around to having the conversation when he was 13, Michael's reaction changed the course of their relationship forever.

The commander scoffed, "You wanna leave? You can't leave."

Eric frowned, his excitement quickly dissolving. "Why not?"

"What do you mean? The Colectiv is your home. You grew up here. You trained here. I raised you to be one of us, and now you wanna leave? I thought we had a deal, E. I protect you, I take you in, and you and Jimmy work for The Colectiv. Just like your mom."

"I can always come back when I'm done," Eric uttered lowly. His voice was starting to drop now that he was getting older. "Besides, you'll still have Jimmy."

"Jimmy is damn good, but so are you."

"No, I'm not," the boy argued.

"Yes, you are," Michael stressed. "You're so close to reaching your potential, E, and you just don't see it. You could get there if you just let go of the fear that's holding you back and let go of those little fantasies. One push. I know it's in you."

The flippant tone he used to talk about Eric's desires made him clench his jaw. He didn't expect the most important man in his life to speak in such a way. In turn, it made him angry and defensive.

"They're not just 'fantasies.' They're real. Other people do it all the time. I've seen it."

"You mean like in those books you read?"

"Yes. I could do it. I might stop aging at 25, what's wrong with wanting to live a normal life until then?"

"'Normal'?" Michael blurted out. "I'm sorry, kid, but I think it's time I hit you with a tough piece of reality...you're *not* normal. Never will be, for a multitude of reasons. You're lucky I found you before you reached high school, otherwise, you'd be under a knife at Area 51."

Eric swallowed thickly. He knew he was right, but he didn't like the way he was throwing it in his face.

The commander went on, "What would a half-vampire like you have to gain out there, huh? What would you do with a pointless college degree? You'd just be wasting your time. Look at you. You've learned more in here than they'll ever teach you out there. Trust me, humanity isn't that fun, especially not for someone like you. Not if the vampires find out about you, either. You're a daywalker, E. You think there aren't people out there waiting to get their hands on you? Kill you?"

"They don't have to know."

Michael grimaced, unconvinced by Eric's words.

"I'm just trying to protect you, E," he told him. "You're not ready. You're just a kid. Whether you like it or not, you were born into this life—this one right now—just like I was. Just like your mother. The Colectiv is in your blood, just like that father of yours. This is what you're destined for. Your brother's accepted it. Why can't you?"

Michael's harsh words were worse than getting a bullet to the chest. The young boy's heart was riddled with a mixture of anger, hurt, and disappointment. To have his mentor, a man he had looked up to for years, say those words and try to shatter his dreams was a different kind of pain.

A lump formed in the back of Eric's throat, and tears sprang to his eyes. He fought them back as well as he could, so they wouldn't fall, and he said the simplest yet most powerful words he could say for a boy his age:

"Because I'm not like him."

And I'm not like you.

"Do you know who your father is?" Michael asked.

Eric frowned in confusion and answered, "Wade MacNamara."

"No, *do you know who your father is*?" the commander repeated with more ferocity.

Eric simply shrugged. "Mom said he was a soldier."

"He was a *murderer*, E. That's who he was. He killed people, and one of those people was a young man by the name of Gabriel Iovaneau. My older brother."

The boy gasped, his stomach dropping down to the floor.

Michael pointed at his face aggressively and said, "*He's* the reason I have this scar, and that's why he's dead now."

Eric's blood turned icy in his veins, his eyes widening in horror and disbelief.

"W...what?"

"It's hard to hear, but it's true. I kept that from you to protect you, and no doubt your mother did the same, but I think you're old enough to know." Michael walked around his desk and put a hand on the boy's shoulder. "You and your brother are different, E. You don't have to be like him. I can—"

"No!"

Eric pulled away, his vision watery with angry tears, and bolted out of the commander's office.

He didn't tell James the truth about their father, mostly because he almost didn't want to believe it himself. He had known his father was dead his whole life, but to learn that he was a monster and that it was Michael who had taken his life was too much to bear. He didn't know who to be angrier towards—Wade or Michael. Wade for being his blood and for making him what he is, or Michael for being so cruel. All Eric knew was that he hated *himself* and the world he grew up in a lot more since that day. In a way, he wanted to protect his twin from the same thing, but eventually, James found out later on—in a less brutal way, at least. As time passed, Eric came to accept the truth, but he was never the same.

Perhaps the commander thought it would force him in the right direction, but instead, it created animosity that hadn't been there before. Over the years, the bitterness between Eric and Michael only grew more and more as the twins got closer to adulthood, creating an emotional chasm between father and son. Michael did his best to handle it, but when James came to Eric's defense, it was clear that the commander had to pick his battles. Of course, it didn't stop him from trying to show Eric his "potential." The training and obligations did not cease, and Michael's punishments for Eric's failures worsened with the years as the boy's hostility increased. The acts of rebellion he committed with James didn't help, although, ironically enough, Michael was more lenient in those cases. If Eric had been human, he would have started a collection of nasty scars long ago, and there came a time when even his brother—who, at that point, got in trouble with the law frequently—wasn't sure if Eric's failure to complete training was out of spite or genuine fear.

At the very least, if there was anything certain in such an uncertain world, it was Eric's unbreakable bond with James. Despite The Colectiv's efforts to keep them apart, they were always there to support each other despite all odds and rules, even when their experiences differed. From an outsider's perspective, they may seem vastly different, but at their core and their roots, they were two sides of the same coin. They were both passionate, loyal, quick-tempered, and had a low tolerance for injustice. One was louder than the other, but odds are, whatever came out of James' mouth was already on Eric's mind, and vice versa. They balanced each other out well, which made them a terrifying pair in and out of the field. They were solace in a world against them, and it was that very thing that almost held Eric back from packing his bags and leaving sooner. However, to his dismay, it was James who encouraged him to leave.

"The Colectiv is all I have, E. I don't have any other dreams, but you do. You should go."

It was the first time his seemingly tough brother expressed any kind of self-doubt, and Eric made a promise to find him a new dream when the time came.

So, with his decision made, Eric got his GED in secret and applied to every university that was as far away from Romania as possible. And as soon as he was of age and got into a decent college, he booked a flight and packed his bags. On the day he left, Michael barely looked at him, and they exchanged a few harsh words. But despite his fear of the unknown and the pain of leaving his brother behind, Eric walked out the door without so much as a glance back, burning the bridge between him and Michael Iovaneau.

That is until fate brought him back to Romania and into the arms of The Colectiv years later.

3

The Train to Bucharest

Eric

[8]Sweat beaded down Eric's face as he eyed James from across the indoor training ring. Each twin held a steel sword in their hand, donning wicked, predacious grins as they circled one another. They wore loose, casual training clothes, opting out of the usual protection the other hunters wore, who, beyond the ring, stood by to watch the show. Training sessions were normal, but when it came to Eric and James MacNamara, everyone always jumped at the chance to witness two daywalkers put on a show.

Learning to use a sword was both a tradition and a requirement for every hunter in The Colectiv. Vampires couldn't be killed by a bullet or even a stake through the heart, but by severing the spinal cord. This meant that every hunter had to get comfortable carrying and

---

[8] Dynasties and Dystopia - Denzel Curry, Gizzle, & Bren Joy

wielding a blade. Although technology has advanced beyond such weaponry when it comes to human war, The Colectiv still believed in earning the right to one's blade through mastery. Hunters were even encouraged to stay in shape and keep each other on their toes, both as a means of improvement and as a form of camaraderie. Of course, the MacNamara twins always liked challenging each other in this regard. After all, there was no better adversary for a daywalker than another daywalker. Not to mention, they didn't have to worry about killing each other.

Eric twirled his sword in nonchalance, watching his brother intently. Then, just as he anticipated, James lunged with animalistic fury, and Eric raised his sword to parry his move. The steel blades clanged against each other again and again as they went back and forth, striking and blocking as they moved in a deadly dance. It was a simple warm-up, but as always, the boys had to up the aggression.

James stepped back and held out his arms in a dare as they circled each other again. Eric snorted in amusement but took the bait and lunged, feinting one way but going the other. James parried him and pushed Eric's sword to the side before slashing the steel across his chest and kicking him in the sternum. With a grunt, Eric fell backward but managed to roll with the momentum and get back on his feet. Crimson blood spilled from the cut, but it was a flesh wound that was already starting to close on its own.

Eric chuckled, finding amusement in this game of bloodshed, and attacked once more. His twin swiped his sword, but Eric jumped over it with ease and then brought his elbow to James' face, his sword following after. He groaned in pain, his hand briefly clutching his face. When James looked up, his nose was bleeding and there was a gash on his cheek. He let out an angry, throaty laugh and licked the blood off his face before charging ahead once more.

Their swords crashed and they pushed against each other, their faces inches apart. Eric sliced downward and James took the opportunity to headbutt him in the face. Eric stumbled back, seeing stars, and now his nose was also oozing blood.

He wiped some of it away and whispered, "You bitch."

The twins continued to spar, slashing with merciless abandon and using every joint and limb to deliver more blows. In the end, it was an even match. The twins knew each other's fighting styles too well, and before they knew it, they were bleeding and bruised on the floor, some wounds already healing and some still fresh. They only moved to give each other a fist bump, which signaled the end of their training session.

"Sunt ca hienele," someone muttered from outside the ring.

They're like hyenas.

"They do this every time," someone else said.

"Le place doar să se arate."

They just like to show off.

James didn't like that.

"Ce ați spus?" he demanded. *What did you say?*

The first one who had spoken responded, "Nothing, *Walker*."

James got up to his feet, all covered in blood, and crossed his arms, saying, "You mean 'nothing, *sir*'. 'Lieutenant' is also fine."

The hunter worked his jaw, glaring at Eric's brother, but it didn't faze the daywalker in the slightest.

At last, the man bit out, "Nothing, *sir*."

The lieutenant gave him a curt nod and with that, the other hunter walked away.

"Close your eyes if you hate it so much, huh," James muttered. He then looked around to the others and said loud enough for everyone to hear, "The next person who talks shit while we're in the ring will get a sparring session with me next. Stop fucking gawking and let's see how you handle it. I know you know I can hear you."

The rest that had gathered around the ring either followed suit and left, or they started milling about, minding their own business. Eric could hear some of the teenage recruits whispering amongst themselves, though he could hardly look at them without feeling a twinge in his chest. Some were bright-eyed and others looked nervous, much like himself all those years ago.

James then turned to him and held out his hand to help him off the ground. Despite how torn his shirt was, the pain from his open wounds was gone now that they were healed. However, the exhaustion from the physical activity would have to be helped with some rest, water, or some blood.

Eric smirked at his twin, beaming with pride.

"What?" James asked with a furrowed brow.

"Considering all those problems with authority, you're pretty good at it."

James rolled his eyes. "Shut up."

"I think you love bossing people around."

His brother motioned to the room and said, "These people? Absolutely. Call it retribution."

Eric chuckled at that.

The Colectiv was structured into ranks and jobs, and while not everyone was an active hunter, those who did were titled "Knights" after training was completed. Michael's First Lieutenant, James, was two ranks lower than his—the Knight Commander—but higher than almost everyone else in the estate. Since Eric left The Colectiv for a time, he had to start from the bottom when he returned and was currently ranked Knight Corporal—two ranks below James.

Most of the hunters in the organization already didn't like them very much, so when James kept ranking up, it peeved plenty of people to no end. Many refused to address him as their superior. They claimed Michael was playing favorites, but James always made sure to remind them who had earned the spot and who had the authority. It was a pain and an uphill battle, but Eric felt like there was no one better equipped to argue his way to the top than him. The only problem was that in an ideal world, Eric would have been Second Lieutenant beside him, but that role, unfortunately, belonged to someone else.

A door clicked open, followed by a familiar voice shouting, "*Walker!*"

Speak of the literal devil.

Eric looked at his brother with mock confusion and asked, "Did you hear something?"

James shrugged innocently. "No, I didn't hear anything."

"Hmm funny."

"Did you hear me, shitheads?" the voice boomed.

Eric cast a lazy glance towards a broad and blonde-haired shape barreling toward them. He tried giving him a well-acted look of bewilderment from across the training grounds.

"Oh, are you talking to us? Sorry, I didn't hear our name."

He rolled his eyes. "You know I'm talking to you, MacNamara."

"See, that wasn't so hard," Eric said with a facetious smile.

The man walked up to the edge of the ring with his arms crossed and a look of disdain. The feeling was mutual.

Caleb Lochmann stood an inch taller than the boys, but his muscular build gave him the appearance of a tank in comparison to their leaner stature. He was 30-something years old with sandy blonde hair and a growing beard, thick around his jaw. He had trained with The Colectiv under Michael Iovaneau since before the man was even crowned Commander. He had been somewhat of a protégée for many years, but as soon as the MacNamara twins came into the picture, they inadvertently took Caleb's spotlight. Like everyone else, he didn't trust them for being daywalkers, but he disliked them for their talent, and he expressly hated that Michael favored their opinion. But it didn't stop him from becoming Michael's second lieutenant.

The boys proceeded to clean their swords on their already dirty clothes as he spoke.

"You both look like shit."

"Better than *you*," Eric teased.

"What do you want?" James asked. His voice was tinged with the usual venom he directed at Caleb.

"The commander wants to talk to you both in his office," he said.

Eric deflated. "About what?"

"He said he needed to tell you something important. He called it an early birthday gift."

Eric quickly straightened back up, only to narrow his eyes at him skeptically. "Really?"

Caleb shrugged. "Don't look at me. I don't know shit. Just meet him in his office when you're done fucking around like a bunch of assholes."

With that, the second lieutenant turned and started walking away.

James scowled and shouted, "Suck a dick, Lochmann!"

"It might be good for you," Eric finished the sentiment.

James choked as a harsh cackle came out of him. Caleb threw back a middle finger before disappearing through the door, which made them laugh harder.

When his laughter died down, James leaned in close to Eric and whispered so nobody else could hear, "Do you know what he's on about?"

If Michael asked for Eric and James specifically and Caleb knew nothing about it, then it could surely mean one thing.

"I have an idea, but there's only one way to find out."

†††

After getting cleaned up and putting on a change of clothes, no one could have ever guessed that the boys had just been in a brutal training session. No longer did they look like something out of a horror movie, as not a single bruise or scratch was left on their skin. It was a perk to their DNA that they didn't mind bragging about.

They walked the corridors of the Brasov estate down the familiar route to Michael's office, side by side. As soon as they reached the commander's door, Eric knocked three times, already hearing his steady heartbeat within.

"Come in, boys," he said from the other side.

One after the other, they entered the familiar room made of mahogany wood. Sunlight filtered in through the tall windows, which were framed with emerald curtains, giving the room a nice glow. A warm fire crackled within a fireplace, enveloping them in warmth. Inserted bookshelves lined the back walls, and in between them was a space dedicated to swords and daggers from around the world, a lot of which Eric recognized to be katanas. In front of the wall was Michael, sitting at a dark wooden desk, leaning back in a big leather chair, looking up at the twins.

James nodded in greeting. "Mike."

"E. Jimmy," he greeted with a smile and motioned to the chairs across the desk. "Please take a seat."

They pulled them out and sank into the soft leather. James found comfort by slouching in his seat, while Eric sat forward with his elbows on his knees, eager with his eyebrows raised.

"Do either of you want a drink?" Michael asked, jutting his thumb at the bar cart by the window.

The boys shook their heads.

"Nah, I'm good."

"No, thanks," Eric said, eager to get to the point. "Caleb said you had something for us?"

[9]"I do, I do, but first," the commander leaned forward on the desk, his gaze fixed on Eric. "I wanted to get something off my chest. I know my methods might be a little questionable sometimes. We've had a pretty rocky relationship, and I know you were pissed when you had to come back, but... I'm happy that you did, E. You've both grown so much in the last few years and you, especially, have trained like a *beast*. You've become better than I ever could have imagined, with little to no guidance from me. I just wanted to tell you that I'm proud."

Michael put his hand over his heart as he said the last few words.

"I'm proud of you both," he reiterated. "Your mom would be proud."

Eric furrowed his brow, not expecting or even used to Michael's words of affirmation. The thought of his mom in that context also filled him with unexpected, pressing emotion. He had returned to The Colectiv for selfish reasons and had improved solely for himself above all else. He hadn't expected any kind of relationship with Michael or even approval from him, but over time it seemed like they had come to rest on somewhat even ground, and the chasm that used to exist between them wasn't so vast. By no means was their relationship the

---

[9] Change (In the House of the Flies) - Deftones

same as it was when he was a child, but at the very least, they didn't constantly want to kill each other.

"Thanks, I guess," he uttered.

Michael continued, "I also know how much it's been killing you to get back out there and find the bastard that attacked you in Italy, so I also commend you on that patience of yours."

"Yeah, well, the reason he got to me in the first place was because I was stupid and woefully unprepared. I just wanted to make sure that wasn't the case this time. He's a vampire, after all. The chances of him being dead are pretty low, and I've got...*all* the time in the world."

Eternity, even.

"That you do," Michael said with a smirk. "And you said you felt ready, so... I'm happy to say that your wait is over."

Eric's heart lurched in his chest. At the same time, both brothers perked up in their seats.

"Wait, what?" James blurted out.

It was true. After almost three years of being back, Eric and Michael thought it was time to think about returning to the task at hand, which was finding and killing his attacker from three years ago.

Dante.

No last name, just Dante, and an apt one at that.

Yes, Eric had exercised an extreme amount of patience, but it wasn't without sudden outbursts or fighting the urge to tear every vampire in the vicinity apart for answers. But he knew he couldn't act out of impulse, especially not with something so personal. Though he had always kept a lookout for familiar faces, he wasn't surprised when he didn't find any. After all, the world had many dark corners. Vampires had a knack for hiding, and it was a hunter's job to search and leave no stone unturned. This piece of information, however, was being saved for Eric as part of the deal he made with Michael, and now it was time for it to be placed in his hands.

The commander reached into a drawer, took out a small piece of paper, and placed it on the desk, sliding it towards them. The twins leaned in closer, their faces hovering over what looked like a business card with the name *Jean Beltremieux*. Underneath was a number scrawled in black ink. They stared at it dubiously.

Is that French?

"Who's Jean?" James asked.

The old hunter leaned back in his chair and said, "Jean... is a vampire."

Eric scowled, and his brother must have made a similar expression, because Michael chuckled as he looked between them both.

"Jean is a respected individual in the vampire community, and he's a pretty valuable asset since he also has a lot of connections and authority," he explained. "He was on The Colectiv's bad side many decades ago, but he's managed to redeem himself in a variety of ways. He's a lot like a mentor for young purebloods, much like I am to all of you, and if you make good with him, he might share some valuable information."

Eric frowned. "And why would *he* share valuable information with The Colectiv?"

It wasn't rare for hunters to work with vampires. If their hands were clean enough or if they made the right deal, they could be great informants for much bigger cases. Much like how civilian authorities work with criminals to take down bigger criminals. But if Jean Beltremieux is who Michael says he is, Eric couldn't help but wonder what the commander had on him or why he would be so willing to work with The Colectiv at all. Vampires weren't exactly trustworthy individuals to begin with.

Michael nodded. "Yeah, he doesn't particularly like us or mess with us, but when he heard that it was you who needed information," he pointed to Eric, "he didn't hesitate to say yes."

"Me? Why me?"

"Because you're a daywalker that works for The Colectiv, E. You both are, and your reputation precedes you, as you know. That's why you're here, because he knows who you are, and he specifically requested to see you both."

"Are you serious?" James asked in disbelief.

"Yeah, I'm serious."

The twins cast a sideways glance at each other. The MacNamara boys were aware, at this point in their lives, that they were known by a vast majority of people on both sides of the supernatural world. However, it was often in infamy. Most people wanted to kill them, not meet with them and have a genuine conversation. Eric knew that well enough.

As if reading his mind, the commander tried to quell his anxieties.

"Jean's not known for being a cold-blooded killer, so I don't think he'll try anything of the sort, but he does harbor a lot of secrets and likes being in the know. He probably wants to know what you're all about. And maybe if you open up to him a little, he'll open up to you."

Eric took the card in his hand, regarding it with thoughtful, steely eyes. The only time he ever had conversations with vampires was when he was pretending to be human to fool them in a hunt. Otherwise, he never sat down with them. He had used their intel before, but the last time Eric had a personal one-on-one was three years ago, and it didn't have a happy ending. Now, to be requested by one was odd, but it was also intriguing.

"How did you even get his number?" he asked.

"We keep tabs on all the major vampires like him. Especially those in the area."

James voiced Eric's pressing thought: "What do you have on him?"

The commander inclined his head and gave a little shrug. "Like I said, he's not a cold-blooded killer, but a vampire like that doesn't live as long as he does without getting his hands a little dirty. Let's just say there's a reason he's not dead or underwater."

By "underwater," he meant Charybdis, which was a medium-sized prison located deep in the Black Sea. It harbored traitors and vampires that The Colectiv wanted to keep alive, either for value or to torture for an indeterminate amount of time. Eric had never been there, but he had heard about it enough to see it as a ghost story. He never had the desire, seeing as getting assigned a job there wasn't precisely an honor either. The thought of it sent a chill up his spine because if things had gone worse three years ago, it could've been *him* in there. Somehow, that seemed far worse than death.

"So, we just...*call him*?" James inquired.

"Yup. He said to call him after sunset, and he'll arrange a meeting with you."

Eric smiled with satisfaction. "Great."

†††

Bucharest, Romania – Two Days Later

After a three-hour train ride, James and Eric arrived at the North Railway Station in Bucharest at dusk. They had two hours to kill before they met with Jean Beltremieux, so they checked into a hotel and got all of their baggage situated for the night.

49

Eric had called the vampire the same night that Michael gave him his number, and it seemed he had been patiently waiting for him. The man had a deep, baritone voice and a charm that he exuded even over the phone. He sounded fascinated by the idea of speaking to Eric, which confirmed what Michael had told the twins in his office. It was disconcerting. Even more so was the fact that Jean called him by his full name: Eric Django MacNamara.

"How the hell do you know my middle name?" he demanded.

Most people knew his father's last name, but no stranger ever knew anything else. Sometimes it was a miracle if they mentioned his first name at all. He didn't think members of The Colectiv cared enough to learn it, aside from the higher-ups. Eric didn't know if Michael had shared things about the boys with Jean or if he already knew them indirectly.

The vampire gave him a simple answer: "All in due time. I want to save our conversation for our in-person meeting with your brother present."

Eric and James approached the meeting like they did with any other hunt: with their guards up and their senses high. Even if Michael assured them that Jean wouldn't try anything, they couldn't take any chances. They didn't know who Mr. Beltremieux was, what he was capable of, or what his intentions were, so they needed to be prepared for anything. They kept the big weapons, like their swords and James' crossbow, back at the hotel, but knives, daggers, and pistols lay hidden in pockets, sleeves, and holsters. They also had their physicality at their disposal, but they saved that for worst-case scenarios, which, hopefully, it wouldn't come to.

When it was time, they went to the address Jean had given them, armed and ready. They walked down the snowy cobblestone path and up the steps of a stone house stuck in between other homes. Eric knocked on the wooden door and listened carefully to what was inside. There was a soft crackling and the smell of smoke mixed with roses. Moments later, a set of heavy footsteps on hardwood approached—no heartbeat—and then the door clicked before swinging inward.

The twins stared up at the man in the doorway, whom they instantly knew to be Jean Beltremieux. Everything about him screamed "vampire." He was a tall man with dark skin and black locs that fell to his elbows. A growing beard covered the lower half of his face, as well as a pleasant smirk. He wore a black coat over a red button-up and the scent of flowers emanated from him. Physically, he looked like a man in his late twenties or early thirties, but there was no way to tell what his real age was without asking.

He stared down at them with his dark brown eyes, which were alight with surprising warmth and excitement. He almost seemed to be examining them with a curious glint, letting his gaze rove over each of their faces. There was something else in his stare, and Eric couldn't tell if it was judgment, recognition, or if he was simply committing them to memory.

"Jean Beltremieux?" Eric broke the silence.

"The very same," he uttered in that deep, sultry voice he heard over the phone.

"I'm Lieutenant James MacNamara," James said first.

"And I'm Corporal Eric MacNamara," Eric said right after.

It was a formality more than anything. A reminder that this was business.

"Wow, you have ranks and everything," Jean mused. "Well, it's nice to finally meet the famous daywalker twins. I think this meeting is *long* overdue."

Eric quirked an eyebrow.

"Famous?" James scoffed. "I wish."

"I think the word you're looking for is 'notorious'," Eric added.

The vampire shrugged. "You'd be surprised. Depends on whom you ask, but living or undead, people have a lot to say about you."

"And what do *you* say, Mr. Beltremieux?"

"That's what this meeting is for, isn't it?" he said, before stepping aside and motioning for the boys to enter. "Come in. We have much to talk about."

The twins shared a glance before going up the stone steps into Jean's Bucharest home, which had similar Romanian architecture to the Iovaneau Estate. However, where the manor was dark, rich mahogany, Jean's house had a bright cream interior and walls adorned with emerald and gold-leafed wallpaper. It was French-inspired, much like his name.

The vampire closed the door and pointed to a table in the middle of the foyer.

"Leave your weapons here. You won't be needing those."

The hunters scoffed and sputtered.

"What?"

"No fucking way."

Jean's cordial demeanor fell, and he fixed them with a severe look. "Hey, this is my house, and in my house, there's a 'no violence' rule, got that? And that applies to humans, vampires, and everyone in between. You are guests here, and I treat my guests with respect, but I expect my guests to treat me the same, so... *no weapons.*"

Eric and James glared at him, perhaps hoping he'd back down or change his mind, but the old vampire was about as unmoved as stone. Instead, he fixed his gaze on Eric and spoke evenly to him.

"I would hope a young anthropologist like yourself would understand the ethics and level of respect an outsider must maintain when in someone else's home."

Eric was taken aback, his eyes flashing with astonishment. He knew for a fact that he didn't learn that from Michael.

How the fuck did he know that?

He stared at him, wide-eyed, with no argument to give, and instead nodded in agreement. "Fine."

"What?" James hissed behind him.

"Just do what he says, Jimmy."

Upon Jean's request, Eric unzipped his jacket and began taking out every concealed weapon with poignancy. James sighed in annoyance and did the same. They took out all the knives and daggers they had meticulously hidden and let them clang against each other on the wooden table as Jean watched. When they were done, he looked between them and stared at James in disapproval.

"You still have one, don't you?" he asked.

"No."

"Yes, you do."

"Fuck you. You know that? Fine."

With a sneer, the lieutenant reached under his boot and took out a small blade from the sole. He raised it for Jean to see and then let it drop on the table with a clatter. Eric was just surprised he didn't throw it at the wall or even his head.

"There. That's all of them," he seethed.

Jean grinned. "Good. Now, let's go inside and get a little more comfortable."

4

The Pureblood from Louisiana

Eric

They gathered in a well-adorned sitting room past a pair of French doors, each man in a plush chair surrounding an old fireplace. Warm embers sizzled from within and cast an orange glow on everyone's faces. It was a welcome comfort at this time of year.

"French name, French house. What's a French man doing in Romania and not, say, France?" Eric asked dryly.

Jean chuckled. "Because I'm not actually French."

"What is it, an alias or something?" James chimed in.

"I'm from Louisiana. My parents were from Haiti, which the French, incidentally, liked taking from a little too much." The twins nodded in understanding as the vampire asked, "Can I offer you something? Water? Alcohol? *Blood*?"

His lip curled as he said the last word. Eric wasn't amused.

"No, thanks. We've got blood back at home."

Jean raised his eyebrows. "So, you *do* drink blood?"

"Sometimes."

"I assume you've hunted? Humans, I mean."

Eric swallowed hard at the idea. "No. We have blood bags for that."

"We're hunters, so it's pretty frowned upon to hurt humans," James added.

Mr. Beltremieux clicked his tongue. "What a shame. Blood packs pale in comparison to what's fresh. They don't taste nearly as good or give you as much energy. Although it does serve as a pick-me-up."

Eric shrugged. "We wouldn't know the difference, so what does it matter anyway?"

Jean hummed in response, studying them like a spectator at a museum—or worse, how a scientist would a specimen. The young hunters stared back with intensity, and Eric especially stood on guard in the presence of a pureblood. He didn't appreciate being watched like an animal or the way the vampire's eyes lingered on James in particular.

"Problem?" the lieutenant muttered.

"No, not at all."

Eric shifted in his chair as the impatience needled away at him. "Michael said you asked for us. Why?"

Mr. Beltremieux turned his attention to him, and the daywalker couldn't help but feel like he could somehow see right into his soul.

"I wanted to see the MacNamara twins myself. Everything I hear about you nowadays is hearsay or something of an urban legend, but I knew it couldn't be true. But it's difficult to tell when those who get too close end up dead... or worse. When Michael came to me and said you needed information, I couldn't refuse. I knew I had to find out for myself who you *truly* were," he explained with a smirk.

"But over the phone, you knew my full name. How?"

"Oh, I know both of your names," he said aridly. "Eric Django and James Danior MacNamara Mészáros."

A muscle twitched in Eric's cheek at the mention of his mother's maiden name. It was even more surprising than the middle names, no less coming from a pureblood. Despite it, the daywalker maintained control, though he could almost feel his brother tensing from a distance.

"Did Michael give you that information?" he asked.

"No, actually… your father did."

Jean dropped the metaphorical bomb so haphazardly that it took Eric a second to process what he had said. After all, he had come here for information on Dante. To have both his parents mentioned wasn't even in the realm of possibilities for topics of conversation. He froze in shock for a moment and glanced at his brother, who shared the same astonished expression.

"What the fuck did you just say?" James demanded.

"I said I learned it from your father. I knew him," Jean repeated. The cool surface of his voice never broke.

After a moment of stunned silence, Eric asked, "You…*knew* Wade?"

No one ever *knew* Wade MacNamara. They just knew *of* him. At least not the people in Eric's circle.

"I did. He was a dear friend of mine."

The young man scoffed in disbelief. *Dear friend? He had* friends?

"Didn't he die before we were even born? How could he possibly have told you that?" James argued.

"He was around long enough to give you your names. Let's leave it at that," the vampire said. "Though I'm not surprised you were led to believe otherwise."

This was news to Eric. He had given up on the concept of his biological father long ago. After all, he was never coming back, and there wasn't much to say apart from what he already learned, and Eric had tried *desperately* to learn. However, the picture painted of him wasn't remotely pretty, in fact, the evidence relayed quite the opposite. Now, even James referred to Wade as their "sperm donor" more often than not. Of course, it didn't mean that this didn't spark some curiosity. And Eric's curious nature often got the best of him.

"How did you know him?" he demanded.

"We met on the battlefield in the 1860s. I was a medic, and he was a soldier."

Eric's eyebrows shot up in surprise. "The Civil War?"

"Yes. Did you know that about him?" Jean asked curiously.

"A bit."

He knew Wade had been a war veteran of some kind, as it was one of the truths their mother told them, but it had been a while since he stopped to think about just how many years his father had lived or how many wars he could've fought. He especially didn't stop to think about the friends he may or may not have made over those years. It was all too human and hit a little too close to home.

The vampire looked between the two of them. "Do you know much about your father?"

"We know enough," James huffed. "He was some angry Irish guy who did bad things, killed the wrong people, knocked up our mom, and got himself killed."

Jean Beltremieux burst out laughing, the sound booming. Eric stared at him warily, suddenly on edge. James, on the other hand, looked vexed and unamused.

"What the fuck are *you* laughing at?"

The vampire shook his head, speaking past his dying laughter, "I'm sorry, I just think it's hilarious how much you remind me of him. And I also find it funny that even after all this time, people still manage to dumb things down for their convenience and leave out important details."

"You mean the details of how he killed Gabriel Iovaneau?" Eric blurted out.

The room fell silent as soon as the cold question left his mouth, and Jean fixed his eyes on him once again. The dark brown looked like amber in the firelight. Though the boy expected some kind of threat or even defensiveness within them, there was none to be found. Eric, however, let his anger bleed into his face.

Jean then narrowed his eyes, asking, "Do you know *why* Wade killed him?"

"Power, maybe. I don't know," Eric answered with a shrug. "Why do vampires do anything?"

The pureblood rolled his eyes. "You hunters act as if we're an entirely separate, inhuman species, but need I remind you that we were all alive once? We were humans before life led us here, so don't speak on something you don't know."

"Fine, but we were born like this," Eric argued, his rage building. "He made us, he disappeared, and then he got himself killed for his own fucked up reasons. So, I'm sorry if there's a bit of resentment."

"And that's where you're wrong."

"How so?"

"Wade was a good man. A complicated man. He was a fighter, a man of war and rebellion, and he carried a lot of pain, a lot of loss, and a lot of baggage, just like many of us vampires do. I think even after getting turned, he had a hard time finding something to cling to in this world. Something other than violence. It was why our friendship was so important. And it was why your mother was important."

"So, what? It got too much for him?" James accused.

"No, I'm just saying he could never catch a break, and when he found something good, he protected it with his life, no matter the costs."

Eric hummed. "I guess it runs in the family."

Jean stared at him, his demeanor turning calm once more. "You've been through a lot, haven't you?"

The young man was caught off-guard by the short yet imposing question. It sent a hot wave of defensiveness prickling over his skin.

"What about it?"

"You know, it's very interesting. Michael may have raised you, but you've both got a lot more of Wade in you than you think. Feel how you feel about him, but you do. That stubbornness and passion—the inability to put up with bullshit. Hell, even the parts you try so desperately to hide. Michael molded you like steel in fire, as he does with all of his students, no doubt, but no amount of fire can truly kill a MacNamara. No matter how hard you try."

After a brief pause, Jean added, with a pointed look, "You've come a long way from the boy you once were, Corporal."

It was a statement, not a question.

Eric scowled. "What the fuck is that supposed to mean?"

"I guess I just imagined you as a boy full of zeal and wonder who wears his heart on his sleeve, but... you're a lot more hardened now. That heart's hidden under a plate of steel, isn't it?"

His words were like an accusation that triggered something profoundly rooted within Eric. It made him lose the remainder of his cool, professional demeanor.

James leaped to his defense first. "Hey, fuck off."

But Eric was already ahead of him.

"How could you possibly know enough about me that you can even imagine anything?" he said harshly, his words as sharp as a blade. "You don't fucking know me. You don't know my life. Just because you knew our father doesn't mean you know me or my brother. And I'm getting real fucking sick and tired of people pretending like they do."

Jean raised and lowered his eyebrows in a rapid motion, his lips curving with mirth.

"Listen, I'm not pretending to know anything I don't. You might be right, but you'd also be surprised by the things that I do know. I've lived for almost two centuries. I know a lot of people."

"Oh, yeah? Enlighten me then," Eric spat. "We came here because we needed information on someone, and Michael said you'd be able to give it to us on the condition that we met with you." He opened his arms wide, motioning to the room. "Well, we're here. And with all due respect, Mr. Beltremieux, I didn't come here for a therapy session. Now...tell us what we need to know, or we'll take it by force."

The vampire sighed, leaning back in his chair. "Fine. That's fair. You're here about Dante, I presume?"

The name made the hunter straighten his spine. "Yeah, we are," he confirmed.

"So, you *do* know him," James said.

"Unfortunately."

"Do you know where he is?" Eric asked with eagerness.

"Actually, I don't. I don't care about that asshole enough to keep track. He's like a Tasmanian devil of destruction, so it's better to keep your distance."

Eric snorted. *Wish I knew that earlier.*

Jean continued, "But... I do know someone who might have a clue as to where he is. In fact, I'm pretty sure she's the only person who could possibly know."

"She?" James uttered.

"Yes, *she.*"

Eric's heart proceeded to sink.

She. As much as he wanted to deny it and hope that he was wrong, he also knew that there was only one person that Jean could be talking about. He would be stupid to not think about it. But even if he already knew, Eric tried to push the idea away.

It could be someone else.

Against his own volition, he started to panic.

No, no, no, no.

"No," he blurted out.

"Yes," Jean said with an apologetic smile.

"There has to be someone else," he argued.

"Even if I could give you other names, I'm afraid she's your safest bet."

He could feel James' eyes on him. "Who is he talking about?"

Eric bounced his leg up and down in a nervous gesture, his eyes on Jean, yet not entirely looking at him.

"Emilia," he whispered.

His brother groaned, "Aww, shit."

[10]All at once, Eric felt like he couldn't breathe.

---

[10] News Today - Phantogram

He shot out of his seat and walked away from the conversation and the heat of the fireplace. He went across the room to stand by a smaller sitting area. He ran his fingers through his hair, taking deep breaths with his back turned to them and his gaze trained on a large painting on the wall. But all he could see were flashbacks to a beach in Italy and that night when she looked at him with horror and betrayal. He pictured glowing eyes as helplessness washed over him. But when he thought about that, he thought about California, and then he thought about brutal training sessions, and then he thought of his mom and his dad, and-

"Hey, E, are you good?" James' voice, though concerned, sounded far away.

"Yeah, just give me a minute," he said, but he knew his racing heart betrayed him.

God, this is so stupid. Get your shit together.

Perhaps Eric had deluded himself into thinking he'd never see Emilia again. He knew he was a fool to think it, but it seemed that no matter how much training he had or how smart of a hunter he became, he was still a fool in other ways. After all, Emilia was Dante's sister, and he knew from his own experience that one never traveled without the other. Still, dealing with Dante was one thing, but dealing with *her* was another. It didn't help that his feelings over what happened were still a tangled, angry mess.

Eric focused on the painting, which was of a woman in a pink dress on a swing. Behind him, his brother continued questioning Jean.

"How do you even know her?"

"She's a very good friend of mine—more than a friend, she's like family. I'm the one that turned her all those years ago."

He really did *know a lot of people.*

"Jesus Christ, who are you?" James whispered sharply.

"Jean Beltremieux, baby," the vampire drawled.

It explained how Jean seemed to know so much about Eric and James, to begin with. Not only had he known their father, but he knew Emilia, of all people, and she trusted him enough to talk about Eric. And the thought of her being out there, knowing what she knew about him, made Eric want to tear off his skin.

When his breathing was even enough, he turned back around and walked back to his seat, but didn't sit down. Jean and James looked up at him in concern.

"There's water if you need some," the vampire offered.

"No, thanks."

"Does that happen to you often?"

Eric crossed his arms and fixed him with a cold stare. "That's none of your business. Tell us what you know."

Jean went on, "Well, I know all about Italy and that night when you almost lost your life. That's why you're here, right? You want revenge."

"I do," he affirmed.

"Then Emilia is your best bet."

"Where is she?"

"I'll tell you, but only if you make me a promise."

Eric furrowed his brow. "What kind of promise?"

"A promise that you won't kill her." The twins scoffed, but Jean proceeded, "I know it might be tempting after everything, but Dante is the one you want. Not her."

"What if she doesn't comply? If she does something shady, you know it's our job to do something about it, right?" James contested.

"Emilia is like a daughter to me. I've watched her grow for decades, and although she's guilty of many things, she is nothing like her brother, and she doesn't play into his wicked games anymore. She's just a lost soul trying to find her way through life. Do what you need to get what you want, but if she doesn't come out alive at the end of all this, I will come for you with everything that I have. I don't care whose sons you are. Is that clear?"

It was the first real threat Jean Beltremieux made in the entire meeting, and Eric had to admit that it was a noble one. He was diplomatic, protective, and commanding, and Eric now knew what Michael meant by him being an authority figure in the vampire world.

He pondered whether he'd be able to kill Emilia if the occasion arose. Similar to what his brother said, it was a possibility if things went awry. After all, it was part of the protocol to take the life of a vampire who was a genuine danger to others. So far, Emilia hadn't done anything to warrant such an execution, at least not like Dante did. But despite the twins' hatred for them both, perhaps they were willing to overlook certain things to take down the bigger threat here.

"Clear," Eric said first.

Jean looked over at James, who simply said, "Clear."

"Good," Mr. Beltremieux sighed. "The last time we talked, she was living in New York."

"Where in New York?" James asked.

"Manhattan. She performs at a club called The Canary, and she goes by the stage name 'Roxie Vega'."

"The last time, she was spending all of her time with Dante. They were traveling the world together. How do you know he's not with her now?" Eric asked thoughtfully.

Jean smiled somberly. "Dante and Emilia haven't talked since what happened in Sorrento."

Eric frowned. "What? Why?"

"They have a dark past, much of which is not mine to tell, but... it's been bloody and tumultuous. Emilia followed in her big brother's footsteps for a long time, and he hurt her in more ways than she could count, but I think what happened with you was her breaking point. They went their separate ways, and the only person she stays in touch with, as far as I know, is me."

So that's what he meant when he said she wasn't playing his games anymore.

When Eric sat back down, his heartbeat was back to normal. He always thought Dante and Emilia had moved on from what they did like it was nothing, but to know otherwise filled him with bittersweet satisfaction. Some dark part of Eric was happy that he wasn't the only one left wounded in the aftermath.

"Is that it?" he asked.

Jean nodded. "That's it."

In a brief moment of silence, Eric looked into the fire as he mulled it all over. While he could've lingered on the thought of Emilia and what seeing her again meant, his mind went back to something Jean said earlier in the conversation. It was something that awakened that deep and ravenous curiosity within him that craved to learn—a part of him that couldn't let certain things go until he knew the answer. It was both a blessing and a curse.

James got up from his seat, eager to go, saying, "Well, thank you for your time, Mr. Beltremieux."

"Wait," Eric blurted out.

He tore his eyes away from the flames and looked toward his twin, who gave him an odd look. He then turned to Jean.

"Why *did* Wade kill Gabriel Iovaneau?"

James raised his eyebrows and looked over at Jean in expectance. Eric could tell that this was something he wanted answered too.

The southern man looked between the two of them attentively and said, "If I told you, it would have to be off the record."

"Off the record? We don't exactly work for the local paper," James derided.

"No, but you do work for The Colectiv, and there are things that they don't like getting spread around. Especially Michael Iovaneau, because this involves his family. You want me to talk? It'll be as a family friend, not as a vampire."

Eric knew all too well how easily The Colectiv covered things up because they did the same thing with what happened to him and even with his mother. Jean Beltremieux may have liked his secrets, but The Colectiv was no better. After all, it made Eric who he is now.

Without using words, the twins reached an agreement with a simple nod and a shrug.

"Fine."

Jean stood up and leaned against the fireplace, looking for the words in the flames. Eric studied the side of his face in anticipation.

"He did it for your mother."

Eric shook his head in confusion. "What do you mean?"

The pureblood turned his head, his brown eyes connecting with the hunter's hazel ones.

"Gabriel Iovaneau crossed a line... and your father had him killed."

5

The Protégé

James

Brasov, Romania

[11]James sat alone in Michael's office, combat boots propped up on the desk, flipping a butterfly knife in his hand. He wore his usual casual outfit, which was a band t-shirt with the sleeves rolled up and black cargo pants. A silver eyebrow piercing glittered in the light, as did the small hoops that hung from his ears against his long brown hair. On his right arm was a tattoo sleeve made up of intricate designs, as well as a ram's skull across his throat. Whether they had any meaning or not was for him to know and everyone else to find out.

The commander had asked to see him before he and his brother officially left for New York to find Emilia. James figured that he wanted a mission debrief for their meeting with Jean. Reporting vital

---

[11] Swerve - Papa Roach (ft. FEVER 333 & Sueco)

information to the commander was a standard part of James' job, though everyone was trained to do it from a young age. Eric was a lot less used to the idea, so James had to remind him to do it, but he didn't mind doing it himself. Although some part of him wondered—he *hoped* if there was something else Michael wanted to talk about.

The promotion, perhaps?

We'll see.

For James, getting summoned into Michael's office was like getting called to the principal's office in grade school. Either you did something good and got an award, or you did something terrible and got reprimanded. Back when he was a kid, 100% of those times were because he did something bad, and he could recall getting dragged into Michael's office for worse things as a teenager.

Breaking & entering, destruction of public property, aggravated assault—the list went on, and it sounded a lot more intense on paper, but in reality, James would qualify it as "stupid shit." While he was a great hunter, it didn't negate the fact that he was a particularly volatile kid, and after the loss of his parents, he took every chance to unleash his emotions through chaos and rebellion. Not to mention, his ego was inflated due to his enhanced abilities, so he felt like he could get away with anything for a long time. Or maybe he thought, "People are gonna hate me anyway, so why the fuck not?" The twins had that in common, although Eric took his anger out on Michael more often than not. Still, if one was trouble, two were chaos, and if it weren't for the power that Michael had, both of them—James especially—would have ended up with jail time and a permanent record. That was one thing he could be grateful to the Silver Wolf for. He always believed in James and managed to knock some sense into him as he got older. Nowadays, he doesn't get into trouble too often anymore because he got his act together enough to rise in the ranks. *Enough*. Because even Michael knew that James' passion came in handy.

"I just think it's hilarious because you remind me so much of him."

That's what Mr. Beltremieux had said to him, apart from the fact that he couldn't stop staring at either him or Eric.

James knew how much he looked like Wade. He had the picture from his mother's locket tattooed in his memory, and he couldn't erase it, no matter how hard he tried. He used to hate the idea of looking like him so much that he shaved his head and started getting more tattoos when he was 19. It wasn't a bad look, but it wasn't a good one either, and it didn't stop him from looking more and more like his "sperm donor" with every passing year. He hardly ever looked into that locket anymore, but he and Eric still carried it around. After all, it was their mother's, and her picture was in it too.

He sighed to himself. When a hunt or an interrogation was done, he didn't think twice about it afterward. It wasn't an emotional job, and heart-to-heart conversations weren't normal on the field, but this meeting stuck with him like glue. He wouldn't admit it out loud, but it did. Jean Beltremieux was a vampire like no other, even if he did make him angry. He just couldn't believe what he said about Wade killing Michael's brother.

James was more than familiar with the story. Everyone who had any ties to The Colectiv was. Michael was 22 when he and his older brother, Gabriel, went on the hunt with a team in the snowy mountains. They were ambushed, not anticipating the attack by such a high number of vampires, and Gabriel was mauled to death before Michael's very eyes. The only reason there were survivors at all was that he killed the remaining attackers with nothing but two swords and led the rest of his team home. It's the story that gave him his scars and his name: The Silver Wolf.

When he was a kid, James saw, as everyone else did, that Gabriel's death was tragic and Michael was a brave hero, but over time, his views on it morphed. When he found out his father ordered the hit, James couldn't help but believe that he was, in fact, the byproduct of some monster, and it made him angry at himself and the world. Then, when Eric - his own brother—almost lost his life, the story gave him nightmares. And now, with this new piece of information, James didn't know how to feel.

Wade had him killed because he crossed a line with Mom.

Wade killed a Iovaneau, an heir, the commander's son...for love? *What kind of person does that?*

For once, he wasn't passing judgment; he simply couldn't wrap his head around it. He could have easily written Wade off as a criminal for the things he did, but it was different when his mother was involved. Their father had been a ghost in the twins' entire lives, and it was easy to forget that, maybe, he *had* loved Anya all those years ago.

James cringed. Even in all seriousness, the topic of love made him uncomfortable. He didn't like thinking about it. And he blamed it on the lack of good examples.

He could hear Michael coming down the hall, the familiar sound of his footsteps getting closer and closer before the door swung open and he stepped inside.

"Hey, kid."

"Hey," he said, his deep voice rumbling.

On the way to his desk, Michael stopped by James's legs and pointed at them in annoyance. "What are you, an animal? Get your feet off my fuckin' desk. Who raised you?"

James scoffed, "*You* did, actually."

"Yeah, but didn't your mother teach you manners?" the commander said as he poured himself a glass of whiskey.

"Must have gotten shredded from my memory to make room for shooting people in the face."

"Okay, wise guy. Feet *off*."

James rolled his eyes but complied and sat back in the chair with his feet firm on the ground. The smell of bitter, smoky liquor filled the air. Michael sat down, and the young man closed his knife with a click and clutched it in his hand.

He eyed the commander for a brief moment before asking, "Is this about the promotion?"

For the past few months or so, he and Michael have been in talks to potentially give James a higher rank in the commander's division. About a year ago, he was promoted to lieutenant, but the role of Knight Captain had been open for a while since the last one had been gravely injured, and currently, two people are being considered: James MacNamara and Caleb Lochmann. It was the second-highest rank in The Colectiv, and James had never wanted anything more in his life.

For as long as he could remember, he had worked tirelessly to prove to himself and Michael that he could get the job done. It was why he had cleaned up his act at all. He started going on more group missions and overseeing training (much to his chagrin). And when he started getting promoted, it was even more incentive to get better. It appealed to his competitive nature and was a chance to show off his leadership skills and gain more respect. Being a daywalker in a position of power could have a far-reaching impact not only on him but also on his brother, and after everything they've been through together, the opportunity was too good to pass up.

Michael chuckled at his eagerness. "We'll get to that. But first," He took a quick sip from his drink and leaned forward against the desk with a serious expression. "Tell me what happened with Jean."

James rolled his eyes. "Oh, that guy."

"I'm assuming you didn't like him?" Michael smirked.

"He's not the worst, but he talks too much. And he speaks like he's in one of those Shakespeare plays or that Aeropostale guy."

"Aristotle?"

"Yeah, that guy."

The commander laughed, "Yeah, old vampires can be a bit dramatic sometimes."

"You're telling me."

"So, what happened? What did he say?"

James relayed the information, just like he always did in these situations. He gave him a play-by-play of what happened while keeping certain details *off the record*.

"He said he knew Dad."

The commander raised his eyebrows. "He told you that?"

"Yeah. He said they met in the American Civil War."

"That's it?"

James furrowed his brow. "Yeah. He said Wade had his reasons for doing things and that he had been through some shit."

"And you believe him?"

"I don't fucking trust him, that's for goddamn sure. Although I kinda have to."

Michael was right about Mr. Beltremieux harboring secrets. It was clear in the way he spoke and danced around information in a way that kept you interested but didn't give too much away. It reminded him of the folklore stories he and Eric had learned about, with creatures that had power over you if they knew your name. And Jean knew more than that.

"It was much wordier, but essentially, he said we were just like him. E told him straight up that he didn't know shit, which I agree with. Did you know he knew him?" James tried reading the commander's expression as he asked the question.

Michael shrugged and leaned back in his chair. "I knew they were connected somehow. Jean was one of the vampires I went to when I was searching for your father, but I didn't know they went that far back. As I said, he keeps his secrets pretty hidden."

Yeah, but something tells me he's not the only one.

James flashed his eyes. "Yeah, it's weird to think about. I'm not immortal yet, so the whole living for hundreds of years thing hasn't really hit me."

"Oh, it will, I'm sure. Did he say anything else? Did you get the information you wanted?"

"Yeah, actually," James said, nodding. "He gave us a lead."

"Okay," Michael said, his eyes bright with eagerness. "What is it?"

For a brief moment, James hesitated. The memory of Eric's episode in the vampire's abode replayed in his mind.

Though they weren't frequent, he had seen his brother have panic attacks before. They happened more after something horrible happened, like when their mother died, during preliminary training, or after Sorrento, but they also happened after a nightmare. James tried to be there for him when he could, but Eric was good at keeping his emotions to himself. Still, he hadn't seen that expression—that *pain*—since the incident. It made his blood boil to even *think* of her.

"Emilia."

The commander's eyes lit up. "Emilia? The girl from Sorrento? The one E—"

"Yeah. According to Jean, she's the only one who would know where Dante is. At least that he knows of. Apparently, she's currently in New York."

Michael scoffed, "Haven't been there in a minute. How'd E take it?"

James' heart faltered. *Not well.* It was a blessing that Michael didn't have heightened senses. The daywalker did his best to find the right words.

"I mean... he's not exactly happy about it, and, to be honest, neither am I. But he knows what has to be done," he replied.

"Really?" Michael asked with an air of surprise.

The lieutenant furrowed his brow. "Yeah, obviously. Why?"

The commander leaned back in his chair. The young daywalker frowned at him, borderline scowling at how long he was taking to say what he wanted to say because that meant it wasn't good. He didn't need something serious right now, not when it came to his brother.

"Oh, God. What?" James' voice rumbled with dread.

"I meant what I said about being proud. You know, E. He struggled a lot with the whole hunting thing growing up, and now he's one of the best we've got."

"But...?"

"*But...* I gotta say I'm a little worried about him."

"Why?"

Michael threw him an unconvinced look. "You're tellin' me you don't know why? You know him better than anyone here, Jimmy. You're tellin' me you're not the least bit worried about what this particular hunt means to him? And now *she's* coming back into the picture."

James crossed his arms and looked off at the books lining the wall. He would be a liar if he said that he didn't worry about Eric. At times, it was like he was the only one who worried about him at all, and he would be loath to admit that Jean Beltremieux was right about one thing: Eric wasn't the same person he was three years ago.

[12]Eric had always been introverted, a dreamer, and more of a thinker, but ever since his recovery, he's been colder, aggressive, and more closed off. It made him a deadly hunter, and James couldn't complain since he was the same way, but it pained him to see that childlike wonder and excitement that Eric used to have get shattered. He couldn't even blame him for being vengeful, because James had felt it since then too, and he knew he would have torn the world apart if Eric had died that day. But he also knew that the reason Michael was worried was not because of Eric's change in behavior, but because there was a possibility that his emotions would get in the way again. And if James was honest, he had a lot of thoughts about that too.

"Of course, I've thought about it," he argued, looking the commander in the eye once again.

"And?"

"I thought you said he was ready. *He's ready.*"

"Is that your honest opinion?"

"What, you want me to talk shit about my brother behind his back? Because I won't."

"No, but like I said, you know him best. I just want to know if I made the right choice."

James scoffed, "And if not, then what? You're gonna stop him? Restrain him? Good fucking luck."

All I'm saying is that the last thing we need is for something to happen like it did with your mom. I pulled him out of the gutter already, but if he decides to go back on his word and do what he did before... I don't know if I can overlook it this time, Jimmy. It's his head or the Black Sea," Michael stressed.

Charybdis.

---

[12] Wires - The Neighbourhood

James clamped his mouth shut tight, nearly breaking his jawbone with the force and the emotions washing over him. He looked down at the mahogany desk, clasping the knife in his hands as he resisted the urge to stab the blade into the wood over and over. It was all he could do to not completely explode at the thought of his brother getting killed or stuck in an underwater prison for all eternity just because he fell for the wrong girl. He'd lose him just like he did his mother, for real this time.

No. No, I refuse to let that happen.

"E's different now," James said after a harrowing moment of silence and proceeded to speak with even ferocity. "He's never made a deal he didn't keep, and he made a deal with you when he came back. He swore he was gonna leave, and he did, even when you didn't want him to. He swore he was gonna become one of the best, and even after all the times he failed, he did it. Emilia broke his heart, and it fucked him up. And maybe that's his fault, sure, but things are different now. He's a cold-hearted, spiteful son of a bitch. I've never seen him fail to complete something he truly sets his mind to. So, if he says he's gonna do this right, he's gonna do this right. And I'll be right there next to him, making sure shit doesn't hit the fan again."

Done with his rant, the daywalker raised his eyebrows at Michael expectantly. In turn, the commander tried hiding a shit-eating grin behind a sip of liquor. James glared at his expression.

"Are you smiling?"

"That's what I wanted to hear, Jimmy," Michael said with a nod of approval.

"Good, because I've got nothing else for you."

"Listen, I admire how much you care about E. Not everyone has the luxury of a solid bond with their siblings, I would know."

The daywalker's eyes briefly flitted to the white scars on his face, feeling a twinge in his heart. He shook off the feeling and buried it like he always did.

"I know," he said simply.

"I'm just looking out for him. I'm looking out for you both," Michael reassured. "But I also want you to know...that there's one more reason I'm bringing all of this up."

"And that is?"

A huge smile spread across Michael's face. "Your promotion."

James' face lit up, and he leaned forward on the mahogany desk. He did his best to still his heart, but the anticipation was already eating away at him. The commander snickered with amusement.

"I'm listening."

"The position is yours—" James sucked in a breath, but he didn't get any words in as Michael continued, "— *If*..."

"'If?'"

Michael nodded, repeating, "'If.'"

"'If' what?"

"If you complete a task for me."

"Oh," James uttered in surprise. "Okay. Done. What is it?"

"Hold on... You can't tell E about it. I know you tell him a lot of things, but this needs to stay between you and me until further notice, alright? I'm asking you as my lieutenant and as my potential future captain."

James gave him a strange look. He had heard these particular words before when he was a troublesome kid. "Don't tell Eric" was usually a suggestion, not an actual order that he followed. But things were different now. Now, it *was* an order, because this meant his entire career, and James didn't know what Michael could be requesting him to do that Eric couldn't know about. Yet, despite his hesitation, he nodded in agreement.

"Yeah. Okay."

The commander took another deep breath before saying, "I think it's about time I tell you a little story...about the case of the 'Hellhound'."

6

Into the Void

Eric

Chains rattled against the sound of heavy metal music as Eric pounded his fists on the vinyl punching bag. He exhaled sharply with each hit, his brow set in a cutting gaze, wearing nothing but gym shorts and black hand wraps. Perspiration ran down his face and body, his skin glistening in the sunlit room. Rage radiated off of him like steam.

Since he returned from Bucharest, his mind had been taken over with thoughts surrounding his meeting with Jean Beltremieux—what he said about his father, about him, and Emilia. He made a strong, desperate attempt to not drive himself insane, but to no avail.

[13]*Of course, it had to be her.*

Eric never told anyone, not even his brother, but Emilia plagued his mind more often than he cared to admit—more than he ever

---

[13] Who Is She? - I Monster

wanted. Soon after the incident, it was worse. Back then, he swore he saw her sometimes, whether it was in the reflection of a mirror or out of the corner of his eye. Every person who resembled her even a fraction caught his attention, making him think she was there when she wasn't and everything that could have possibly reminded him of her seemed to taunt him. He had obsessed over her when they were dating, but after they broke up, it was like the idea obsessed over *him.* Emilia may not be dead, but she haunted Eric all the same, except she was more of a demonic presence than a friendly ghost. And knowing that he had to see her again after three years, those thoughts came creeping back.

Wasn't time supposed to get rid of this?

He knew it was all in his mind. Those thoughts didn't torment him like before, but every so often something would catch him off guard, especially in his dreams. Emilia appeared in them sometimes, as if Eric didn't already have enough nightmares of his past. The dream was often a blurry memory or something out of a psychological thriller and either took place on a beach or an abandoned cityscape. The latter made her being in New York that much stranger. After all, they never met in New York. Sorrento had been far from it. The only time he experienced strange phenomena like that was when he and James had "twin telepathy."

How am I still tied to you?

Eric pushed the thought of her away. He had to if he was going to move forward with this job, because he'd been waiting three years, training arduously, and working himself to the bone to become someone worthy of his name. The last thing he needed was to lose his head the same way he did in Bucharest, or even before because it would result in a downhill spiral. He couldn't lose again—he *wouldn't.* He would simply cross that bridge when he got there. Emilia was a means to an end, and anything he thought he was feeling was rooted in a past that was based on lies. A past that no longer existed.

Still, Jean Beltremieux words lingered.

"Michael may have raised you, but you've both got a lot more of Wade in you than you think."

Perhaps, at some point in time, Eric would've loved to be compared to Wade MacNamara. Lord knows, his mother did it all the time, with a mixture of pride and exasperation. It was a pillar to hold onto during uncertain times, but things are different now. Resentment didn't just go away in the blink of an eye, for the living or the dead. Even if the truth moved him. Even knowing the reason behind Gabriel Iovaneau's murder left him reeling. He had been in denial about it, thinking that perhaps Jean was lying, but he had no reason to.

It almost made him want to laugh out loud.

[14]For a long time, he wanted to be *better* than his father, only to find out that maybe he was worse.

"You've come a long way from the boy you once were, haven't you?"
Yeah, no shit.

Half-breed. Bastard. Walker. Leech. Freak. Demon. Traitor.

Maybe they were right, or maybe not. Either way, those insults were like water off his back at this point. Eric had grown accustomed to such things before joining The Colectiv. Certain things didn't affect him anymore, but Jean's observations were a bit more cutting and precise. It made his blood boil.

He started punching the bag with more aggression, using his knees and elbows to deliver blows.

Did everyone expect me to stay the same forever? Did they expect me to keep taking their shit? To not hit back? Was I supposed to be the same

---

[14] CODE MISTAKE - CORPSE & Bring Me the Horizon

naive shithead who didn't know any better? Who saw the world as some fairy tale? Was I supposed to stay weak and scared? Was I supposed to keep proving them right?

I'm just leveling the playing field.

With a grunt, Eric kicked the punching bag forward before finally pausing and letting it swing back and forth. His chest heaved from the exertion as he grabbed his water bottle from the floor and chugged half of it.

At that moment, a knock came at the door.

Eric rolled his eyes, irritated by the interruption. "Who is it?"

"E, it's me. Can I come in?"

He hoped it was his brother, but to his disappointment, it was Michael's voice on the other side. The last thing he wanted or needed was a "talk" from the commander, but he didn't have a choice in the matter. So he put the bottle down and lowered the music to a whisper before striding over and opening the door. Surely enough, standing in the hallway was the Silver Wolf.

Eric could still recall when he felt like Michael towered over him like a giant, but now he was almost level with his silver eyes. With his casual attire consisting of a black sweater and some jeans, he didn't look like he was in charge of a small army, but the scar and the way he carried himself said otherwise.

The commander donned a fatherly grin and Eric fixed him with a quizzical look.

"Yeah?"

"Sorry to interrupt, but I was hoping to talk to you," Michael said.

"It's not every day you make visits. You usually call or have me sent to your office."

"You know, I tried, but you have a bad habit of putting your phone on Do Not Disturb."

Eric closed his eyes for a moment, baring his teeth apologetically. "Yeah, I forgot that was on. I'm surprised you didn't send Caleb or Jimmy."

"Yeah, well, I wanted to talk to you myself."

A pit of dread began to fester in Eric's stomach.

Great. I think I'd prefer a phone call.

"You can keep doing your thing if it makes things easier," he added.

"Sure."

Eric stepped away from the door, letting the commander into his room. Eric took another drink of water and stood before the punching bag once more. Michael closed the door, sealing them inside. All the while, Eric could sense him eyeing the space. The only person allowed in his room was James, but of course, there were exceptions to be made. Instead of focusing on the discomfort, Eric started hitting the bag at a slow and steady pace.

"What's up, Mike?" he asked coolly.

"I wanted to ask you how your trip to Bucharest went."

"It was fine," Eric answered in between grunts.

"Just 'fine'?"

"Yeah. You were right about Jean. He gave us what we needed."

Eric was being vague on purpose. He knew he was supposed to give the commander all the details, but this case was different. He knew better than to share too much, but to his chagrin, Michael liked being one step ahead.

"Yeah, Jimmy told me everything," he said.

Eric paused for a brief moment, eyeing the commander from the corner of his eye. "*Everything?*"

"Yeah, he told me about what he said about your dad...and about Emilia."

"Huh."

The daywalker stared at the bag rigidly before punching it again.

Sometimes, Eric forgot just how close James and Michael were. It wasn't a total surprise, but Eric couldn't help but feel a little irritated and resentful about it. He trusted James to never say or do something that would put either of them in harm's way, but Eric wished that he kept more things to himself. Even then, he knew it was mostly due to their slightly different upbringings. Some habits weren't so easy to shake.

"What? Were you hoping he didn't?" Michael asked.

"No, I'm just wondering why you came to me at all if Jimmy already told you everything."

"I wanted to make sure you were included in the conversation."

"Well, consider me included," Eric said aridly, eager to move on.

There was a brief pause before the commander asked, "Wasn't it you who told me that lone wolves didn't survive in the world? That it was all bullshit, and they need a pack to survive?"

Eric shot him a strange look. "What? Did I?"

"Yeah, you learned it from one of those books you read a long time ago. When you were just a kid."

"And you remember that?"

Michael gave him a soft grin. "Of course I do."

Eric let the bag swing back and forth, suddenly deep in thought. As a child, he blathered on about a lot of the things he learned and was hyper-fixated on. That trait carried on as an adult and even helped when he went to college, but he didn't do it as openly or as often anymore. Back then, Michael always seemed too preoccupied with turning him into a hunter to ever listen. So the fact that he remembered even a fraction of it was surprising.

"And you're bringing it up now because..."

"I know you like keeping to yourself. I won't bother you for very long, but icing me out doesn't benefit either of us. I'm only trying to help you, E. We're a team. It'd be nice if you were more communicative. I don't appreciate feeling like you purposefully keep things from me."

"Who said I keep things from you?"

"I'm not an idiot. I get paid to notice this shit. You play the mysterious card well. You don't talk unless you're spoken to. I used to think it was an obedience thing, but now I know better. It was fun when you were a kid, but things are different now."

"From what I recall, you keep secrets too, Commander," Eric contested.

"That's different."

"How?"

"Like I said... I get paid for that. It's in the job description. *Our relationship is different, E.*"

"Right." *The whole not being my dad while also being my dad thing.*

Eric glowered at the punching bag and raised his hands in a defensive position as he could feel his anger burning within him once more.

"I don't talk, because if I do, I'll say something we'll all regret," he uttered as he threw a punch, causing the chains to rattle once more.

"That shouldn't be a problem. Jimmy says what's on his mind all the time, and look where he's at."

That's different. My words won't make you happy.

Michael went on, "I don't care if you're a cold-hearted asshole, as long as you put it to use. You want to be a sergeant one day? Lieutenant? You need to be a team player."

"I report to you. I'm trying."

"Eh, you run away from it more often than not. Don't think I don't notice. It's not any different from when you were a kid."

Eric clenched his jaw. Memories of his childhood flashed before his eyes—of time spent hiding in the library or secret rooms, only to be inevitably found by the commander and do tasks he had abhorred, failed, and was then punished for. It had him fighting against a flare of panic and fury.

Running to the point of passing out. Sitting in the gravel on his bare knees. Standing in the snow until his skin was cracked and bleeding. Broken fingers. Broken noses. Shocks to the ribs. On and on.

"I'm *trying*," Eric bit out. "I thought you said you were proud of me, Commander."

Passive aggression oozed into his words. He had allowed himself to feel some semblance of hope in Michael's pride, but it was turning sour. It always did.

"I know. And I am," the Silver Wolf said. "I meant what I said, but you understand that I'd be doing you a disservice if I didn't help you improve or rise even further. As your commander and as your mentor."

Ah, as per usual, it never stops. Can't celebrate for too long because there's always something to pick at. There's always something I'm doing wrong. Something I'm not doing enough of.

"You want to be a sergeant, don't you?" he asked.

Eric let his eyes trail across the many items across the room as his mind turned. He had to admit that the idea was enticing. To be the second daywalker to rise to power after years of getting beat down sounded like a sweet victory. If he was going to stay in The Colectiv, it seemed like the obvious goal. After all, he'd be standing next to his brother, just like they had always dreamed of. And yet...

Just like when he looked at himself in the mirror, there was a disconnect between Eric and his future. There was no desire, but a necessity—an *obligation*. He *should* want this. He *should*. It was the next logical step, but the fact of the matter was that Eric didn't think that far into his future at all. Not anymore. Not like he used to. The only thing on the horizon was revenge.

"I just don't appreciate being micromanaged," he muttered.

"It's called raising a kid, E."

The young man scoffed, "You know, I seem to recall telling you that I wanted you out of my way three years ago."

"I'm letting you and your brother go on this hunt with no team," Michael argued. "That's about as 'out of your way' as I can be, considering this is a fugitive who attacked another hunter. I gave this to you and let you train for this long when I could've easily handed it to someone else who would've done it already. You wanted revenge, E, and I'm giving it to you, but everything comes at a price, no matter how small. You knew what you signed up for when you came back. Don't get mad at me because you hate the way the game is played."

As the commander spoke, Eric wailed at the punching bag over and over and then threw one final hit before it gave out. The wood ceiling cracked and one of the chains broke, causing the bag to go lopsided. Eric grabbed it and looked up, assessing the damage.

"Shit," he whispered.

Not again.

Michael, however, paid it no mind.

"This is a big job for you, E, and I just want to make sure we're all on the same page. With that girl involved, it's easy for me to be a little worried, but Jimmy trusts you."

And there it is—the point *of the conversation.*

At the mention of Emilia and James, Eric looked at Michael once again. "Is there a reason he shouldn't?"

"I don't think there's anything on this earth or any plane of existence that would keep him from trusting you, but... I had to make sure. He made a damn good argument, and I can't help but trust him."

So James *hadn't* told him everything. *Good.*

"She means nothing to me anymore," Eric said with cold apathy. "I learned from my mistakes. She's just a means to an end."

Michael smirked, his eyes turning to steel, the fearsome eyes of a commander. "So, if she does something out of line, you'll know what to do, right?"

Kill her, you mean?

Not if Jean can help it.

"Yeah, I know what I'll have to do. I'll do anything I have to. I don't care who I have to break or who I have to kill. I've done it before, and I'll do it again."

A half-truth.

"Good."

Once Michael left, Eric bore his eyes into the wooden door, listening intently as the commander's footsteps got further and further away until they were gone. Only then did Eric relax, his shoulders falling. He raised the music's volume once again and walked over to the other side of the punching bag, debating how to take it down.

That voice in the back of his head spoke once more—the one that disguised itself as her.

You're a goddamn liar.

Eric hissed. "Shut the fuck up."

He punched the vinyl bag as hard as he could, causing the last chains that were holding it up to break and send it flying across the room. It fell with an aggressive thud, and sand leaked out onto the hardwood floor from a newly formed tear.

He sighed.

Great.

†††

Eric, *she whispered in his mind.*

Eric! *She raised her voice until it echoed over and over, louder and louder, until suddenly...*

"Eric!"

He opened his eyes and found himself in a dark, desolate street. He was in a metropolitan city again with skyscrapers towering above him, except it was completely devoid of life and human existence. There was no sun, no stars in the black hole sky, and no moon to light the way. Nothing but a singular lamppost amongst the abandoned cars and businesses of this post-apocalyptic world. Its light was just enough to let him see that he wasn't alone and that there was someone else standing across from him. She was a blur at first, slowly coming into focus before she became recognizable.

Eric's breath caught in his throat.

Emilia.

It was always her.

Her raven hair cascaded down her shoulders as she wore nothing but a tattered red dress, her feet bare and dirty. She looked as breathtaking as ever, yet absolutely and utterly wrong. *She cradled something in her hands, which were dripping with crimson blood. When her big brown eyes connected with his, she smiled and giggled in a way that unnerved him.*

Eric reached for a weapon—for anything to defend himself with—but found himself bare of any. In fact, he looked nothing like a hunter at all. He was a thin young man in a hoodie, jeans, and sneakers. His skin was devoid of tattoos.

"What do you want?" he demanded.

"Come find me," she uttered, her voice echoing despite the setting.

Eric furrowed his brow. "You're already here."

"You have to come the rest of the way, silly. You have to see."

"See what?"

"Everything."

When she spoke, it sounded nothing like Emilia at all, but a caricature.

Eric shook his head. "I don't know what you're talking about."

Emilia grinned and held out her bloody hands, opening them up to expose what was within their grasp. Eric's eyes widened when he noticed that it was a beating heart.

"Don't you want this back?" she whispered, jutting her chin toward his chest.

He looked down to see a large, gaping hole right in the middle of his chest. Eric fell into a panic, suddenly unable to breathe. He tried placing his hands over the wound in a futile attempt to stop the bleeding, but all he got was pain and bloody hands.

"G-Give it back," Eric choked out.

"Here, I'll help," a deep voice said. It sounded like Dante, but also like Michael, Caleb, and other people, all at once.

A split second later, a pair of hands shoved Eric forward. He prepared to stumble and hit the hard ground, but instead, it turned into liquid, swallowing him whole. With a gasp, he fell into a deep, dark abyss as Not-Emilia laughed at his demise. He moved his arms and legs, trying to swim out of it, but he had no sense of up or down, and his agitation worsened. His lungs begged for oxygen, and before he knew it, he was inhaling water. All he could do was give in until his body fell limp.

Just before his untimely death, there was a flash of brown hair, and then a large tattooed hand grabbed his wrist. With little to no effort, they pulled him up to the surface, and as soon as he was out of the water, Eric fell to his knees on a sandy beach and coughed up seawater. The city was gone and bright, imposing sunlight illuminated the space, making him squint. Waves crashed, and he watched the water pool beneath him and then recede backward.

Eric looked down, only to see, with a shock of terror, that his hands were covered with blood. He tried scrubbing them with sand and water, but it wouldn't come off no matter how hard he tried. They were stained. More than stained.

He sat up on his heels and stared down at them in horror.

"Eric!"

He looked up at the sound of the voice, and Eric jolted as Emilia appeared before him like magic. She was kneeling on the sand in her red dress. Before he could do or say anything, she grabbed the sides of his face, boring her brown eyes into his, and whispered,

"Find me. I'll take you where you do need to go."

Eric woke up with a start, his mind feeling heavy from the intense, vivid dream. He sat upright, in total shock, taking deep, even breaths to still his pounding heart, and then proceeded to sit in stunned silence.

Fuck my life.

7

Beyond the Grave

Jean

Bucharest, Romania—Days Earlier

Jean Beltremieux closed the door behind the twins, leaving them to the night and the world beyond. With his hand resting on the doorknob, he momentarily contemplated what just transpired. He chuckled to himself, feeling a mixture of excitement and, for the first time in decades, *hope*.

The old vampire returned to the sitting room and went to a shelf stacked with a variety of glass bottles containing liquids of different shades. He grabbed one and poured himself a glass of red blood. He took a sip of the sweet drink as he walked back over to his plush chair and sank into it, facing the fire. He basked in the warmth of the flames spreading across his cold skin.

Fire was the closest thing to the warmth of sunlight without the consequence of it sapping his energy. It was why every home he's ever lived in in the last 200 years had at least one, and why he liked sitting in front of them more often than not.

With a sigh, he leaned his head against the upholstery.

When it came to Eric and James MacNamara, Jean had his preconceived ideas. Before meeting them, he had thought about a lot of things, like where they came from and who and what they were, but he tried to keep an open mind and not harbor too many expectations. Yet, somehow, they managed to entirely exceed them. It seems his own words were true:

"No amount of fire can truly kill a MacNamara."

Oh, they're your kids, alright.

The idea filled Jean with great satisfaction. Call it intuition, but he had a feeling. Because despite the hostilities, he could see it in them both—that flame that refuses to go out. Even when it was hidden, it was never concealed from his wise eyes. He had lived long enough to spot it, and this flame was all too familiar, especially to himself. He called it "the inherent inability to stand by and do nothing."

The vampire put his drink down on the table next to him and took out a phone from his pocket. It was one of many burners that he cycled through for the sake of anonymity and safety. As an immortal, keeping unwanted eyes away was integral, whether it was The Colectiv, other vampires, or humanity as a whole. Now, he needed that privacy for the important call he was about to make.

He dialed one of the many numbers he had committed to memory, put the phone to his ear, and with anticipation, listened to it ring over and over until, finally, there was a crackle. The hushed voice of a young man started to speak.

"Yeah?"

Jean perked up. "Jonas. Where are you?"

"We're on the coast of Bulgaria, waiting to check in with you before we do anything."

A smile graced the vampire's lips. "Do it. The timing is perfect."

"I'm guessing the meeting went well."

"As good as it could have been, considering the circumstances. I couldn't exactly say everything I wanted."

"Well, hopefully after tonight, that'll change. If things go well."

"If things go well, *everything* will change, brother," Jean replied. "Just make sure to get everyone out of there and take him east, like we said. Michael might be distracted with his boys, but as soon as he gets the news, there's no telling what he'll do."

"What about you?" Jonas asked with concern.

Jean looked around his Bucharest home, shaking his head. He had been living near the wolf's den in hopes of getting a glimpse at the MacNamara's while never being able to reach out under certain parameters. Until now, that is.

"I've gotten good at letting things go, so it shouldn't be too hard to leave this place behind," he reassured. "Besides, when he's finally free, I'll be free...and so will they."

"How do you know he won't tell them when it happens?"

He huffed, "That their father's been alive this whole time? I highly doubt it."

8

The Lost Girl

Emilia

Manhattan, New York

[15]Emilia woke up at the crack of dusk, her nightly alarm jolting her awake. With her face crushed into the pillow, she swiftly turned it off and contemplated the souls she'd be willing to sacrifice to the devil for another 10 minutes of sleep. Or, perhaps, 10 million. It was an everyday battle at this point. She couldn't remember when life started feeling like such a chore, but it seemed endless.

Don't be so dramatic.

With a grumble, Emilia rolled out of bed. She grabbed a red silk robe from her closet and threw it on over her naked body, slinking into the kitchen to start her evening. With a clatter of cabinets and drawers, she put some of her favorite grounds into the coffee machine. As it

---

[15] Lilith - Halsey

brewed, she took a quick shower, brushed out her raven hair, made her bed, and then fixed herself the first of many cups of coffee for the day.

Vampires couldn't keep down most human food, but the list of things they could were specific herbal teas, caffeine, or a handful of foods with natural sugar. It had something to do with their digestive tract that changed with being turned, and because blood didn't contain much sugar to begin with, vampires developed a bit of a sweet tooth to compensate. Cane sugar, honey, and specific fruits were good to enjoy as a pick-me-up, though they would never be a meal supplement, and too much would make them sick. Emilia, herself *thoroughly* enjoyed coffee with honey. It was delicious, but also provided her with a sense of human comfort, so taking them together became a vital part of her routine (because routine kept her sane). She called it "The Vampire Special": coffee, honey, and some blood from the fridge.

With her steaming mug in hand, she traipsed into her large walk-in closet. It was filled with racks, shelves, and drawers of clothes, shoes, handbags, and jewelry. Most of the items were either black or red, though there was a section dedicated to bright and glittery pieces, which were mainly for work. Emilia liked looking good, and she liked having options, so her assortment was vast, and she chose every outfit she wore with diligence. Tonight was no different.

She picked out a long-sleeve bodysuit and a fitted leather skirt, which she paired with a black coat, black Louboutin's, and a matching purse. Gold jewelry hung from her ears and around her neck—minor but essential details. And with a travel mug in hand, she exited the apartment and went on her usual route to work.

✝✝✝

Midtown Manhattan—The Canary

Girls in pasties and lingerie conversed and giggled amongst themselves in the illuminated dressing room. Some of them were running about getting in and out of costumes, while others did stretches in a corner. In the background, a performance could be heard from the stage along with the occasional applause.

Emilia sat in front of her vanity mirror in a deep red wig styled with big Hollywood curls as she adjusted some false lashes on her eyelids. She then lined her lips and threw on some gloss before leaning back and smiling, pleased with how she looked.

She loved doing this—getting to be someone else for a few nights of the week. She was never allowed to put on makeup or go out when she was a child, so she made up for it when she got older. She loved getting dressed up and calling herself "Roxie." Not Emilia, not Alejandra, not anything else. Not because she didn't love how she looked—she had come a long way from hating her physical appearance—but because she didn't quite like *herself* at the moment. Besides, it was a good source of fun, and Emilia always liked to have fun.

The vampire left her makeup station and slipped into her costume for the night. It was a beautifully detailed black corseted dress decorated with sleek red feathers and a thin, black tulle skirt that fell to her feet. When she put it on, it gave her a stark hourglass silhouette and pushed "the girls" right up. She handpicked jewelry with beautiful fake gems—a velvet choker with rubies and black diamonds hanging from it. It was dramatic and beautiful. After all, it was all for the show, and she didn't get paid to look like a pedestrian.

"Roxie, you're on in five!" the stage manager called.

"Thank you, five!" Emilia answered with a gasp.

She waited offstage in anticipation, adjusting her costume where necessary. A few of the dancers gave her words of encouragement. Their bubbly smiles were contagious, though the others didn't pay her any mind. Some didn't bother saying words to her at all, but Emilia didn't take it to heart. After all, for personal reasons, she was a bit of a recluse these days. Some took it as her simply being shy, while others took it the wrong way. Of course, she wouldn't be surprised if envy had something to do with it. Regardless, she thought it was better for her to keep a safe distance, specifically from humans. "Roxie" went to the club to rehearse, perform, make money, and repeat. After that, Emilia went back home at the end of the day.

[16]For tonight's show, Roxie Vega sang and danced to a mixture of old-school and pop favorites. It was all equal parts sexy, sultry, and fun, and just like every show, Emilia put all of her passion into it. Her performance was met with thunderous applause, as it always was, and the feeling it gave her was like a drug. She felt powerful, unstoppable, and like, for once, she could do anything in the world.

†††

The Canary was a swanky burlesque club located in Midtown. There, Emilia did anything from group performances to main stage solos. Like most of the other performers, Emilia was a dancer, but her biggest talent was her voice. She drew in many patrons for that reason, as she shined the most when she was singing and there was no one else on stage but her. Though it was only half the battle, she couldn't have found a more fitting job for her life in the meantime.

---

[16] Feeling Good - Nina Simone

Over the two years that Emilia worked there, she's garnered a lot of attention from people—men, especially. A lot of them were scoundrels, but some of them had a delicious amount of wealth. Sometimes they even wanted a "private session," which she declined because she didn't do "that kind of work." It irritated her that just because she was a dancer for something as raunchy and revealing as burlesque, she was now somehow open to selling her body for the sexual pleasure of others. Men did that regardless of their occupation, but it was still prevalent in this area in particular.

Others who frequented The Canary simply wanted her attention, which was a conquest in itself. They brought her flowers or even expensive gifts like a pair of designer shoes or a Prada bag, and it was all in exchange for her time and energy. It wasn't, by any means, a job requirement, and the dancers had every right to turn anyone down. However, they were encouraged to play nice with regulars and high-level patrons if possible, within the safety of the club, of course.

Emilia, frankly, *loved* taking advantage of men—the rich ones, the dumb ones, and the dumb rich ones. She saw no harm in accepting as many gifts and extra money from those who offered them. As long as they didn't come home with her at the end of the night, how bad could it be? It was their money, and they chose to splurge on a woman they didn't know. Not even a woman—a *fantasy*. They didn't know her real name, where she lived, or what she looked like underneath, so it didn't matter. Not unless, of course, they crossed a line.

She may have been a performer, but as a vampire, Emilia had to keep a lookout for any potential victims she could feed on for her next meal. And, well, being a small Latina woman who put her body on display a few nights a week gave her a whole buffet to choose from. She did her best to be discreet, and she didn't always pick from The Canary, but sometimes she came across someone she just couldn't help herself with. Of course, she never considered the rich ones because it was too risky, but she did keep in mind the ones who *wouldn't* be missed.

Those were often the lonely, overeager men who threw away money they didn't have. They'd make some lewd comments, either to her or one of the girls. If they got a little handsy, then it wasn't even a question. Even if it took everything in Emilia not to tear them to shreds right then and there, she'd spin her web instead. She'd put on her biggest smile, tell them at what time she got off work, and instruct them to meet her at the corner down the street. And they never hesitated, keen to get their hands on her, not knowing they were playing into *her* game and not the other way around. She'd tell them they were going to her place, only to stop at some dark corner so she could subdue them with her venom and drain them of their blood.

With people like that, it never weighed heavily on her conscience.

After her meal, Emilia arrived at her apartment, reeking of blood. She tried her best to get cleaned up before going out in the street, but luckily, everyone minded their business in New York. Still, without a proper shower, she knew it would be hard to get it all out. The makeup around her mouth was almost gone, and her brown skin was stained with a tint of red from the tip of her nose down to her chin. Her fingers were stained, too, and some blood glistened in a piece of hair that framed her face. The glitter on her eyelids, however, was somehow still intact.

Although she was energized and invigorated by the meal, some deep part of her was also extremely exhausted. Now she was ready to scrub herself away. So, she peeled off her clothes and turned on the overhead shower and some music. She let the water get hot enough to practically burn her skin off, and as she washed off all the makeup, blood, and sweat, she imagined that the dirt from her mind would somehow flow down the drain along with the rest.

†††

When she first moved in, Emilia knew she wanted to create a space that was true to her—a space that felt like home. It was her goal with any place she inhabited. In terms of creams and neutrals, you'd find none of those in her abode. No, the vampire preferred darker colors, gem tones, and anything brass or gold. Most of the furniture had a variation of velvet, satin, marble, or dark wood. And instead of going the minimalistic route, Emilia was a self-proclaimed maximalist. Any space on the walls was filled with mirrors, artwork, and movie posters of her favorite films. Bookshelves flanked either side of her TV, containing a wide array of literature that was merely a fraction of those she had read thus far. A well-used record player sat next to a stack of records she loved from recent decades. And everything, from the coasters to the glasses to the kitchen appliances, was carefully picked to match her specific tastes. It was by no means the biggest dwelling she had ever lived in, but it was perfect for what she needed right now. No one else but Emilia ever got to see it anyway, and she liked it that way. It was for her eyes only, and a place for her to call home.

Like many nights, she'd make herself another cup of coffee, do some reading, and partake in some self-pleasure using her box of toys. More often than not, she sat on her wine-red velvet couch and watched something that brought her joy. Emilia did her best to keep up with new media, but sometimes she'd put on something from her childhood to bring her comfort. Today, it was a show called "The Munsters" from the 1960s. She had the plot of every episode memorized by now, yet no matter how many times she had seen it, it always made her giggle.

Sometimes, the night seemed a little too long, and then all at once, she'd begin to feel lonely again. Although her time alone had given her room to grow these last few years, it seemed she got too comfortable in the isolation. It wasn't every day, but there were times when it almost seemed to drown her. No matter how hard she tried to cope, the loneliness—and the root of it—always crept in the shadows, waiting for the opportunity to strike. On days like this, she liked to phone a friend. Being that it had been a while since they last talked, she chose to go out onto the balcony to give him a call.

"Emilia." His familiar, deep voice came through the other end.

"Hey, Jean," she smiled as she greeted her oldest and most trusted friend.

"How's my girl doing?"

He sounded groggy as if he had been asleep. Still, he sounded thrilled to hear from her, which warmed her heart.

"I'm doing alright. I had another show today and ate some food, as usual. Sorry for waking you. I know what you like to say about isolating myself, so I decided to let you know I'm still alive. To my misfortune."

"Well, *I'm* glad that you're alive, if that means anything."

A small smile played on her lips. "It does. How are you?"

"Good, good. I made some new friends."

She rolled her eyes. "Of course you did. Living or dead?"

Jean Beltremieux always had a knack for making connections with others. It was a talent that not many people had.

"Mmm, dead. They're very interesting," he said.

"How'd you meet them?"

"Through an old friend. By the way, I'm meeting up with Misha in a few days. She misses you."

Emilia pouted despondently. Misha was a 200-year-old vampire that Emilia met through Jean decades ago. She had given her places to stay all across Europe and was the first person to tell Emilia that she had any real talent. Misha was a very flamboyant and theatrical person, and she was about as stereotypically old-school as a vampire could get. Much like Jean, Emilia found a home with her and her clan of misfits.

"Tell her I miss her too," she said. "She made going out fun."

"She also told me to threaten you to go to as many Broadway shows as possible or else."

A giggle bubbled in Emilia's throat. "Tell her it's already being done."

After all, she couldn't be in New York and not go to Broadway.

"Bucharest is beautiful, by the way. I'd ask you to come visit if it weren't for the circumstances."

Emilia sneered, groaning in disgust. "Romania? You're already crazy for choosing to live in that circle of hell. There is no chance I'm touching that place with a ten-foot pole."

"I know, I know."

The mere thought made her skin crawl. Emilia had been to Romania many decades ago in her more reckless days, and she agreed that it was wonderful and gorgeous. At one point, she tried making plans to go back, but that was before a *certain someone* lived there.

"Are things at The Canary going well?" Jean asked after a moment. She appreciated the change of subject.

"Yeah, it's great. I'm good at what I do. Everyone seems to love it anyway."

"You're a beautiful performer, Emilia. I'm sure you're the best they have."

Emilia didn't always like to brag, but she was confident enough in her skills to agree with him.

"Have you made any new friends?"

She cast her gaze at the streets below, where the city was awake even this late at night. In a place where she never got to see the constellations, the building's streetlights created stars of their own against the darkness. The cold breeze swept up pieces of her dark hair as she mulled over Jean's question, dreading having to give him the same answer she always did.

[17]"You already know what I'm gonna say, Jean." She sighed, "No."

"Why is that?"

"They're humans, Jean. I'm a vampire. It creates a complicated dynamic and a conflict of schedules. It's for their own good."

"I know plenty of vampires on the Upper East Side who would love to meet you."

Emilia scowled. "No, thank you. I need a break from immortal assholes for the time being."

Jean clicked his tongue in annoyance, saying, "And how would you know they're assholes?"

"All immortals are assholes. You and I included." She then quickly added, "With peace and love."

"I object to that."

She groaned, "Oh, Jean, you know you're insufferable. You're the embodiment of the Cheshire Cat when you want to mess with people. There's a reason you and Wade were friends."

Jean cackled—a sound that was young and jovial. "Well, if I'm the Cheshire Cat, then he's the Mad Hatter."

"Oh, undoubtedly."

They both laughed until all that was left was that familiar pang of sorrow over an old friend who was long gone. She didn't like to think

---

[17] Brand New City - Mitski

about Wade often, but when she did, it was like a slap in the face, regardless of how many years passed.

"I miss him," she said somberly.

"Me too."

Immortals weren't used to the death of their people. Not because it was impossible, but because they always assumed they had more time. More decades, more centuries, more millennia, and yet...

Wade was never supposed to die.

"Back then, you loved being the life of the party, Emilia," Jean told her.

Somehow, he pulled her out of her grief only to remind her of a different woe.

Emilia furrowed her brow. "Did I? I don't know anymore. Maybe I was just used to constant chaos, compensating for other things. And now that it's gone... I don't know." She swallowed hard against a lump in the back of her throat. "Sometimes it feels like I have nothing left."

"That's not true. You have you. You have me, Misha...and Jaya too."

She frowned, tears stinging in her eyes.

Another friend left behind.

"Have you heard from her?" Emilia asked, her voice soft.

Jean made a thoughtful sound. "She doesn't keep in contact with me as much, but the last time, she seemed to be doing well. She still helps a lot of people with her business."

That, at the very least, gave Emilia a sense of relief.

"Good. Good," she said.

"You should call her, you know."

"I don't know if I'm ready for socializing or making connections again just yet. I've got a pretty solid routine, and I really like my apartment."

"So, what you're saying is... you're happy where you are right now."

Emilia ran her tongue over her teeth in anger, because once again, her old friend knew her too well. He was more familiar with the cracks in her armor than anyone else.

"Is anyone ever really happy or satisfied?"

"Yes, I know a few who actually are," Jean argued.

"Well, good for them, but unfortunately, I don't think I'll ever be one of those people. I think I'm doomed to live an unsatisfactory life until the next fucked-up thing happens, and then the cycle repeats itself."

"You're not the only one who has those thoughts. I have a hard time believing that that is your fate. I *refuse* to believe it."

"It's just hard to not be a bit cynical after 70 years of literally no fucking peace," she whispered sharply.

From birth to the present, going from sorrow to sorrow, she was bred out of violence and torment long before she turned. Most of her pure happy memories were in the rearview mirror, out of reach, and she couldn't remember the last time she had a real sense of happiness, except...

Memories of a boy with brown hair and hazel eyes flashed in her mind, making her heart constrict in anguish. Emilia closed her eyes, grimacing at the reminder of *him*. He was there, in her mind, sitting on a beach, smiling at her—an image now tainted with blood.

No. Don't think of him. He's the reason you're here.

"My heart can't afford another heartbreak right now," she uttered. "Vampire, human, or anything in between, I can't afford to get hurt, and I can't take someone else getting hurt because of me."

Jean let out a long, heavy exhale before saying, "I know how you feel, Emilia. I know that feeling all too well. Trust me, you're not alone.

But I'm going to say something that you won't want to hear, but you need to... You can't keep letting Dante hold you back even when he's gone."

Red, bloody tears welled up in Emilia's eyes at the mention of her older brother, staining her vision pink. They inevitably spilled over, tracing crimson tracks down her cheeks. And for the first time, she had no smart retort to give.

"It's you and me against the world, Alé. Nothing can stop us or get in our way. Remember that."

She shook her head and pushed his voice away. It didn't matter that she hadn't talked to him in years. A lifetime spent together was difficult for the mind and body to forget.

"I know."

9

Reunion

Eric

Manhattan, New York—Present

Eric lazily rested his hand on top of the steering wheel, his fingers tapping along to the music. James was next to him with his feet up on the dash, their eyes tracing over the East River and the towering skyscrapers up ahead as they passed over the Brooklyn Bridge. The buildings looked golden against the blue morning sky, and their reflection in the water created an abstract painting.

After a 16-hour flight from Romania, the boys arrived at JFK airport the night before and immediately settled into their cozy, unassuming hotel on the Lower East Side. Even though The Colectiv had a lot of money, hunters always preferred smaller lodgings because they stood out less and could hide their true whereabouts with ease.

After all, it was a job, not a vacation, and there were many weapons that had to be dealt with.

It was tricky, but not impossible, to get weaponry overseas. They just had to know the right people and time it well. While some swords could be checked in as cosplay or Renaissance props, when planning a widespread hunt, the amount they needed wasn't so subtle. Instead, they shipped their prized pieces to a secret location—in this case, Brooklyn—where a member of The Colectiv kept them until the twins arrived. They would take daggers, knives, crosses, and other things they required from the hunter's arsenal and then load them into a borrowed car. Now, they were on their way back to the hotel to store their items and kill time before the night began. It was just the two of them, and they were on a mission of search and destroy. In order to do that, they had to do a bit of interrogating first. Once they had a clear lead, they'd plan their next move.

Despite growing up here, it was strange for Eric to be back in the U.S. this time around. Including his teenage years, Romania had been his home for a decade. Three years ago, it was California, and before everything began, New York had been their family refuge until Anya passed away. Anything prior to then was a blurry mess of temporary dwellings scattered across the map. Somehow, every city he ever lived in was a different era, lived by a completely different person than Eric was now. Queens was east, along with a house that was no longer theirs and a childhood that was long gone. The twins didn't like paying frequent visits since nothing but pain tied them to that place. There wasn't even a grave, as their mother's ashes were kept in the estate's columbarium. Yet, despite the bad, New York would always have some sentimental value to them.

Eric glanced at the rearview mirror, where a golden heart-shaped locket dangled from it. It was the very same one that contained Wade

MacNamara's picture and the one their mother had always worn. It was one of the few things Anya had left behind, except now it included a picture of her as well. Eric and James carried it with them everywhere they went and switched it off between themselves. They didn't consider themselves superstitious, but they did think of it as a good luck charm of sorts. Still, they avoided looking inside it too often.

He then eyed James curiously. He couldn't help but notice that his brother had been unusually serious the last few days. James had his moments, but he wasn't known for being quiet for long unless he was exhausted or something was bothering him. At least not around Eric. The former made sense considering how much air travel stressed him out, but Eric pondered the latter. There was an inkling in the back of his mind.

"You good?" he asked.

James, who had been deep in thought, blinked a few times. He glanced over at Eric with a frown.

"Yeah, why?"

"I don't know. You haven't complained about anything in the last hour, and I'm getting worried," Eric smirked.

His twin rolled his eyes. "I'm just exhausted. Jet lag following that shitty 16-hour flight is fucking with my head. Add that to the list of shit we're not immune to."

Eric nodded. He too felt the weighty effects of their travels. It had been a while since they took a trip this far, and who knew how much farther the road would take them?

"Yeah, we're gonna need some rest and some food before we do anything else."

And by "food," he meant blood from the cooler in the trunk, right next to their weaponry. They were "ethically sourced" blood bags, as Michael would say, and specially ordered just for them. He hadn't gotten a chance to replenish yet, and now the mere thought of blood made his thirst double.

"Yeah."

For a moment, Eric debated whether to tell James about his nightmare with Emilia. He often told him about his dreams, but considering what they were about to do, he decided against it. He thought about all the promises he had made and the stakes involved and didn't want to risk sounding deranged or unhinged. Especially since he already felt that way half of the time. He just wanted to get the interrogation with Emilia over with.

†††

Manhattan, New York—Comfort King Inn

He sat on his stiff double bed, scrolling through his phone, while James flipped through TV channels in the bed next to him. He found himself going to Instagram and, without even thinking twice, visiting the page for The Canary—the club where Emilia was supposed to perform that very night.

She didn't have any social media herself, which didn't surprise him. It was a risk to immortalize oneself on the internet when you were, well, *immortal* and so many eyes were on you. There were, however, several pictures of her on The Canary's profile. In them, she looked almost unrecognizable and was dressed in a wig or an extravagant costume. It was clearly done in the name of selling the persona that was "Roxie Vega," but Eric could still see Emilia underneath. Her striking brown eyes and memorable expressions were hard to miss.

"Find me," her voice echoed in his brain, and he swore he could feel her hands on his face still.

Eric scowled in discomfort, feeling sick to his stomach. He locked his phone and set it face down on the bed next to him. He put his training to use and tried to keep his heartbeat under control, but his brother had a way of reading him like no one else could.

"You weren't looking at her pictures again, were you?"

"No."

"If you keep doing that, you're only going to make this worse for yourself."

"The worst has already happened. I'll be fine."

"If it makes things easier, I can do the initial handling. It would be a pleasure to kick her ass for you."

Eric scoffed, "As much as I appreciate it, I don't need you to do that. I think I've prepared enough to handle myself just fine. She's just another vampire. How bad can it be?"

James turned off the TV and sat on the edge of the bed to face his twin seriously.

"Yeah, a vampire that we promised not to kill, remember? And one you were in pretty deep with," he said, fixing his brother with a stern, knowing look. "E, you know I trust your gut more than anyone, but I also know how special this job is for you. Bro, it's personal for me too, alright? I'm the one that got the call when you were dying."

Eric furrowed his brow as a troubled look passed over his twins' eyes.

James was Eric's best friend. Considering they were twins, it most likely sounded obvious, but they had an unbreakable bond that not many understood. They grew up together, trained together, traveled together, and they even came into this world together. They knew each other and confided in one another like no one else. In an emergency, they were each other's first call, and the last time there had been an emergency, Eric, a daywalker who they thought couldn't die, nearly bled to death. James was arguably better at keeping his emotions in check than he was, but Eric knew how much the traumatic experience affected him. He remembered the haunted look on James' face when he woke up in the hospital like it was yesterday.

"I know," he said, his expression grim.

"I'll follow you into the depths of fucking hell, E...but if something happens and your life is on the line again, I'm getting you out. I'll kill Dante myself if I have to."

Eric faced him fully to say, "That's not gonna happen. He only ever got that close the first time because I let my guard down. And I promise you that won't be a problem again. I've been ready for this. I'm not going back until it's done."

James nodded, and then for some reason, became hesitant.

"Listen... I know we made that deal with Jean...but if something happens..."

Eric frowned. "You're not thinking of doing something crazy, are you?"

His brother shrugged. "No. Yes. I don't know. What I'm trying to say is that if it comes between you and her, if I feel like the only option is to take her life... I want you to know that I'm gonna do it. Fuck what Jean said."

Any normal person wouldn't feel the deep sense of affection that Eric held for his brother after saying such a brutal statement, but *he* did. In fact, he wouldn't have expected anything less. And he knew that, despite everything, he would do the same thing if it meant keeping James alive. Whether it happened or not didn't matter, because the thought held a lot of weight on its own.

"Same," he responded with a nod.

"One word, E. One word while we're out there tonight, and I'll knock her out myself. You got that?"

"Without a doubt."

†††

Later that night

The sleepless city was always teeming with vibrant life, but the nights were especially wired. The urban streets of midtown were packed with people, and the scent of humanity was borderline overwhelming to the McNamara's immortal senses, but it made their ability to blend in that much easier.

For their special night out, the boys put a little more effort into their outfits. Their leather hunting attire and distressed clothes were tucked away in exchange for something more fashionable. Pants, boots, and winter coats - all black. They both wore turtlenecks to hide their tattoos (despite how much they loathed them). It made them look older, yet somehow still lethal. What mattered was that they didn't stand out too much amidst the trendy locale. The main differences were the hidden knives in obscure places.

Eventually, they reached the street corner where The Canary resided. It was hard to miss, with its sparkly red sign, glittering lights, and the sound of old-school music coming from within. People filtered into the club, buzzing with excitement; a lot of them were dressed up for the occasion. Eric stopped just far enough to get a look at the big, white marquee with the list of performers for the night. Among them, in big black letters, was none other than Roxie Vega.

With a little extra money, they skipped the line and paid for their entry. Once inside, they walked down the lit-up hallway toward the club interior, the music and chatter swelling with their approach. And as soon as they stepped into the main room, the twins had to stop and take a moment to marvel in awe. The pictures online didn't do the place justice and Eric couldn't help but think that this was exactly the kind of place he'd find Emilia in.

Everything about the Old Hollywood burlesque club was equal parts sexy and glamorous, from its red leather seats to the chandeliers with golden lighting, the art-deco wallpaper, and the mirrored ceiling up above. Along the side was a sleek, black bar with bartenders and servers dressed in satin clothing. Tables and booths made up the center, facing the red-curtained theater up ahead. The air had a faint smell of vanilla and liquor.

"Holy shit," James whispered next to him.

"Yeah."

After all, it wasn't the kind of place they'd go out of their way to find in their free time.

They paid their way into the VIP room, which was on the second floor and had a bird's-eye view of the stage itself. They were given a red leather booth that overlooked the stage from the balcony, which made it easy to watch and hide if need be.

Eric had never been to a burlesque show before, but he knew *of* them, and from what he came to witness that night, it was about what he expected. People performed a variety of acts, from dancing and singing to gymnastics, acrobatics, and even comedy. Most were dressed extravagantly in feathery clothing or even lingerie. He didn't expect to be surrounded by so many half-naked people at once, but he didn't mind. It was entertaining, and he had a good time...until the underlying unease kicked in.

Even though the shows were fantastic, the anticipation of it all had the boys exercising a lot of patience. They ordered non-alcoholic drinks and some fries to have something to snack on. A few club-goers tried flirting with them and starting conversations, which they politely had to steer away from. For the most part, they were waiting for the main event with bated breath until finally… the time came.

The lights dimmed once again, bringing everyone's attention to the spotlight on the stage. Overhead, they announced the name of the next performer.

"Ladies and gentlemen, for our next and final act, we bring to you the one and only Roxie Vega!"

The twins shared a knowing look and they both sat upright, peering over the balcony. Eric zeroed in on the stage, maintaining a cool demeanor as the show began. The curtains lifted, and a familiar melody filtered in through the speakers. A spotlight came to life, and there, sitting over a grand piano beneath the glow, was Roxie Vega. Her hair was icy blonde and a shimmering red bodysuit hugged her figure, a feathery boa draped around her. The makeup around her eyes was red and glittery, like flames. The audience clapped at the reveal as she started to sing a cover of "Toxic" by Britney Spears.[18]

Eric watched her with laser focus, the sight of her making his jaw clench.

Here she was, the physical manifestation of his nightmares. Much like in the pictures, "Roxie" looked nothing like Emilia, yet the more she moved, the more he recognized her beneath it all. Even on stage, she was like a siren. Her outfit was even a similar shade of red to the one in his dreams and what she wore when they first met. And just like that first night, Eric couldn't take his eyes off of her. She slid off the piano and moved around the stage as if she owned it, in perfect rhythm, dropping to her knees and dragging herself across the floor in

---

[18] Toxic - Yael Naim

a seductive dance. Even her voice was sultry and smooth. Two men came in from the wings, joining the routine, but the hunter didn't pay them any mind.

Eric had to give it to her; she was talented. He always knew she was. After all, her dancing was what grabbed his attention all those years ago, but it was never like this. When she sang, it had always been in bits and pieces, for fun, but now it was obvious she had been holding back. *Again*. Eric didn't know whether to be impressed or angry.

Two more elaborate dances followed, and when she reached the end of her performance, the club erupted in thunderous applause. Of course, Roxie Vega reveled in it. She stepped forward, center stage, bowing and blowing kisses into the audience like some kind of pageant queen. Her eyes roved over every face and then, suddenly, flitted upwards to the VIP area. And in that brief second, she made direct eye contact with Eric. Her expression faltered and he immediately pushed himself away from the booth and the view of the stage.

†††

As soon as Emilia got off-stage, the boys left the club to get ahead of her for what came next. They went back to the Jeep that they left down the street, gathering everything they needed. They switched to more comfortable clothing and traded out their fashionable jackets for hunting ones, which were layered with Kevlar and lined on the inside with an intricate pattern of filigree and wolves. James took his crossbow in a duffle, while Eric grabbed a pair of silver daggers instead of his heavy sword. Deal or not, he wouldn't be needing it, and the small blades were less of a hassle to obscure anyway.

Aside from the obvious, hunters also used a variety of other means to weaken vampires enough to take them down. These items consisted of religious symbols, holy water, UV lights, concentrated dog rose spray, and silver (bullets, knives, and chains). Not all vampires were affected by religious objects since not all shared the same beliefs, but it was always good to have them just in case. Wild dog rose water, in its purest form, was like poison and made them cough up blood (somehow, vampires found a way to dilute it into a form of consumable alcohol). Silver, when on a vampire's skin, was hot to the touch, and any wounds created by it would heal half as fast. If shot by a silver bullet, then that or any other wound present wouldn't heal until it was taken out. There was also sunlight, which didn't burn vampires alive but depleted them of energy when standing in it for too long.

Of course, the one true way to kill a vampire was to sever the head. In certain parts of Europe, they liked to use battle axes or even scythes. Eric found them fascinating, but he didn't personally like the look for himself. Even so, sharp, double-edged daggers could do the trick just fine if used correctly, but few hunters were skilled with smaller blades because not everyone was brave (or insane) enough to confront a vampire in such proximity. Considering Eric had been in the same boat when he was a child, it was a wonder he even mastered them at all. Although he was sure spite had something to do with it. Ironically enough, he preferred them now since they allowed better mobility.

Since 99% of the hunter population was human, the vast arsenal came in handy, but Eric and James had less to worry about. Daywalkers had abilities that nearly equaled those of purebloods but were impervious to most things that debilitated them, which made them a little more unstoppable. Starvation, decapitation, and, apparently, pureblood venom were the only ways to kill or impair them. The twins didn't like to put it to the test, though.

"I'll stick to the rooftops and watch from above," James said when they were ready to go.

"Good. Leave the rest to me."

"Yeah, yeah," James sighed. "I'll wait for your signal."

"No hesitation."

His brother scoffed, "When have I ever?"

Eric held out his hand, and James took it in his. They did a short signature handshake before nodding to each other and going their separate ways.

†††

[19]Eric waited patiently across the street from The Canary, his eyes trained on the entrance to the club. Every time the door would open, the sound of jazz music poured onto the street. As soon as someone came out, the hunter would raise his chin in question, only to deflate when it wasn't who he was hoping for. It was a waiting game, but he was used to it. However, this time around, he was a little more anxious.

After some time, Emilia eventually stepped through the door. Upon immediate recognition, Eric squared his shoulders. She was out of her wig and fancy costume, donning her natural black hair that glistened like oil underneath the lights. The makeup around her eyes was gone, and she wore a short black dress with a coat around her shoulders and a red purse on her elbow. She glanced up and down the sidewalk, and Eric stuck to the shadows of a closed shop, lest she see him. Emilia then walked down the sidewalk, rounding the corner as her heels clicked on the pavement. When she was far enough, Eric, quick and stealthy on his feet, crossed the street and followed.

---

[19] Animals - Maroon 5

He kept a safe distance, knowing that if she ever got too far, he could catch up to her in an instant. Even in a city like New York, it would be hard to lose her with not only his eyes but James' eyes watching from above. Eric kept his hood up to obscure his face and pretended to look at his phone to sell the act. He had every intention of cornering her when the opportunity arose. The gears in his head turned as he worked out what he would do, just like always. But, of course, vampires had heightened senses too, so it was only a matter of time in any hunt when they started to realize they were being tracked. And when there was a safe distance between them, The Canary, and the hub of people around the area, Emilia took a sharp turn into an empty alleyway.

Here we go.

With a deep breath, Eric put his phone away and pulled his mask over his face before following her into the darkness. After that, muscle memory took over.

Emilia whirled around, swinging her purse at Eric's head with all her might. He dove under it and sidestepped so that he was right behind her. He took out his daggers, and a second later, Emilia bared her teeth and swung the bag again. He quickly blocked it with his blades and slashed at it. Its mangled carcass fell to the ground and her stuff littered the floor. Emilia's eyes went from the bag to the blades, then to his face.

"Hunter," she hissed. Her dark irises glowed a pale, deadly blue.

"Exactly."

"You owe me a new purse!" she barked and then lunged at him in full force.

Emilia shoved him against the brick wall with all her strength and Eric grunted as his back made contact with the hard surface. She then raised her manicured hand and tried swiping at his face with her sharp nails. The hunter raised his arm to block it, and her claws scratched at the material of his jacket instead. With his other hand, he jabbed her in the stomach with his silver-tipped blade. She gasped in pain, instinctively clutching at the wound and Eric took the opportunity to shove her away. He sidestepped her once again, slicing at her arm in the process. But if Eric thought subduing her would be easy, he was sorely mistaken because Emilia fought like an animal.

Without hesitation, she threw a mean punch squarely at the side of his face. He stumbled a little, his groan turning into an amused chuckle from the surprise. Part of him almost wanted to compliment the hit, but Emilia threw herself at him again, this time aiming for his neck. Eric raised his daggers in an "X" to block her, but she managed to knock him down on his back with her full weight and momentum. She straddled him, scratching and punching despite the blades cutting her hands. It wasn't anything Eric couldn't handle, but it was positively infuriating. Most of the vampires he dealt with didn't fight back *this* hard.

With an angry snarl, he slashed at her cheek, making her cry out and stop just long enough for him to buck his hips and roll over until she was the one pinned to the ground beneath him. Before she could do anything else, he crossed his daggers over each other and pressed them against her neck, threatening to decapitate her if she moved. In the aftermath, their chests rose and fell heavily as they stared icily at each other.

"Move again, and you'll lose your head," Eric hissed.

"Just do it," she spat out. "You're already here. Why waste precious time?"

"Because I'm not finished yet."

Her expression was a perpetual scowl, her pale blue gaze like a laser. The right side of her face was covered with blood.

"What are you gonna do, torture me?" she asked.

"Who says I'm gonna torture you?"

She scoffed, "Isn't that what you people do? Whether you kill us fast or slowly, only one gets out alive in the end."

"Maybe if you give me what I want, you'll get lucky."

"What makes you think I'll give you anything?"

"Then that's where the torture comes in," Eric replied, flashing his eyes deviously.

Emilia narrowed her eyes, the irises reverting to dark brown. Somehow, he swore there was recognition in them.

"Who are you?"

"The Grim Reaper," he teased dryly.

That look in her eyes only seemed to solidify.

"Show me your face," she demanded.

"No."

"Then I. Won't. Talk," she said indignantly.

Eric groaned in exasperation. Emilia was brave, despite being under two knives and having her life on the line. He couldn't tell if she was that unaffected by his hostility or if she had some sort of death wish.

The hunter worked his jaw, thinking long and hard about revealing who he was. There was some distance involved in hiding his identity. In a world where too many people knew his name, he liked the anonymity, but she wasn't making it easy. He knew she wasn't going to budge, and he had a feeling that she could tell who he was, regardless.

With a resigned sigh and one dagger pointed at her throat, he pulled down his mask. Emilia inhaled sharply, her eyes widening. Heartache and heartbreak washed over her face in an instant. At that moment, he saw a piece of her he hadn't seen in years.

"Eric," she whispered.

It was like a curse, the way she said his name.

"Emilia," Eric uttered.

A curse of his own.

"I knew it," she said. "I knew I saw you back at the club, but I thought I was going crazy."

Here, in this proximity, and without the costume, he got a good look at her after all this time. She was here, in the flesh, both everything and nothing, like the image that had lived in his head all these years. He had half expected her to age, but of course, her face was the same—caramel brown skin, fox eyes colored brown like the earth, high cheekbones, and lips like a flower. Her black hair fell against the surrounding gravel, blending in with the night. The one difference was the absence of a ruby cross around her neck, which she used to wear back when they first met. Her expression, however, was no different from the one she gave him *that night.*

Emilia looked back and forth between his eyes now, as if searching for something, but when she didn't find it, all that pain and heartache turned into bitterness in seconds.

"So, it was all true," she said, her body limp beneath him. "You *are* a hunter."

"And you're a vampire."

"And you're a daywalker," she shot back angrily. "That's how you survived, isn't it? And now you've come back to...what...kill me?"

Eric grimaced. "Sorry to burst your bubble, but I'm not here for you. I'm here for your brother."

Emilia rolled her eyes and groaned before saying, "Well, sorry to burst *your* bubble, *MacNamara*, but Dante isn't here."

He wondered if it was Jean who told her his last name, or if she found out just as everyone else ultimately did. He had deliberately hidden it from her back then, just as he had with everyone else, and now that she said it back to him, it sounded like an insult too.

"I know that," he growled. "That's why I'm here. I want you to tell me where he is."

She cackled a low sound, finding something funny in his words. Eric observed her without an ounce of amusement.

"Emilia," he uttered her name like a threat, inching both daggers a little further into her skin.

She winced, stopping her laughter to look at him with a fury that could burn. "I don't know where my brother is. I haven't known in years."

He leaned in closer to her, menacingly. "Bullshit. Don't lie to me."

"I'm not," she asserted. "I don't know shit and I don't want to know shit. And even if I did know, why would I tell *you*? Just so you can kill me anyway? So, you can get revenge? So, you can kill *him*? Get in line. You're not the first person to want Dante dead, and I doubt you'll be the last."

"Well, according to my source, you haven't been on good terms with him in a while," Eric said with a shrug. "He's fucked you over quite a lot. What does it matter what I do with him?"

Emilia's lips twisted in distaste. He looked back at her in kind. It was like she couldn't recognize him, and some dark part of him felt satisfaction over the idea.

"Well, I don't know who the fuck your source is, but they sent you on a wild goose chase. I don't know where my brother is, nor do I care to know. I'm done getting dragged into his bullshit, and quite frankly, I don't want to get dragged into yours. You wasted your time."

"Trust me, we both got roped into something we didn't want."

She tore her gaze away from him and looked off to the side as if she could escape him that way.

"Just kill me already. I know you want to," she muttered.

Even if he could, Eric had other ideas. Seeing as she wasn't going to comply, the hunter exhaled and retracted his daggers instead.

"Fine," he said coldly, rising to his feet. "You don't wanna talk? I guess that's how it's gonna be."

The hunter sheathed his weapons casually, and Emilia stood up in confusion. She slowly got up on wobbly legs, narrowing her eyes as she watched him in bewilderment.

"What are you doing?" she asked warily.

With his eyes trained on her, Eric raised a hand in the air and said loud and clear, "Jimmy!"

Emilia's eyes widened, but before she could react, a whistle echoed through the air. Not a second later, a bolt made contact with the side of her skull with a thud. Her eyes rolled to the back of her head, and her knees buckled as her body went limp. Before she could hit the ground, Eric caught her in his arms.

"It's nothing personal," he whispered.

10

Butterfly Effect

Emilia

Sorrento, Italy—3 years ago

The first time she ever saw him, it was at a place called La Farfalla.

That evening, Emilia was as she always was—dancing and having a good time. On the dance floor, she was in a world of her own that no one could take her out of. She moved her body and swayed her hips to the rhythm of the beat, and when there was a song she knew by heart, she sang every word at the top of her lungs. She smiled, laughed, and shouted because there was nothing more freeing for her than getting lost in music. In that space, it was like she was still 22, and life hadn't happened yet—*death* hadn't happened yet. And Dante was nowhere in sight. For now.

Normally, Emilia paid no mind to the men who ogled her when she was out. She paid no mind to human men in general unless she found one that piqued her interest, but the most attention they ever got from her was when they were on the receiving end of her bite. Other than that, she barely looked at them because she knew that if she did, they'd take it as an invitation that was never even sent. But if Emilia wanted someone, they would *know* because she wouldn't hesitate to get her hands on them. And that night, she found herself desiring someone like no other.

At some point, she got this gnawing feeling at the back of her neck, like someone was watching her, and a voice in her mind was telling her to turn around and take a peek. So she looked over her shoulder, feigning casualness, and there, at the bar, was a young man who grabbed her attention. Even from a distance, she could tell he was attractive. He looked to be in his early 20s with shaggy, dark brown hair and a button-down with the sleeves rolled up. She wasn't sure if he was Italian or not, but he didn't look like any of the white American tourists that were around. They locked eyes briefly and smiled at each other before he shyly looked away.

For some reason, it made Emilia feel giddy. She hadn't even spoken to him, and his smile drove her wild in the best way. Yet, for a long moment, she contemplated whether she should approach him at all or if she should just leave him alone. After all, he looked like a nice boy and nice boys belonged with nice girls, which Emilia was not. Still, it wasn't like her to back down or shy away, and despite her better judgment, something pulled her to him. She didn't know why, but she *wanted* him.

One night couldn't hurt. [20]

Emilia peeled away from the dance floor and made her way to the bar to talk to this stranger. He was busy speaking to another young

---

[20] Make You Mine - Madison Beer

man at his left, so she tried sneaking up to his right, but it was like he sensed her from five feet away. His head snapped in her direction, eyes wide with surprise, as she sidled up next to him with a smirk. His heartbeat quickened, which made her grin wider. She rested her elbows on the bar, never taking her eyes off of him.

"Hi," she uttered.

He was even more beautiful up close, and his eyes were like honey, with flecks of green in them. There was also something about him that seemed oddly familiar.

"Hi," he responded, giving her a big, dimpled smile.

"I'm Emilia."

"That's a pretty name."

"Thank you," she grinned coyly.

"Hi, Emilia. I'm Eric."

She liked the way her name sounded coming out of his mouth. His voice was on the deeper side and had a rich, husky quality to it.

"Eric," she repeated the name as if committing it to memory. "This is gonna sound weird, but...have we met before?"

He shook his head. "No, I'm pretty good with faces, and I think I'd remember meeting you."

Emilia hummed curiously but, in the end, let the topic go.

"I saw you dancing out there, by the way. You're really good," he said.

"Thank you. Do *you* dance?"

He snorted, "Not well."

"That can be helped."

Eric raised an eyebrow. "Are you offering?"

"Only if you want."

"Hmmm... I wouldn't mind a few lessons."

He looked down at her through long lashes, his gaze beckoning her to dive right in. Even in a noisy, crowded room, it was as if they were the only people there. And she wanted to do more than just dance with him.

"So, Eric... to ask the age-old question...What's a guy like you doing in a place like this?"

He chuckled breathily. She enjoyed the sound, even more so that he laughed at her joke.

"A guy like me?"

"Yeah."

"Why is anyone here? To have fun, right?"

She rolled her eyes. "I mean in Italy."

"Ah. I'm, uh, on a study abroad trip from California. I major in anthropology. We study history and ruins and shit. It's my last year, actually."

Emilia's eyes widened in surprise. "Oh..."

That sparked genuine intrigue in her and pulled at a side of her that always loved art, museums, and history.

Eric must have taken her reaction as a negative one because he looked at her warily and said, "That probably sounds really boring, doesn't it?"

Emilia shook her head. "No, quite the opposite, actually. I was gonna compliment you on it."

Now it was his turn to be pleasantly surprised. "Are you just saying that to be nice, or...?"

"Trust me, Eric, I'm never nice just to be nice."

"Somehow, that doesn't surprise me," he said with a curious smirk.

Oh, is he reading into me now? Please, keep going. Tell me more.

"I'm just glad you're not a psychology or a business major. You'd be surprised how many of those come around," she told him.

Eric laughed. "Actually, I wouldn't be surprised at all."

Emilia giggled and his hazel eyes flitted to her lips. All at once, the air around them seemed to electrify. She looked between his eyes and his mouth, then back again, and in that moment, she heard his heart falter. It was like they were playing a metaphorical game of chicken. She wanted him, and it was clear he wanted her too, except he was just being maddeningly respectful about it, leaving the ball in her court. Emilia wasn't used to that, but she liked it.

She took the hit.

"Well, if you want, we can get out of here, and you can tell me all about yourself and your studies and what does and doesn't surprise you about me."

He swallowed thickly, his heart stuttering again. "And what about you?"

"I'll say or do whatever you want," she uttered lowly.

Eric chuckled nervously as his eyes pierced hers. "Promise?"

"I promise."

"Then it's a deal."[21]

---

[21] Death of Me - PVRIS

11

The Interrogation Game

Emilia

Undisclosed location, New York—Present

An incessant pounding reverberated on the right side of Emilia's skull, and her skin felt like it was on fire.

Her eyes fluttered open as she gradually awakened from her unwanted slumber, but everything was a blur. She blinked a few times and slowly but surely her vision started to sharpen, the pain in her head subsiding. The dull burning, however, was constant, and it wasn't until she tried moving that she realized why.

Chains clinked against each other, squeezing her tight. They were wrapped around her torso and legs, binding her to a metal chair and biting into her skin. She stared down at them in confusion and tried using her strength to break free, only to be met with painful, scorching heat. It was akin to a hot blanket suffocating her.

Silver.

"The more you struggle, the more it's gonna hurt."[22]

It was a familiar voice from a dream or maybe a memory.

The vampire jolted against her restraints and snapped to attention. She needn't look very far for the source of the voice, because as soon as she looked up, she made eye contact with the last pair of eyes she saw in the alleyway before everything went black.

Eric MacNamara. Her attacker, an old flame, and the boy she thought had died but turned out to be just as venomous as she was. He sat by a barrel of fire just a few feet away in a fitted charcoal sweater with the sleeves rolled up and a dagger in his hands. They were in an abandoned structure, with pillars, graffiti, and boarded-up windows, but all she could focus on were his eyes, which looked like hellfire in the light of the flames.

Emilia's heart split apart many times that night in Sorrento and thereafter. Once, when she found out about Eric's ties to The Colectiv; twice, when she realized he was a daywalker; and three times, when she was sure her brother murdered him. The nail in the coffin was learning the full truth about Eric's true identity. Back then, she knew him only as "Eric Leone," an innocent college boy who was studying in Italy, but now she knew better. Jean told her as much not long after what happened.

Eric *MacNamara*. A liar. A traitor. A wolf in sheep's clothing. A hunter and a daywalker—a lethal combination.

Now that she knew the truth about his infamy, Emilia couldn't help but feel stupid for how oblivious she had been. She didn't know what was worse: for Eric to have died and for her to live with that pain and guilt, or for her walking heartbreak and betrayal to be alive and

---

[22] Eyes On Fire - Blue Foundation

become something to watch for at every corner. She always had the sinking feeling that their paths would cross again, considering his vampire DNA. That was why she stayed away from Europe, especially Romania. It was too easy to run into people in a place that was so accessible. Emilia even thought that by cutting off her brother and hiding away in a big city on the other side of the world, she'd be hard to find, but alas, Emilia's past always had a habit of coming back to haunt her.

"Eric."

"Emilia."

"Where did you take me?" she asked.

He shrugged. "That's for us to know and you to find out."

She glared at him.

How strange, she thought—he looked just as she remembered him, yet completely different.

He really does look like Wade. How did I miss it before?

It was Eric, but a little older, colder, and rougher around the edges. He was more muscular and had a few new ear piercings and even more tattoos. Even from what she could visibly see, his skin was covered in art. There was a skeleton hand inked over his real one and a solar eclipse on the side of his neck. Most of his fingers had a mixture of silver and gold rings. His brown locks were in the same style, but his eyes, which were once sweet and welcoming, were now piercing and sour.

In many ways, this wasn't the same boy she fell for in Sorrento.

No, he wouldn't look at me *like* that.

"Did you shoot me in the head?" she muttered.

"No, that wasn't me."

"That was me," a different, but similar voice answered.

Emilia's gaze darted over Eric's shoulder, landing on another tall figure hovering by the doorway. He was staring back intensely with his arms crossed. She blinked in confusion as she found herself looking at another version of Eric. A clone. A *twin*. It took seconds for the realization to dawn on her.

Though she never met him in person, Eric talked quite a bit about his brother while he and Emilia were together. He always mentioned him in a positive light, but she always gathered that he was unfiltered and intense. His looks and demeanor alone confirmed that.

Eric's resemblance to Wade was a shock on its own, but James' was uncanny. She blamed it on the longer hair length. He was much edgier than Eric and even more rugged due to the stubble on the lower half of his face. He had more piercings, and the cut-up sleeveless t-shirt he wore revealed tattoos that ran up his right arm. One was a similar eclipse to Eric's, and he had a large ram's skull that spread across his throat with lotuses.

His contempt for Emilia was very visible on his face. She returned his expression in kind.

"James," she said.

He huffed, "So you *have* heard of me."

"Unfortunately."

The vampire returned her attention to his twin.

"Eric," she bit out, a little more amicable than before. "Let me go. I told you I don't know anything."

"And I said that's bullshit," he snapped. "There has to be something that you know that could help us find your brother. Even something you don't know that you know."

Emilia scoffed, "What are you gonna do? Read my mind? Go into my subconscious?"

"No," he said, resting his elbows on his knees and letting the dagger hang casually from his fingers. "I'm gonna ask you some questions, and you're gonna answer them."

Emilia's eyes flitted between the blade in his hands and his eyes. It was one of the two he had pressed against her throat earlier in the alleyway. In the light, she could now see how unusually eye-catching the design was. It didn't look like any normal dagger she had seen before, as the hilt looked iridescent white and had a cross-guard that almost looked like butterfly wings. It was also sharp and coated in silver, and she remembered how easily it cut into her skin.

"Are you gonna torture me with that pretty knife?" she asked.

Eric shrugged. "That depends on you."

He played with the dagger in his hand like a toy, flipping it around with ease. It was both a warning and a threat. Emilia did her best to hold her ground as the hunter pierced her with his eyes, but if she was honest, she would have preferred physical torture to this.

"Where's your brother, Emilia?" he asked evenly in that low voice of his.

She repeated the same answer she gave him earlier, "I. Don't. Know."

Eric sighed, the muscles in his jaw twitching as he clenched his teeth. He leaned back in his chair, never looking away.

"You know, we have all the time in the world. I could slice you up, or... I'm pretty sure we have a UV light in the trunk that'll do wonders for your skin. How about that?" He smirked like a demon. "Or... you can cooperate."

The cold ease with which he said the words made Emilia's mouth twist into a scowl.

"Are you really capable of that, Leone?"[23]

She threw the fake name out in spite, and Eric's eyes darkened. She couldn't help but notice the steadiness of his heartbeat thus far.

---

[23] do you really want to hurt me? - Nessa Barrett

Hunters had a knack for hiding their feelings, even in their physical bodies. He had been practicing since they last saw each other. It was unsettling.

"There's a lot I'm capable of that you know nothing about," he muttered.

Emilia ran her tongue over her teeth as they stared each other down with vehemence. It was like she was meeting him for the first time again. Back then, he seemed like such a playful and kind soul, but not now. Now, there was a giant fortress built around him, and at a glance, she couldn't find the way in. She should have run away or backed down, she should have surrendered, but some twisted part of her wanted to find the cracks. She wanted to break through his shell to finally discover the truth. Maybe it was vengeance, or maybe it was her twisted way of desiring closure after all this time, but if she couldn't appeal to Eric the old way, then she'd have to get a little creative.

"How about we play a game?" she said with a smirk. Her voice was honeyed, feigning innocence. Emilia all but laughed maniacally.

Eric glowered at her. "What are you on about?"

"I don't think it's fair that you get to ask the questions while I just sit here chained to this stupid chair. Either you torture me already or... you let me ask questions too."

"No. No fucking way," he argued.

"Why not?"

"Because it's stupid, and I'm not playing a fucking game with you, Emilia. This is an interrogation. It's not exactly how it works."

"You haven't even let me explain the rules."

He exhaled in exasperation. "What rules?"

"For every question you ask, I get to ask whatever I want. If you don't answer my question, I won't answer yours, and vice versa. It's a win-win situation. Deal?"

The hunter narrowed his hazel eyes but fell silent. Emilia could see he was genuinely pondering her proposition as he gripped the dagger in his hand. James, however, was having none of it.

"Don't play into her silly little mind games, E. She's just trying to get to you," he blurted out. "I say we get this over with and get the knives out. She's wasting our time."

"Hold on," Eric grumbled.

Seeing as he hadn't disagreed yet, Emilia chose to drive her point forward.

"If you say yes, I'll do and say *whatever you want*."

She made sure that her voice oozed insinuation, hoping that it would trigger a familiar memory. And it must have because Eric's eyes flashed for a brief moment.

"Only if you tell the truth this time," he said.

For once, she didn't lie. "Okay. That goes for you too."

"Promise?" It was more of a demand than a question.

"Promise."

Eric looked down as if to ponder. She couldn't quite place what was going through his mind. He almost seemed to be weighing his options, considering her idea, and for a moment, she thought he'd back out, until...

"I'll do it. But only until I get what I want, and only if you stick to your own rules. If I answer a question, you have to answer mine, *or else*. Got that?"

"Got it."

James grumbled, "This is so fucking stupid."

"Jimmy, it'll be fine. Trust me, I know what I'm doing," Eric assured his twin, and then said to Emilia, "Me first."

She frowned. "Fine."

Eric leaned forward again, his eyes dead set on her. James watched from the side, lingering like an attack dog, ready to pounce at the first sign of danger.

"Where. Is. Dante?" he asked for the millionth time.

Emilia rolled her eyes and groaned, "What a waste of a first question."

"Answer it," he ordered.

"I told you! I don't know where he is!" she shouted and sat up straighter in her seat. "New rule: no repeating questions. So that's the last time you get to ask that one."

She ignored the hateful expression he gave her.

"My turn," she said with a smile and fired off the first of many burning queries she'd had since that night. "How long have you been with The Colectiv?"

"14 years," he answered simply. "My turn. When was the last time you saw Dante?"

Emilia huffed at his short and vague answer but kept the game going, "Three years ago, after what happened in Sorrento. My turn. How long have you known you're a daywalker?"

He chuckled. "14 years."

"A lot happened then, huh?"

"Maybe you can ask that question when it's your turn." He gave her a condescending grin. "*Where* did you last see Dante?"

"Sorrento, Italy," she sighed. She then tilted her head to the side, and her next question came out more like an accusation. "Why didn't you tell me that you were a daywalker?"

Eric hummed angrily. "I didn't tell you that I was a daywalker for the same reason, I assume, that you didn't tell me you were a vampire. Rejection. Trauma. Immortality. All that bullshit."

Emilia bit her lip but nodded in understanding. Maybe she had expected something more sinister, but he had a point.

"My turn. Where were you and your brother born?"

"You actually know this. My brother was born in Mexico, but I was born in L.A. after our parents immigrated."

"Well, at least that was true," he muttered.

"I didn't lie about everything, Eric," she whispered, avoiding the look he gave her as she kept going. "My turn. Why are two half-vampires working for an organization dedicated to hunting other vampires?"

Many people had the same question when it came to the MacNamara twins. Most vampires knew *of* them, but they didn't know how they got into The Colectiv in the first place, and they were left to assume the worst. As far as everyone knew, they were shameful and traitorous for doing what they did, especially to those who knew their father. Emilia included.

But all Eric did was shrug and say, "It's complicated."

She scoffed, "That's it? That's all I get?"

He rolled his eyes. "Everyone always wants to treat it like some tabloid gossip, when, honestly, it's none of your fucking business. You had your chance to hear that story, but now it's a little too late."

The statement was like a slap in the face.

She remembered it vividly, much to her detriment. That night, when she found out who he was, he tried explaining everything, but in the overwhelming chaos, she didn't know how to respond. Emilia hated hunters and everything they stood for. She was meant to fear them, yet she had slept with one without knowing it, so at that moment, all she could feel was betrayal and rage. She didn't think she needed to hear the story, not at the time.

"It wasn't exactly an easy situation," she said.

"Oh, you mean with big brother present?" Eric said tartly. "Yeah, I know. He tried to kill me, remember? But I'm pretty sure there's a valid reason for letting your boyfriend bleed to death after he literally begged for his life."

Emilia's jaw dropped. "I didn't—" She stopped to laugh in disbelief, overcome with a sudden fire in her veins. "Gee, I wonder why, *Eric MacNamara*. Everyone knows who *you* are, where *you* come from, and what *you* do, and you managed to fool me into thinking you were some normal schoolboy. How was I supposed to know you weren't going to kill me?"

"If I wanted to kill you, I would have."

"And why didn't you?"

Eric opened his mouth, but no words came out. He paused for a surprising moment before saying, "Because I was stupid. And I was retired back then... I recall trying to tell you that."

"Maybe you should've tried earlier," she spat.

"As if it would've made a difference."

Emilia seethed in her chains, her skin now burning hotter with her rage. By the door, James looked uncomfortable and whispered something under his breath that she couldn't understand.

Would it have? Made a difference? If Eric had told her earlier who and what he was, would she have reacted differently, or would she have felt the same shock and betrayal? If Dante wasn't there, would it have ended differently? She wanted to believe it could have, but she was miles away from the girl she used to be three years ago. It wasn't good to dwell on what could have been. There was only what was in front of her. And what was in front of her wanted her dead.

"This is an interrogation, not a heart-to-heart conversation," Eric said, squaring his shoulders. To remind her, and perhaps even himself. "Let's get back to the questions. What year were you born?"

Emilia snorted. "Never ask a lady her age."

"Just answer the question."

She rolled her eyes but continued to follow her own rules and replied, "1950."

The corners of his lips turned down for a brief second. "You're not even a hundred yet," he said in surprise.

She smirked playfully. "Is this your way of telling me I'm young?"

"I mean, we know of plenty of vampires pushing 200, so by immortal standards, yeah."

"What about you? When were you two born?"

"1997."

Emilia blinked a few times in surprise at this shocking revelation. "I thought you were immortal."

"Not yet. Daywalkers stop aging at 25, allegedly. After that, we live forever."

The pureblood narrowed her eyes, looking between the twins in bewilderment. She didn't know anyone familiar with the biology of daywalkers compared to that of purebloods, so everything was speculation. Now, it made sense why she felt Eric looked older than before. It was because he *was*. You didn't see that when you were surrounded by other vampires who didn't age.

Another thing he didn't lie about. Add that to the list.

"The more you know," she whispered.

"You have no idea," he mused, and then continued, "Does your brother go by any aliases or names that we can track?"

"I mean, he obviously goes by Dante. There's also Ricky Velez, Dorian Black, Victor Creed... there's also his birth name."

He chuckled. "Victor Creed, as in from the X-Men?"

"Yup."

"And what's his birth name?"

Emilia hesitated before saying, "Daniel. Daniel Antonio Bernal. He hasn't gone by that name since we got turned, so good luck finding anything new under that."

"And what's *your* real name?" He pointed the dagger at her, waiting expectantly.

She glared at him. "Wouldn't *you* like to know?"

"You know *my* name now, so I don't see a problem," he argued.

"It's different," she snapped. "Besides, you already asked too many questions, and it's my turn. You said you left The Colectiv. Why?"

Eric worked his jaw in and looked down at the iridescent dagger in his grasp. His leg started bouncing unconsciously as he looked for his answer, a nervous habit peeking through, and Emilia wondered just how bad this response was.

"We didn't see eye to eye anymore," he finally responded, his words slow. "I wanted to do other things, and they weren't happy about it. So, I left."

"Why did you go back?"

He stared at her silently, his gaze poignant. Without words, there was a clear message in his eyes. Emilia's face fell, her dead heart constricting as guilt started to wrap itself around it.

She whispered the answer for him: "Revenge."

"Revenge," he repeated, nodding along with her.

"Of course." Her voice came out thin.

He went back because of Dante...and because of me.

She had no idea that the change in him was the direct result of her actions. The idea of having pushed Eric to such extremes overwhelmed her with shame, and she found herself fighting against oncoming tears.

No. Don't cry in front of hunters. Don't cry in front of him.

"It's my turn," he said. "Did your brother say anything about where he might go before he left?"

Emilia cleared her throat and said, "No. My brother rarely tells me his plans. He just impulsively decides to do them without caring about the consequences. That and he basically told me to go die in a hole, but you know…"

The humor in her voice did nothing to hide the pain in her eyes.

"Pudrete." Rot.

That was the last thing her brother said to her before he walked out of her life. The final blow in an earth-shattering conversation that still torments her to this day.

Emilia looked up at the dirty, cracked ceiling of the abandoned building to give her mind some relief. She was already growing tired from both the silver and the interrogation. Her dress had holes in it, one of her heels was gone, and her skin was sticky with blood. Her energy was depleting, which meant that if she was to survive this, she'd need to get some food into her system fast.

"It's your turn, Emilia." Eric's impatient voice cut through her thoughts, jolting her back to reality.

As she looked back into his eyes, she asked, "Did you know that I was a vampire?"

It had plagued her a little more than the rest, and she often wondered if the reason he came into her life at all was because of some sick plan to kill her for The Colectiv. After all, it was the idea Dante had planted in her head, and it didn't seem that far-fetched all things considered.

Eric stared at her long and hard for a second, his expression stone-like, before responding, "No. Not at first. But, I mean, by the end, it was pretty obvious. You can thank Dante for that."

Emilia narrowed her eyes. Even though his heartbeat was even and he fought to keep his features neutral, something in his eyes told her that he was hiding something.

"Did you ever suspect that I was anything other than human, or that I was a hunter?" he asked.

Emilia shook her head. "No. Never."

At least not entirely.

Funny things, daywalkers. They had heartbeats and could go out into the sun without turning purple from livor mortis. At a glance, they seemed human, so Emilia never suspected anything supernatural. If anything, she suspected health problems before vampirism. Eric was never good at taking care of himself and while the truth now explained his behavior and the slower heartbeat, back then, it seemed normal for him. After all, he wouldn't be the first human with a blatant disregard for their biology. He was nothing like any hunter she ever encountered, and perhaps now there was a reason for that. It didn't make her feel any better about being fooled. She had been too caught up with her own problems to even notice.

"So, you thought I was human?" he asked skeptically.

"Basically."

To her dismay, he snorted. "How did you think *that* was gonna end?"

Emilia sneered at him and resisted the urge to shrink away as he drove the metaphorical knife into her chest. She knew how selfish she had been back then, giving attention to a man that she knew could never have her. She knew how temporary it was. She had plenty of opportunities to stop and leave, and she didn't. But Eric was different, or so he appeared to be. Even so, she wasn't the only guilty party here.

"Not like that, obviously," she spat. "I know what I am, Eric. But you're not any different. You didn't think I was going to find out? Your family are hunters! Your brother is a hunter! And you were going to stop aging eventually, too. You're as much of a vampire as I am. I was going to find out your name. You said you figured out what I was eventually, and you said nothing. How did *you* think it was gonna end?"

Eric grimaced, and Emilia could hear his heart falter for a moment.

"I was reckless and naive, but I've learned from my mistakes. What we had was just doomed from the start."

"Clearly."

It didn't surprise her, with her dumb luck in the romance department. "*You picked a real winner this time*," Dante had said. *He wasn't wrong.*

With the hunter's patience wearing thin, his following questions were asked with a heightened level of irritability.

"Are there any places he could possibly have gone that had any meaning to him?"

With the tiredness wearing away at her, Emilia tried applying what little brain power she had left to this interrogation to break free from her chains.

"There are a few, I guess. He always talked about Mexico, Brazil, or even Cuba. He loves Vegas and New Orleans. And he used to love Milan, Barcelona, and a lot of other places in Europe, but I highly doubt he'd be there right now after everything."

"Why?"

"Because he's my brother, and if there's anything we have in common, it's that we like running away from our demons." Emilia flashed her eyes. "If he thinks I'm still there, he's staying away."

Eric furrowed his brow. "So... Vegas, New Orleans—anywhere else in this *country* that we should know about? Any other cities we should check out?"

Dante and Emilia had been to so many places over the last 50 years that it was often hard to keep track. With immortality and the world at their disposal, there were few limits to how far they could go. They just needed time and money. They had plenty of time, and money was just a means to an end.

"I mean, he always liked places that were fun or luxurious. Casinos, clubs, concerts, beaches..."

Emilia suddenly trailed off as her own words triggered a memory—no, *too many* memories. Violence, bloodshed, and pain. Mania and heartbreak. How could she have forgotten? Perhaps, after so many years, she had blocked it out somehow.

"Emilia," Eric elongated the last vowel, growing restless. "What is it? What do you remember?"

"A beach," she whispered. "Crimson Beach."

"Crimson Beach? As in Crimson Beach, California?"

"The very one."

"And what's special about Crimson Beach, Emilia?"

She hated the way he used her name. She liked it when he said it back in Italy, but now it was like he had power over her by saying it so many times, and she wished he would stop. Everything was becoming too overwhelming.

"I don't wanna do this anymore. I plead the Fifth." Her voice shook as she squirmed in her restraints.

"This isn't the court of law," Eric snapped. "Besides, the only law you're stuck under is The Colectiv's, and they're not very merciful."

She scowled. "I know."

Still, she was too afraid to answer the question, even now. Crimson Beach was nothing but a river of blood and tears for Emilia, and it was the darkest part of her past as of late. There was a reason she kept it hidden. She refused to look Eric in the eye.

"Emilia," he repeated, his voice drilling into her skull.

"Stop it," she hissed. "I don't want to talk about it, okay? Just know that it's a place he might be. Now let me go, so we can both be on our merry way."

James spoke up then, "E, let's just end this. We got enough to work with. I'm tired of this bitch."

Eric, however, was relentless when it came to the truth.

"No," he said sternly. "I wanna know what's so special about Crimson Beach."

He leaned forward again, his stare burning into her skin. Emilia glared at him now. He always had a habit of reading into her as no one else could, and he also had a habit of pulling at loose threads. It benefited him as a scholar, and now it seemed to benefit him even more as a hunter. She abhorred it.

"I need to know you're not sending us on a wild goose chase. Tell us what we need to know," he ordered.

Emilia closed her eyes, preparing herself to talk about something she swore she wouldn't talk about again. She writhed in her seat, whining like a child being forced to do something she didn't want to do. Finally, she snapped her eyes open.

"Do you know who 'The Hellhound' is?"

Eric went rigid, the fury dimming for a moment. "Yeah..."

"What do you know about him?"

He rolled his eyes. "Is there a point to this?"

"You wanted to know why Crimson Beach is special? Do you want to know who you're dealing with? Then you need to know who 'The Hellhound' is," Emilia stressed.

She raised her eyebrows at him expectantly. He was always good at finding connections and figuring things out, so this should be easy for him.

"What do you know about him, Eric?" she repeated.

"He was a serial killer in Crimson Beach who killed a fuck ton of people in the 70s and 80s," he answered.

"How did he kill them?"

"By slitting their throats and draining their blood. They also called him 'The Vampire,' ironically enough."

"Correct."

"Where the hell did you learn *that*, E?" James asked.

Eric shrugged. "I took a criminology class in college, and I know a little too much about true crime cases."

That sounds about right.

"What else?" Emilia urged him on.

He scoffed, "I don't know. His targets were...*specific* to say the least—dirty cops, shady businessmen, traffickers, gang members, bigots, rapists, you name it. This case was such a gray area for the people because, as far as they knew, the victims were real pieces of shit that deserved it."

"And did they deserve it?"

"Depends on who you ask."

"I'm asking *you*."

"Let's just say I won't lose sleep over it," he told her.

Emilia fought back a smirk. "Do you know what happened to them? The Hellhounds?"

"No. Eventually, the murders stopped, decades passed, and they called it a cold case. It wouldn't be the first time it happened in history, so..." Out of nowhere, Eric faltered, and then some realization struck him before her. His eyes flashed before his expression turned grim. "What's so special about this case, Emilia?"

The vampire shrugged. "I don't know. You tell me."

"You referred to them as more than one," he said. He straightened up a little, his gaze turning to steel. "You know... they used to speculate that 'The Hellhound' didn't work alone. Based on the evidence, the crime scenes, and the number of deaths, it didn't seem plausible, but they never proved it. So how can *you* say that? What do *you* know about 'The Hellhound' Emilia? What are *you* hiding?"

With every question, his eyes grew bigger and angrier. He was getting a little too close for comfort.

An anxious giggle came out of her. "Can we go back to playing the game instead?"

Having thoroughly snapped, Eric bolted from his chair. Emilia gasped as he wrapped his large hand around her throat and pointed the dagger under her chin. Her chair tipped backward, balancing on its hind legs, as Eric steadily held her there. All she could manage was a high-pitched squeak. Any other exclamations were cut off by the sight of his glowing yellow eyes—the eyes of a daywalker that she had seen once before. Except this time, he was rage-filled and predatory.

It seemed Emilia had sufficiently poked Eric MacNamara enough to make him break.

"Stop fucking around, Emilia," he said through gritted teeth, his face hovering over hers. "I played your stupid game, and I'm over it. Tell me what I need to know, or I'll break your fucking neck."

Instead of looking at him in terror or even animosity, like any sane person would, Emilia couldn't help but feel a mixture of mania, amusement...and *attraction*. It was something primal and deep-rooted. In other circumstances, she would have liked this position. After all, they had been this close many times before, with him touching her and his breath fanning over her face, but not like *this*. She may have missed the nice boy, but she had to admit that maybe she liked seeing this side of him too.

Emilia choked out a laugh and said, "I've never seen you so angry before. I think I kinda like it."

With a growl, he squeezed her neck even harder and put the blade further into her neck, drawing blood. His silver rings burned into her skin and she could feel her windpipe breaking as her vision filled with stars. She tried fighting against his grip, but she was left at the mercy of her chains and his strength. When the pain overwhelmed her, she caved in.

"Okay. Eric. Let go. I'll tell you. Safeword. Peaches," she wheezed.

Just when she thought she'd lose consciousness, Eric released her with an angry groan. She grunted as the chair fell back to the ground, jolting her body. She fell into a coughing fit, her vision still hazy as she regained her ability to breathe.

She didn't tap out because she was afraid of dying, but because she knew if she got knocked out, she'd have to start this over again.

With her composure intact, she looked up at Eric once more, her throat slowly healing. He stood tall before her, his eyes no longer glowing, but his wrath was palpable as he kept the dagger pointed at her neck.

"Who... Is... 'The Hellhound'?" he barked.

Emilia swallowed thickly before finally admitting,

"It was me. Me and Dante. We were 'The Hellhound'."

12

Hellhounds

Emilia

[24]Emilia was born on August 11th, 1950, as Alejandra Jimena Bernal and her older brother Dante was born on November 28th, 1947, as Daniel Antonio Bernal. Their parents were Antonio and Dolores, and they crossed the border into the U.S. from Mexico when Dante was two years old and Dolores was seven months pregnant with Alejandra. They settled in Los Angeles, where they lived in a small house for the majority of their lives.

The Bernal family came from traditional Mexican Catholic roots, and they raised their children in the same way. Both children were baptized as infants and had their first communions when they were a little older. They went to church every Sunday and were taught to pray to God, Jesus, and the Virgin Mary, as well as confess their sins

---

[24] Eleanor Rigby - Cody Fry

regularly. Antonio and Dolores were devout believers, and the strictness with which they raised their children was not only apparent in their religious beliefs but in other areas of life as well.

Alejandra's father, in particular, was what was commonly known as a "machista," which is a word in Spanish that directly means that he had a "strong sense of masculine pride." It was also another word to call a hypermasculine man who was sexist and viewed women as objects that were meant to serve them. This meant that while Antonio adored his firstborn son for being born with a penis, he hated his daughter for being born a woman. So, after he prayed to Jesus' mother, he'd turn around and treat his daughter—and his wife—like trash. And Dolores had become so submissive and accustomed to the way things were that she didn't even flinch.

For Alejandra's entire life until adulthood, this was how it was: Daniel was the favorite, and she was lucky to be born. Daniel had the love of both parents, while Alejandra was constantly picked apart. Daniel got to go out with friends while Alejandra was forced to stay home and do chores. He was coddled, served, and babied, while she was berated and asked to do the serving. He got his father's praise, while she got the back of his hand to her face. Daniel had everything, while Alejandra lived on the edge of a knife.

The young girl did her best to escape her reality. She turned to music, movies, and TV shows that ran at the time. She loved classic rock, books, and comics, and she fantasized about life away from her parents. Alejandra would dance alone in her room while listening to Fleetwood Mac, or if she got a chance to go to a family party, like a quinceañera, she'd spend all night on the dance floor without care. And if she needed to vent, she'd journal, or, surprisingly enough, she'd go to her older brother.

Although Daniel was on a pedestal that was too high for Alejandra to reach, he always treated her with more kindness than both of her parents combined. He played with her and brought her back comics, fiction books, and records from his outings with friends. He'd introduce her to new music and movies, and he would even sneak her out to the drive-in to watch a film or two. When their father wasn't watching, they'd dance, sing, and laugh together. And it was in those moments that she felt like there were no differences between them at all and like they were brother and sister, as brothers and sisters should be. But, of course, at the end of the day, they lived different lives—one with chains and one without—and come adulthood, things only complicated themselves further.

At a certain age, Antonio and Dolores expected their children to get married and settle down, and it was normal for that pressure to come as soon as they turned 18, if not before. Without question, Alejandra suddenly went from being forbidden from seeing boys to being matched up with a family friend named Mauricio, who was raised in the same traditions as her parents were. Alejandra was expected to marry him, have his children, and serve him as his wife, while Daniel was expected to marry a respectable woman, have children, and provide for his family. However, Antonio and Dolores realized that their children were not what they had raised them to be and were gradually becoming what they, and so many others like them, feared.

Daniel had a few girlfriends in high school, but his interest in women seemed to be less than normal as he never seemed to want to commit. When he went to college, the condition worsened, and the rest of the family started to talk. "Chisme" spread like wildfire that Antonio's son might not be as "macho" as his father was, and while they were at it, they thought his daughter might be a little queer too.

People in the community started viewing Daniel and Alejandra differently, and unfortunately, Mauricio made it personal.

Alejandra's first real date was in the year she was supposed to turn 23, and it was a nightmare she would never forget. It was with Mauricio, and since her parents didn't question his integrity or trustworthiness, they left their daughter in his hands. There was no reason to be concerned, as long as she returned by a certain time. They went to the movies and watched "The Poseidon Adventure," and everything seemed fine until the drive home. Instead of going to her house, Mauricio drove up to the hills and stopped at an outlook overlooking the valley. He had feigned romance, speaking sweet nothings, until, out of nowhere, a switch flipped. And it was in that car on that night that Mauricio decided to assert his masculinity and power over Alejandra without her consent. She went home that night feeling used, broken, and hollow. And when she got home, she cried to her mother and begged her to understand, but all Dolores said was, "It happens to the best of us."

From then on, Alejandra did not seem to exist for the months that followed. She was but a shell and she even contemplated taking her own life more than a few times. She couldn't imagine living such a horrible existence only to basically be sold off and repeat the cycle with a predator. But in the summer of 1972, all of that changed after one horrible night that transformed her life for eternity.

[25]It was a normal Saturday evening and Daniel had gone out with some friends, just "boys being boys." Everything was as it was. Alejandra and her mother were cleaning up after dinner while her father sat on the couch watching TV when, suddenly, the phone rang.

---

[25] Ptolemaea - Ethel Cain

Her father picked it up, and as he listened to what he was being told, Alejandra witnessed his face transform into that of a monster.

"¿Qué?" he shouted. *What?*

According to a nosy neighbor that had been in town, someone had caught Daniel walking out of a gay bar, and he was kissing another man.

Alejandra's heart dropped, not because she couldn't believe what she was hearing but because she instantly feared for her brother's life. She had every reason to because as soon as her brother came home, Antonio turned on his favorite child. He started yelling at him, calling him names and slurs, which then escalated to a physical altercation. Daniel looked terrified, which affected his little sister. Their father hit him while Dolores cried, and it was at that moment that Alejandra was overcome with a wave of courage she didn't even know she had in her.

She screamed at her father to stop and just as he raised his hand to strike again, she put herself in between them and grabbed his arm. She tried pushing him away with all her might, but unfortunately, she wasn't strong enough to stop him. All Antonio had to do was hit her in the face, and Alejandra fell to her knees on the floor.

"¡No la toques!" Daniel shouted.

Don't touch her!

Her brother sank down next to her, his hand finding her shoulder. They shared a look of absolute terror. Bruises were already forming on his face and his lip was bleeding. At the same time, Antonio marched to the kitchen and rifled through a drawer, taking something out that he had been saving for a special occasion.

A revolver.

And he pointed it at his favorite child as their mother screamed in the background.

Daniel stood up with his hands raised and tried pleading to his father, but Antonio was already pulling the trigger. A loud gunshot pierced through the house, and the young man grunted as a bullet hit him in the stomach. Alejandra let out a blood curdling shriek, the blood in her veins turning to ice.

"No!"

She bolted to her feet and caught Daniel around the torso to keep him from collapsing. The girl placed herself in front of him, creating a shield with her small body before her father could pull the trigger again.

Antonio bared his teeth, saying, "Quítate o te mato a ti también."

Get out of the way, or I'll kill you too.

Salty tears ran down Alejandra's face, her lips quivering.

"No," she said with all the courage she couldn't muster until now.

At that moment, she was ready to sacrifice herself for Daniel. She was ready to die *with* him. But as Antonio was about to put a bullet in his daughter, Dolores came up behind him with a frying pan and struck him in the head with all of her strength. Her husband's eyes rolled to the back of his skull, and he fell unconscious to the floor. The gun clattered out of his limp hand, and the house fell silent.

Alejandra and Daniel stared at their mother with matching expressions of astonishment.

"Váyanse. Váyanse y nunca regresen," she ordered with tears in her eyes.

Leave. Leave and never come back.

With a shaky nod, the Bernal siblings ran out of the house and fled into the dark street as fast as they possibly could. Both powered by adrenaline, Daniel managed to run while his sister carried half of his weight. They ran and ran until Daniel's legs gave out, and they ended up at the corner of a closed church. Alejandra screamed for help, holding her brother's body in her lap. She kept pressure on his wound with trembling hands to keep him from bleeding out.

"Danny—Danny, stay with me, please. Please don't leave me," she cried.

She didn't know what she would do. She didn't know if she could live without him.

Daniel held onto his sister's arm gently and said, "It's okay, Alé. It's okay."

His eyes fluttered shut, making her sob. Alejandra closed her eyes and turned her face towards the sky, begging God to save her big brother. But God was not the one who answered.

"What's going on here?" a deep voice rumbled.

Alejandra jolted, her attention going to a tall figure standing before her. He almost blended into the night, but the singular lamppost on the corner allowed her to get a good look at him. He was a dark man in a brown coat with an Afro that resembled a halo around his head, and while it seemed like a trick of the light, she swore his eyes glowed for a brief moment.

He crouched at their feet, looking down at them grimly. His demeanor was a little too casual for her liking, yet she clung to his presence for dear life.

"Help. Help us, please. Help him. He's dying," she pleaded.

"Who did this to you?" the man demanded.

Alejandra scowled. "Our father."

"Do you have anyone you can go to? Anyone who is safe?"

"N-no, they wouldn't..." she looked at her brother and then back at the man. "They wouldn't understand either. Nowhere is safe."

He hummed dourly. "I can help you, but it comes at a price."

The girl shook her head. The rest of her body shivered, but she couldn't tell if it was from adrenaline, terror, or the cold air.

"We-we don't have any money," she stammered.

The strange man looked at her with surprising compassion. "I don't mean money, darling girl. I mean your life, your mortality."

She frowned. "I don't understand."

"Do you know what a vampire is?"

Despite her bewilderment, she nodded. Alejandra had read stories and watched movies about vampires enough to know. "*Cosas del diablo*" or "devil stuff," her mother had called it.

"Well, what if I told you they were real? And what if I told you that I *am* one?"

His eyes then turned a pale blue, and he smiled to show fangs. The siblings gasped, clutching onto each other. But they didn't shy away from him. They couldn't.

"Holy shit," Daniel whispered.

"I know," the vampire said but kept his eyes on Alejandra. "I can save your brother and you. I can take you away from this life, from your father, but it means you have to abandon everything. That means who you are, who you thought you were going to be, and any sense of normalcy you could've possibly had. You'll have to feed on blood for the rest of your life, but you'll never die, and you'll be strong—stronger than any human—and...if you want, you can make them pay."

Alejandra had always fantasized about being someone else. She imagined herself in another world that was unlike her own, where nobody could touch her and her power was hers alone. She wished and prayed for the day she'd be able to leave her horrible life, and now... the opportunity was being handed to her on a silver platter. After the nightmare she and her brother went through, this man was offering them escape...and *redemption*. The vampire should have scared her, but she knew far more terrifying men who hadn't treated her with such kindness and respect. It wasn't even a question. She'd do anything to save her brother, and she'd do anything to break out of her cage.

"What do we have to do?" she asked.

Jean—Alejandra soon came to learn his name—gave them both a taste of his blood, but for the transformation to begin, they had to die. So, he let Daniel bleed out from his wound and, with her permission, snapped Alejandra's neck. The next thing she knew, they woke up to their new home in Crimson Beach, both alive and fully healed—and with a newfound *hunger*.

Their new friend warned them about the side effects of being freshly turned—the venom tended to amplify certain traits and emotions one had as a mortal, especially strong ones. And after the hell the Bernal siblings endured, getting turned unleashed a part of them that became hell-bent on *revenge*. Like a caterpillar destroying itself to become a butterfly, Daniel and Alejandra destroyed a part of themselves to become something powerful and untouchable. They changed their names, severing ties with their family and their old life, and started going by Dante and Emilia.

Dante and Emilia were bound by blood, trauma, and rage. They made a pact to hurt anyone who ever hurt them, even the people just like them. Their first kills were Antonio and Mauricio. Dante left Mauricio's torture to his sister, but they split their father's demise between the two. Their mother they spared, leaving her with his money and the freedom she never had. But it was these crimes of passion that opened the door to a much bloodier path. They never planned on it. It just turned out that way. They had the power and skills to take down the vermin of humanity, and they took every chance they had. After all, if they needed the blood to survive, why not pick victims who deserved it? Thus, the case of "The Hellhound" was born.

With reckless abandon, they terrorized the southern California coast. All Emilia could remember from that time was constantly being covered in blood and feeling high from the sweet nectar. And by the time the 80s came, Dante and Emilia reigned supreme in their own little bubble. It was them against the world. Until... that bubble burst.

At the time, the Crimson Beach clan consisted of young vampires led by the experienced Jean Beltremieux and his best friend, Wade MacNamara. Considering they had a century behind them, people easily flocked to them. Emilia especially grew very attached to Jean from the start. He was an excellent judge of character and saved those he believed had a bright future, Emilia and her brother being two of them. Jean did his best to teach Emilia the same ideology, which is how she met her best friend, Jaya. Because of people like them, Emilia learned that perhaps she could be good at helping others in different ways—ways that *didn't* involve selfish murder. Yet she was still hung up on having "fun" and was always torn between herself and her brother's lifestyle. That was until, in late 1985, when The Colectiv caught up.

After years of getting away with it, the Hellhounds officially drew so much attention that the Crimson Beach clan had to flee and scatter throughout the country. Dante and Emilia lived life on the run across the U.S. until they eventually decided to leave their American lives behind and move to the other side of the world to escape. It was effective enough to throw The Colectiv off guard and put an indefinite end to their pursuits. Dante, however, seemed to worsen over time.

[26]Emilia knew his toxic and shameless behavior was a response to what had happened to him. Emilia was no different and had acted in a similar way for a long time, but no matter how much time passed,

---

[26] Labour - Paris Paloma

Dante never seemed to want to get better. On the contrary, he was determined to become what the world wanted him to be: a devil. With "The Hellhound" long gone, he had too much time on his hands and soon became possessive of his little sister. It had been them against the world for decades, so when she'd venture out on her own, he took it personally. He'd get overbearing and controlling, claiming that it was for her own good while also shaming her for not loving him like she used to. Those who truly cared for Emilia despised Dante, as they quickly noticed the negative effect he started to have on her life. Yet she'd forgive him despite their warnings because he was her brother and she loved him like no one else, but it didn't stop her from resenting him.

She dreaded his presence and hid things from him, just as she had with her father when they were kids. Even when he went off to do who knows what, he'd only return to drag her back into the chaos. It was a constant roller coaster that had Emilia wondering if she simply needed to accept that this was her fate. Perhaps the darkness was as inevitable as he said it was. But everything changed when she met Eric MacNamara.

13

The Pot & The Kettle

Eric

Staten Island, New York—Present

"What the fuck did you just say?" Eric stared down the blade of his dagger at Emilia in complete disbelief.

"You heard me," she said. "It was us."

He looked over his shoulder at James, who was surprisingly silent through all of this. His brother shrugged, his eyes wide.

"You're not just fucking with us, are you?" James asked.

Emilia scoffed, "Why would I lie about something so horrible and so specific? A minute ago, I didn't even want to tell you."

Eric regarded her for a piercing moment, searching for the lie in her eyes. He thought it could've been another game she was trying to play, but as she looked up at him, he could see a brokenness in her.

From the moment they met, she had fought tooth and nail to keep that secret from him, and what a secret it was to bear.

So, as it turned out, Emilia was the infamous "Hellhound." Rather, she and her brother were the pair that committed the crimes. It would be a blatant understatement to say that Eric was shocked. For the second time this week, life was catching him by surprise.

He had always found the case intriguing, and he'd be lying if he said that he hadn't considered the possibility of vampires being involved. He thought about it often when he looked at unsolved murders, disappearances, and strange urban legends. It was normal for humanity to either sensationalize or rationalize things, but as a hunter and a daywalker in hiding, Eric knew better. He could see the signs of something more...*supernatural*. So, finding out that two vampires were behind this particular case was plausible, but never in a million years could he have predicted falling for one of them. He meant it when he said that the lives "The Hellhound" took didn't bother him, but knowing the truth made him rethink everything.

Emilia, out of all people?

He could never imagine going that far. For a vampire to kill for survival was one thing, but to go on a murder spree was another. Eric himself hunted and killed people who did that very thing, and it was a shock to his system to know that Emilia fell into that category. It painted her in a new, bloody light and added another layer to their already tumultuous story.

He shook his head in bewilderment. "Why? Why did you do it?"

Emilia's smile was somber. "Revenge, Eric. You would know something about that."

"But I would never kill that many people," he argued.

"Oh, really?" she scoffed. "You're the trained killer. 14 years, you said? How many vampires have you killed in that time, huh?" She turned her fierce gaze on James. "How many have *you*?"

His twin had killed more vampires than Eric, that was certain.

James growled, low in his throat, "You shut the fuck up. You don't know shit."

"Don't I?"

Eric clenched his jaw, seething.

He didn't like to think about it. In fact, he had lost count, especially in the past three years. There was a level of distance and prejudice that hunters felt toward vampires. After all, they didn't get paid to like them. In fact, quite the opposite. They were raised to believe that what they were doing was for some greater good, and Eric, for the most part, believed it. James believed it. Most of the vampires they set out to kill were the scum of the earth, and by getting rid of them, he made the world safer. Even his own blood was tainted.

So, why did he feel offended by Emilia's accusation?

[27]His old flame turned back toward him to say, "Don't go around being the pot and calling the kettle black. Living or dead, lives are lives. I killed people because, after the hell I went through, I was given a second chance. Now I get to live with that nightmare in my head. *I* live with who I am now."

Emilia leaned forward until the tip of Eric's dagger pressed into her skin, her eyes like blades themselves. The hunter didn't move.

"What about *you*, Eric? Will you be able to live with yourself? When you finally kill Dante, will you stop? Or will you keep going? Because I know I didn't stop. I had two on my list going into this, but

---

[27] I Don't Care - VIOLENT VIRA

then it turned into tens more, and that's not even counting the ones I've killed just to survive since then."

"Stop it," Eric hissed.

Try as he may to keep his composure steady, he could feel himself starting to lose it again. She had already broken his patience once. Even if it got him the answer he wanted, he hated unraveling like this. He promised that he wouldn't, but Emilia had a knack for getting under his skin, and she knew the right buttons to push. It drove him up the wall. But he didn't let it take away his focus.

"We come from completely different worlds, Emilia," he said evenly. "I don't kill for the same reasons you do, so don't pretend like we're the same. What I do is business. It's a necessity. Dante is *unfinished* business, and I promise you, I won't lose sleep over that either. Once I'm done with him... I'm moving on. You're dead to me, and I'm dead to you."[28]

He withdrew the dagger and turned away from her, briefly catching sight of her frown.

Eric didn't know what happened that could have pushed her to such extremes, but he wasn't going to act like he did. He'd be a hypocrite, considering his own rage. No matter how intriguing, hearing Emilia's story was the last thing he needed or wanted to do. With every shocking truth, he became more aware of the lies and felt like he knew her less and less. Yet, somehow, he found peace in that. Having the remnants of an old illusion burn away made it easier to feel nothing.

"Who even are you?" she whispered.[29]

---

[28] SPIT IN MY FACE! - ThxSoMch
[29] Decode - Paramore

That's a hell of a question, isn't it? With too many answers and so little time.

All he did was look over his shoulder at her and say, "I could ask you the same thing."

He sheathed his weapon and glanced over at James. His twin raised his eyebrows and looked about as irritated as Eric felt.

"Let's get out of here. We got what we needed."

"Fuckin' finally," James muttered, throwing a scowl at Emilia.

"Wait, what?" she sputtered behind him. "That's it?"

"Yup," Eric said, pulling on his jacket.

"Aren't you gonna kill me? Or turn me in to The Colectiv?"

Eric huffed and turned around to look at her. She was on the edge of her seat, her face riddled with panic.

"You know, in other circumstances, we would have, but... unfortunately, we made a deal with our informant to not kill you in exchange for your location. Turning you in would guarantee that," he explained.

Emilia shook her head in confusion. "'Informant'? Who the fuck is your informant?"

"Jean Beltremieux, baby."

Eric's lips widened into a wicked grin as Emilia's jaw dropped upon hearing the news of her mentor's betrayal.

"Jean?" she shrilled.

"Yup."

"He knew you were coming after me this whole time?"

"Seems like it."

Eric grabbed his duffle from the ground and threw it over his shoulder before heading toward the door.

"Wait! Stop!" Emilia shouted. "You're not just going to leave me here, are you?"

"Obviously," James rumbled.

"You bastards! I told you everything I know! You made a promise! But you're just going to leave me here until I starve, and then what do you think happens then? I'll die!"

She screamed in frustration. Eric could hear the sound of the metal chair scraping against the floor and the silver chains rattling as she tried to break herself free. The twins paused and shared a sigh of annoyance and a knowing look. As tempting as it was to leave her to rot, they knew she was right.

"How are we supposed to know you won't run off and tell Dante all of this?" Eric questioned.

"I told you, I haven't talked to him in years. I've made my peace with not caring about what happens to him. I'm not his fucking mom."

He twisted around and raised his eyebrows at her. "He's your brother. I have a hard time believing that you stopped caring about him just like that."

Immortal or not, Eric still worried about James. He couldn't imagine a scenario where he would stop caring about his brother, no matter how bad of a fight they had. He couldn't imagine not caring if he lived or died.

"You only know our relationship at a glance, Eric," she argued. "You don't know what else we've been through. You're not the only one he's hurt."

That still doesn't mean I can trust you.

Regardless, the hunter rolled his eyes and reached into his pocket to fish out a small ring of keys. He raised them in the air, tauntingly jingling them in his hand. Emilia focused on them, frozen in anticipation.

Eric smiled darkly at her and said, "Beg."

Emilia sneered. "Drop dead, you piece of shit."

"Well, then, I guess you'll have to get used to your new home," he said with a shrug, and he turned away from her once more. He was almost through the door, but then...

"I didn't leave you for dead, you know!"

Eric stopped dead in his tracks once more, his brow furrowing. "What?"

"You said that I left you for dead, but I didn't," she repeated, her voice hoarse. "You ever wondered who got you to the hospital that night? Or who called James? It was me."

Eric's face dropped, and he spun around to look at her.

So it was *you.*

That night, after he had accepted his imminent death, Eric woke up in a hospital bed, hours later, with his brother by his side. Apparently, James had received a phone call from a girl who told him what happened. Allegedly, she knew Eric from school, but considering how the events played out, one of the people they suspected was Emilia. They were never entirely certain...until now. Why she did it, Eric would never truly know.

For selfish reasons, probably.

"Why should I believe you?" he demanded.

Emilia shrugged, her shoulders heavy with exhaustion. "I don't know. You have every reason not to."

Looking at her now and being reminded of what happened, memories of that night flashed before Eric's eyes. He looked away quickly as his heart raced and suddenly, the room seemed smaller.

Italy. Going to Emilia's place that night. Talking to James on the phone. Dante coming out of the shadows. Finding out his secret. Screaming. Being practically torn to shreds as Emilia watched. Waking up at the hospital to find his life destroyed. The pain. The scar. The heartbreak.

He felt a hand on his shoulder.

"E. Hey, it's okay."

James' voice was enough to somewhat pull him out of the noise and stop the dull ringing in his ears. Eric blinked a few times and shook his head before looking into the familiar face of his brother, who was watching him with care. All at once, Eric was back in the abandoned building, in the present day.

He tapped James' hand in a grateful gesture as he nodded. His twin pulled away, and Eric took a moment to compose himself. When he glanced back at Emilia, she looked confused by the whole ordeal.

Perfect fucking timing, as usual.

"What just happened?" she asked.

"Nothing you need to worry about," he muttered.

Wanting this night to end, Eric put his duffle on the ground and marched over to Emilia, keys in hand. As he got closer to her, she shrank back in her chair, as if preparing for the worst, only to be taken aback when he stopped before her and pointed the keys at her. With how irritated he looked, they may as well have been a weapon.

"You try anything, I don't care what Jean said. You're losing your head, got that?"

Emilia nodded. "Of course."

Eric rolled his eyes, mostly at himself, and went behind her to release the lock that secured the restraints. The chains fell loose around her and with a pleased sigh, Emilia tugged them away until she was free to stand up and move around.

"There, you're free to go," he muttered, ignoring her wary look.

"Thank you."

Her skin was starting to take on a cool purple tint. It happened when pureblood vampires went too long without eating or spent too much time exposed to things that drained their energy, like UV rays or silver.

"I'm sure you'll have no problem finding a way out of here or someone to eat," he said dryly.

"W-What?" Emilia sputtered. "I don't even know where we are. How am I supposed to get back home?"

"We're in Staten Island."

He walked back to his bag and picked it up again. To his chagrin, Emilia followed close behind.

"Staten Island?!" she exclaimed. "You think I know my way around this hellhole?"

"Use a GPS."

"You took my phone, you asshole. You could at least give me a ride."

James scoffed, "What do we look like, a ride-share service? We had you tied up to a chair. You're lucky we let you go. Talk about Stockholm syndrome."

Emilia sneered at him viciously. "Fuck you. At least take me to the train station or something. You took my purse, my phone, and my wallet. And even one of my shoes. I'm not a wild animal who knows how to survive in the wilderness."

"Actually, we have those in the car, and I'd be more than happy to give them back if it means you let us leave," Eric told her.

"Or, I can take them with me when you drop me off at the train station," she said with a sugary tone.

Eric couldn't help but laugh. "It's kind of hilarious that you think you can tell us what to do."

"It's kind of hilarious that you're a condescending prick."

He raised his eyebrows in shock and put his hand over his chest dramatically. "Wow, now I'm *really* not letting you ride in the car."

Eric let his expression drop, and the twins walked out the door, leaving the dim light of the empty structure behind. But now that she was out of her chains, Emilia was as unrelenting as ever. Eric sensed her barreling toward him, and with a growl, she grabbed his arm and pulled him to face her.

"Hey!" James shouted. In seconds, he pulled out a pistol, cocked it, and pointed it at her head.

Emilia glowered at him sidelong but didn't look particularly alarmed. Eric pulled his arm away from her and stared down at her severely. The vampire looked up at him in kind, looking venomous despite her size. A muscle feathered in the young daywalker's cheek as he fought back a shaking wrath.

"You really shouldn't touch a hunter like that. They could kill you," he growled.

"You'll live," she hissed. "Listen here... You ambushed *me*. You kidnapped *me*. You tied *me* up to a chair. Now, the least you could do is give me a ride, or I will snap both of your necks and steal your car. Or even worse, I'll slash all of your tires and strand all three of us here, so you can suffer!"

James gave Eric a sharp look and started speaking in Romanian.

"Am de gând să o omor."

I'm gonna kill her.

He pressed the gun into her skull, and Eric's heart dropped.

Before he could pull the trigger, he pointed a warning finger at his twin and shouted, "No! Ține minte Jean!"

Remember Jean!

James groaned in exasperation. "La naiba cu Jean. Am spus ce am spus!"

To hell with Jean. I said what I said.

"This is not life or death, Jimmy," Eric argued.

"It could be!"

Eric shook his head sternly and turned his attention back to Emilia, who surveyed them with bemusement before returning to her fury.

The former lovers stared each other down once more. It was just like when he threatened her earlier, except now the roles were reversed. Eric was used to having the upper hand against purebloods because he had methods of getting what he wanted, but this was *Emilia,* and the circumstances complicated things. It was aggravating, and he was beginning to understand why hunters were told not to make things personal. He was deeply regretting every single decision he had ever made because of her. Perhaps he wouldn't be here at all, dealing with any of this or the *stupid* deal with Jean. But Eric was not one to give up, and he was determined to have as much control over himself and the situation as possible. He just needed to get Emilia away from him quickly so she wouldn't become any more of a problem. If it meant taking her to the train station, then so be it.

"Train station. That's it."

James sighed, retracting the gun. "I'm gonna kill myself."

Emilia smiled like a cat. "Perfect."

14

Dead To You

Emilia

Emilia was completely disheveled, sitting in the back of the twins' car. Her face was covered in blood, and while there was no pain, she was sore, exhausted, and, above all, extremely irritated. Up ahead, Eric was in the driver's seat, with James as his brooding passenger. They all sat in deafening silence, their disdain palpable. The only thing that alleviated the tension was the soft sound of music.

From what she could gather, the boys had taken her to Staten Island, to what looked like an old brick building in the woods that was forgotten years ago. How they knew about it, she didn't know, but she wouldn't have been surprised if hunters somehow kept track of empty spaces for their shadowy business. Emilia couldn't remember the last time she was interrogated, but she knew for a fact that it was nothing like *that*.

I should've known better than to play a game with him. I should've known he'd never back down. Eric was always stubborn. It's my fault. I thought it was cute back then.

Now, Eric knew one of her darkest secrets—a secret only a handful of people knew—and Emilia felt like she had been stripped naked. Even if she found satisfaction in pushing his buttons, at the end of the day, he had the upper hand. He secured precisely what he needed out of her—no physical torture required. It was maddening. But at the very least, she wasn't the only one left rattled.

The vampire's gaze flitted to the rearview mirror. There, she could see Eric's eyes in the reflection as he stared out the windshield. Emilia couldn't help but wonder about the episode he had earlier. After keeping his heart steady for so long, all at once it was beating so fast that even his brother was concerned. She knew she shouldn't care, but it was hard to forget.

As if sensing her, Eric glanced into the reflection, and their eyes briefly connected. Emilia looked away to save her dead heart. Instead, she focused on a piece of jewelry that dangled from the mirror itself. It was a necklace with a golden, heart-shaped locket. She furrowed her brow, wondering who it could belong to. The last thing she wanted to do was ask, so she kept her curiosity to herself.

Beside her was a duffle bag. Though she didn't know who it belonged to, she couldn't help but notice that one of the zippers was partially open. Within, she could see pistols, a few knives, and a crucifix (which made her roll her eyes). There was also a bottle of brown liquid, which she knew to be pure rosewater. The sight of it made her cringe, knowing firsthand the awful effects it had. She paid no mind to most of it until she caught sight of a wallet sticking out of a small pocket.

Emilia's curiosity was piqued. She didn't intend to steal anything. No, she just wanted to see if she could learn anything of value. It seemed only fair to her, considering what she was forced to share.

So, she sat upright in nonchalance and glanced at the boys. James looked over his shoulder, giving her a once-over. They glared at each other and then straightened up once more. When all seemed fine, Emilia reached into the duffle with nimble fingers and snatched the wallet out. While staying on high alert, she opened it and flipped through its contents, her touch as light as a feather.

The bag was Eric's. She could tell from the New York driver's license with his face on it, which she could tell was fake from the name alone: *Christian Hofstetter*. There were also various credit cards, all with different aliases, and a room key for a hotel called Comfort King Inn. The key came in a little sleeve with a room number written on the back: *244*. But what truly caught her attention were two pictures in plastic sleeves.

The first was a picture of a woman with brown skin, dark hair, and hazel eyes. At first, Emilia assumed it was a romantic partner of some kind until she saw a second picture of the same woman standing with two little boys. Twin boys.

Her eyes flashed with recognition, and she bit back a gasp.

Eric and James. It was so obviously them, even though they were significantly younger.

Was this before The Colectiv took them in? Did that mean... Was that their mom? I mean, who else? Why else would he have this picture?

Seeing them all standing side by side, the resemblance was there. They had their mother's features too, especially her smile, and she was absolutely beautiful.

So, this is who Wade fell in love with. I wonder what happened.

If what Eric had told her was true, then Emilia already knew what happened to his mother. The reminder overwhelmed her with sorrow now that there was a face to the woman's memory. And the more she thought about it, the more she felt like she was heavily violating this woman's privacy somehow, even if it *was* Eric's wallet. So, when she was sure they weren't looking, Emilia carefully closed it shut and swiftly put it back in the duffle. Just as she straightened up, Eric caught her eye but didn't catch *her*.

†††

Instead of the train station, the twins dropped Emilia off at the St. George Terminal, where a ferry would take her and her alone back to Manhattan. Eric parked by the curb and looked over his shoulder at her. His side profile was a silhouette against the night lights outside the windshield.

"This is as far as we go, Emilia."[30]

To her surprise, she frowned. *This is as far as we go.* She knew he wasn't referring to just this moment, but every other after.

"You're dead to me, and I'm dead to you."

He had said it earlier with such cold finality, and Emilia realized that, for the second time in their complicated relationship, she didn't know if she'd ever see Eric MacNamara again. She didn't know if she should even want to, yet there was a sudden disappointment weighing her down. Perhaps it was the past again, dressing itself up as something new to trick her heart. Of course, she maintained her composure. She wouldn't dare give her feelings away, especially as he looked at her through the mirror once more.

---

[30] Simple And Clean - Utada Hikaru

"I guess I won't be seeing you again, then, huh?" she asked.

Eric snorted. "Don't count on it."

The quick and steady reply was like a soft stab in the heart, but she told herself it was for the best.

"Good. I think I like being left alone."

With her things in hand, she opened the door and hopped out onto the sidewalk. She pulled her coat tight around herself to hide the holes in her dress. One of her shoes was broken, and though she did her best to get rid of the blood on her face, it was obvious she had a pretty rough night.

With her hand on the door, she took one last, long look at Eric, as if she could compel him to look at her without words.

"Good luck," she told him. "You're gonna need it. Oh, and try not to die...*again.*"

He threw her a glare, but before he could respond, Emilia slammed the door and put as much distance between her and the hunters as possible.

15

Deal with the Devil

James

Brasov, Romania—Three days ago

For what could have been the first time in his life, James was at a complete loss for words.

Michael had just spent the last hour telling him all about the story of "The Hellhound," an unsolved case involving a serial killer in the 1970s on the southern California coast. What made this case significant, however, was the fact that, despite civilian speculation, the killer was not human, and he hadn't done it alone. In actuality, "The Hellhound" was a pair of vampires that worked together to terrorize humanity, and The Colectiv knew all about it.

As it was technically still an ongoing case, a lot of the details were on a need-to-know basis, and only those who lived through it knew the full details. Michael himself had been a teenager in training at the time, but even he didn't know everything until he got higher in the ranks.

And now, as James was on the precipice of potentially becoming captain, Michael was bestowing the information upon *him*. Yet, the most astonishing piece wasn't the murders themselves, but the intel that Michael had on who exactly the culprits were.

"Emilia?" James whispered sharply once he finally found his voice. "Emilia...and Dante...*they're* the 'Hellhound?'"

"I'm not 100% certain, but after what happened with E, I'm a little more than positive," the commander confirmed with a nod.

James sat in silence for a long moment. Emilia, Eric's ex-girlfriend—the one they were about to go to the other side of the world to find—was a wanted criminal. His twin brother slept with a killer. Not only that, but *her* brother, the *other* killer, almost made him their next victim.

What are the fucking odds?

The thought made the daywalker hot with fury.

"How do you know that it's them?" he asked.

Michael leaned back in his chair. "Well, we always knew they were a duo, and they were always together. At first, everyone thought they were dating—some fatal attraction story—but we heard through the grapevine that they were brother and sister. Pair that up with the description we received a long time ago, and it makes sense."

James exhaled slowly, trying to steady his mind. He had to remember that this was brought up because of the promotion and the fact that the commander had a task for him to complete. So, now that they were at the end of the story, he had to know the point, even if he was hesitant to know it.

"And what do you want *me* to do about it?"

The commander looked at him seriously and told him, "I want you to take her out."

James exercised every last bit of control he could muster, lest he explode. He fought to keep his face still and held back his genuine reaction because, on the inside... he wanted to scream.

"You want me...to *kill*... Emilia? That's what you're saying?"

"That's exactly what I'm saying," Michael replied with a nod. "Is there a problem?"

Yes. Yes, there is! He wanted to shout it. There were a multitude of reasons, many of which he couldn't voice.

"Yeah, funny thing," he said with a dark chuckle. "E and I sorta promised Jean that we wouldn't kill her...in exchange for information."

Michael scoffed and rolled his eyes. He waved one of his hands as if swatting James' words away.

"Don't worry about that. He tries anything, we'll take him down. As a matter of fact, now that you say that, I'll make sure to send some people over to his place and keep an eye out."

James furrowed his brow. He asked Michael once before what he had on the old vampire, but he didn't give a straight answer. Confidential information, no doubt. He wondered if he'd let him know after the promotion. Considering how unbothered he was by Jean's threats, the daywalker couldn't help but be curious. After all, the vampire made it seem like he'd rain hellfire if Emilia lost her life. But even if Michael told him not to worry about it, Jean was the least of James' worries. No, his biggest concern was *Eric*.

He knew just how much Emilia had meant to him back in Italy. It was more than even Michael knew because the commander didn't know Eric the way his brother did. Even if Eric hated Emilia now, and even if the thought of killing her was enticing to James, this all created conflict within his psyche. And not being able to tell Eric any of it felt wrong and like some kind of betrayal. Yet, his promotion hung in the balance. It was what James had worked for his entire adult life thus far—a new leadership role and one step closer to taking over as commander. It was still years away, but it was right there when, before, it was barely a possibility. This goal—this dream, this *one thing*—was within reach at last, and Michael was offering it to him... for a *price*.[31]

Despite everything, in the face of the commander, James lied.

"Okay... I'm just wondering how I'm supposed to keep this from E when this is his hunt, after all."

"It is," Michael reassured. "Dante is all his, and so is anyone else that stands in his way. I have no doubts that your brother will follow through on his end. But Emilia? Emilia is in your hands."

"What if it's not her?"

"I'm sure you can find a way to confirm her identity, but as I said, I'm pretty certain it is."

The daywalker nodded, his skull feeling heavy as he didn't know what else to say or do. Michael seemed to sense his apprehension.

"I know you don't like keeping things from your brother, but from here on out, this is just the way things are gonna be. Even you know that there's a level of covertness to this job, Jimmy. And the more you rise, the more secrets you need to keep. You need to keep your cards hidden and always be one step ahead of your enemy and those around you. Because if certain information gets out, it can mean your life or the lives of your people, and that includes E. You need to be strategic. You understand?"

Despite the discomfort, James knew it made logical sense.

"I do," he said.

"Good. Look at it as just another job. A big one at that, and with a big reward. If you follow through, which I'm sure you will, then the promotion is all yours." He gave his son a smirk, silver eyes sparkling. "Deal?"

---

[31] Circle With Me - Spiritbox

With sickness in the pit of his stomach, James accepted the challenge just like he always did.

"Deal."

†††

"Is there a particular way you want this to go?"

The commander shook his head. "No. All I want is her head on a platter. I don't care when, where, or how, as long as it gets done before you come back."

Manhattan, New York—Present

Fuck. Shit. Fuck. Fuck. Fuck.

That wasn't supposed to happen. How did I let that happen? I should've killed her when I had the chance.

Fuck!

James seethed in the passenger seat of the Jeep, his mind going a million miles a minute. They had just dropped off Emilia, an act he never could have anticipated, yet Eric, in some act of compassion, chose to give her a ride. As if he wasn't already livid over the interrogation itself. To James' misfortune, not only did this go against his entire code, but it also put a dent in his plan.

Ever since Michael gave him the mission, James had been driving himself insane, trying to come up with ways to get away with it without Eric finding out. Not to mention, he was stuck in a perpetual mental battle over the stakes of it all and his brotherly guilt. It pained him to lie to his twin, but he knew it had to be done. Until now, his brother didn't question his excuses, but Eric was extremely perceptive, especially when it came to him. The lieutenant wanted to believe that, at the end of the day, his brother would understand. James never did

185

anything halfway or without reason, and Eric knew that. He had to. James' intentions were never ill.

Right?

He figured that he'd have a chance at completing the act sometime after the interrogation. The plan was always to abandon her on Staten Island and leave the key at the door. That would've bought some time for James to sneak back, find her, and cut her head off. It was the perfect plan—quick and easy—and it would have been over before they found Dante at all. Emilia would have been one less vampire to worry about, one less nuisance, and yet...

They had been *so close*. He could see it in Eric's eyes and hear it in his voice. He had been ready to leave Emilia behind despite the shit storm of an interrogation, but then she had to open her mouth. Eric was triggered and something shifted long enough for him to let her go. James couldn't even blame him. *That night* was traumatic for everyone involved. After all, he was the one who got the call, and it was most likely Emilia's one act of mercy that saved his brother.

Goddamn it.

Now Emilia was God knows where and James had no way of knowing where she could be or how he could strike next. Not without deviating from the current mission and without alerting Eric to the fact that something was wrong.

Fuck you, Emilia. And fuck you, Michael.

In any other circumstance, this would've been one of the easiest jobs of his career. But by default, this was the hardest thing he'd ever had to navigate. Still, in James MacNamara fashion, he wasn't going to back out. He wasn't going to let Emilia win. He wasn't going to let *Caleb* win.

16

Dead To Me

Eric

It's over. The worst part is over. She's gone.

Eric's hand rested on his brow as he kept his eyes trained on the road ahead. Despite his focus, none of that was enough to appease his racing mind or take away his awareness of the very obvious rage that was radiating from his twin like a furnace on high. James wasn't one to keep his mouth shut for very long, so the anticipation was driving Eric insane. He would rather have him blow up now than back at the hotel when he'd be trying to wind down.

He let out a long, tired side.

"I know you're pissed off, Jimmy. Just spit it out."

James scoffed, "That's a fucking understatement."

"Just say it."

"Okay. What the fuck was that?" His brother blurted out with a motion of his hands.

"What do you mean?"

"What do you mean, 'what do I mean?'" James exclaimed, his voice getting higher.

"A lot of weird shit just happened, so I'm gonna need you to be more specific."

"Exactly. A lot of weird shit just happened. That was the weirdest interrogation of my life. The whole time, I felt like I was interrupting something I shouldn't be a part of. Like a fucking couple's counseling session, but worse. It took everything in me not to put an end to her stupid little game."

"You think I wanted that to happen?" Eric argued. "We knew this was a special case. I did what I had to do."

"Yeah, but at what cost—finding out that your safe word is 'peaches'?"

Eric cringed at the word that came out of his brother's mouth. It was a private, personal thing from a long time ago, and of course, Emilia just *had* to say it out loud for his brother to hear. The reminder infuriated him all over again.

"Say that word again, and I *will* crash this car," he threatened. "It's not like I expected any of that shit to go down at all."

In fact, he didn't know what he expected from a reunion with his vampire ex-girlfriend, let alone an interrogation, but it certainly wasn't what unfolded. To say he felt strange and conflicted was an understatement. He felt emotionally violated, despite having somehow survived.

"It didn't mean you had to play into it," his brother hissed.

"I was fine. I *am* fine."

"Yeah, that's what you always say, but we both know that's a fuckin' lie."

Eric glared at him, but all James did was meet his intensity.

"We got out of there. That's all that matters," he reassured.

"Yeah, but not before you had us give her a ride! We were supposed to fuck with her, not be her Uber. Letting her go would've sufficed."

Eric growled lowly in the back of his throat. He was less angry at James and more furious with himself...and Emilia.

"I know," he muttered.

"Then?"

"I don't know."

But Eric knew he had to give a logical answer, even if the decision hadn't come from a logical place.

"Let's just call it 'getting even', alright? 'Unfinished business,' whatever. I know it doesn't make sense, but you heard what she said. You of all people should understand why I let her go."

"Yeah, I heard what she said," James uttered. "I get it, but I also heard everything else and saw how completely unhinged she is. She's a wanted criminal, E. If it weren't for Jean, we'd be putting her down or at least reporting her to Michael. For all you know, she was just trying to get into your head. I would've let her rot in there."

They put a brief pause to their conversation as they approached a toll booth to pass under the East River. Once they were in the dark, subterranean tunnel, they sat in tense silence for a moment.

Eric's sudden panic attack from earlier came to mind. It frazzled him and maybe that, mixed with the emotions of the entire evening, was enough to mess with his decision-making. And there was nothing Eric hated more than doubting himself. He knew he could've easily knocked Emilia out and left her long enough for her to wake up on her own and find her way back home by herself. But that one tiny detail...

"We're even now," he reiterated. "And if it bothered you so much, then why didn't you do something, huh, Lieutenant?"

His twin snorted. "Oh, I wanted to. But I'm not a mindless monster. That rank shit doesn't apply here. You're my brother and I trust you. Even if your tactics are fucking weird sometimes."

Eric couldn't fight back the soft smile on his face.

He may not always agree with the ways of The Colectiv, but if there was anything that made James the perfect hunter in Eric's eyes, it was that he had his own code. And while he may be rough around the edges, there was a big heart underneath it all. It didn't seem like it to most people, perhaps not even himself, but James fought back because he cared. He was protective because *he cared*. It was more than Eric thought he deserved, but it didn't go unnoticed.

†††

By the time they arrived at their hotel room, the exhaustion had truly settled in. Eric, in particular, was drained after his emotional rollercoaster of a night, and before even thinking of their apparent cross-country road trip, he was ready to take a cold shower and fall asleep. Unfortunately, James was quick to beat him to it.

"Dibs on the shower," he blurted out as soon as his bag hit the floor.

"Ugh, fuck you!" Eric groaned.

James cackled maniacally as he grabbed a pair of underwear and dashed for the bathroom.

"Serves you right, *peaches*."

Eric snarled, his expression taking on a vicious wrath. He swiftly drew one of his daggers and threw it at his twin with a flick of his wrist. With quick reflexes, James slammed the door shut, and the blade embedded itself into the wood with a thud. Eric could hear his laughter from the other side.

"Yeah, you better hide, pussy, or I'll drive a knife through your fucking skull!" he shouted.

"I'd like to see you try!" his brother yelled back as the shower turned on.

Eric rolled his eyes and pulled the dagger out of the door. He eyed the very visible hole he had made.

Probably gonna have to pay for that. Again.

He sat down on his bed and placed it beside him with a dejected sigh. He peeled off his jacket, took off his shoes, and, seeing as his plans were thwarted, chose to busy himself by turning on the TV and taking on the task of cleaning his blades in his spare time.

In most vampire-hunting organizations, the unique design of a hunter's weaponry was just as important as its practical use. After all, most of what is forged at the beginning of a hunter's career was what they used for the rest of their lives. Symbolism, thought, and patience were encouraged. And as much as he hated the job when he was younger, Eric grew attached to his blades and pistols. It was a form of expression that he didn't fully appreciate until he got older, but while he designed his sword himself, the daggers he carried came from his mother, Anya.

They were anelace blades that were wider at the base and sharp on both sides. They were made of steel for durability and coated in silver. The hilt was a mother-of-pearl spiral with gold detailing, and the pommel had a shape that resembled a half-blooming rose. However, what made them unique was the crossguard that was made in the shape of thin butterfly wings (because Anya loved butterflies).

Before they became part of his arsenal, Eric was terrified of close-contact weapons and had been too hesitant to learn them at all. But when Michael told him that it was one of his mother's weapons of choice, the boy was determined to master them. After her death,

Anya's weaponry was stored in a box for safekeeping, but on the twins' 16th birthday, the commander gifted her blades to Eric and her crossbow to James. To this day, they never did a job without them, and it was Anya's weaponry that inspired the design of their swords.

While he and James loved their mother's design, the twins wanted to make something more personalized. They chose double-edged bastard swords, which were easy to carry, easy to wield, and easy to take heads with. Not to mention, the name seemed ironic and fitting to them. They kept the rose and the spiral hilt, but instead of mother-of-pearl, Eric's was made of black stone, and James' was blood red. And while the butterfly was Anya's symbol, the boys chose to place a solar eclipse on the crossguard instead—Eric's in silver and James' in gold.

The idea for using the eclipse as a symbol happened by chance. They were never actively looking for such a thing, but when they found it, it became obvious how perfect it was. It was the embodiment of the moon overlapping with the sun. Night and day coming together. Human and vampire. Mészáros and MacNamara. So, they adopted it as their own, both separately and together. They engraved it on their weapons and etched it into their skin. It was a reminder of who they were, where they came from, and their unbreakable bond (even if they did get on each other's nerves sometimes).

Eric gazed at his warped reflection in the blade of the now-clean dagger. He twisted it in his hands, admiring its beauty, when...

"Are you gonna torture me with that pretty knife?"

The memory of Emilia's voice came to him so unconsciously, it made him wince. Her face flashed before his eyes, bringing him back to when he had the very same dagger in one hand and her throat in the other. He could see her in his mind, looking up at him with that fiery, deranged smile.

A groan rumbled in the back of his throat, the thought of her almost causing him physical pain. He closed his eyes and tried forcing the memory away, but it didn't stop the lingering feeling and the sudden quickening of his heart. It was hard to fight now that he was alone, especially when he had seen her for the first time in so long.

While Eric did his best to keep the interrogation professional, just like he had hundreds of times before, Emilia had to take a hard left and make his life a lot more difficult. She always liked keeping him on his toes, and he obliged by playing her game in hopes of getting information. For the most part, he kept his answers vague, but other times the pent-up emotions he kept meticulously hidden broke through against his will. His anger got the best of him. Jean Beltremieux may have pushed some buttons, but Emilia made Eric feel on the verge of exploding at any given second.

In some form of messed up irony, it was also, somehow, the most Eric and Emilia had ever opened up to each other in their entire relationship. No stone was left unturned, and everything was laid bare. Back then, he had hidden anything having to do with his upbringing or his DNA, not just from Emilia but from everyone else. Keeping it from her in particular, however, almost got him killed. But at the very least, he could say with utmost certainty that she didn't get *all* of his secrets.

Of course, I knew.

Eric was a daywalker, and he could sense people from afar and hear their heartbeats as clear as day—or the lack thereof. He knew how to sense a vampire. Of course, he did. He would have been stupid not to. Only a human—a civilian—wouldn't have known. When Emilia asked him if he did, for a moment, he contemplated telling her the truth, but lies and blissful ignorance were always easier.

Why?

It didn't benefit anyone. In fact, it would make things worse. And he didn't need her asking him more questions that he couldn't answer. She didn't need to know why, because it didn't matter anymore. Things were different. That door was closed, and if he chose to keep her identity a secret now, it was for his own sake.

Eric knew James was right—Emilia was a wanted criminal. They should have been turning her into Michael by now, but strictly following The Colectiv's laws wasn't in his nature to begin with. After all of his hard work, the last thing he needed was for Michael to get in his way and ruin it for him. Not when they could be moving forward with what they have.

17

Seeing Red

Emilia

A ferry and a train ride later, Emilia was able to get back to her apartment in almost one piece, but while she managed to survive two hunters with her head intact, she was hollow in every sense of the word.

She pressed her back against the door, her lips quivering as tears filled her vision. Her eyes fluttered shut just as her world turned pink, and she let her tattered bag fall to her feet before sinking to the floor with it.

Because vampires couldn't produce tears of salt, what came out in times of extreme emotion was blood. It was uncomfortable compared to the tears shed by the living, and it created a mess that was challenging to cover up. It was the reason Emilia did her best to maintain her composure in the public eye because if anyone caught sight of her bloody tears, they'd surely suspect something was wrong on multiple levels. It was also why most vampires came across as apathetic to humans. Only in private did the floodgates ever truly open.

So now that Emilia was alone, every emotion she had been holding back the entire night rushed out like a tidal wave. In the safety of her home, she finally allowed herself to crumble, and red tears poured out of her eyes. She pulled her knees against her chest and sobbed into her hands, her shoulders shaking.

[32]Seeing Eric again, after all this time, was a complete and utter shock to her system. Emilia had mourned him when she thought he was dead, and she mourned their relationship even when she found out he was alive. The events of that night had affected her so profoundly that she went so far as to cut her brother off and isolate herself in New York. To have both Eric *and* Dante betray her in different yet detrimental ways had been too much to bear. It was the straw that broke the camel's back and made her already shaky world come falling down.

She knew, deep within, that the day she saw Eric again would be painful, and she was right. Eric may not have tortured her, but he may as well have. It confirmed the hard truth that she had learned that night: he's a devil in disguise. Not only was he a daywalker—a fact that she could have gotten over—but he was the enemy. He was a hunter, a cold-hearted killer, and stood for everything Emilia swore to hate. And if it wasn't clear to her back then, then it is clear to her now. He made sure of it by going back to The Colectiv three years ago.

Emilia couldn't help but mourn once more. She remembered a time when it seemed like her heart was safe in his hands, but now he held no remorse for crushing it. Eric MacNamara may not have died, but a part of him did die that night in Sorrento, and it pained her to

---

[32] No Time To Die - Billie Eilish

think that she had any part in it. Her guilt solidified into indomitable steel, but at the very least, she could find solace in knowing that she wasn't who Eric thought she was, either.

She remembered the look in his eyes when she told him about "The Hellhound" with vividness. It was not merely horror—no, it was worse. It was a look of disappointment and disbelief at witnessing an old fantasy die before his eyes. At this point in her life, Emilia wasn't surprised, because they all looked at her that way in the end. She had warned him long ago, after the first night they spent together, that he didn't know what he was getting himself into, but he refused to listen. She was a demon underneath the surface, just like her brother was, and if people weren't bound to get hurt, it would be a matter of time before they ran away. Very few people stayed...or survived. Somehow, Eric was proof of both.[33]

Had he truly seen her as nothing but good back then? Had he failed to see the darkness? Or had they both deluded themselves into thinking it wouldn't end in ruin? Age was but a number, after all, and Emilia knew too well that learning was never-ending.

The vampire lifted her head and wiped her face with her hands, transferring the mess to her fingers and then to her clothes. Her stomach rumbled, and her throat was dry from how parched she was. She mustered up some strength and pushed herself off the floor, kicking off her broken shoes as she stumbled into the kitchen. Led by hunger, she wrenched open the fridge, took out a blood bag from the shelf, and tore it open with her teeth. Like a starving animal, she sucked the sweet liquid out of the bag until it was dry and then tossed it onto the counter with a gasp, gripping the edges.

"Who even are you?"

---

[33] Bells in Santa Fe - Halsey

"I could ask you the same thing."

I am what I've been hiding all along. That's what her answer would have been, and no doubt it was Eric's answer too. They had both been in hiding when they found each other, accustomed to lying, and it was a ticking time bomb for a relationship. *"Doomed from the start,"* he said. She wondered if any of it had been real at all, but it didn't serve her well to ponder such questions now.

Then why can't I stop thinking about his face?

Emilia knew she had a habit of clinging to the good in people, so she tried not to read too much into it. But it was hard not to notice changes in people like Eric, who, unlike her brother, was the embodiment of a brick wall. Sure, he had a hard shell, but Emilia managed to poke and prod him enough to catch a glimpse of what was underneath, and what she had seen were parts that were familiar to her—the emotional and *human* parts.

She hadn't planned on mentioning her phone call to James. She could've made up a lie to get out of her chains or even sparked up some deal, but that was always more up Dante's alley. No, when she saw that Eric was planning to abandon her in that building, Emilia knew she needed to say something that would gain his trust enough to set her free. Perhaps some part of her wanted him to know that, despite the deceit, she cared enough to save his life. She just didn't want to say the words themselves. What she didn't expect was his physical reaction.

It reminded her of when he'd wake up from a nightmare, which, considering how little he slept, she didn't witness often. He never told her what they were about, but she remembered how his heart sounded like it was about to burst. Even tonight, when he tried to compose himself, she could see and hear how unnerved he was. It was like finding a crack and seeing the old Eric beneath it. And that was the hardest part of it all.

But...it was *real...wasn't it?*

Being an immortal vampire, some things were blips in the entirety of eternal existence, yet this felt so different to Emilia. She knew that she shouldn't dwell on the past and that people change just as much as the seasons do. So much can happen in just three years, and she's changed a lot in the five decades since she was turned. However, there were moments in time that left a permanent scar on your soul, and Eric wasn't just a scar but a wound that Emilia had convinced herself was already healed, but as soon as he came barreling back into her life, he tore her stitches right open.

And now he's gonna kill Dante.

Dante. Another wound that hasn't healed.

Emilia downed another blood bag before making a beeline for the shower. She tore her clothes off on the way there, leaving a trail in her wake. Under the heat of the water, she washed off her dried blood and the feeling of Eric's touch. Tears continued to flow down her cheeks, turning the water pink as it went down the drain. At the same time, a dilemma formed in her mind.

She had told him that she didn't care about what happened to her brother. She told him that she had made peace with the idea of his death, but now that she was alone with her own mind, an aching dread filled her chest. It was a feeling that she was all too familiar with when it came to Dante.

Yes, Dante had hurt her. Yes, she cut him off and ran away in hopes of finding some semblance of bliss or a way to die. And in some ways, it didn't matter what happened to him, as long as she wasn't in the crossfire. But knowing that Eric and James, with their skills and abilities, were on a mission to take his life? Dante didn't stand a chance. Even worse was the fact that she was the one who led them right to him. Emilia didn't know if she could live with the weight of that guilt for the rest of eternity. Out of everything she had done, that was a pain she couldn't imagine carrying with her.

She tried telling herself that it shouldn't matter, that in a life like theirs, death was everywhere. It would've been easier to be cold and apathetic, but that was where she and Eric differed. Ironically enough, it was also where she and her brother differed the most. It wasn't in her nature. And, in the end, Emilia found herself reaching the same conclusion:

She couldn't let Dante die.

Emilia pushed her face against the shower wall, balling her fists on either side as she let out a groan of frustration. The groan turned into a scream, which grew louder and louder until she pushed herself away and punched the tile with all of her strength. Pieces of the ceramic rained down to her feet in chunks, leaving a hole behind. Her hand came away torn and bloodied from the impact, but she couldn't care less. She then heaved a sob and fell to her knees on the shower floor.

Why do I care so much about the people who hurt me?[34]

No, she couldn't let Dante die. He was her brother after all, and the only family she had left. There were too many memories and too much love that nothing could ever vanquish. They made a promise to keep each other safe, and Emilia would have done anything to keep that promise. She already had countless times. It was the one thing they ever agreed on. Even what Dante did to Eric was done out of his twisted version of love and protectiveness for his beloved sister. He always made sure nobody put their hands on her, not even himself, even if he often took it too far.

So, Emilia took the pain of her bloody tears and let them flow, seeing red, until she had nothing left in her. She hugged her knees

---

[34] Lonely is the Muse - Halsey

against her chest beneath the water, looking at the wall numbly as she thought of what this meant.

If she didn't want Dante to die, then she couldn't let Eric kill him, but she knew she couldn't march up to his hotel and tell him that she had a change of heart. With his newfound hatred for her and James' murderous intent, it was a losing game from the get-go, and they'd kill her without hesitation.

Perhaps she could fly over to Crimson Beach and warn Dante, which, after a rocky reunion, would no doubt result in them fleeing once again. But Emilia wasn't even sure if Dante was there to begin with. In reality, there were so many places he could've been, so if she didn't find him there, what then? Something told Emilia that Eric would never stop looking for him, and unlike his human counterparts, there was no waiting for his eventual death either. So it was safe to say that the MacNamara twins were a vampire's worst nightmare.

They're Wade's sons, after all, and that's what scares me.

She knew she needed to put a stop to this. She wasn't one to stand by and let things happen, and there was an old, chaotic part of her that was determined to find a way, by sheer force of will.[35]

---

[35] Bad Idea - Ariana Grande

18

The Stowaway

Eric

Comfort King Inn—Present

Eric didn't know how long he'd been asleep when the knock came at the door, but it felt like his head had barely hit the pillow.

His brother groaned, and Eric hoped that if he just ignored it, whoever it was would go away, but the knocks persisted, and they grew more incessant.

"You answer it because if I do, I might actually murder them," James muttered into his pillow.

With a disgruntled noise, Eric forced himself out of bed and grabbed a knife from the bedside table before making his way to the door. He hid the blade behind his back and took a quick look through the peephole. When he saw raven hair and big brown eyes, his heart sank and his eyes widened.

"You've got to be fucking kidding me," he whispered.

He wrenched the door open, and he set his gaze upon Emilia, letting the hand holding the knife fall to his side. She was all cleaned up and in much better condition than when he last laid eyes on her. She stood with her arms crossed and a look of determination, which was briefly replaced with shock at the sight of him. Her eyes bounced between his face, the knife, and his bare torso. Eventually, they landed on his scar, and Eric instantly regretted not having put on a shirt before answering.

"Is that-?"

He casually hid half of his body behind the door and interrupted her question, "Am I having a nightmare? What the fuck are you doing here?"

She raised an eyebrow at him and said, "Do you always answer the door half-naked and with a knife?"

"What. Are. You. Doing. Here?" he repeated with a steely glare.

Emilia sighed, "I need to talk to you."

Eric scoffed, "I feel like we did enough talk for one night, don't you think?"

"I know, but this is important."

"What could possibly be so important?"

There was a groan from inside the room. "Please tell me that's not who I think it is."

"Unfortunately, it is," Eric answered with a scowl.

His twin cursed.

There was rustling and then footsteps as James marched over to the door. He held his arm out and kept a hold on the door frame in anticipation. Just as he expected, his brother came up behind him with a knife in his hand, pointing it at Emilia, but he didn't get farther than Eric's arm.

"What the fuck are you doing here?" he hissed. "Did you follow us after we dropped you off?"

Emilia rolled her eyes and said, "No. I saw your room key in your bag. Be grateful that I didn't take it and sneak in while you were asleep."

"How thoughtful of you," Eric derided.

"Listen, I wouldn't be here if I didn't think it was important, okay? The last thing I wanted was to ever see you again, and now I'm willingly at your door after you had me tied to a chair, so I think that should mean something."

The volume at which she spoke put Eric on edge, and he instinctively looked up and down the hallway, tuning into his senses to make sure no one was listening. Luckily, there was nothing of alarm.

He gave her a sharp look and said, "Please, by all means, say that louder so that New Jersey can hear you."

Emilia narrowed her eyes at him. "You're lucky I'm trying to be civil because you make it very hard to not wanna punch you in the face again."

"I mean, you can certainly try, but it would probably end the same way," he said, twirling the blade like a threat.

"What do you want, Emilia?" James demanded, cutting through their bickering.

"I wanna talk," she reiterated simply.

"About what?"

Now, it was her turn to look up and down the hallway. "I think we should take this inside."

Both hunters gave similar answers.

"No fucking way."

"There's no chance in hell we're letting you in here."

"Oh really?" Emilia sang. "Even if what I have to say has to do with my brother?"

Eric froze at that. He glanced at James, who shared a look of bewilderment, but the intrigue was clearly there.

†††

Considering how much leeway James had given him already, Eric let his twin make the final decision on whether to let Emilia talk. He trusted his judgment and wouldn't have cared either way. After all, they've gotten by with far less. However, to his surprise, James decided to give Emilia a chance. He must have seen some value in what else she could say, but Eric also knew that he'd shut it down at the first sign of trouble.

They convened in a corner of the room. James sat on the edge of his bed with his holsters on, while Eric was in an armchair with a knife, now in a t-shirt. Emilia stood before them, anxiously nibbling at one of her nails.

Eric eyed her curiously, taking in her strange behavior. Whatever was on her mind was putting her on edge, and he didn't like it.

"Whatever you have to say, make it quick, because I'd really like to get some sleep," he said.

She looked between the two of them and said, "You're gonna think I'm crazy, but I need you to listen, okay?"

"Too late, but go on," James mumbled.

Emilia ignored his comment.

"Why would we think you're crazy?" Eric asked.

"Because what I'm about to say is a little crazy."

"Crazier than being 'The Hellhound'?"

She shook her head. "Not like that, no, but you're not gonna like it."

Eric scowled. The last thing he needed was more "crazy."

"You said this was about Dante..."

"It is," she reassured with a nod. Emilia then clasped her hands in front of her, suddenly the epitome of poise. "I know my brother like the back of my hand. He's the most shameless and spiteful person I've ever met, but he's also clever and ruthless and knows how to slip through the cracks."

"Obviously," Eric whispered.

"I also know Crimson Beach like the back of my hand. I lived there for almost two decades after I turned, and I also grew up in L.A. before then."

"And your point is?" James pressed.

She shrugged and then, to their complete and utter dismay, responded with, "You need me."

James snorted and Eric immediately burst out laughing, taken aback by the outlandish statement. Emilia stared icy daggers at them, zero amusement in her eyes.

"Oh, you're being serious," Eric said amidst dying laughter.

"Yeah. I'm being dead serious."

"We already got what we wanted. Why the hell would we need you now?" James challenged.

"You're planning on going across the country to find Dante, who you know nothing about, in a city that you know nothing about. How do you expect to find him without a proper lead?"

"We're good at our job, that's how," the lieutenant argued. "What do you think we do—sit on our asses all day? Please."

"Yeah, but what if he's not in Crimson Beach? What if he finds out you're on his trail and he runs off? What if he kills you before you get a chance to kill him?"

The twins scoffed.

"Yeah, that's not happening ever again," Eric assured her.

Emilia looked at him with arms crossed, seeming rather unconvinced by his statement. "So, you're just going to spend ages trying to find him?"

He shrugged, leaning back in his chair. "As long as it takes."

She ran her tongue over her teeth—either thoughtfully, angrily, or both—and took a deep breath.

"I could make it easier on you," she said. She kept her voice cool despite their arguments. "I know how my brother's mind works. I know every secret tunnel, every hideout, and every possible place that he could be, in and out of Crimson Beach. I have connections—people who would only talk to me. Not to mention, I know how to blend in with purebloods better than you daywalkers can. Even a faint heartbeat is a dead giveaway that you're not a normal vampire."

Eric couldn't argue with that one. Since vampires had no heartbeat and humans did, daywalkers were stuck somewhere in the middle, with a beating heart that pumped blood half as fast. Drinking blood regularly, like any vampire, helped regulate it and replenish their energy to the fullest. Nevertheless, he tried to find a flaw in Emilia's reasoning.

"That doesn't matter because we don't pretend to be purebloods anyway. We just need to blend in enough with the crowd to get intel and then make an attack."

"We have other ways of making people talk. As you know," James added with mirth.

"Yeah, I gathered," Emilia muttered. "Your methods aren't bad, but with me, your plan could be better. Wanna know why? Because I can get really close without anyone suspecting a thing. I mean, after all, the only person Dante trusts is me."

It was a stupefying task for Eric to try and make sense of all of this. Emilia was fighting hard for this strange plan of hers, and it didn't sit well with him. He refused to give in out of pure bullheadedness.

"Why? Why are you doing this?" he demanded, shaking his head. "Why do you wanna help us all of a sudden?"

The vampire fell quiet, looking down at the floor seriously. For a moment, Eric thought she was going to retreat, just like she tried during the interrogation, but to his surprise, she didn't.

"I don't need any more blood on my hands. Dante is an animal, and he has a knack for surrounding himself with people just like him. We used to kill people we thought deserved it... but he's far more careless than I ever was. If I can save at least one more person from getting murdered, then great. If I can keep you assholes from dying, even better. After all, what would be the fun in that?"

Her lips curled into a playful smirk. She looked at James, whose brow was furrowed, and then locked eyes with Eric once again. They stared at each other intensely, playing an invisible game of chicken. He didn't trust her, not one bit, but he could tell that there was truth to what she said.

While Eric was busy mentally processing, James did his processing out loud:

"So what you're saying is, you want to come along with us to Crimson Beach to help us find your brother...so we can kill him?"

"You can do whatever you want to him. I don't care," Emilia said with a shrug. "Although I don't actually plan on being there when the deed is done. You know, for obvious reasons."

"How do we know you won't try to kill us before we get there?"

She gave him a strange look. "Why would I go through all this trouble to kill you in Crimson Beach when I could have just killed you here? I've had plenty of opportunities. I could have broken in if I wanted to."

"You know this is a cross-country road trip, right?" Eric blurted out.

Emilia whipped her head towards him, her jaw dropping as she sputtered in shock.

"*What?*"

He chuckled at her reaction. "You didn't think we'd be flying first class to California, did you?"

"I thought you'd at least be taking a plane!" she exclaimed.

"Do you know how many weapons we carry around?"

"Our arms guy in California is a bit indisposed at the moment," James said. "It's easier to drive. It's how all hunters do it."

"But I mean, if that's too much for you," Eric teased, his mouth pulled into a smirk, "I won't blame you if you don't wanna go. Living between motels and gas stations can be a bit much for *some* people."

He recalled her very expensive outfit and the designer purse he had destroyed. It came as no surprise to Eric that Emilia had extravagant tastes. He just wondered where—or who—she got them from. After all, he hadn't failed to notice the number of wealthy men at The Canary, and it was hard not to overhear the things they talked about. She and a few of the other performers were a favorite topic of conversation.

Emilia flipped him off with one of her manicured fingers and Eric bit back a smile.

"Fuck you. I've been on the run before, okay? I know what it's like to live on the road, especially in this godforsaken country. I can handle myself just fine," she retorted.

Ah, yes, when you were running from The Colectiv.

Eric grimaced. "You see, the thing is, I don't know if it's a good idea that the two of us are stuck in a car together, let alone in a room for a few nights."

The thought made him want to pull his hair out. The last thing he wanted was to be that close to her for days on end. It was the most absurd thing he had heard all day.

"As if I'd sleep in the same room as the two of you!" she scorned. "This is strictly business, Eric. I'll be in the back seat the entire time. I'll have my own room, and I'll spend my own money."

Eric scoffed in disbelief, and his body started to shake with panic and rage.

"You're really just inviting yourself, aren't you? What about your job at The Canary? Isn't your boss gonna be angry if you don't show up for a show? Aren't your rich boyfriends gonna miss you? Don't you have a life here of your own now, Emilia? Doing whatever the fuck you want? Why would you wanna fuck that up?"[36]

He didn't mean to sound so bitter, but some deep part of him *was*. It was hard to be patient when Emilia was wearing him down to the bone once again. Words came out of him like vomit.

"Boyfriends?" Emilia giggled. She pointed a finger at him, leaning closer, saying, "First of all, they're *patrons*. Second of all, The Canary doesn't own me. I'm not the only performer, and I'm sure they'll be fine if I call in sick for a weekend or two. And like you said, I do whatever the fuck I want anyway."

All Eric could muster was a cold, dirty look.

"And what if we say 'no'?" James said aloud, interrupting their argument. "What then?"

---

[36] Dummy - Cheat Codes & Bring Me the Horizon

Emilia straightened up.

"I know a few of Dante's friends. Pretty shady ones who hate hunters. I'm sure one of them can pass the word that you're coming." Eric clicked his tongue irately, but she kept going, "And before you even *think* about killing me, just know that Jean *will* deliver on his promise. He's a powerful vampire who knows a lot of other powerful people, and he'll make you wish eternity was much, much shorter."

She was saving that one for last.

If looks could kill, then Emilia would be dead twice over with how the twins looked at her now. It was a miracle the room didn't burst into flames from Eric's rage alone. Even if they *could* argue their way out, Emilia wasn't giving them much of a choice in the matter. She was a vampire that they interrogated so that already made her unhinged, but the fact that she and Eric had a history made things more complicated.

He wanted her out of his hair for personal reasons, but he also knew that the second Michael caught a whiff of this, they'd be in deep trouble. Especially after what happened three years ago. He couldn't possibly agree to this. He *shouldn't*. Yet Emilia's next statement was enough to make him think otherwise.

"Take me with you, and I'll take you where you do need to go," she said with finality.

Eric blinked a few times, unsure if he had heard her correctly. It was like déjà vu. For a moment, he thought it was some kind of hallucination. He wouldn't have been surprised if it was all in his head, but no, it wasn't. She said that to him before, in a dream somewhere. And he didn't want to base a decision on something that wasn't real, but it made that solid exterior of his falter again for a swift moment.

He glanced over at James, and his twin had an intimidating, pensive look that Eric had seen on Michael's face many times. He was going over everything in his mind, strategizing, and trying to make a solid decision.

"*Tu* ce crezi?" Eric asked.

What do you *think?*

James groaned lowly, "Nu-mi place asta... dar este decizia ta."

I don't like it... but it's your call.

"Suntem în asta împreună, Jimmy."

We're in this together, Jimmy.

Despite his disdain for Emilia, James wasn't outright rejecting the idea. Either he saw value in it, or he was at as much of a loss as Eric was, which was concerning.

"I don't think we have a choice," he muttered. His eyes flitted to Eric. "Tu?"

Eric narrowed his eyes at Emilia, who was looking between them in anticipation.

Her offer to help find Dante was extremely useful, but he badly wished that it was anyone but her. If it was anyone else, he and James wouldn't have resisted so much. It was like picking between two evils. But if one thing was certain, Eric had a mission to complete. Nothing was ever going to make him back down from achieving his goal, and he was going to take anything he could get. Even if it meant taking it from Emilia.

The hunter leaned forward and signed, "Fine."

[37]*I'm gonna regret this.*

---

[37] This Is A Trick - †††(Crosses)

19

Extra Baggage

Eric

[38]The urge to snap Emilia's neck could not have been stronger than it was now.

This is so fucking stupid. Why am I doing this?

They gave her 24 hours to get ready for the trip, and at 9 a.m. the following day, they'd be leaving with or without her. Perhaps it was callous to force a pureblood to get up in the morning when the sun was out, but Eric knew it wouldn't kill her, and they were operating on their time, not hers. He also wasn't particularly worried about being nice or accommodating to her. At the very least, it gave the boys enough time to both physically and mentally prepare for the cross-country drive with their unwanted company.

The entire time leading up to the departure, Eric did everything to distract himself, but no matter how hard he tried, his thoughts

---

[38] Ghost In My Home - Point North

increased in volume. He was uneasy and got little sleep, and it was due, in big part, to the fact that, for the first time in a while, he was truly doubting himself. Eric's confidence as a hunter had grown significantly since returning to The Colectiv, and he hardly ever second-guessed his decisions at all. It was, perhaps, to a fault, but it got the job done. However, right now, he was starting to feel like a teenager all over again, and he abhorred it.

Eric was going on a week-long drive with his ex, who was not only a vampire but a wanted criminal on all fronts. If his relationship with Emilia almost cost him his life before, then this would cost him that twice over. He, of all people, knew what would happen if he went through with this and got caught. His mother lived her life on the run after having an affair with their father. Even if Emilia was nothing but an informant now, their history, along with her own twisted past, made that completely null and void. It was why, to some degree, part of him would always dislike the organization that raised him (though he wouldn't say it out loud), but in reality, he worried more about his brother than he worried about himself.

"You don't have to do this, you know," he said as he zipped up his duffle.

James was fixing his damp hair in the bathroom mirror when he stopped mid-motion. He frowned at Eric through the reflection.

"What are you talking about?"

"I'm talking about doing this job with me...and with her," he stressed. "Lines are getting a bit blurry, and I don't want you getting caught in the crossfire because of me. I can do this on my own. It's fine."

James whirled around and scowled at him. "You're insane if you think for one fucking second that I would ever let you do this alone."

"Jimmy, the last thing I want is for you to lose your place in The Colectiv, or worse, get killed."

"Oh yeah? And what about you, huh?" his twin shot back. He crossed his arms and leaned back against the sink. "I know you don't care about what happens to you, but I do. I'm not letting you die, either. Not if I can help it this time."

Eric rolled his eyes in exasperation. "You don't need to protect me. I'm not the same kid as before. I'm probably the last person that needs protecting."

"It's not about that, and you know it."

Eric fell silent because he knew his brother was right. It wasn't about how capable either of them was. They went through a lot of their lives feeling invincible, but now they were both well aware of what exactly could kill them. Like some sick twist of fate, it happened to be the two things that made them who they were: hunters and vampires. And now Eric was on a mission to tempt both.

He worked his jaw seriously. "Nobody can know what we're doing, alright? Not even Mike. Whatever other weird shit happens stays between you and me."

James turned back around and continued to mess with his hair.

"My lips are sealed. Mike's not gonna find out shit."

†††

Emilia arrived 15 minutes before nine, much to their sheer disappointment, as they had been hoping she wouldn't show up at all. When Eric opened the door—fully clothed this time—Emilia was standing in the hallway, covered head to toe in a black turtleneck, coat, sunglasses, and bucket hat.

He snorted, giving her an odd expression. "Are you hiding from the paparazzi?"

"From the sun, actually," she derided. "You're the one who told me to get up at 9 a.m. Desgraciado."

Disgraceful man.

Out of all the languages Eric picked up, Spanish was the most obvious one. Though he wasn't entirely fluent in speaking it, he understood what Emilia said.

"Yeaaah, sorry about that," he said with a fake apologetic smile.

"No, you're not."

[39]*No, I'm not.*

"We're gonna be in a car most of the time anyway," he said. "You won't have to worry about the sun too much on the road."

"Uhh, UV rays go through windows, Eric. I thought you'd know that, being a genius and all."

He narrowed his eyes at her condescending tone.

"Now, excuse me," she said, pushing her suitcase forward, which he now noticed was a large, full-sized monster on wheels and was bigger than anything the twins were taking.

Eric sputtered in disbelief. "What the fuck is this?"

"My suitcase, obviously."

"Yeah, I can see that. Why the fuck is it so big?"

"This is a perfectly normal-sized suitcase," she contested.

"Yeah, for an orc."

James came up behind him with a cup of coffee in hand. Eric stepped aside to let him get a better look and his eyes grew wide.

"What the fuck? Are you going to Paris after this or something?"

Emilia rolled her eyes. "We're traveling for six days to *Crimson Beach*. Including stops. I'm coming fully prepared."

"We're gonna be on the road most of the time. You don't need a constant outfit change. How much shit could you possibly need?"

---

[39] Gives You Hell - The All American Rejects

"Wouldn't you like to know?" she huffed. "I don't need men like you—who probably use 5 in 1 shampoo—questioning me and my needs."

The twins started muttering defenses, but Emilia was having none of it. She put her hand on Eric's chest and pushed him backward into the room. With a sigh, he moved out of the way and let her through, only to see her pulling what looked like a square chest on wheels with her other hand.

"Okay, what the hell is *that*?"

Emilia turned around with a grin. "Food for the road."

She lowered the handle on the case and lifted it onto the bed. James and Eric looked over her shoulder as she opened it to reveal a cooler filled to the brim with blood packs.

Eric furrowed his brow. "Where did you get these?"

"The blood bank," she said, shrugging.

James scoffed, "Did you break in and steal from the Red Cross?"

"No. I know a guy who works there. A vampire, ironically enough. He sets blood packs on the side for when vampires need them, and I stopped by before coming here. You guys drink blood, right?"

Emilia looked over her shoulder, glancing between them warily as if hoping she hadn't made the wrong assumption.

The corners of Eric's lips lifted for a second. "Yeah, we do."

They never had *this* much on hand, though. Most of it would go to Emilia, no doubt.

"Great!" she said, shutting the lid with a thud. "I figured it would make things easier, you know, without the necessity to hunt."

"Mmm, right," James hummed, and Eric simply nodded, sharing a look with him. "We don't need you leaving a trail of bodies across middle America."

Emilia glared at him and whispered, "*You're welcome.*"

Little did she know they'd never hunted for blood a day in their lives.

20

Burning at Both Ends

James

James wasn't a spiritual person or a believer in any all-powerful entity. He considered himself a realist and focused on what he could see in the present moment. But if he were ever to think that there were some magical forces at play, it would be now.

Emilia had somehow found her way back into his sights without James having to lift a single finger. She, of her own volition, came to their hotel in the middle of the night and presented herself on a silver platter. She was offering assistance in finding Dante, and while James wasn't against having an informant, it was, of course, *Emilia*. He didn't trust her, not one bit. But no matter what her twisted intentions were, she was going to be there for the taking—all the way to Crimson Beach. He couldn't make this up on his own. And he couldn't say no, even if he would have otherwise.

This is insane.

James didn't consider himself a mindless monster; he had told Eric as much. Even if he was good at his job, he liked to follow a moral code. He didn't kill without reason, but he also had to stay objective despite any personal feelings he might have. So even if Emilia had a modicum of a soul (for saving his brother) and wasn't the raging lunatic she used to be (although she very well might be), he couldn't change his mind.

He still had to kill her.

It's nothing personal.

†††

As they were packing everything into the trunk of the car, James' phone went off. He fished it out of his pocket and grimaced upon seeing the name.

Michael.

"Aw shit," he muttered.

Eric frowned. "Who is it?"

James lifted the phone, showing him the screen. Eric deflated and rolled his eyes in annoyance.

"Perfect timing," he whispered.

"I know."

Odds were that Michael was calling to check on their progress, but most importantly, *James'* progress. Again, it was nothing new or out of the ordinary, but considering the circumstances, it was the last thing they both needed right now.

He cast a brooding glance at Emilia—their current problem—who was eyeing the phone in his hand with a quizzical brow.

"Start the car. I gotta take this," he said to his brother before stalking off to the other side of the parking garage.

"Hey, Mike."

"Hey, Jimmy," the commander sang. "I just wanted to call in real quick and check on you and E. How's everything going on the other side of the world? Any updates?"

"Yeah, actually, we got the lead that we needed, and we're heading out to chase it right now."

"I'm guessing things went well with the girl, then?"

James made sure he was hidden and far away enough to not be easily heard by anyone, especially his twin.

"Yeah, they did," he replied.

Depending on your definition of the word.

"Have you...*handled her* yet?" Michael asked, the insinuation as clear as day.

The daywalker grimaced. "No, not yet, but I'm *in the process* of trying to handle it. It's not exactly easy with E around."

"I know, but it's part of the challenge, Jimmy. You gotta learn to rely on yourself first."

"Yeah, I know."

"Have things gone smoothly, otherwise?"

"Yeah, she's a royal pain in the ass, but we got what we needed," James told him.

"What about E? How'd he do?"

"He's the one who did most of the work. I barely had to step in."

Even if I wish I did.

"He didn't take it easy on her, then?" James could sense the smirk on the commander's face through the phone.

A muscle twitched in his cheek as he remembered Emilia's game.

James had conducted plenty of his own interrogations before, but when it came to levels of discomfort, all of them paled in comparison to this one. It said a lot about him, but he would've rather pulled someone's fingernails off than have to endure what Eric did with

Emilia. James wouldn't have lasted very long in Eric's position, and it was a testament to his brother's talents and abilities. Granted, James didn't think it did him any good to put himself in that position, either. Not with someone like her.

The lieutenant's eyes flitted to the car, where Emilia herself was waiting. And, leaning against the car door, was Eric, also awaiting his return.

James coated his words with honey, keeping his tone jovial as he said, "Hell no. You know, E. Taking it easy isn't his forte. 'Psychological warfare,' as I would say."

It wasn't entirely false. "Psychological warfare" was about as accurate as he could describe what happened in that building. Rather, "emotional warfare," yet despite how certain things affected him, Eric held his own pretty well. It was why James didn't fully insert himself into the situation.

"Yeah, that boy's sharp. I'm happy to hear that," Michael said. "Where are you headed next?"

James hesitated, and he *hated* hesitating.

He didn't know how much to tell him or whether he should be vague. Michael had told him about Crimson Beach before this trip, and it was a mere coincidence that it became his next destination. He wanted to earn this promotion but he also wanted to be careful. He didn't need the commander to know precisely where they were, because if he did, he'd find out that Emilia was tagging along with them, alive and unchained. James had a plan, but he didn't want him to think he was stalling when, in fact, he was working on his own schedule.

"California," he said simply.

"Ah, I see. Do you know what city?"

"L.A., actually."

"L.A. is a big place, Jimmy. It's not gonna be easy to find one person."

Exactly.

"E knows the area pretty well from his college days. I've been there a few times myself. So together, we've both got some ideas about where any vampires could be lurking around. It shouldn't be hard to narrow it down."

"We've got some connections out there too, so if you need them, just give me a call."

"Will do."

"But if things get out of hand, you know I'll send the cavalry, alright? Major cities are a cesspool for vampire activity, especially in California."

"E and I can handle ourselves just fine," James assured him, oozing arrogance.

"Yeah, but you know what I mean. Keep an eye out. Be careful who you trust," he stressed.

James furrowed his brow and looked off toward the Jeep once again. He locked eyes with his brother. Even if he was far away, James could sense his curiosity.

"I don't trust anybody, Mike. You know that. We'll be alright," he told him, and he tried changing the subject. "How are things on your end?"

To his surprise, the commander let out a long, tired exhale before saying, "There's been some...complications."

The daywalker straightened up at that. "What kind of complications?"

"There's been a minor breach down in the Black Sea that we've been having to deal with."

"Charybdis?" James blurted out.

"Yup."

"I thought that place was fortified."

"It is. Or at least it should be. Don't worry about it. It's nothing I can't handle. Just...like I said...be careful who you trust."

"Tell me all the details when I get back?" His own curiosity was piqued.

"Yeah," Michael said, his voice hesitant, "just don't go blabbering about it."

"No, sir."

After hanging up, James met his brother by the Jeep. Eric watched him over the top of the car from the passenger's side, his eyes expectant.

"What did he say?"

James wrenched the door open and said, "Oh, you know, to be careful who we trust."

Eric ran his tongue over his teeth in irritation. They both got into the car, and James made sure to give Emilia an irritated look as he slammed his door shut.

"Who was that?" she asked.

James put his hands on the steering wheel and stared ahead. "That was Michael."

"Who's Michael?"

He glanced at his twin sidelong, asking him with his eyes whether he was going to do the honors of saying it himself. Eric rolled his eyes and leaned back on the headrest, looking out the windshield seriously.

"Michael is the man who adopted us and took us into The Colectiv after our mom died," he explained.

James examined Emilia's expressions in the rearview mirror. Her eyes were trained on Eric, eyebrows raised in surprise as she listened intently.

He continued, "He's the Knight Commander, which is the highest rank you can get in this line of work. He's good at what he does and holds a lot of power."

"Yeah, and I just had to lie to him about a few things," James interjected. "Because if he knew we were bringing *you* along, he'd send an army after you. So, if you don't want that to happen, I suggest you keep a low profile."

Emilia nodded vigorously, saying, "You don't have to ask me twice."

"Good. Now, let's get the fuck out of here."

†††

[40]James considered himself good at lying. He had enough practice as a rowdy kid, but hunters for The Colectiv were *literally* trained to be good at it. He was raised to live in stealth and deception and learned to pass polygraph tests with flying colors, but this was different. He wasn't used to lying to the people he cared about so easily, not about things like this. Stupid shit? Yes. High-stakes information? Not so much.

Eric had his reasons for not trusting Michael, and James didn't blame him, but the lieutenant's relationship with the commander was a different kind of complicated. Michael was the only human James respected other than his mother. He could have very well written James off for his behavior, just like everyone else, but he never did. Instead, he taught James everything he knew, raised him in his teenage years, and was the closest thing he had to a father. He wasn't perfect, and his methods were questionable, but he always delivered. Deceiving him

---

[40] TERMS & CONDITIONS - Bad Omens & Bob Vylan

felt wrong, but never did he think he'd have to choose between him and his twin.

There was a particular ick in James' soul over how much he was keeping from Eric already. Not only did he have duty as a lieutenant and future captain, but his duty as a brother held more weight. Their mother taught them long ago to look after each other at any cost, and James took that job seriously to this very day. It's become even more prevalent in the last three years after almost losing Eric forever. It was even harder when, despite having almost died, Eric seemed to have even less regard for his well-being.

"I'm the last person that needs protecting."

James didn't know if it was confidence in his survival skills or if Eric didn't care about his survival at all. At times, he seemed cool and in control, but other times it was like he was ready for the flames to swallow him up. After what he went through, Eric should've feared death, but he only seemed deeply apathetic, which is what scared James the most.

Eric had been so focused on this hunt for years, training for this moment, that James often wondered what would become of him when it was over. After all, his sole reason for returning to The Colectiv was vengeance. When Dante was dead, what then?

He remembered what Emilia asked him back in Staten Island:

"When you finally kill my brother, will you stop? Or will you keep going?"

That's the thing, James thought—*does E even know the answer to that?*

He tried not to think any further in that direction. His brother was strong. He knew he was. He had been to hell and back, after all, and James trusted him.

He can get through this. We can get through this.

James wanted to rise. He wanted Michael's respect, but he also couldn't let Eric down. Not now, and not when Emilia was around to mess with his head. He meant every single word that he said to him at the hotel, and he intended to keep it that way.

21

A Life for A Life

Emilia

Six days. It took approximately six days to drive across the U.S. by road, and Emilia would be stuck in a car with two hunters the entire time. One of them was her ex. Who would've thought it would come to this? Surely, Emilia did not. Even if it *was* her wild idea that got her here.

After much consideration, she decided that if she couldn't stop the boys from seeking out her brother, then she'd simply join them and get involved in their pursuit as much as possible. Then, as soon as she could pinpoint Dante's location, she'd gently lead them astray in the opposite direction. Perhaps, if she had the guts, she'd give him a personal warning should the chance arise. But that was a bridge she'd cross when she got there. Emilia was aware of how insane it was, but she'd be damned if she didn't get through this like any other phase of her life: by sheer force of will.

Luckily for her, the first day of travel wasn't as horrible as she expected. They drove a whopping eight and a half hours from Manhattan to Columbus, Ohio, and despite any discomfort, Emilia managed to rest through at least half of it. Granted, sleeping in a moving car wasn't the most comfortable, but at the very least, their different sleep schedules proved beneficial (Emilia being nocturnal and the twins not). She also took precautions to protect herself from the sun, even bringing a shawl to shield herself from its harsh light. However, while Emilia put all the effort into making things easier, the boys made little to none, refusing to lower the volume of both their music and their voices.

In between periods of sleep, she tried taking advantage of her waking time to ask them questions, but of course, they made it practically impossible to do so. Eric more so seemed to have made it his personal mission to keep as much distance from Emilia despite their proximity, only speaking to her if necessary. Even though the vampire knew it was better this way, it still irritated her, gnawing at her skin. However, considering how he blew up during the interrogation, she resisted the urge to push his buttons lest she cause a collision or, worse, get abandoned on the side of the road. Everything she said was always met with a harsh "no."

Emilia would scoff and say, "No? 'No,' what?"

"No."

"You're not funny."

"Wasn't trying to be."

In the end, it was James that answered in his brother's stead, "It's none of your fucking business. Now, shut up."

The vampire scowled at him and stuck her tongue out when he wasn't looking. Annoyed, she sat back in her seat and looked out the window instead. That was how most of their conversations went until she gave up.

Emilia despised the twins in similar yet different ways. What she felt towards Eric was spiteful and personal, while her hatred for James was genuine anger and dislike. He was like a wild dog with no leash, eager to bark and bite anything he deemed a threat. It was clear from the beginning that he lacked a filter and wasn't afraid to be unkind, much to her chagrin, considering she was left to interact with him the most. It made her not want to speak at all, which was most likely the twins' plan all along. Their hostility proved hard to work with, their walls as strong as the steel of their blades. Still, even if they were hunters, she was hoping they'd warm up somehow. Unlucky for them, even when she doubted herself, Emilia was relentless.

Before she knew it, she was awakened from one of her naps upon arrival at their first motel. The shawl had been rudely tugged off her face, exposing her to the light. Emilia groaned and opened her eyes to James staring from the passenger seat.

"Wake up!" he shouted..

She grumbled, "Fuck off."

He snorted and disappeared out of the car. When she sat up, Eric looked at her from the driver's seat, with his body still halfway through the door. The last of the afternoon light filtered in through the windows, casting a halo around his head.

"We're here," was all he said.

Emilia slid out of the vehicle, half asleep with her shawl draped around her and her things in hand. All three of them checked in at the lobby, and as promised, she paid them for her separate room. They walked to their shared floor, and just as she was about to disappear into her motel chamber, Eric uttered his first full sentence to her in hours.

"We're leaving at the same time tomorrow, so be ready by then. It'll be a longer drive, so prepare for that."

Emilia frowned. *Ah, business as usual.*

"Where are we going next?" she asked.

"Oklahoma City."

"Tornado country. Great." Her voice oozed sarcasm.

She couldn't recall the last time she set foot in Oklahoma in her entire life. She was more of a metropolitan girl, to begin with.

"Yeah, well, at least it'll cut a day out of our trip," he said.

Emilia's face lit up at the hopeful piece of news. If it meant having one day less to deal with everything, then she didn't mind the long drive at all.

"Thank God for that," she said. She went into her room, calling over her shoulder, "Have a good night, boys."

I know I will.

†††

Columbus, Ohio

[41]Emilia's eyes lingered on the fountain before her and the two small elephants that sat on top of it. She was on a bench in a now-empty park, surrounded by trees, dressed in much flashier clothing, and with her hair and makeup done (she felt more like herself that way). Nightlife continued on beyond, but at the moment, she had a small pocket of nature to herself. It was a breath of fresh air, especially after being in the confines of a steel box on wheels. And after having to avoid the sun for hours, she had a deeper appreciation for the night.

One of the upsides of this torturous road trip was the fact that Emilia was traveling again. And the thought of going out and seeing the sights was the one thing that had kept her going for those eight long hours. She'd been isolated in New York for a small eternity and had missed experiencing new places. It's been decades since she stepped

---

[41] People Disappear Here - Halsey

foot in her birth country, and there was a strange bittersweetness to being back. So much had changed in so little time.

Emilia was not the same woman she used to be—that much was clear. Now, when she looked back at her life, she could spot red flags and broken pieces where she couldn't before. She could see where and why everything went wrong. Yet, like a masochist, she yearned for those nostalgic days. Part of her missed living life with so much carefree and reckless abandon, but one can only be reckless for so long before they start to destroy themselves and everything around them. She and her brother were proof of that.

She took out her disposable phone and swept her gaze around the park, making sure she was alone. She tuned into her hearing but simply caught the sound of cars and the occasional bystander walking by. Nothing of concern.

Oh, yes, she was very grateful for the alone time. As long as the twins were asleep, there was no tension, and at least now she could guarantee some privacy. Because while Emilia wanted to enjoy herself, she also wanted to take the opportunity to confront the real reason she was here in the first place:

Jean.

She knew that it was most likely morning in Romania by now, but she didn't care. She'd let the phone ring, or she'd call as many times as necessary until he answered. However, to her surprise, she only needed to call him once.

"Emilia?"

She frowned in confusion. "Jean? I thought you'd be asleep."

"Ah, yes. I actually decided to take a little spontaneous trip west."

"West? Where? I thought you were meeting up with Misha."

"I did. I'm currently at her place in London."

"Hmmm. Well, at least you're out of Bucharest."

Good riddance. Now it was Emilia's turn to be caught in the snare.

"Why'd you call me?" he asked.

Her rage came back twofold. Emilia ran her tongue over her teeth, pressing her tongue against the place where her fangs retracted as she gathered herself for what she was about to say.

"Do you know where I am right now, Jean?"

"Your apartment, I assume?"

Emilia, hoping that he could sense it. "No, Jean. I'm in Ohio. Columbus, Ohio."

"Ohio!" he exclaimed in disgust.

"Yeah. Do you know *why* I'm in Ohio, Jean?" She spoke in a sugary voice that could cut like a knife. She paused but spoke too soon for him to answer. "Because I'm on a fucking road trip with Eric and James MacNamara!"

She shouted in anger but then paused to check if anyone heard her. Fortunately, there was still no one of significance. There was a moment of silence on the other line, followed by a peal of booming laughter. It made her livid.

Emilia pulled the phone away from her ear, saying, "You're such an asshole. I'm hanging up."

"No, no, Emilia, wait," he said in between chuckles. "I'm sorry."

"Yeah, you better be fucking sorry because this is all your fault! And don't even try denying it because they already told me it was you," she whispered sharply.

Jean's laughter subsided as he let out a heavy sigh, his breath crackling against the speaker.

"Why'd you do it?" she asked somberly, a lump forming in her throat. "I didn't think you'd sell me out to hunters so easily."

"And you're right, Em, I would never do that to you," he reassured, "not to betray you. But as you can tell, these aren't just any ordinary hunters, so I had to make some...*interesting* decisions. Besides, I made them promise to ensure your safety."

Emilia scoffed bitterly, "Mmm, right. My life in exchange for my location, which sounds like an oxymoron."

"Then you *do* know why."

"Something tells me you have your own twisted reasons for leading him to me, of all people. I know how much you love your secrets. I just never thought I'd be part of one. Literally, any other hunter would have been better. *Death* would have been better, but I can't even have that," she spat.

"And yet, you're currently going with him to... where?"

Emilia got quiet, biting her lip to stall answering him.

"Emilia?" he urged on.

"Crimson Beach."

Jean sputtered, "Crimson Beach? Emilia—"

"I know!" she exclaimed, on the verge of tears.

"Wasn't it you that said one of the circles of hell was in the depths of that godforsaken city?"

"Yeah, I did," she said with a nod.

"So why are you going back there after all these years, with *them*? Do they *know*?"

Emilia swallowed hard as once again she recalled Eric's expression when she told him the truth.

"Yeah. Not everything, but yeah. I didn't really have a choice. Eric had me chained to a chair and was ready to crush my windpipe. He wanted to know where Dante was, and...the name slipped out. He's a little too good at what he does, Jean."

"So, he's a lot more like his father than I thought," he mused.

Emilia chuckled darkly. "You have no idea.".

"And do you think you'll actually find Dante when you get there?"

"I mean, it's one city out of thousands on the planet. I know the chances are low, but..."

Emilia put a hand over her collarbone, where she once wore a ruby cross that matched her brother's. She took it off when they cut ties and hadn't put it on since, but every so often she found herself reaching for the empty space.

"I might have a way of finding out for sure," she replied.

"You mean Jaya?"

Jaya, the friend she left behind. From what she knew, she still lived in the area, and contacting her had crossed Emilia's mind a few times in the last 24 hours. But that was another bridge she'd cross when she arrived.

"Yeah."

"You know what Eric will do, don't you?"

Her lips fell into a dismal frown. "I do."

"You may have known him one way, Emilia, but he is far more than the boy you fell in love with."

"You don't think I know that?" she argued.

"No, because there are things about him and his brother that you don't understand. They are soldiers, and The Colectiv is all they have in a world that wants them dead. If Eric wants revenge, he's going to get it. Especially with his brother by his side. They're not beat cops."

Emilia furrowed her brow.

Jean had given Emilia a brief summary of how Eric and James came to be. Wade had fallen for a hunter, and when she got pregnant, they ran, never to be seen again. Since Wade seemed to have disappeared off the face of the earth, Emilia was only faintly aware of it at the time. And Jean was so protective of his best friend that he never shared anything aside from basic details. Of course, now she knew why.

"Wade was a soldier too," she argued with fire in her heart. "You think *he* would've wanted this?"

Emilia loved Wade and cared about him just like everyone else did. She should care about his family and maybe many decades ago or in another life, she would have, but these men before her were something else. They were his blood, but they were not raised by him. They are the opposite of everything he believed in. How was she supposed to be okay with that?

"For them? Absolutely not, but that's why you need to understand, Emilia," Jean stressed.

The sorrow it gave her weighed heavy on her chest. Emilia never thought about it from that perspective until now. She didn't want to. She didn't want to feel empathy for the hunters who were trying to kill her brother, but she was too close to the story to not know that there was more to it than she could ever imagine.

"I can't just let it happen, Jean. I *can't*. He's my brother. I have to try."

"Are you sure that this is just about Dante?"

"Of course it is," she said defensively.

"Then why didn't you go and find him on your own?"

Emilia scowled, rolling her eyes in annoyance. There were a multitude of reasons why she didn't try finding Dante on her own. She was afraid of seeing him again, and this was an excuse to do so. She was using the twins' expertise to locate him, which was true, but...there was another part of her *without* malicious intent, a part of her that was still haunted by the things she had done.

A memory flashed in her mind's eye.

Trembling hands pressing down on an open wound to stop the blood from pouring out of it. Her vision was tinted pink with bloody tears. Broken furniture. Pale skin, a dwindling heartbeat, the smell and feel of blood.

It was quick yet as jarring as a slap to the face. It made her grateful that Jean wasn't present to see her fighting back tears.

"Eric and I have unfinished business," she whispered, repeating what the hunter said to her.

"And what business is that?"

Emilia shrugged, holding at bay things she could hardly admit to herself.

"That's a secret for me to know and for you to find out."[42]

---

42 You Asked For This - Halsey

22

First Night

Eric

He was falling again and then drowning again. His hands were covered in blood, but this time, he held a sword in his grasp. He saw Emilia on the beach, but blood poured out of her eyes as Eric watched in horror. Even the ocean was bloody red. All of a sudden, he was a child, sitting by his mother's bedside as she deteriorated. "My sweet boys," she whispered. Now, he was a teenager, bound to a chair. "Give me your hand." Crack. "You're weak." Stop it! "Hit him." Crack. "What even are you?" I am what they made me. "I trusted you!" "We're not gonna stop until you get it right." Find me. "You're a wolf." "Look who's a dirty little liar."

Eric!

The nightmarish dissonance of voices swelled until they were all but a swarm of bees from hell. At the sound of his name being called, Eric's eyes snapped right open, and suddenly he was back in the dark and quiet motel room in Columbus, Ohio. His heart was pounding, his breathing shallow.

Eric sat up against the headboard with his eyes closed and curled his shaking hands into fists. He inhaled, held his breath, exhaled, and repeated in intervals. As usual, it took a moment, two, or more, until his body fully relaxed. When he managed to calm down, he checked to make sure his brother was still asleep, but James had barely stirred, sleeping like a log.

Eric had never been happier to be in a dingy motel in a strange city than at this very moment.

He quietly made his way to the bathroom to splash cold water over his burning skin and to shock him back to reality. He then ran his fingers through his hair and leaned against the sink, jaded.

I can't keep living like this.[43]

He tried making sense of his nightmare, but as always, it never did. There were voices from his past, voices of fiction, and voices that had nothing to do with one another. They meant nothing and everything at the same time. It was every bad thing that had ever happened to him, clinging to his skin and his mind, threatening to drag him down. And he was over it.

Eric exited the bathroom, grabbed his water bottle from the bedside table, and took a long drink. His gaze wandered to the wall that separated their room from Emilia's, and out of curiosity, he expanded his mind, using his abilities to listen in beyond the wall. But all he heard...was nothing.

He frowned. *That can't be right.* Emilia was nocturnal, and she wasn't exactly a quiet person, so if she were awake, Eric would have heard *something*.

---

[43] Broken Machine - Nothing But Thieves

He put the bottle down and walked closer to the wall, listening in once more for any signs of life. But again, he sensed *nothing*.

What the fuck?

Feeling a sudden sense of alarm, he decided to investigate. Without waking up his brother, he threw on a hoodie and shoes, grabbing the extra key card to Emilia's room. He went next door and knocked. No response. He called her name several times, but again there was no response. Eric used the key card to let himself in, and when he opened the door and looked inside, it was just as he had feared: empty. Her bags were still there, but Emilia was not and from what he could tell, she left recently.

Eric's eyes widened. *She left? Where the fuck did she go?*

He immediately assumed the worst.

"Shit."

He bolted back to his room, letting the door slam without care as he started changing out of his pajamas in frantic haste, intent on going after Emilia. The ruckus was enough to finally wake up James.

"Where the fuck are you going?" he muttered.

"Emilia's gone," Eric seethed.

"What?"

"Emilia. Is. Gone!" he growled. "She left!"

Eric threw on a jacket and grabbed as many concealable weapons as possible.

"Aww, shit," James cursed, jumping out of bed. "Do you know where she went?"

"No, but I'm going after her." Eric went to the door, ready to go. With a look at James, he said, "I'll let you know when I find her."

His twin looked at him in confusion. "Don't you need me to come with you?"

"I'll give you a heads-up if I do, but I think two men going after a small woman is gonna draw a little too much attention."

James groaned, "Point taken."

†††

Knowing what he knew about Emilia, there were a number of things she could've been up to, but then again, as of late, he felt like he knew nothing, which made him more anxious. He didn't like the idea of her running around a strange city at a time like this. Emilia, as far as he knew, could have been blowing their cover, which could mean the end of their lives. She could've been out feeding on someone, causing mayhem, or perhaps secretly plotting against them with someone they didn't know. Maybe it was Jean, or worse, maybe it was her brother. Call it paranoia, but it's what fueled his search as he scoured the city for her, and he wouldn't know peace until he found her.

It was well into the night, so most establishments were closed, save for the clubs, bars, and breweries. Eric didn't know much about the city, so he started asking around for points of interest. He was starting to feel lost and frustrated until someone pointed him in the direction of the arts district. And if there was anything that Eric knew about Emilia for certain, it was that she could always be found where the art was. After that, it was easy to track her down.

On the way to the district, Eric passed by a huge tree-filled park when he caught a familiar figure making their way out towards the sidewalk. It was Emilia, as clear as day. She was dressed in different clothes from this morning, in smaller, tighter, and more fashionable clothes that were attention-grabbing in a place like this. She was talking on the phone with someone, which made the hunter stop in his tracks. He slowly backed away, hiding against the trunk of a tall tree. Hoping that he could find out who she was talking to, he held his breath and listened intently.

"I think you have too much faith in them. I don't know how far they're willing to go to uphold your stupid deal."

When the realization hit, Eric's eyes widened.

Jean.

The older vampire responded on the other line, and though it sounded broken up and far away, Eric could recognize the baritone voice anywhere.

"Something tells me they're men of honor, but I didn't exactly take *your* actions into consideration... You're playing with fire, Emilia...like I said, they're soldiers..."

The hunter narrowed his eyes. It was obvious they were talking about the twins, which didn't sit right with him.

There was something else he didn't catch, and then Emilia said, "No, I don't. But that's never stopped me before, has it?" She sighed. "I don't wanna talk about this anymore. I'll call if anything crazy happens."

"Be careful with them, Emilia...know... I still care about you... I hope that you know...very similar goals. One day you'll understand. Stay safe."

"I sure do hope so, Jean."

By the end of the call, Eric's hazel eyes were set in an icy glare. He may have only caught the tail of it, but it was enough to raise his suspicions. Jean Beltremieux harbored secrets, and the fact that Emilia was talking to him at all was a cause for concern.

He took a peek from behind the tree just as the vampiress put her phone in her purse and made her way toward the arts district. Seeing the opportunity, Eric locked his eyes on Emilia and took long, even strides towards her. Before she could cross the street, he took her arm and spun her towards him. She reacted as he expected.

"Hey, don't fucking touch me!" she pulled out of his grasp and aimed a punch at his nose.

The hunter, however, caught her fist before it made contact. When she saw who he was, her face fell in shock and then morphed into a scowl of disdain.

"You?" she growled, snatching her hand away from him.

Eric, despite his fury, tried to remain calm as cars drove by.

"What the fuck are you doing here?" he hissed under his breath.

"What does it look like I'm doing? I'm enjoying the city. Did you follow me here?" she demanded.

"Kind of. I woke up and realized you were gone, so I came looking for you."

Emilia scoffed, "Why? You psycho."

Eric grabbed her by the wrist and pulled her into the shadows, away from the streetlights and cars. There were a few lingering eyes, but he tried smiling at them to save face and draw less attention. Emilia pulled away from him again.

"Don't touch me," she repeated, pointing a manicured finger at him.

Eric kept his voice low but sharp as he spoke, "Emilia, you're supposed to keep a low profile. Do you know what the fuck a low profile is?"

"Yeah, I do, actually. I'm not an idiot."

"Then what the fuck are you doing?"

"I'm trying to have a good time," she argued. "What did you want me to do—stay cooped up for hours?"

"I didn't think you'd be running around the city all night."

"News flash, I live by night. You know this."

"Yeah, but I also said you needed to stay hidden. You're our responsibility while we're doing this. If someone recognizes you or sees you with us, then we're all dead," he stressed.

"*You* should've stayed in your room, then. I'd worry more about *your* face than mine, MacNamara."

Eric rolled his eyes at the blatant mention of his name. He inhaled to calm his anger, but it did very little.

"Have you ever thought of shutting the fuck up for once?" he whispered sharply.

Emilia's lips spread into a cat-like grin, her eyes wild. "No, but I *can* leave."

She spun around and tried walking away, but Eric grabbed her arm again and pulled her back. Emilia hissed and leaned in close to his face, with a menacing glare. Her sweet and flowery perfume filled his nostrils as she proceeded to threaten him under her breath.

"I am going to tear—not break, *tear*—your fucking hands off, and then I'm going to gouge your eyes out if you do that again."[44]

Eric looked down at her, clenching his jaw to hold back a smirk.

At that moment, a car pulled up next to them, breaking their focus from each other. The passenger window rolled down, and a man leaned over, looking between them with concern.

"Ma'am, is this man bothering you?" he asked.

At the same time, Eric and Emilia blurted out, "No!"

They both paused as they quickly became aware of how much attention they were drawing to themselves. In that moment, Eric watched Emilia straighten up and, with the ease of an experienced actress, react in a way that both scared and impressed him.

---

[44] Kiss With A Fist - Florence + the Machine

"Sorry! My boyfriend and I were just having an argument. I swear, there's nothing to worry about."

Her voice took on a higher pitch as she placed her hand on Eric's chest in an act of affection. The hunter fought the urge to visibly recoil.

"Are you sure?" the stranger asked, still wary.

The middle-aged man looked them both up and down, but his eyes lingered on Emilia a little too long. Eric noted the obvious way in which his gaze snagged on her body, his eyes doing what his hands could not. As if he wasn't already irritated by his interruption, at that moment, something dangerous sparked within Eric, and he didn't know why. His feelings must have been clear on his face because when the man glanced at him once more, fear passed over his eyes.

Why don't you just mind your fucking business?

He opened his mouth to say it out loud, but Emilia instinctively put a hand over his lips before he could get a word in. He glared at her but didn't fight it.

"Yeah, he just gets a little jealous sometimes," she assured. Her voice was the epitome of polite femininity. "He's an asshole, but he's harmless."

Eric snorted.

"Okay, just making sure. Have a good night," the stranger said.

"You too," Emilia answered with a smile.

With that, the meddlesome man drove off. When she knew the car was gone, Emilia dropped her smile and her hand and gave Eric a questioning look.

"You should really work on your people skills."

He rolled his eyes. "That guy was a creep anyway. It doesn't matter."

She crossed her arms, raising an eyebrow at him. "So much for low profile."

Granted, Eric used to be better at dealing with civilians than this, but it had been a while since he'd left Romania and was away from the estate. Living in a hostile environment tended to rub off, even on a former "college boy." But the current circumstances weren't necessarily bringing out the best in him, either.

"I don't exactly deal with people like you on a regular basis," he said.

"That's because I'm one of a kind." She flashed him a dazzling smile before saying, "Now leave me alone."

"No."

For a moment, she squeezed her eyes shut and groaned through gritted teeth. "Why?" she whined.

"Because I'm doing my job, Emilia," Eric contested, barely speaking above a whisper. "You literally asked for this. You knew what you were getting yourself into with me and Jimmy. I'm just making sure you don't get us killed. And that *you* don't lose your fucking head."

"You're being dramatic. I'm not gonna eat anyone if that's what you're insinuating. That's what the cooler is for. And I'm not trying to make friends or get noticed. I'm simply trying to *exist* when I'm not stuck in the car with *you*. You're not my dad or my bodyguard, and I'm definitely not some young, dumb child. I'll do as I please."

Eric rubbed his hands over his face and resisted the urge to scream. He looked around and pulled Emilia further into the park, amidst the grass and trees.

"You're not a hunter, Emilia," he stressed. "You don't know these people like I do. You don't know what they're capable of. And we both have a reputation, so we can't afford to be seen by the wrong people."

"I've been chased by hunters before."

"Yeah, in the 80s. But now there's a new guy in charge, and a lot more shit has happened since then." He motioned to himself.

To her, it could have meant what happened three years ago, but Eric was referring to everything that led to his entire existence, which was more than 25 years' worth of history. There were things that she couldn't even begin to understand, but he didn't have the patience or the time to explain that to her.

"You're talking about that Michael guy?" she asked.

"Yeah," he nodded. "You know what they call 'that Michael guy'?"

"What?" There was a wary look in her eye.

"'The Silver Wolf of Romania.'" Eric made sure to enunciate every word. "Not only does he hunt vampires, but he and his father, and his father before him, operated under the gaze of communist rule. They don't fuck around."

The young daywalker allowed some urgency into his voice in hopes that Emilia would understand, and for the most part, it seemed to work. The fury in her expression was now replaced by a mild look of fear, the corners of her lips pulling downward. Eric didn't blame her. The Iovaneau's came from a long line of cold-hearted men; it was in their blood. Although what they achieved was admirable, Eric didn't need to like it.

"You know, I could've done with this information prior to all of this," Emilia said after a moment of silence.

He shrugged. "I thought you knew, considering your history."

"I don't know the ins and outs of The Colectiv, Eric," she admitted, shaking her head. "I didn't stop to ask *who* was chasing me. I just ran. The real world's got enough politics as it is."

"Yeah, well, now you know."

Emilia ran a hand through her hair in what he assumed was exasperation. There was a storm in her brown eyes as she looked off, a conflict he couldn't quite read. Eric watched her with thoughtful intensity.

"I heard you on the phone with Jean," he said.

She threw him a sharp look, her eyes flashing with shock. "You were eavesdropping on my phone call?"

"I only heard the end, but, you know, forgive me for being a little skeptical about your intentions when you're talking to the most secretive man on the planet. And then you just left without saying anything. Of course, I'm thinking the worst."

"I wasn't aware that I was supposed to ask for your permission to go out. But for the record, I called Jean to let him know what's going on and to yell at him about what he did. Which I think is valid."

Eric inclined his head in a small nod. He couldn't disagree with that. But just from the small sliver he had caught on Jean's part, his skepticism couldn't be completely helped. He didn't like the idea of anyone talking about him or his brother in secret, so he'd make a mental note of it.

The hunter pointed a finger at Emilia sternly and said, "From now on, as long as we're doing this, you tell us where you're going. Got that?"

Emilia let out a long, irritated sigh, but he swore he caught a hint of amusement in her eyes.

"Fine."

"Good."

23

Hotel California

Emilia

Only a day into the trip, Eric and Emilia had managed to ruin each other's night. He barely even looked at her the entire drive to Ohio, and then all of a sudden, he was manhandling her in public and telling her what to do. He preached about not drawing attention, but if it hadn't been for her, he would've put his foot in his mouth and made things worse (even if he wasn't wrong about the man who approached them).

After three years, Emilia could still tell when he was on the verge of saying something hostile. Eric may have been sweet once, but he was never one to stay quiet if he thought something was wrong. It was one of the things she admired about him—his protectiveness and sense of justice. He was ever the introvert with something at the tip of his tongue, but it seemed that being a hunter made it worse. Or perhaps it was the fact that their feelings towards each other were now on the opposite end of the spectrum. It was no-holds-barred, and most of that sharpness was directed at *her* now. And Emilia was no better.

If one thing was certain, it was that Jean was right—there *were* things about the twins that she didn't comprehend. She almost wanted to deny it, until Eric told her about The Silver Wolf, the man who raised them. The name alone sounded like some kind of urban legend. Even now, the thought of Michael Iovaneau sent a chill up her spine. Not many men scare Emilia anymore, but just from his description alone, she couldn't help but feel terrified.

What the fuck did I get myself into?

If Michael Iovaneau was who Eric said he was, then the twins weren't simply working for The Colectiv...they were sons of the most powerful man there...and that meant something completely different.

She thought of the picture in Eric's wallet of the woman with her two boys.

How did they end up like this?

Emilia found herself aching for the truth, but knowing about The Silver Wolf made her more eager to save her brother. The last thing she wanted was for him to fall into his hands somehow. She just had to act fast as soon as they arrived at Crimson Beach. And if she wanted to get to Crimson Beach at all, she needed to follow Eric's regulations, even if it hurt her.

†††

The following morning, they all headed out for their 13-hour drive to Oklahoma City. It sounded unbearable to Emilia, but at least she wasn't the one driving (not that they'd let her). The day started off as the one before, with Eric uttering minimal words to her, James being insufferable, and Emilia trying to ignore them by sleeping. However, while they stopped at a gas station, she was jolted out of her slumber by the sound of booming rock music.

[45]The bass and aggressive drums shook the car, and Emilia scrambled awake with a deep gasp. She pulled off her shawl and looked around frantically, only to find James cackling as he lowered the volume.

Emilia went feral.

"You bitch!" she screamed and lunged over the console to strangle him.

"Jesus fucking Christ!" he exclaimed.

James tried fending her off, but the cramped space and their matching strengths made it no easy feat.

She smacked him incessantly as she said, "I've! Had! Enough! Of you!"

"Don't! Fucking! Touch me!" he growled in between hits.

Emilia tried wrapping her hands around his throat when, suddenly, there was a sharp jab at her side. She yelped and clutched her now bloody abdomen. Her eyes were wide in disbelief as she looked between James and the knife that was now in his hand.

"Did you just stab me?"

"Yeah, I did!"

She hissed and lunged at him again with even more fury, getting a few scratches in. On cue, the driver's side door opened, and Eric looked at them in complete and utter bewilderment with a tray of coffee in his hand.

"Hey, hey! What the fuck is going on here?" he yelled.

"What does it look like? She's trying to kill me!" James exclaimed.

"What did you do?" Eric demanded.

---

[45] Welcome Home - Coheed and Cambria

"*Me*? Why do you assume it was me?"

Eric groaned. The backdoor opened, and with little to no effort, Eric grabbed her by the waist, wrenching her away from James. Emilia struggled in his grip, but the more she fought, the more Eric wrapped his arms around her and squeezed.

"Emilia, stop! Chill or I'll leave you on the side of the road," he said through gritted teeth.

With that, she went limp in his grasp, her chest heaving. She glared at James from across the car, who was wiping away some blood from his arm. Despite her rage, the heat radiating from Eric's body and the sound of his voice in her ear did a good job of bringing her back to reality. If it still worked, her heart would've skipped a beat.

How embarrassing.

"You good?" he asked, still holding her.

"Yeah," she muttered.

His hands slipped away from her waist, taking his warmth with him. When she turned to look at him, he eyed her expectantly with his hand resting on the door frame. Emilia frowned in confusion until she realized that he was waiting for her to sit properly.

When she finally did, he said, "We have a few more days out here. I know it's tempting, but try not to kill each other in a confined space." He pointed to James and said, "You stop being such a dick."

His twin scoffed, "Hey, what?"

Eric ignored James' protests and then pointed his finger at Emilia. He fixed her with a commanding look, and she bit back the urge to smile.

"You? You're already on thin ice."

With that, he shut the back door and got into the driver's seat with his tray in hand. Emilia cast a glance at James, who was in a quiet rage now that Eric had called him out too. The sight pleased her.

Eric sighed. "Why the fuck is there blood on my hand?"

Emilia looked down at the hole in her shirt, which was stained from a wound that had already healed.

"James stabbed me," she blurted out.

"She attacked first," James argued.

"Jesus fucking Christ," Eric whispered.

†††

After that debacle, Emilia managed to sleep with little to no interruptions, except the next time she woke up, they were still on the road.

She sat up and ran her fingers through her hair as she blinked herself awake. When she looked out the window, the sun was setting low on the horizon, and the plains outside were bathed in its orange light. Everything was quiet except for the constant soft music, the humming of the car, and faint snoring coming from the passenger seat.

James is asleep. Thank God.

Emilia looked towards the driver's side, where she could see Eric's silhouette. Considering he had been driving when she dozed off, she couldn't help but wonder if he had been doing so the entire time.

"Good morning," she whispered.

Eric huffed in amusement. "Good morning."

"How long have you been driving?"

"Just a few hours," his deep voice rumbled as he talked above a whisper. "We switched while you were asleep."

Emilia nodded. *Good.*

"How long before we get there?" she asked.

"About—" he peered down at his phone's GPS, "—Three more hours."

She exhaled wearily. It wasn't too bad considering the other 10 hours they had already driven, but three hours seemed like a lot when it was just Emilia and Eric awake at night. All at once, the car felt smaller and the quiet made the air thick. Still, she tried being amicable now that his twin was out of commission.

"If you're tired, I can drive." It was a genuine offer.

Eric scoffed, "No fucking chance."

"What do you think I'm gonna do—drive us off a cliff, Thelma and Louise style?"

"I wouldn't put it past you at this point."

Emilia hummed. "That's fair."

"Besides, I'm not tired. I had a blood pack earlier, and I'm used to running on little sleep."

"Ah, of course you are," she said, sitting back against her seat.

I guess not everything has changed.

Emilia recalled many nights when Eric would stay up past 3 a.m. to spend time with her, do homework, or just because. It was convenient back then since there was a huge overlap in their lifestyles, but she did worry about him sometimes. Even if he *was* a daywalker, vampires needed sleep too, but perhaps it wasn't her place to care now.

"Is there any chance we can stop by for some coffee?" she asked. "I could really use some right now."

"As you can see, it's a barren wasteland over here, but if I see a coffee shop in a cornfield, I'll let you know," he said in that dry tone of his.

Emilia rolled her eyes. "A gas station would suffice."

"Don't get your hopes up."

She leaned against the door, gazing at the sun as it disappeared beneath the skyline until the world went from orange to purple to black. Soon enough, the only remaining sources of light were the dashboard and the stars twinkling above. She marveled at them from her window. She didn't get to see the stars often in the big city, so when she did, it filled her with childlike wonder.

Eventually, she started rifling through her bag and pulled out one of the many books she brought along with her when the heart-shaped locket caught her attention again. Emilia eyed it many times on the drive but never asked about it. After the rest of her rejected questions, she focused on keeping her head down, but that didn't mean she didn't want them answered. Perhaps, with one twin sleeping, her curiosity could be satiated if she was careful with her words.

"Whose necklace is that?"

Perhaps it belonged to an old lover of James, or maybe Eric (although Emilia hated the idea).

Through the mirror, she found Eric's eyes. They glanced at the necklace and then back at the road. The pause that followed made her think he wasn't going to answer at all, until...

"Our mom's."

He didn't elaborate, and from the part of his face that Emilia could see, a muscle feathered in his cheek. Considering what little she did know about her, she wasn't surprised that it was a sore subject. It made her sad all over again.

"Oh," was all she uttered.

Emilia envisioned the woman in the picture once more and thought of how she must have worn that same necklace day after day. It made sense that it was hers, yet it was still surprising to see how sentimental the boys were to carry it around long after she was gone. It warmed her heart.

The vampire let a moment of silence pass, wondering if she should push the subject further or any subject at all. She found herself deciding on one more simple question.

"What was her name?"

At the very least, she should know her name. Even after all this time, she never came to learn it. Eric never shared it with her, the same way he never shared who his father was either. Though Jean may have mentioned it in passing, it only seemed right to ask someone who knew her personally. And it seemed only fair that she had her name along with Wade's.

Eric tensed, and again, Emilia thought he wouldn't respond, but then...

"Anya," he whispered. "Anya Mészáros."

Meh-zahr-osh. She sounded it out under her breath. It was obviously Eastern European.

It reminded Emilia of something she had somehow forgotten about.

"She was a hunter too, wasn't she?"

The question almost came out like a gasp.

"Yeah...she was."

It didn't fully register until now that *Wade fell for a hunter*. It must have been why Eric said their reason for joining The Colectiv was complicated. Their mother had been a hunter, which meant that it was part of their history and bloodline. It was part of hers too, no doubt, yet, despite it all, she still managed to fall for a vampire. She gave it all up.

Emilia glanced at the locket again, admiring the engraved design with fresh eyes. Anya had been a faceless being for years, and now she knew her face and her name. It made the fact that she was gone even worse. She had so many more questions to ask—so many to ask *her*, but she couldn't.

"Anya," she whispered. "That's a pretty name."

Emilia went back to her book and got lost in the words as silence fell between her and Eric once again. She had to admit that it was relieving to have a peaceful exchange for once and to have at least one of her burning questions answered. She figured he was exhausted, and that's why he was being nice. Or maybe their conversation from last night broke the ice somehow.

For a while, she thought that would be it. She didn't expect much else to happen for the next three hours until a very specific song from Emilia's past started filtering in through the speakers.

"Hotel California" by The Eagles.[46]

Emilia went rigid, her attention no longer on the book before her or anything else. She could feel her dead heart constrict as the song triggered a memory—no, a *plethora* of memories from a time in her life that was long gone. She was both in the present and yet almost five decades in the past all at once. The unexpected wave of nostalgia and bittersweet sorrow nearly knocked the wind out of her.

For the second time, she chose to break the silence.

"Is this your playlist?"

"Yeah, why?"

"Nothing... I just... I didn't know you liked this song."

Emilia saw Eric's brow furrow through the mirror.

"Yeah, of course, I like this song. Why?"

"No reason."

Emilia made a noise of discomfort. She tried ignoring the music but, instead, found herself restless and fidgety. She thought of asking Eric to skip the song but didn't want to make a big deal out of it. In the end, her anxiety must have been too obvious for him to ignore.

"You good back there?"

---

[46] Hotel California - The Eagles (obviously)

For a moment, Emilia hesitated, wondering if she should open up to him at all. The last time she did, the circumstances weren't ideal, and it didn't end well. She wasn't quite certain if she knew how to put her feelings into words at all. But then she remembered Sorrento, the interrogation, and how hiding things about her life had caused her more problems. There was nothing wrong with sharing a piece of her past with someone who already knew the worst about her, right? After all, she didn't have a perception to uphold anymore, and he couldn't hold it against her. Eric told her about his mother, so, surely, she could talk about a song.

"I just..." she began, "this was one of my favorite songs. I remember when it first came out."

"Oh, right." Eric sounded surprised. "You grew up in the 70s. I forget what that means sometimes."

Emilia smiled softly. "60s and 70s, yeah. Although this song came out in '77, which is about 5 years after I got turned. I remember hearing it on the radio and just...bawling my eyes out."

"Why?"

"I don't think I really knew why back then. The lyrics don't make sense unless you want them to. I just remember thinking it was beautiful. We used to listen to it all the time on drives like this."

"'We'?"

"Yeah, me and Dante," she gushed, but as soon as the words left her mouth, she snapped her mouth shut.

The reminder of her brother made Emilia's smile drop and a hush went through the car. It had been so casual and accidental. It was as if, for a second, she forgot about everything that had happened between them. She internally berated herself for it, especially for doing it in front of Eric.

"Sorry," she mumbled.

Her eyes stung with tears, and she bit her lip to keep herself from talking lest she start truly crying. Instead, she looked down at her fingers, fiddling with them in quiet sorrow.

[47]Until recently, Emilia hadn't talked about Dante in a long time, not out loud. It was too painful as it brought about so many memories like this—of old road trips filled with loud singing, laughter, and good conversations. That was all behind her now, and when she looked back, they were an indistinct dot in the distance, unreachable.

Eric sighed before asking, "Are you okay?"

Both his gentle tone and the question itself surprised Emilia enough to make her find his eyes in the mirror once more. To her dismay, he was already looking right back. His hazel eyes were softer than before, leaving her breathless. Not many things or people make her feel that way nowadays.

"Yeah, it's fine," she told him with a sad smile. "It's stupid. It was a long time ago. Obviously, things have changed since then."

Irreparably so.

That night in Sorrento, everything that her friends had ever warned her about finally clicked for Emilia, and as soon as she and Dante were alone, she laid all of her feelings on him—every single emotion she held back over the last few decades over how he treated her. At the very least, she thought she'd receive an apology, but in the end, he used that last moment to tell her to rot. Since then, that argument often replayed in her mind, plaguing her day and night, but not once did she regret what she said. Severing the tie she had to her brother was the most liberating thing Emilia had done since getting turned, even if it left her feeling like she was doomed to free-float in space forever.

---

[47] My Immortal - Evanescence

The vampire returned her focus to the plains outside, but she could still feel Eric's attention on her.

"You're not stupid for missing it."

The words were so soft, that a human may not have caught them, but Emilia did.

Her eyes flitted to him in surprise, just as he averted his gaze and focused on the drive. Even so, Emilia continued to stare at him long and hard. His simple but powerful statement managed to validate her feelings while simultaneously doubling her longing and melancholy.

Was he being kind out of obligation? Boredom? Or was he being purely genuine? Was he speaking from experience? After all, he had lost people too, hadn't he? And technically...*she* had been one of those people. Or was she stupid to think she was ever that special?

"Always the smart one, Leone," she whispered.

His eyes found hers again, but this time, it was she who had to look away.

†††

About an hour later, Emilia noticed Eric take an exit much earlier than anticipated, in a city that looked much smaller than she expected. She frowned and closed her book to look around at the small suburban town they were driving through.

"This isn't Oklahoma City, is it?"

"Nope."

"Are you getting gas?"

"Nope."

"Then why are we here?"

"You wanted coffee, didn't you?"

Emilia furrowed her brow. "Yeah..."

Eric pulled into a shopping center and pointed out toward a small building they were now approaching.

"Coffee."

She gasped and leaned forward, resting her hands on the back of Eric's seat. Her eyes lit up like a Christmas tree at the sight of a 24-hour donut shop with a glowing sign. Having her nightly cup of coffee brought some semblance of consistency and joy into Emilia's life, and with how relieved she was, you'd think they'd discovered an oasis.

"Oh, my god. You actually found one," she marveled.

"You're lucky there was one on the way."

Emilia had accepted that Eric was going to purposefully forget to stop anywhere for coffee, so she was amazed that he even went out of his way to find a place at all.

She rested her chin on the corner of his seat and looked at the side of his face. "You didn't have to be nice. I would have settled for shitty gas station coffee."

He leaned his head toward her and said, "I wanted some anyway. Take it as compensation for the food."

Emilia narrowed her eyes skeptically. "Okay."

Eric proceeded to shake his twin a few times, shouting, "Jimmy, wake up!"

James groaned, his face twisting into a scowl. "What? Why? Are we here?"

"Nah, we're getting coffee. Want any?"

His brother sat up, looked at the time, and fixed Eric with an incredulous look. "Coffee? What the fuck are you getting coffee at 8 p.m. for?"

"You say that like that means anything to me."

"Right," James scoffed. "I forgot you used to drink this shit like water back in college."

Eric snorted. "Amongst other things."

They made their order at the drive-thru: Emilia, a black coffee with a side of sugar, and Eric, a cappuccino with an extra shot of espresso. James opted out of any drinks, but he did order a chocolate-frosted sprinkled donut to snack on. The sight of him eating it made Emilia miss being able to eat normal people's food, and she desperately wished she could snatch it out of his hands in an act of vengeance.

†††

At last, they reached Oklahoma City, which was a small metropolitan town with a big skyscraper standing in the middle and a river running around it. When they arrived at their hotel, Emilia knew they were all thankful to have a place to rest after being on the road for so long. According to Eric, their next destination was Amarillo, Texas—their shortest drive of the trip. All was normal and they bid each other goodnight.

It was an uneventful end to the evening and yet, when Emilia was all alone and getting ready for the night, her conversation with Eric replayed in her mind over and over. She couldn't stop thinking about it. It had been years since he spoke to her with such deliberate compassion. The entire time, she was waiting for the other shoe to drop, but it never did.

She tried not to linger on such things, but it was hard not to as she eyed the now half-empty coffee cup he bought for her earlier that night.[48]

---

[48] Coffee - Chappell Roan

24

Nothing More

Eric

Eric couldn't help but feel guilty for the obvious discomfort his brother was feeling. He knew it had to do with Emilia's presence, which felt like his fault in the first place. It didn't help that he had scolded James for messing with her, but Eric knew that the last thing they needed was another feud between them. Even if James' hatred for Emilia was warranted, it would only make things worse. Eric would just have to make it up to him when this was all over.

Amarillo, Texas, was their longest stay, which would give them some much-needed rest. However, Eric wasn't very fond of the place (the government, really) or any of the other conservative states they were passing through for that matter. It made him blatantly aware of how much he and his brother stood out, not because they were hunters or daywalkers, but because they were heavily tattooed non-white men. The twins had a colorful background, but a lot of their mother's side—

from what they knew—had Romani heritage, and they inherited a good chunk of those features. Having Emilia around didn't help either. And Eric would rather be vigilant against vampires than ignorant human beings.

That's their fucking problem.

He had more pressing things to think about, like his last conversation with Emilia.

Eric even surprised himself with the way he treated her. Since reuniting, he carried nothing other than contempt or bitterness towards her, but not this time. Perhaps it was the respectfulness with which she asked about his mother, or maybe it was seeing how affected she was by the mention of her brother. Whatever it was, Eric couldn't bring himself to be cold, not when he knew what it was like to be attached to someone who hurt you—someone who was supposed to be family.

It was a brief, short interaction, yet...it lingered in the back of his mind.

It's nothing.

Getting coffee was an afterthought, an olive branch, and like he said, he wanted some anyway. Nothing more.[49]

†††

"God, I forgot how fucking boring it is to drive through this part of the country," James said in their hotel room. "Why couldn't he have been in Oregon or some shit?"

Eric snorted. "Dante doesn't strike me as the type to isolate himself in the woods."

---

[49] Say It Right - Nelly Furtado

"He should. It would make everyone's lives easier."

"Agreed."

James eyed him curiously. "How are you doing, E? Have the nightmares gotten better or worse with her around?"

"They haven't gotten better, that's for sure, but they technically haven't gotten worse, so...the same, I guess. When all this is over, I might check myself into a psych ward."

"The estate's pretty much like a psych ward already."

"Yeah, but a padded room and a sedative would be nice right about now."

They burst out laughing. The shared moment was a welcome joy amidst everything, but as it died down, Eric's eyes lingered on his brother's face.

"What about you? I know this isn't what we signed up for, but... Emilia's not fucking with your head, is she?" he asked.

"Nah, she's just annoying."

"Are you sure? I wouldn't blame you."

The question was asked in complete sincerity, and something passed over James' eyes before he inevitably shook his head. Eric held onto that thing, but of course, his brother had to make a joke.

"Yeah...yeah, I'm sure," he assured. "Although I will say one thing. You have questionable taste in people, bro. No offense."

Eric scowled. "Hey, fuck you. I was in college, and I was trying to have a good time. Give me a fucking break."

"A little more than a good time," his brother whispered.

Eric rolled his eyes and lay flat against his bed.

"I don't wanna fucking hear it," he said, staring up at the ceiling. "It's been three years."

I was wrong. I fucked up. He ruined everything, and she's no better. I already know.

The boy found himself battling against a racing heart and tried slowing down his breathing to keep from blowing up. In the end, he got up from the bed and moved towards the door.

"I'm gonna get some fresh air."

25

Nothing Less

Emilia

Due to their longer stay, Emilia had arguably the best sleep this entire week. There were uncomfortable car seats, no bumpy roads, and no noisy hunters. It was perfect, and she reveled in it as much as she could.

Considering the way things were going, Emilia decided to take a jab at inviting the boys out to town. She knew they stayed in to avoid her and to "lie low," but she couldn't imagine it was particularly enjoyable for them to do so (even if she did despise them and wish them harm on most days). She argued that they could keep an eye on her and enforce their rules if they tagged along.

Was she doing it out of the kindness of her heart? Maybe. Was she hoping to get them to open up a little more? Most definitely. It was all part of her plan.

The way they protested, she felt like a disgruntled parent forcing her children to have fun on a family vacation. But it was the third night on the road, and it wasn't the last, so she knew she was right.

"You're lucky I'm bored as fuck," James said. Eric, of course, was his usual annoyed, broody self.

So, they walked around the southern town with scarves, hats, and jackets for disguises. Emilia walked ahead, while the boys trailed behind, pretending they weren't together. Luckily, they didn't stand out too much since the desert nights in January were freezing. She stopped at as many open shops as possible, although the boys drew the line at bars and clubs since there were too many people. As a compromise, Emilia settled on a coffee shop, where she practically dragged them inside towards a booth where they sat in silence (as always).

During their stay, Emilia couldn't help but notice that the waitress was overly...*attentive*. Her eyes roved over the boys while she, aside from pleasantries, completely ignored Emilia. James, for the most part, looked bored and uninterested, but Eric was all bright smiles and playing the amicable customer. All the while, the vampire sipped her coffee, trying to hide her feelings behind the cup.

Emilia didn't know what came over her, but her face and chest started to get...*hot*. It could've been anger, or it could've been something else. She knew it wasn't her place to feel any kind of way now that their relationship was over, but it was almost instinctive. Now *she* was the wild dog, ready to snap at a threat. And while she reserved such feelings for men, for the first time in a while, she had the urge to sink her teeth into that pretty girl's neck until she passed out.

Of course, Emilia didn't voice any of these feelings, but sometimes they slipped out in small ways.[50]

"Will that be all?" the waitress asked.

Yes. That's it. Now leave.

Eric smiled. "Yes, thank you."

Emilia ran her tongue over her teeth, his very normal response having pissed her off. Eric rarely smiled these days, and now here he was, doing it with such openness. She knew it was irrational, yet...

The waitress left, and Emilia put her cup down, looking out the window with a thoughtful hum.

"Problem?" James muttered.

She thought it was interesting how she could tell which one of them was speaking without having to look. There were differences in their voices and the way they talked.

"No, not at all," she replied, feigning innocence.

She sank back into the booth as they both gave her an odd look. James didn't seem to care for longer than a few seconds and quickly returned to his pastry. Eric, however, kept watching her, picking her apart with his eyes like a mystery to solve. Emilia wondered if he could tell what she was feeling, but even if he could, he didn't address it. The quiet stretched, and the vampire said nothing.

Instead, Emilia waited until Eric took a sip of his coffee to say, "So when somebody flirts with the both of you, do you do a coin flip, play a game of rock paper scissors, or do you take turns?"

Eric inhaled sharply, causing him to breathe in some of his drink and fall into a coughing fit. James patted his back with a firm hand to help him clear his airway. All the while Emilia smirked with glee.

James glared at her. "I hate you."

---

[50] Kill Bill - SZA

"Emilia," Eric choked out.

"What? It's a valid question!" she said defensively.

"Shut up."

"You better decide fast because I'm pretty sure she's coming back to ask if you need CPR."

"Stop!"

"Okay!"

After the coffee shop, they chose to part ways, so the hunters could sleep. According to Eric, their next destination was Arizona.

"It'll be the last stop before Crimson Beach," he told her.

A pit of dread opened up in Emilia's stomach as everything seemed to be speeding up all of a sudden.

"How long?" she asked.

"9 hours, give or take."

Emilia bit her lip in thought before saying, "You know, I can take a turn driving to help with the load."

The twins grimaced and both made noises of uncertainty. Emilia raised her hands in question and looked around to make sure no one was listening.

"I got my license 50 years ago, and I've driven more vehicles than either of you have combined. I know how to drive. I can get us there in one piece."

She couldn't exactly turn left toward Mexico and hoped to keep her head, even if it was tempting to do so.

The twins both shared a look that held some conversation she couldn't hear.

"Unless you're okay with me being useless in the backseat and doing none of the work," she added.

Eric rolled his eyes, and at the same time they both said, "No."

The way they spoke in unison was both unsettling and amusing, and it wasn't even the first time.

"It's like you're robots or those twins from The Shining."

Again, at the same time, they muttered variations of "Shut up." Emilia giggled and motioned that they had basically proved her point.

"Exactly," she whispered and started backing away with a dramatic salute in their direction. "Goodnight, boys. See you in the morning."

James grumbled, as usual. Emilia turned around to go, expecting nothing else, but then, right behind her, Eric uttered a simple, "Goodnight."

The sound of his soft voice made her breath hitch, catching her off guard. She looked over her shoulder, thinking she'd see him still standing there, but he was already walking away, following his brother close behind.[51]

---

[51] BITTERSUITE - Billie Eilish

26

Stay

Emilia

Sorrento, Italy—3 years ago

[52]Eric and Emilia sat side by side on the sand, overlooking the sea. She rested her head on his shoulder, their towels laid out beneath them along with their personal items—phones, a sketchbook, and some pens among them. The waxing moon illuminated the night and painted the water in silver as it crashed and receded. The breeze tousled their hair, making it unruly, and music played from a restaurant some ways away, creating a fitting ambiance.

Aside from the moon, their only other source of light was the one from Eric's phone, which he used to read the book in his hand. It was a collection of Italian poetry that Emilia had picked up from a small bookshop. She wasn't fluent in the language, but Eric was, which is

---

[52] Romance - My Chemical Romance

why she bought it. Apparently, he learned it from his uncle, and his accent was perfect. He even navigated the city much better than she ever could, and she found it very attractive, to say the least.

She also loved the sound of Eric's voice, so she asked him to read it for her when he had the time, but, of course, Eric didn't want to wait. Even though it was dark outside, he took out his flashlight and insisted on doing it right there on the beach ("What's more romantic than that?"). He was strange, but Emilia liked that about him. Men tended to brush off her interests, but Eric never did. In fact, he was the complete opposite, and he loved books about as much as she did. Now, listening to him read poetry with that voice that made her melt, it felt like they were in their own little bubble.

"'Rimani' by Gabriele D'Annunzio. Rimani! Riposati accanto a me. Non te ne andare. Io ti veglierò. Io ti proteggerò..."

Emilia looped her arm through his, resting her chin on his shoulder. Occasionally, she'd cast glances at his beautiful face, watching him at the same time.

[53]No matter how many times she looked at Eric, she never got over how perfectly shaped he was inside and out. She loved his Greek-like nose, the sharp line of his jaw, and the way his hair curled at the ends. And those dimples when he smiled. Her heart ached more and more for him with each passing day, and she was in deep. He gave her butterflies that made her feel like a young schoolgirl with a crush. It was both dangerous and exhilarating.

Eric Leone had been nothing but kind to Emilia since the day they met, and she wasn't entirely sure why. She didn't know what she did to deserve it, and quite frankly, she didn't think she did, but she refused to let him go. It was selfish of her, she knew. Eric was human, and she knew there was no possible way that what they had could ever last, yet

---

[53] Seventeen - Bunny Lowe

she couldn't bring herself to end it. It was difficult when he did things like *this* and when she was falling for him faster than anyone else she had ever met.

When he finished the poem, Eric looked at Emilia and raised his eyebrows to see her staring back. Emilia didn't look away, holding his gaze.

A smile played on his lips. "What?"

"Nothing," she said coyly, shaking her head.

In actuality, there were *too many* things she wanted to say, but there weren't enough words or time.

"What does the poem mean?" she asked.

Eric glanced down at the book, suddenly hesitant, and then translated, "Stay! Rest beside me. Do not go. I will watch you. I will protect you. You'll regret anything but coming to me, freely, proudly. I love you. I do not have any thought that is not yours; I have no desire in the blood that is not for you. You know. I do not see in my life another companion, I see no other joy. Stay. Rest. Do not be afraid of anything. Sleep tonight on my heart..."

With every line, the vampire's dead heart swelled. Even if it wasn't Eric's poem, hearing it from him somehow made it more profound. For a long time, she could only hope that someone would feel such a thing for her.

That was certainly one *way to find the words.*

Stay.

When Eric lifted his attention to her again, the look in his eyes took her breath away. His pupils were blown out, and his face softened. She could even hear his heartbeat quicken. She almost couldn't believe that he was looking at *her* like that, so lovesick. If she could bottle up the feeling it gave her, she'd drink herself to perdition.

"That was beautiful," she whispered when she managed to find her voice.

He nodded. "Yeah. I told you you'd like it."

"Thank you for reading it to me."

"I like reading to you," he said with a shrug and a smirk.

Emilia bit her lip, feeling those butterflies again. She followed the urge to touch him and let her fingers graze his chin. He was too close to not touch, and his lips were too enticing to not kiss them, so she did.

She pressed her lips to his, saying, "I like you."

Eric smiled against her mouth before letting the book and his phone fall next to him.

"I like you too," he said.

His hand went to the back of her neck, his touch making her gasp as he deepened the kiss. It made her toes curl and took her breath away. Eric slowly pushed her back against the towel, and Emilia pulled him along by his shirt. They made out on the beach for a while, the poetry long forgotten, with her half-pinned beneath him.

When it inevitably became too heated, Eric pulled away. He rested his forehead against hers, his warm breath fanning over her face as he panted, his lips swollen. Emilia stared into his hazel eyes, which were drunk with desire. It made a familiar desire of her own unfurl within her.

She played with the hem of his swim trunks, letting her fingers brush against his bare skin and playing with dangerous territory. He shuddered, which quickly turned into a dark chuckle, bright teeth flashing in the night.

"You're gonna get me in trouble," he rumbled.

"I don't know what you're talking about," she smiled.

"Oh, yeah? You know...if I could..."

"If you could, what? Hmmm?" she teased.

He licked his lips and shook his head, clearly fighting back whatever wicked words he wanted to say. It brought Emilia immense joy to know that she drove him crazy as much as he did her.

Eric suddenly tore his eyes away from her to take a sweeping glance around the beach. He looked over his shoulder as if he were scanning the area. Emilia wondered what was on his mind until he looked back at her with a mischievous smirk.

"There's no one around. Wanna go for a swim?"

The question was unquestionably suggestive.

Emilia scoffed, but a grin brightened her face. "Look who's the troublemaker now, schoolboy."

Eric was bolder than he let on—a fact Emilia came to learn soon after they met.

He laughed, tilting his head in agreement. "I may have been told that once or twice before. The question is whether *you* think it's a good or a bad thing."

"Oh, I like it. I've always liked a little trouble."

Eric's face lit up. "Then follow me, *mia cara*."

Her giddy reaction to the pet name made him giggle. He then stood up and tugged off his shirt, leaving only his swim shorts. Emilia's eyes roved over his body hungrily, frozen in place. It was another thing she never got tired of, even if she saw him like this countless times.

Eric snapped his fingers in his face.

"Hey, my eyes are up here," he scolded.

Emilia rolled her eyes. "You're an idiot."

He held his hand out to her with a smile and helped her to her feet. Emilia took off her thin beach cover, revealing her red bikini underneath. Eric took his turn ogling at her, but when she caught him, he blushed and looked away.

A giggle bubbled in Emilia's throat.

"You're so cute when you're shy," she said, lightly tapping his cheek.

She marched past him towards the sea with all the confidence in the world, but before she could get too far, Eric came up behind her and scooped her up in his arms. Emilia let out a screech, which turned into a cackle. He shushed her but couldn't help his own laughter. She then wrapped her arms around his neck, holding on for dear life as he carried her into the water. Salty seawater splashed her skin, feeling young and jovial and free as if she were a girl on the cover of a contemporary romance novel.

Eric didn't put her down until they reached the area just before the waves broke, where the water stopped at his waist and her chest. They proceeded to swim a little further until Emilia's toes were grazing the sand below. By then, they were far enough from the beach that they were barely visible in the darkness to the human eye.

For a moment, Eric and Emilia watched each other across the black abyss of the sea with sparkling eyes and playful smiles. Eventually, Emilia inched towards him, closing the distance until they were a foot apart.

"Hi," she whispered.

"Hi."

"I like your face."

He chuckled. "I like your face too."

Emilia paused. Looking at him now, and at the mercy of nature, she was overcome with the urge to say whatever was on her mind.

"Hey, Eric?"

"Yeah?"

[54]She hesitated before saying, "Have I ever told you what a great guy you are?"

He furrowed his brow. "I don't know. You may have said something like it."

"Well, you are. You're a really great guy." Then, in a whisper, she added, "I like that."

---

[54] Safety Net - Ariana Grande (ft. Ty Dolla $ign)

Emilia didn't know what compelled her to say such a thing, but he needed to know. Even if she could never tell him the truth about what she was, she could at the very least tell him this. Emilia had never met anyone who was genuinely kind and cared about her as much as he did. He was like the missing piece of a puzzle she had been looking for all along. It was a rare find. It made her emotional thinking about it.

To her dismay, Eric seemed to falter, his expression almost unsure. "I don't know about that...but thank you."

Emilia cocked her head and frowned.

"I mean it," she stressed.

"I know." There was silence, and then all of a sudden... "Hey, Emilia?"

"Yeah?"

"You're amazing, you know that?"

That took her by surprise. She didn't expect him to pay her back in kind or for such simple words to hit too close to her heart. A lump formed in her throat, and she had to look away lest he see a hint of red in her eyes.

"Stop," she whispered.

You don't know that.

Eric followed her face, trying to catch her gaze so she wouldn't hide. It wasn't hard when they were out in the water, and running away wasn't easy. And she did a lot of that—running. Back in her apartment, she could lock herself in the bathroom if she needed to shed a few tears, but even then, it was hard when he was around. She could never hide when something was wrong from her perceptive boy.

"Hey. *I mean it,*" he said, repeating her words back to her with more firmness.

Emilia blinked back her tears before daring to look back at him. There was nothing but sincerity in his soft, hazel eyes. It was almost too much.

"How can you be so sure?" she asked in a small voice.

He shrugged. "I just am."

Awash with emotion, all Emilia could do was move towards him and wrap her arms around his waist. Without hesitation, Eric took her in his embrace. She let his warmth envelop her for a few moments as she fought back tears. He and his beating heart were like a solid, unmoving pillar in the waves.

I think I could love you, she wanted to say. *I think I could love you so much, and it scares me.*

Emilia liked to think that she was a confident person, especially compared to who she was before. That girl was easy to take advantage of and easy to kill, and this one, *Emilia*, was not. She had proven that over and over again, yet it was always love that revealed the cracks in her armor. It was ironic how something that was supposed to bring happiness could threaten to tear her asunder. She wanted it with every fiber of her being yet was absolutely terrified of it. But at the very least, in his arms, Emilia felt certain that Eric wouldn't let her drown.

When she managed to pull herself together, she looked into his eyes once more. And that lovesick expression softened his features again. Her gaze flitted to his mouth, and without another word, she crashed her lips into his. The kiss was fervent as Eric and Emilia poured their unspoken feelings into each other.

I love you. Stay.

She ran her hands up his chest, shoulders, and neck, tangling her fingers in his damp hair. Eric's hands caressed and massaged her body, making her sigh. He bent down and kissed her neck, making her sigh. He then looked deep into her eyes and with one hand holding her against him, he slipped the other into the bottoms of her swimsuit. His fingers brushed her core, and Emilia's lips fell open with a gasp as pleasure coursed through her. Then, all of a sudden, she was losing herself in his touch.

27

The Anthropologist's Lament

Eric

[55]*Eric dug his fingers into Emilia's thighs as he thrust in and out of her. She moved up and down on him, mirroring his movement, with her legs wrapped around his waist. Her sharp nails dug into his back while her other hand tugged on his hair, clinging onto him for dear life. The water sloshed around them with their motions, the moonlight providing the perfect backdrop for their forbidden excursion.*

He tried his best to stay quiet and not draw attention, but the feeling of her around him and the sounds coming from her mouth made it impossible—the panting, the moaning, the whimpering. Knowing that her reactions were because of him made him never want to stop. It was like a drug he could get addicted to.

---

[55] Go Fuck Yourself - Two Feet

You're amazing. You're amazing. God, you're amazing. It repeated itself in his mind and fell from his lips over and over in whispers and moans.

Emilia licked the shell of his ear, making him grunt and inch closer to finishing.

"Eric."

It drove him wild.

Fuck.

†††

Flagstaff, Arizona—Present

When the dream was over, Eric sprang up into a sitting position and put his face in his hands. He repressed every agonizing sound that he wanted to make, lest he wake up James and have to explain himself.

Fuck, Fuck, FUCK!

It wasn't just a dream, but a memory.

Out of all the memories, this one? Really? Right now?

For once, Eric would have preferred literal nightmares to *this*. He didn't know what was worse—the actions or the words exchanged from that memory. He blamed it on the forced proximity and recent conversations.

What, I can't utter words to someone without having a sex dream, now?

But it wasn't just "someone." What Eric and Emilia had was more than just these last few days, and there were many things he had locked away in his mind.

Every day this last week, he tried not to think about Emilia in any shape or form that wasn't purely professional. For the most part, he managed to brush any unwanted feelings away to stay composed, but in pure honesty, being near her made him feel like he was on fire. It used to be an invigorating feeling, but now it threatened to turn him to ash at any second. It equally frightened and infuriated him. He shouldn't be so affected by things like the smell of her perfume or the shape of her lips anymore, yet he was.

Eric continued to sit in bed for a while, picturing horrible things to calm certain parts of his body down (which wasn't too difficult). When he was back to normal, he ruminated in the darkness for a long while. He knew he could've tried going back to sleep, but he didn't want to risk dreaming about *her* again. So, instead, with a glance at his sleeping brother, he got up to distract himself.

Eric MacNamara already operated on very little sleep. Though he tried his best to get in as many hours as possible to keep himself in good shape, it was hard when his past haunted him. It made him question whether sleep was worth it at all, and it was why he turned to caffeine at a young age to keep himself awake. Still, it frustrated him that even in his attempts to make good decisions, his mind was against him. In times like these, he tried his best not to bother his twin. It seemed logical for at least one of them to be well-rested throughout the day. In the meantime, Eric figured that now was a better time than any to get some exercise in.

The places they stayed in rarely had a gym, but as luck would have it, this one did, albeit it was not a great one. It was tiny, but at the very least, it gave him something to work with. So, the hunter put his headphones in, turned his music to full volume, and ran on the treadmill for a while. He then did some weight lifting and calisthenics using the equipment provided. If it were up to him, he would've practiced with his blades, but it wasn't exactly subtle. Instead, he chose to take a dip in the pool and get some laps in. It was supposed to be closed during certain hours of the night, but nobody ever followed the rules anyway.

Without waking his twin, he rinsed off his sweat in the shower, threw on some swim trunks, and grabbed a towel before heading down to the indoor pool area. From what he could tell, there were no signs of life, which seemed perfect. However, upon entering, he realized that he hadn't been able to detect the one person who wasn't technically alive.

Aww, fuck.

Right next to the pool, sitting in the hot tub, was none other than Emilia herself. She was relaxing amidst the bubbles in a swimsuit and with her hair tied up, and she immediately locked eyes with Eric from across the way.

"Oh, hi," she uttered in surprise.

"Shit. Sorry," Eric muttered and turned to leave. "I'll just—"

"You don't have to go," she said.

"Yeah, but I don't wanna step on your alone time. You're clearly enjoying yourself."

"No, you're fine, really. Use the pool. Unless you were planning on using the hot tub, then *I* can go."

"No, you're good."

They stared at each other in awkward silence, the pool casting a rippling light across their faces. Eric swallowed thickly, debating whether it was a good idea to be alone with her at all. He was already trying to fight the imagery that wanted to repeat in his mind, and being half-naked in the water wasn't going to help at all.

Emilia groaned, "For fuck's sake, Eric, just get in the fucking pool. I'm not gonna kill you."

That's not what I'm worried about.

Eric scoffed, "Right."

For once, he chose to ignore the nagging voice in his head, convincing himself that he was stronger than this. He put his towel down on an empty lounge chair and approached the pool without a word. He could feel Emilia's eyes on him, burning into his skin, so he cast a quick glance in her direction. She averted her gaze casually, and again Eric was very aware of how bare he was.

He rolled his eyes at himself.

Don't do that.

With a deep breath, Eric dove into the pool. The cold water was a slight shock to his system, but after the workout he had, it was also very refreshing. He lingered beneath the surface for a moment, letting the water muffle any thoughts and sounds from above, and then eventually swam back up into the cool air. He rubbed the water out of his eyes and pushed his wet hair out of his face.

"I saw you working out earlier before I came in," Emilia said.

Her eagerness to fill the silence and take every opportunity to ask questions didn't escape him for a second.

Eric furrowed his brow, treading water. "Really?"

He must have been so deep in the zone to not even notice *her* watching.

"Yeah, I passed by the gym on the way back. You were kind of hard to miss. You're uh... You're really intense," she chuckled.

"So, I've been told."

"What are you doing up this late anyway? I thought you were supposed to be asleep."

When he dared to look at her, she was resting her elbows against the edge of the hot tub, her eyes trained on him. Eric didn't let his gaze linger.

"I was, but I, uh...had a nightmare. I didn't want to go back to sleep."

I was trying to avoid you in my dreams but still ran into you in reality. Go figure.

Emilia hummed in thought. "You still have those?"

Despite everything, it seemed that familiarity was unavoidable. He didn't know if he liked that.

"Yeah. Unfortunately."

Wanting to avoid any more talking, Eric started swimming back and forth across the pool, ignoring the way Emilia watched him.

Back and forth, back and forth. He did this until he was too tired to continue and then sat at the shallow end to take a break. His eyes instinctively went to the hot tub, only to find it empty. At first, he thought Emilia had left, but his senses told him otherwise, so he scanned the pool area and found her sitting by the deep end. She was dipping her feet in the cool water, her eyes on the sky through the glass ceiling. Eric's focus, however, flitted to her body.

It was hard not to look when she was in a two-piece bikini and her curves were on display. And it was even more difficult knowing that he had seen her in less—many, *many* times. Unwanted thoughts clawed at a door in the back of his mind, dirty ones that had no business being this *alive*. His pulse stuttered for a moment—only a moment—and it was then that Eric was reminded how much of a simple man he was at his core.

Stop it.

Emilia snapped her attention toward him and frowned. "Are you okay?"

"What are you doing?" he asked, like an accusation.

"I'm dipping my feet. What does it look like I'm doing?"

"Nothing. I guess."

"Is there a problem?"

"No, of course not," Eric muttered in annoyance.

To make his life easier, he too looked through the glass ceiling and focused on the sky above. With his eyes, he could see the stars pretty clearly and the constellations they made. Since he was a kid, he thought it was both fascinating and amusing that, one day, people were so bored that they assigned stories and names to random shapes in the sky. Of course, Eric knew them by memory at this point and had them mapped out in his mind.

The North Star, Big Dipper, Little Dipper, Orion's Belt, Draco, Cassiopeia...

"I've never seen a vampire get a scar like that before."

The abrupt statement pulled Eric out of the stars and back to earth. He turned to Emilia once again, her eyes fixed on the scar at the crook of his neck—the one her brother gave him. She had tried pointing it out before, but Eric refused to acknowledge it with her. To his surprise, she hadn't addressed it in a while, but he imagined that the curiosity plagued her. He'd commend her for her patience if it weren't for the sad look in her eyes.

Instead of hiding it this time, Eric brushed his fingers over the familiar, damaged skin. It was numb and rigid as usual. The memory of the attack was still fresh in his mind even now.

"Yeah, it seems like I'm a walking phenomenon these days," he said.

"Do you know why?"

He hesitated for a moment, considering whether to share valuable information that could, without doubt, kill him. For some reason, in the end, he concluded that he didn't care.

"Pureblood venom," Eric answered, his eyes watching the water ripple and wave. "Apparently, it's the one thing that slows down our healing. My injury was so bad that it left a scar. If I were human, I would've died."

Vampires had venom similar to snakes that incapacitated humans long enough to draw blood from them. Since the dawn of purebloods, this information has been known, but it wasn't until recently that it was found to have another effect on daywalkers. Much to his misfortune, Eric MacNamara was the guinea pig for such a test. When he was attacked—*and bitten*—by Emilia's brother three years ago, it slowed down his healing enough to almost take his life.

Emilia became eerily quiet, so much so that Eric had to make sure she was still present. But when he looked at her, she was frozen in place, bearing a deeply haunted look in her brown eyes. Eric's face fell because it reminded him of the expression James had when he woke up in the hospital *that night*.

"So, I was right...you did almost die," she whispered.

"Yeah... I did," he answered slowly.

"And you didn't know that would happen?"

"No, nobody did."

"Huh."

The hunter couldn't help but be confused by her reaction. He didn't think that his potential death could have affected her so much. Now, he wondered if maybe, at one point, she did think he was dead and she did care about what happened to him. Eric had always assumed Emilia would be so angry and disgusted by his existence that she would *prefer* he died. He figured she called James and took him to the hospital because she wanted to save herself and didn't want blood on her hands. But knowing that she cut off her brother and seeing her reaction now, he was starting to think maybe it wasn't entirely true.

He almost wanted to reach out and reassure her, but he resisted the urge.

"Do you hate me?" she blurted out.

Her question took him utterly off-guard. "What?"

Emilia repeated, dead serious, "Do you hate me?"

Eric shook his head. "What kind of question is that?"

"It's a valid question," she argued.

"But why would you ask me that?"

She rolled her eyes. "Please, you know why I'm asking. It's because, after everything, it seems like you do. I mean, it's understandable if you do. I hurt you. I've hurt other people. I've *killed* people. I'm what you're *supposed* to hate. I guess I just..." She trailed off, looking out onto the water somberly.

Eric studied her with a severe expression as he found himself battling with her question. In the past, it had been easy to boil down his feelings for Emilia to something as simple as hatred, but now he couldn't use the word with certainty. It was a lot more complicated than that.

He could've let her think otherwise. He could've continued to be cold. But for what?

"I don't *hate* you," he told her, the words bitter. "The person I hate is your brother, not you."

Dante was an easy person to feel that way towards. In fact, Eric knew a few people he loathed with ease. Emilia, on the other hand, is, and always has been, a different case.

"I'm just..."

"Hurt?" Emilia tried finishing for him.

"Pissed off," he bit out, correcting her. "I'm angry, and I'm not really sorry about it."

"I get that. I do. You have no idea," she said. "You know, Jean says those are the same thing: anger and pain."

Eric rolled his eyes. "How? From what I remember, he likes to say a lot of things."

As helpful and wise as the old vampire was, Eric was still sore about what he had said about him in Bucharest. He already had one domineering adult in his life, and he didn't need another telling him what he was or wasn't.

"He gave you a read, didn't he?" Emilia asked with a giggle.

"Nothing that matters to me now," he muttered, his hand causing ripples in the water.

"Well, Jean does say a lot of things, but in the time I've known him, he's usually right. Whether you realize that now or years later just depends. He's the one who told me that when someone's angry, it often means that they're covering up underlying pain. Which makes sense because I spent the first decades of immortality being angry."

"Is that why you did what you did?"

Eric had been holding back his burning questions about as much as Emilia had, if not more, but it was hard when it was so natural for him to do so. As much as he shouldn't, he *wanted* to know. What else was he supposed to do on a night he couldn't sleep?

Emilia stared into his eyes, her bottom lip caught between her teeth in a nervous habit. No doubt she was debating whether to keep her secrets hidden once more. He wouldn't have been surprised, but it seemed things were different tonight.

"Yeah," she confirmed with a nod.

He could see years of anguish in her face, just as he had back in New York. He didn't want to pry. Eric, of all people, knew what it was like to carry burdensome trauma, but some part of him wanted to understand.

"For the record, I didn't spend all of my time partying and killing people back then," Emilia started. "That was Dante's full-time hobby. I used to help people, or at least I tried. I wanted to be like Jean. He sees people for who they are and for what they can be, and he's saved many lives, including mine. But my judgment is fucking horrendous, as you know. Even Dante said it. I guess you can blame the trauma for that."

That makes two of us.

She continued, "It took a lot for me to get to where I am. I haven't always been a crazy bitch, but you know, you kind of have to become something else to protect yourself from the world. And I *had* to protect myself. Especially after everything."

She trailed off for a moment, and Eric couldn't help but resonate with her words.

"You probably think I'm nothing like the girl you knew in Italy, but if you met the younger version of me, the one that I was before I got turned... I would be *unrecognizable*."

Emilia took her legs out of the water and hugged her knees up to her chest.

I wouldn't say that.

Eric was spiteful, but he wasn't blind, and his memory was more or less photographic. Now and then, he caught sight of the girl he knew in Sorrento. When they weren't fighting in an alleyway or bickering at a park, he could see it. In fact, he saw her even now as she spoke to him. It reminded him of a different, bittersweet time.

"How was she different?" he asked, now fully invested.

She sighed drearily, "That girl was treated like the scum of the earth. I would say she was invisible, but being invisible would have been a mercy. Her mother loved her out of obligation, and her father hated her for existing, yet they controlled every single thing she did. She was used and abused her whole life. And Dante, well..."

"Was he always like that?"

"No, no," Emilia shook her head, "the opposite, actually. He was really kind, despite everything. At least, he seemed that way to me at the time. Of course, when you grow up, you see things differently. Like I said, my judgment isn't always great."

Dante, kind? *Hell must have been frozen over.*

"I know you probably think that's insane," she said, as if reading his mind, "and to be honest, you probably met him at his worst. God knows what he's up to now."

The hunter found himself scowling at the mention of her brother and to his dismay, Emilia laughed at him.

"If I had a dollar for every time someone made that face when it came to Dante…"

"The guy did ruin my life, so…"

Once again, Emilia got ominously quiet, and then, out of nowhere, she said, "I'm sorry."

Her voice was small but genuine, which made the statement all the more jarring.

Eric threw her a strange look. She was watching him with sad eyes that made him feel like his chest would cave in on itself. It brought him back to his harsh reality, and he found himself overcome with conflicting, overwhelming emotions once more.

"What? What are you doing? Why are you being nice all of a sudden?" he asked defensively.

She craned her head back. "Jesus, can't I make an apology?"

No. No, you can't, because it complicates things.

Eric shook his head and looked away from her, saying, "I'm not here to make amends. This shouldn't even be happening right now."

"What are you even talking about?"

"This. This conversation," he hissed.

With urgency, he stood up and walked up the steps, out of the pool. Goosebumps dotted his skin from the cold air, and water dripped from his body all over the concrete floor.

"Why?" Emilia demanded.

"It's against the rules."

"The Colectiv's rules or yours?"

Eric glared at her, but he knew it was both. "The Colectiv forbids close relationships with vampires."

"Didn't stop you before," she scoffed.

"That was different." He picked up his towel and started drying himself off. "The circumstances were different."

"You can't even make friends?"

"Not with you."

"Why?"

Eric said nothing, but he knew the answer. *We can never just be friends.*

"I'm not lying or being sneaky right now. I meant what I said. I'm sorry for everything. *I am!*" she exclaimed.

When he looked at her again, she was facing him in full, her expression tender. All at once, Eric had a hard time breathing and needed to leave before he lost control again. However, his silence only seemed to anger Emilia further, and she groaned in frustration as she got up to her feet.

"You know, you didn't always have a stick up your ass. Or was that a lie too? Aren't you basically royalty in The Colectiv? You would think it gave you some kind of leeway in all of this. Some *benefits*."

Eric, who was on his way to the door, halted in place. Her words and wrongful assumptions triggered something profoundly rooted as if struck by lightning. A fire ignited, coursing hot through his veins. Without thinking, he whirled around on her.

"*Royalty*? Is that what you just said?" he blurted out.

"Yeah!"

"Where the fuck did you get *that* from?"

"You said you were raised by the guy who runs the place. Your mom was a hunter too. Legacy and all that. I'd say that's pretty close to royalty," she argued, crossing her arms.

Eric let out a big, hearty laugh, but there was nothing jovial about it. He then stopped and fixed Emilia with a vicious, cutting glare.

"Well, that's where you're fucking wrong, Emilia," he growled. "You really think that *I* have leeway in The Colectiv? That my life should be *easier*? That who I am means *anything*? On the contrary, being a daywalker has made my life a living hell!"[56]

He all but barked the last words, and Emilia's incredulous expression vanished. Eric was shaking with fury now, untethered.

"I am burdened by the curse that both of my parents bestowed when they were stupid enough to fall in love. They had us. They fucked everything up, and then they died, leaving me and my brother to *this*," he ranted, spreading his arms out wide. "Because of them, everyone's eyes are on us. Everyone's waiting for the half-breeds to fuck up because we shouldn't even be alive. If we step one toe out of line, we're as good as dead. I was lucky enough to survive after Sorrento, and not just because of Dante."

"But I thought you weren't with them when it happened," Emilia whispered.

"Doesn't matter, apparently," he said with a shrug. "If it wasn't for Jimmy or the fact that I'm an *asset* by blood, then it would have turned out differently. I could've lost my head for being with you, or worse, I'd be in a cell underwater, rotting away. Because I'm indispensable until I'm not."

Emilia's eyes widened in horror as Eric continued to speak with cold intensity.

---

[56] Running Up That Hill - Placebo

"I know everyone thinks I'm some kind of abomination, and maybe I am, but I didn't choose to be a killer. Not initially. You were right. I wasn't *capable*... not like Jimmy...but that didn't matter. If I wasn't born a killer, I had to be made. I was pushed to places no kid should ever be pushed and forced to do things I didn't want to do. I was poked and prodded, shot and stabbed, mocked and beaten down until I broke..."

His voice shook as memories of every training session he ever endured against his will flooded him. Every time Michael yelled at him to go again and again, every life he didn't want to take, and every failure that was met with animosity and disappointment. What happened three years ago wasn't the beginning—it was a breaking point.

Looking at Eric now and how far he had come, it probably seemed like a success story, but he often wondered: *at what cost?*

Tears sprung in the daywalker's eyes, but he blinked them away. He balled his hands into fists to keep them from trembling and didn't dare look Emilia in the eyes for too long.

She made a step towards him, reaching out. "Eric—"

He took an equal step back. "Don't."

Emilia didn't move any further and kept her distance as she hugged herself.

"How old were you?" She sounded afraid of the answer.

Eric furrowed his brow as he thought back to it all and said, "I don't think I was 12 yet."

She inhaled sharply. The appalled look on her face was too much for him to bear. It broke his heart.

"Why do you still do it?" she asked.

The hunter looked off gravely. At this point, the floodgates were wide open, and everything he had pushed back into the recesses of his mind was at the surface.

"You know how you said that you had to become something else to protect yourself?"

"Yeah."

This is who I have to be.

"Well...no one beats me down anymore," Eric told her with a sad smile. "I'm Corporal Eric MacNamara. *I* do the beating, *I* do the shooting, and *I* do the killing. *I* make the decisions. It's all on *my* terms now. *I* get to choose how I go. And I'm good at what I do... so I'm told. Maybe I like being good at it. Whatever it is, there's no going back now."

What's a little more self-hatred?[57]

Eric gave Emilia another pained, tight-lipped smile. He didn't know what came over him. This was the most he had ever opened up about anything in the past few years—no, his entire life. Not even James knew the extent of his feelings about any of this. Maybe it was because he didn't want to burden him, or maybe he had been so shut up in his own head that he just didn't know how.

There goes Emilia, pushing the right buttons again.

"I didn't know," she whispered.

"Of course you didn't."

He put the towel around his neck and ran his fingers through his damp hair, looking down at the floor. He pondered leaving once again but somehow stayed rooted to the spot as his emotions came down.

"Thank you," he told her, "for the apology."

As much as it had shocked him, he appreciated it. It was more than most people had ever given him.

Emilia looked surprised by his gratitude but didn't question it.

"Of course."

---

[57] Monster - PVRIS

"And I'm sorry."

She furrowed her brow. "For what?"

"Back then. I lied, and I hurt you too. And I'm sorry for what happened to that girl. She didn't deserve any of that," he said, referring to her past self.[58]

Emilia's eyes threatened to swallow him whole, just like the abyss in his dreams. For a moment, he wanted to let himself drown in them.

"You didn't deserve any of that either," she said.

"Don't worry about me. It's nothing I can't handle."

On his way out, Eric grabbed the folded-up towel lying on one of the other chairs. He tossed it to Emilia, who deftly caught it. Eric finally reached the door, and with his hand still on the doorknob, she called out to him one last time.

"Eric?"

He looked over his shoulder at her to see where she was still standing by the pool's edge, hugging the towel against her chest.

"Yeah?"

"I'm glad you're still alive."

Eric worked his jaw as a lump formed in his throat. It was such a simple statement, yet not at all. All he could do was give her a curt nod before leaving the building.[59]

---

[58] Daylight - David Kushner
[59] Sleep - My Chemical Romance

28

Positive Reinforcement

Eric

Brasov, Romania—12 years ago

Eric MacNamara sat on the second floor of the estate's library, wedged into a corner between a bookcase and the balustrade. He was on the carpet with his legs crossed, reading a book on Greek mythology that was about half the size of his 13-year-old body.

The Colectiv's library was one of the safest and most peaceful places in the entire grounds. It provided the young boy with books to indulge in and also a sense of comfort and quiet (although none of them cared for it as much as Eric did). The bookshelves made the room essentially soundproof and alleviated most of the sensory overload from the rest of the estate. It was the easiest way for Eric to shut himself off from the rest of the world, his duties, and, most importantly,

Commander Iovaneau. Even so, it was always a matter of time before someone found him.

The library door creaked open, and Eric held his breath.

"E?" The commander's voice echoed from afar.

The boy's heartbeat quickened with the sound of heavy footsteps on the hardwood floor. In a futile attempt to hide, he pulled his legs up to himself and tried shielding his body with the large book. Even from that height, he could smell the scent of cologne, gunpowder, and whiskey that followed his mentor everywhere. He listened to him get closer and closer with dreadful anticipation until suddenly he stopped and chuckled to himself.

"Did you really think I wasn't gonna see you up there?"

Eric sighed, his shoulders falling in disappointment. "Maybe."

"There's all these couches and chairs, and you chose to sit up there?"

"It's different. I like it up here," he muttered from behind his book.

It's safe.

"Of course," Michael said. "You can't keep hiding, E. I've been looking for you everywhere. It's your turn to do the polygraph test."

The boy clutched the edges of his book until his knuckles turned white. The reason he was in the library at all was to delay another dreaded task that he didn't want to complete.

"I know," he whispered.

"E, look at me."

Eric didn't move or say a word.

"*Look* at me," Michael repeated sternly.

It was an order.

With a roll of his eyes, Eric shut the book and looked through the balusters, towards the commander. He was staring at him from below in his usual black coat, and his jet-black hair was now streaked with gray at his temples. His silver eyes were serious, as always.

"The longer you stall, the more you prolong the inevitable. This is one of the easiest tests you can do, E. There's no killing, no blood, and it's a skill you need to hone in order to survive. It's better to get it over with."

"You always say that, and then when I fail, I get punished," Eric contested.

"It's called positive reinforcement. It's not any different from making soldiers do push-ups when they do some stupid shit in military training. You do well, you get rewarded, and when you don't, I push you to do better. It's motivation."

"I don't think that's the proper term," the boy mumbled under his breath.

"What did you say?"

"What if I fail?" Eric asked loudly to cover up his comment.

"You go in there thinking you'll fail, then you'll fail," Michael told him. "Now, put that book away and get down here, or I'll take away your library privileges."

The commander walked off without saying another word. The little boy frowned, glaring at Michael as he disappeared. He knew where to hit Eric where it hurt, and he knew that there was nothing else the boy could do but comply.

†††

They went down into an interrogation room on one of the subterranean levels that looked nothing like the rest of the estate. It had white walls, a concrete floor, and a single table in the middle. Even before Eric walked in, there was a lingering scent of bleach that heightened his nerves.

In total, there were four people in the room: Eric, Michael, a hunter named Adrian, and a woman sitting in front of a laptop with wires attached to it. The thought of having an audience made the boy sick to his stomach, but he couldn't help but notice that someone was missing.

"Where's Jimmy?" he asked.

"He already passed his test. He went with Caleb to learn archery," Michael said.

Eric deflated. He was hoping his brother would be around for moral support, but of course, he couldn't even have that.

The commander directed him to sit down on the other side of the table, and the woman began to strap his body with the wires before her. She put one around his forehead, a few on his torso, and the rest on his fingers. Eric tried assuaging his heart and telling himself it would be fine...but all he could think about was the long baton that was in the other hunter's hand.

"What's that?" he inquired.

"That's the motivation, E," Michael said and then proceeded to explain what was about to happen. "This machine is going to read your heartbeat, which these wires are detecting right now. I'm gonna ask you a series of questions, and Maya here is going to keep track of any spikes. Spikes mean that the wires detected a lie. The goal is to keep a steady heartbeat even when you're lying. Do you know why?"

"Because vampires can detect heartbeats," Eric answered without hesitation.

"Exactly. If a vampire catches you in a lie or finds out who you are, then you're as good as dead. That's why we train you to control it. All kinds of service agents and soldiers learn it for different purposes, and we use it for this. You got that?"

Eric nodded.

"Now, I'm gonna start with easy questions to get a base reading. You don't lie about these, okay? You tell the truth. Simply answer yes or no."

"Okay."

The commander stood in front of Eric on the other side of the table, arms crossed.

"Is your name Eric MacNamara?"

"Yes."

"Were you born February 13th, 1997?"

"Yes."

"Do you have a brother by the name of James MacNamara?"

"Yes."

Michael continued with the personal, yet easy questions until he was satisfied. He then glanced at the screen and nodded. Eric couldn't see what was on it, but he assumed he did well. However, the hard part was only about to begin.

"Now, I'm going to ask you questions again, but this time, you have to lie," the commander told him. "You keep a steady heart rate, we move on to the next one, and you get a point. But if we detect a lie..." he motioned to the hunter with the baton, who approached Eric's side, "Adrian here is gonna shock you."

On cue, Adrian pressed a button, making the end of the baton crackle with sparks. Eric flinched, and the hunter grinned deviously.

"The goal is to pass at least five times," Michael went on. "Five times, and it's over. If you don't, we'll keep going until you do... or we get tired. Okay?"

The boy clenched his jaw, anticipating the worst. His insides were screaming, but all he said was, "Okay."

Michael's eyes flitted to the screen once more, and he cleared his throat before saying, "First question. Are you human?"

"Yes."

The answer shot out of him quickly, as it was the easiest response he could give considering he wasn't technically wrong. He was, in fact, half-human, so it was a half-truth.

He watched as the commander shot Maya a look. The woman gave him a simple, curt nod. He raised his eyebrows at the boy, a smirk pulling at his lips.

"Good job. You get one point."

Eric exhaled in relief. For a moment, he was filled with a shining sense of hope. He thought that perhaps he *could* get through the test with flying colors. Maybe this time he could make someone proud...but his logic could only get him so far.

"Are you a vampire?"

The correct response was to deny it. It was the lie he'd have to tell for the rest of his life, not just on the field. But in his 13-year-old mind, logically, he knew it wasn't correct. He *was* half a vampire, and he was aware of it every day. Still, to pass the test, he had to remain calm.

"No."

That time, his overthinking and his heart betrayed him. Maya shook her head, and Michael grimaced. Eric immediately panicked at the sight of their expressions.

"Not fast enough, E, and not very convincing either," the commander said in disappointment. He nodded towards Adrian, and the baton crackled with electricity.

Eric gasped, "Wait!"

His protest fell on deaf ears, and Adrian jabbed it into his arm. It sent a painful shock through his body that made him convulse in his seat. Although it was brief, it was unlike any sensation he had ever felt before. Eric's heart pounded in his chest like a jackhammer, and he wondered how many spikes it made on the screen. When the uncomfortable feeling passed, he stared at Michael, completely speechless, but the commander looked unfazed.

"Do your breathing and steady yourself, E."

The boy tried doing what he was told, but it was difficult when he had just been tasered a few seconds before and when he was trying so hard not to shake with anger.

Before he knew it, Michael was repeating the question, "Are you a vampire?"

"No," Eric growled.

The commander rolled his eyes. He didn't even check with Maya this time and instead nodded to Adrian once more. The hunter sent another unexpected shock through the young daywalker.

He cried out, "What? What did I do?"

"There's no point to the test if I can see your emotions in your face, E. It's obvious that you're pissed," Michael scolded.

"Yeah, because it hurts!" Eric shouted.

"You'll get over it," his mentor told him coldly. "It's not the worst pain you'll feel in your life, so get used to it."

Tears started welling up in Eric's eyes. He looked around, wishing he could flee into the forest, but he knew he wouldn't get very far. He hated being alone, trapped in a room with hunters he didn't know.

"Where's Jimmy?" he asked again.

Michael clicked his tongue in annoyance. "I told you, Jimmy's not here. You can't keep expecting your brother to be around to help you, kid. You can't depend on *anyone* to help you because, in the end, the only person you can depend on is yourself. It's better to learn that now than later. You have to get yourself out of this on your own, especially if you want to catch up to where he is."

This was Michael's version of being a father. This was his parental advice, because only with his boys did he have such merciless patience. Only with them was he so determined and attentive to the point of control, overshadowing any real affection he once showed.

Eric averted his eyes and focused on the steel table before him.

"We'll try a different question. Is your name Eric MacNamara?"

"No," he whispered.

Zap.

"Do you have a brother?"

"No."

Zap.

"Do you know what The Colectiv is?"

"No."

Zap. Zap. Zap.

Eric wasn't sure how long the test lasted. All he knew was that it felt more like torture before Michael finally decided to pull the plug. [60]

---

[60] R.I.P 2 My Youth - The Neighbourhood

29

That Night

James

Flagstaff, Arizona—Present

It was the final stretch to Crimson Beach, and James could almost cry with relief.

Almost.

Even if the thought of sitting on his rear end for nine hours didn't sound appealing, it was a much better alternative to extending the trip by another day. He was more than ready to get to their final destination because getting to Crimson Beach meant two things: Eric could get rid of Dante, and James could get rid of Emilia.

The last few days, he had been playing the long game. It was obvious he couldn't kill Emilia before she helped them find her brother, so James endured the agony. Emilia had been nothing but a nuisance the entire trip—calling Jean, running off, asking too many questions, and trying to literally strangle him unconscious. Eric did a better job at handling her, but considering the circumstances, he wasn't sure if that was a good thing. But if it were up to *him*, he would've put a bullet in her head by now, even if all it did was put her to sleep.

He was well aware of how messed up it all was. His worry over the mission seemed to worsen with time, but he did his best to hide it. Ironically enough, Emilia served as a good distraction, but it didn't stop him from dreading the next inevitable phone call he'd receive from Michael soon enough.

On their way to California, Emilia chose to reveal a vital piece of information about her connections in Crimson Beach.

"Her name is Jaya. She might be able to help us find Dante... and maybe even give us a safe place to stay."

"Let me guess, she's a vampire," James drawled.

"Obviously."

"There's no chance in hell we're staying at a fucking vampire's house. Especially if she's anything like your brother," he argued.

"Jaya is nothing like Dante," Emilia protested. "Quite the opposite. In fact she hates him. So, you both have something in common with her."

"What makes you think she'll even let us in?" Eric asked.

"Well, for starters... The house she lives in now is the one I used to live in back in the day."

"Which is where exactly?"

"The Pacific Coast Highway."

James threw her an incredulous look over his shoulder. "You lived on the PCH?"

"Yeah," she said casually.

"I fucking hate you," he hissed, his voice oozing with envy.

She laughed at him, and he worked his jaw. When he glanced at Eric to share a look of annoyance, he found his twin smirking to himself. James frowned at that.

"I don't care who she is. We're not staying at her house," the lieutenant continued firmly. "There's a reason we do things a certain way around here. Or do you wanna risk The Colectiv getting on her ass too?"

The last thing he needed was another tangle on the web, another obstacle in his way.

Emilia groaned in annoyance, but James paid it no mind.

Eric spoke up then. "We *should* talk to her, though. We can't stay there, but if she knows where Dante is, it *could* be valuable to check it out."

James couldn't help but notice that he was uncharacteristically calm and reasonable, compared to his attitude of the last few days. Even if he had a valid point, he never agreed with Emilia so easily. James took note of it but said nothing, not in front of *her*. Instead, he chose to humor them both. After all, it would be foolish to disregard useful information that could benefit them in the long run.

"Fine," he conceded, sighing. "We'll pay Gina a visit."

"It's Jaya," Emilia corrected him.

"Jaya, whatever."

"Okay, but we can't have a repeat of the last interrogation. Keep the silver chains and knives to a zero."

The twins scoffed.

"No promises. Especially if she doesn't cooperate," James said.

"As if I'd let you," she spat. "Besides, Jaya is nothing like me. She won't give you a hard time if you don't give her a reason to."

"We'll see about that."

†††

He knew it was a problem, but if James didn't like someone for one reason or another, being in the same room with them was enough to make him angry. He's been like that for as long as he could remember, and it was why it was so hard for him to "play nice" with people. It seemed wrong and fake, so in the end, they always knew how he felt about them. Even now, it was better to lean into his hatred because it was like fuel for the road ahead.

James glanced over at Eric, who was reading a book in the passenger seat. Unlike James, his twin loved books, and it wouldn't surprise him if he had devoured The Colectiv's entire library. Growing up, it was normal to see him with a book in his hand, but on this day in particular, Eric's silence seemed louder than before. The twins partook in conversation and bantered more often than not for it to not mean something. He knew his brother, and he knew what holding something in looked like. And after their conversation in Texas, James couldn't help but feel concerned.

"You good, E?" he finally asked.

Eric looked up from his book, brow furrowed. "Yeah, why?"

James shrugged. "I don't know. Did you get any sleep last night? I thought I heard you come in late."

Eric's nightmares were another common occurrence that James grew up around. It wasn't rare for hunters to have them, especially those who lived through a nasty mission. James had a few of his own, but not to the extent that Eric did. It worried him because he knew there was very little he could do to help him. As much as he wanted, he couldn't fight something that wasn't real.

"Yeah...another shitty dream," he answered, looking out the window.

"Was it...*bad*?"

James took careful note of his brother's expressions. He knew that sometimes talking about his dreams helped, which was a step up from not talking about his feelings at all. Not that James did, either.

"They're always bad," Eric said.

But then, to James' dismay, he glanced at the rearview mirror, towards the backseat where Emilia slept.

James clenched his teeth and tore his eyes away.

"Ai visat la *ea*?" he uttered lowly.

Did you dream about her?

"No, yeah, I mean...kind of," Eric stammered before saying, "It was another one from Sorrento. Nothing new."

James worked his jaw seriously and muttered, "Yeah, we'll get him, E. Don't worry."

He faltered for a moment, remembering their short conversation in Amarillo. He glanced over his shoulder, making sure Emilia was asleep, and then he started speaking in Romanian once more.

"The other day..." He hesitated and could feel Eric watching him as he spoke, "I didn't mean to be a dick. I didn't mean it like that."

He truly hadn't. He was used to saying things like that, things that he perceived to be out of honesty. Eric wasn't exempt from it. He just didn't think it would affect him the way it did this time. It was a rare thing for James to feel like a genuine asshole, but at that moment, he did.

"I know."

James tightened his grip on the steering wheel. "I just worry about you, E."

His twin scoffed, "You and the entire fucking world."

"Not like *that*," he argued, giving his brother a serious look.

Eric worked his jaw and looked down at the book in his hands.

Everyone was "worried" about Eric because he was either "failing" at something trivial or not doing what he was supposed to. James, however, worried about his well-being. *They* didn't see the mental toll everything took on him, even if Eric himself denied it.

"I just don't want you to get yourself killed," James told him.

"I'm fine," Eric stressed. "I'm doing the best I can. I *do* the best I can, but even then, it's a cause for fucking concern."

"I'm not talking about you or whether you're good enough, E. I'm talking about..." He cast another glance at a slumbering Emilia, and then he said, "I'm talking about her."

His brother gave him a sharp look. "What? What are you talking about?"

James went over everything in his head. He had been able to hate Emilia and disconnect himself from the relationship she had with his brother because he wasn't there when it happened. For a long time, he thought it was stupid, a fling, but now, seeing them interact with each other in front of him, things seemed a little more real. It was undeniable. Even through the hatred, he could see the familiarity and the chemistry. Time did nothing to get rid of that.

He almost didn't want to say it out loud, but considering what had to be done, perhaps he needed to get it out in the open to deal with it.

"E..." He said lowly, still in Romanian, "You don't still have...*feelings* for her, do you?"

"What? No!"

"Are you sure?"

"Yeah, Jimmy, I think I'm fucking positive."

"I don't know," James sang, unconvinced.

Eric let out a long, angry sigh. "You know what? How's *this* for concerning? You're starting to remind me of Mike, and that's the last thing I need right now. Fuck off."

He returned to his book with cold finality, and James cursed under his breath.

For the second time, he felt like a genuine asshole. This wasn't what he wanted. He didn't want to push his brother, but what was he to do if Eric was lying? If his fears were true, what then? It wasn't just James' promotion at risk, Michael made that abundantly clear. There was dread in the pit of his stomach that he couldn't ignore. It reminded him too much of something that he was terrified was going to happen again.

†††

Italy—3 years ago

That night, he went on a hunting trip in Italy with a small group. They had just finished their mission and while most of them had gone out for drinks, James was alone in his hotel room. He took the time to call his brother and pitched the idea of visiting him since he was also in the country for school.

"Oh, shit! No, yeah, come over!" Eric said excitedly.

James smiled. "Maybe you can introduce me to your girl."

Eric had only been blabbering about her since the day they met. It was only fair that James got to see her in person, especially since he was wary about the whole relationship. He merely wanted to scope things out and see for himself who this Emilia girl truly was. Eric may have been in love, but he was a daywalker, and that complicated things.

He sounded hesitant on the other line. "Yeah...yeah...we'll see."

James frowned. "Did you guys break up or something?"

"No, no. It's just… Her brother's in town, so it's a little weird right now."

"Oh, is he a dick?"

"Yeah, a bit of dick, yeah."

"Do you want me to kill him?" James offered with a smirk.

Eric snorted. "No, *don't*. It's fine. It can just be you and me."

"Fine. I'll leave first thing in the morning and let you know when I get there."

They ended the call, and James put his phone on the nightstand, not thinking much else of the situation, and then, suddenly, there were light, rapid footsteps followed by a knock. There was mixed whispering and rapid heartbeats. With a tired sigh, James went to the door, already dreading who was on the other side. As he expected, standing in the hallway was a smiling, 14-year-old girl with brown skin and curly hair in two puffs at the sides of her head. Her name was Sasha Şimşek, a new recruit with the hunting party. In her hands was a white box with a sweet scent emanating from within.

Despite James' protests, Michael assigned a few trainees to his group whenever he saw fit. The ones that were allowed, that is, as most of the parents didn't want their kids anywhere near him. James saw it as grunt work, but Michael argued that he did it because the kids liked learning from him. The reason was a mystery to James, but Eric concluded they probably found him funny and liked his directness.

"What do you want?" James muttered.

"Can you eat real people's food?" she asked in a thick accent.

He narrowed his eyes and said, "Yeah, I can eat real food."

Sasha's face lit up. "I knew it! We bought cannolis. Do you want some?"

James ran his tongue over his teeth as he tried to hide his genuine surprise and eagerness for a pastry—his one, true guilty pleasure.

"Suuure."

The girl opened the box to reveal half a dozen tube-shaped pastries with white cream inside. James deftly grabbed one for himself. Sasha then closed the box and smiled up at him.

"Do you not get lonely being here by yourself?"

"Okay, you can go now," James said as he started closing the door.

She protested, but before he could fully shut it, James was hit with a sudden wave of unease. His heartbeat quickened for seemingly no reason, and he froze in place.

What the fuck was that?

"Eşti bine?" Sasha asked. *Are you okay?*

"Yeah, yeah..." He said slowly.

However, a few seconds later, a sharp pain shot through his left shoulder. His hand flew to it, and he dropped the pastry on the floor. He gasped and stumbled back as the sharpness was followed by a burning sensation.

"Oh, what the fuck?"

"Sergeant MacNamara?"

Sasha carefully put the box on the ground and ran to his side. James pulled down the collar of his shirt to look for some kind of wound or injury, but what he found was nothing but a patch of inflamed skin at the curve of his neck. The recruit's green eyes were wide with fear.

"Should I call for help, or...?"

He shook his head. "I don't know..."

James couldn't even find a sarcastic retort or something humorous to say. He was too busy reeling, and he instantly thought the worst.

Eric.

†††

Somewhere in the Southwestern U.S.—Present

James' eyes fluttered open as he abruptly woke up to reality. He sat up groggily, casting a quick look around. Eric was at the wheel, and Emilia was still asleep. They were about seven hours into the drive, and the sun was starting to dip low on the horizon. He was bewildered and not entirely present as he still processed the dream he just had. It was distorted bits and pieces from that night in Italy, and he felt sick to his stomach all over again. Even as he started to wake up, the real memory was always there.

"Rise and shine," Eric sang, completely unaware of his turmoil.

"How long was I out?" James mumbled.

"Three hours. I don't know how you get comfortable enough."

"I'm used to it, I guess."

The semi-nomadic life of a hunter was something his mind and body adapted to a long time ago. Or maybe it was before then...

He eyed his twin. "How about you let me drive? You could use some sleep after last night."

"It's fine. I'm not that tired."

The exhaustion in his eyes told James otherwise.

"Bullshit. Pull over. I'm driving. We still have—" he checked the time, "At least three hours left. I'm not letting you do that."

"These seats are uncomfortable. It's not like I'm gonna get any rest anyway," Eric argued.

"You can sleep back here."

The sudden sound of Emilia's voice made James nearly jump out of his skin. "Jesus Christ," he hissed.

They glanced back at her. She was rubbing the sleep out of her eyes.

"Back there, with you?" Eric scoffed. "No, thanks."

"Not *with* me. We can switch seats. James can drive. I'll take the passenger seat, and you can spread yourself out back here. It's a lot better than up there."

James grimaced. "I don't know how I feel about you being up here."

"What? You're afraid I'll get back at you for stabbing me?" she teased.

"I wouldn't put it past you."

She leaned across the console and James pulled away from her in disdain. But her focus was on Eric, and she spoke uncharacteristically kind.

"I'm just saying, if you need to sleep before Crimson Beach, it's not a bad idea." She then turned to James, switching her tone to something hostile as she said, "And if it makes *you* feel any better, you can keep a better eye on me from up there anyway."

James was loath to say that he agreed with her.

Why is she being so nice all of a sudden?

Eric sighed, "Fine."

He pulled off at the side of the road, and despite his irritation, James didn't complain.

†††

Italy—3 years ago

James didn't spiral often, but that night, he had the closest thing to a breakdown in his life. He must have called Eric about 20

317

times, and all of them went to voicemail. Even his texts went unanswered, which sent him into a full-blown panic. His brother seldom missed his calls, and when he did, he always called back or let him know that he was busy. So, for there to be radio silence after what just happened...

James didn't believe in things unless he saw them with his own two eyes, but if there was anything he did believe in, it was the connection he and Eric shared. "Twin telepathy," people called it. It could be as simple as saying the same thing at the same time or being able to detect each other's feelings. And when they were children, sometimes they would feel when the other got physically hurt. It didn't happen as often anymore, but when it did, it meant something serious.

From a young age, Michael always warned the twins about people who could kill them if they had the chance. Vampires were at the top of the list, but for a long time, James didn't worry about it. He was a trained killer, after all, and he could handle himself just fine. Eric, on the other hand, was living like a civilian, and James feared the day when he would become a target.

After his episode, he gathered his things with haste and told Sasha to inform the rest of the team that he was going to Sorrento to find his brother. And it was right as he got in the car that he received the call.

His phone vibrated in his hand and his heart quickened with hope. As clear as day, it was Eric's face and name on the caller ID. James answered it with lightning speed, but to his sheer disappointment, it *wasn't* his brother on the other line.

"E? Where the fuck have you been, you asshole? I've been calling you—"

"James?" a woman answered instead.

He stopped dead in his tracks, taken aback by the sound of a stranger's voice. Any relief in him was briskly wiped away and replaced by harsh overprotectiveness.

"Who the fuck is this? How do you know my name? Why the fuck do you have my brother's phone?"

"Eric told me who you were. We go to school together. I—" She was crying and fighting to keep her words together. "I didn't know what else to do. He's—something happened to him."

James' panic came rushing back like a tidal wave. "What? What happened?" he demanded.

The woman rambled despite her shaking voice, "I don't know. He got badly hurt, and he was bleeding everywhere, and it wouldn't stop, and he wasn't responding. I took him to the hospital, but I do—I don't know."

She held back a sob. James couldn't believe his ears. Surely she was exaggerating. Surely, Eric would be fine. He was always fine.

"How? W... Are you sure?" he asked, enunciating every word.

"Of course, I'm sure! I...found him on the street, and he wasn't waking up. He's in the ICU at Sorrento Hospital. You better get here quick." She got the words out fast before hanging up the phone.

"Wait—"

James cursed and then tried calling the number back, but was met with an automated message telling him that the number was unavailable. In an act of desperation, he called the one person who could possibly help:

Michael.

†††

Somewhere in the Southwestern U.S.—Present

No more than 30 minutes passed since they switched seats, and Eric was already fast asleep in the back of the car. James would've been grateful if he wasn't also irked by it.

Emilia peeked over her shoulder, a small smile grazing her lips.

"I told you," she whispered, straightening her back.

"Yeah, yeah," he muttered.

Up until this point, she had been scribbling away at a notebook, with few words exchanged between them. Of course, he was a fool to think it would last very long.

"You're unusually placid," she remarked.

"That's because I don't like talking to you."

"Why not?"

"You're annoying."

Emilia scoffed, "I don't think we've had a long enough conversation for you to truly say that."

"Eh, I've heard enough."

"I could say the same about you."

"A lot of people don't like me, and, to be honest, I really don't care."

The vampire responded with a noise of uncertainty but didn't say anything else.

He had done a good job at keeping a distance from Emilia, and with his brother around, it was easy. But James got bored easily, and with Eric asleep, he felt like he might go insane the more the silence and the road seemed to stretch. He didn't like Emilia, and he most definitely did not want to talk to her, but he didn't see any other option.

"What are you doing over there anyway?" he rumbled, eyeing the notebook in her hands.

"Journaling, obviously."

He snorted. "Like a diary?"

"Yeah, like a diary," she said defensively. "You should try it sometime. Maybe it'll help you work through all that rage."

"Oh, like it helps you? I don't need to work through shit. I'm perfectly fine."

"That's funny."

"You don't know anything."

"I know a little."

James scowled. "Like what?"

Emilia looked up from her journal and said, "Like, you and Eric are daywalkers. You were born on February 13th, 1997, which makes you Aquarius's. You became hunters after a man named Michael adopted you into The Colectiv when your mother died. Your mom was a hunter too. You never met your dad. Amongst other things." When she saw his stunned expression, she grinned. "What? You think because I talk, I don't know how to listen?"

He brushed it off and said, "It's still the bare minimum."

"Enlighten me then."

"No, thanks. I don't need you to know my secrets."

"I shared mine. It only seems fair."

He shot her a deadly glare. "You can play that game with my brother, but not with me. You might as well be talking to a brick wall."

Emilia groaned and whispered something along the lines of, "...all the same."

"What did you say?" he demanded.

"I guess I'm just wondering what your deal is. I mean, I know Eric's deal, but not yours. Are all hunters emotionally constipated, or...?"

"No, we're just trained to keep our mouths shut around vampires."

"'Trained'? Like a dog?" she teased.

A muscle jumped in his cheek. "No," he growled.

"Okay then, do you have hobbies? A favorite color?"

James sputtered, "What? You're trying to make small talk? Good fucking luck."

Emilia kept going despite his protests, "Favorite movie? Are you dating anyone? AlthoughIfindthathardtobelieve."

"Stop."

"What's your moon sign? What do your tattoos mean? What—"

Unfortunately, the hunter's patience was already paper thin, and it was only a matter of time before he snapped.

"Oh my god, shut up!"

Emilia closed her mouth but had an evil smirk on her face. They both checked to make sure they hadn't woken up Eric and to James' relief, they hadn't. He looked forward once more and sighed, trying to contain his anger.

Trying.

"I'm just gonna keep asking questions until you answer one," she said. "I might look 22, but I am 70 years old, which means my ability to give a fuck left a long time ago."

James ran a hand over his face and groaned. He had half a mind to knock her out or maybe kill her to get it over with. Of course, he knew he couldn't, because he was pretty sure that Eric wouldn't be too pleased to find her dead when he woke up. It would also defeat the point of bringing her along at all. So, for his sanity, he chose to humor her with the bare minimum, nothing more.

"Okay. Fine," he seethed. "You get three. Three questions and that's it."

When he glanced at her, Emilia's eyes lit up. He didn't like how excited it made her to know things about him.

"Okay... What's a hobby you enjoy doing...*that has nothing to do with hunting*?"

"Drums."

She huffed, "Drums?"

"Yeah, drums."

In fact, he had a drum set in his room back at the estate. Being a metalhead, he had wanted one for as long as he could remember and bought it with his own money when he was 15. He used it to let off steam, but nowadays, it goes unused more often than not.

"What an elaborate answer," she derided. "You and Eric both have an eclipse tattoo. What does it mean?"

"It's our daywalker symbol. The sun and moon, night and day, vampire and human, all together. E came up with it."

"Hmmm, interesting... *Are* you dating anyone?"

He had been hoping that she would skip over that question altogether.

"No... I am not dating anyone," he replied curtly.

"Can't say I'm surprised. Is there a reason?"

He groaned in the back of his throat. "Because," he bit out, "relationships fucking suck and, you know, I have a 'charming' personality."

Between the chaos of his parent's relationship, Eric and Emilia's dumpster fire, and the fact that Michael was a divorced man, it was enough to put James off of romance entirely. In his mind, relationships ended in flames, and he didn't think it was possible for someone like him anyway. Not only was he a workaholic, but he was a bit much for most people. Being a hopeless romantic was always up Eric's alley to begin with.

"Maybe if you acted like you cared. It's pretty obvious that people throw themselves at you all the time," Emilia muttered.

"Ah, are you talking about the waitress?" he teased with a smirk. *The one that flirted with E?*

He had seen that murderous look before, and her reaction wasn't subtle either. James would've found it funny if she hadn't roped *him* into it. He knew the waitress was being overly friendly, but he didn't pay it any mind.

"I'm talking about how you didn't seem to care. Like at all," she said, veering around the subject.

"Because I don't. Shit like that makes me uncomfortable."[61]

Emilia seemed surprised by his answer. "Is it because you aren't attracted to women, or is there another reason?"

There was hesitance to the question. It was clear she was trying to be open and careful about it, which James found amusing.

"Oh, trust me, it's not that," he snickered. "I am very attracted to women. I wouldn't say I'm straight, but it's a bit more...*complicated* for me." He was uncomfortable just thinking about it.

Still trying to be respectful, Emilia struggled with her next words, "Are you...do you..."

"I'm on the ace spectrum. I think E said the proper term is demisexual," he explained, putting her out of her misery.

"Oh, okay! I was gonna ask, but I wasn't sure if you were gonna kill me."

James figured it out in his early twenties when Eric was in college. Though he had a few crushes growing up, it felt different from how others experienced them. For Eric, it was instantaneous and visceral, but for James, it was almost the opposite. Where his brother liked sleeping around, James never found himself feeling very "horny" over anybody. People *did* throw themselves at him, expecting physical

---

[61] Cat Girls Are Ruining My Life! - CORPSE

intimacy, and while he'd indulge now and then, the spark fizzled out. He had to get to know someone and connect with their personality first, but how could he do that if he hated most people to begin with? How could he ever be sure?

All of a sudden, Emilia asked, "So, you've never done it before?"

That question could have gotten her killed.

"Hey, I'm ace, not a fucking virgin, alright?" he snapped. "But I'm not gonna sit here and talk to you about my sex life, because quite frankly, I'd rather kill myself."

"Okayyy! I'm sorry! I don't want to talk about it, either. I was just curious."

"Yeah, well, let that curiosity die. You've exceeded your limit."

Emilia clicked her tongue in annoyance, and they fell quiet once more. She was smart enough not to push him, and fortunately, he didn't share anything he was trying to hide.

†††

Sorrento, Italy—3 years ago

[62]When James arrived at the ER, they told him his brother had been in surgery for an *hour*.

Eric never had surgery before. He's never needed it. By then, he should have healed, but if he had healed, then the hospital would be crawling with scientists and the military. However, Michael arrived in record time and quickly intervened with a board-certified surgeon who worked closely with The Colectiv itself.

---

[62] The Day The World Went Away - Nine Inch Nails

They took over the operating room and made the hospital a place for them to do their work. The commander reassured James that they were doing everything they could, but it didn't help with his growing anxiety. Nothing like this had ever happened to either of them before, and James abhorred hospitals as is. They reminded him of when his mother was sick, and that fact alone terrified him more.

I can't lose you too.

After yet another hour, James sat in one of the waiting areas outside the ICU with his face in his hands. He was on the verge of tears. The anticipation was killing him.

He should've healed by now, repeated in his head.

You can't die. You're not supposed to die. You're not allowed *to die.*

Suddenly, the double doors leading into the ICU banged open. James' head snapped right up and he bolted out of his seat as Michael walked in.

"What happened?" he blurted out.

The commander held out a calming hand. "E's fine. He's out of surgery and stable. They put him in a private room."

James let out a huge breath of relief. "And? What the fuck happened?"

"And..." Michael shook his head grimly. "The wound didn't heal properly, Jimmy."

"What do you mean?"

"I mean, the entire time he was in there, his healing never kicked in. Not fully anyway."

The daywalker shook his head in disbelief, asking, "W-what? How? Why? Did they say what happened?"

"No, but from the looks of it? It looked like something—or some*one*—tried taking a big chunk out of him."

"What do you mean?"

"I mean... I'm pretty sure a vampire attacked your brother."

[63]James stared at Eric's unconscious form with a blank expression as he stood beside his hospital bed. His brother was in a hospital gown, his left side was bandaged up, pale, and bruised. James had never seen him in such a state.

He looks so human.

It was all overwhelming. The sound of the monitors, the dripping of the IV, and the fluorescent lights—it all brought him back to a time he tried so hard to repress when he was just an eleven-year-old boy who didn't want to lose his mom.

Eric's breathing was even, his vitals were good, and he was stable, but James knew he wouldn't know peace until he woke up.

Then, finally...

His twin sighed and started fidgeting. James perked up, and his pulse quickened when Eric's eyes fluttered open for a moment.

"E?"

His twin blinked a few times, his eyes looking a little hazy. It took him a while before he was wide awake, but his eyes caught on to James almost immediately.

"Jimmy?" His voice came out hoarse.

"Hey," James whispered.

"What are you doing here? Where am I?"

Eric furrowed his brow and started taking in his surroundings. The more aware he was, the more confused he got, and the more confused he got, the more agitated he became. The monitors started going off as his heart rate spiked. He tried sitting up but hissed in pain. James had to gently push him back against the pillows.

---

[63] The 30th - Billie Eilish

"Yo, easy, you're gonna hurt yourself. You're in the hospital."

"The hospital?"

"Yeah. You were in surgery for two hours."

"*Two hours*?" Eric exclaimed.

James nodded, his lips pursed. His brother looked around frantically for a moment as if searching for something. When he looked back at James, his eyes were wide.

"Where is he?"

"Who? Michael?"

"No. Dante."

James shook his head. "Dante? Who's Dante? There's no 'Dante' here."

"What about Emilia? Where's Emilia?"

"She's not here," James said with a frown. "Do you want me to call her, or...?"

"No!" Eric snapped, surprising him. There was an intense fury in his eyes that James didn't expect.

Trying to take some control of the situation, he put a reassuring hand on Eric's uninjured shoulder and gave him a serious look.

"E, you need to breathe. You almost died. If you can remember anything, I need you to tell me what the hell happened."

His brother got quiet and his eyes dimmed with hollow pain. It was clear he was remembering something James couldn't see— something horrible.

"Jimmy...there's something I didn't tell you about Emilia," he whispered, his voice shaking.

James frowned. "Oh God. What?"

His brother curled his hand into a fist and looked down at the sheets in shame.

"She's a vampire."

"What?" James blurted out in disbelief. "She—she's a vampire? *She* did this to you?"

Eric shook his head. "No, no, it wasn't her. It was her brother, Dante, but...she just *stood there*. She watched him do it."

James MacNamara could have set the entire world on fire with the sudden wrath coursing through his body. The very girl that Eric had been enamored with had been a monster the entire time, and her brother nearly took his life. Eric almost *died* because of them, and James was out for blood.

With his jaw set, he took a step back, aiming for the door. "I'm telling Mike. He needs to hear this, so we can catch them before—"

"Wait, no, Jimmy, stop!"

Eric grabbed his wrist to detain him, and James looked back at him in bewilderment. His twin winced in pain as he tried sitting up, and James tried pushing him back against the pillows again.

"Easy. What? What is it?"

"I knew."

The sergeant blinked a few times in disbelief. "What?"

"I knew the whole time," Eric reiterated more firmly, yet completely broken. He was fighting back tears and guilt. "I knew Emilia was a vampire, and I didn't do anything about it."

James' face fell, and a chill ran down his spine.

Of course, he would have known. Of course.

"Why?" he whispered sharply.

Eric lifted his shoulders in a weak shrug. "I thought she was different."

James stared at his brother in astonishment as he processed a rollercoaster of conflicting emotions he'd never felt before. The twins never kept anything from each other, so to learn about such a monumental secret was world-shattering. Considering the laws of The

Colectiv and their shared history, this could mean life or death. It *did* mean life or death. Their childhood and every horror story revolving around their lives were proof of that. Their parents' affair and their birth had been drilled into their heads as a cautionary tale to never repeat, and yet here Eric was, playing with fire and getting burned.

"Why didn't you tell me?"

"Because I didn't want to put you in danger, and I thought I could handle it on my own."

James scoffed. He turned away from his twin, stepping away to run his fingers through his hair. Eric hadn't been a member of The Colectiv for years, but who knew what they would've done if they found out he was in a relationship with a vampire? To not have known was one thing, but *this* was inexcusable.

His mind ran a million miles a minute, already thinking of the best plan of action.

"Jimmy—" Eric began.

James whirled around and pointed a stern finger at him, saying, "We're gonna fix this. I don't care what we have to do. We're gonna fix this, okay?"

Eric's eyes flashed with surprise, but he nodded in agreement. "Yeah. Yeah, okay."

"Let me handle it."

And handle it, he did.

†††

Somewhere in the Southwestern U.S.—Present

The memory of what happened plagued James even now and after the dream he had, it was at the forefront of his mind.

"You know, we figured it was you that called me back then," he said, speaking mindlessly. "You knew my name, you knew to call me, you found him at the scene, and then you just...disappeared. I was so caught up in everything...but you have no idea how many times I thought about tracking you down and killing you and your brother myself, while E was still in that hospital bed."

Maybe I should have. Then we wouldn't be in this mess.

Emilia gave no response, and when he glanced at her sidelong, she was surveying him like a wild animal, waiting for an attack.

"You're a 70-year-old pureblood on The Colectiv's shit list. Why the fuck did you risk it by taking him to the hospital? Why did you risk it by calling me?" he demanded.

From his personal experience, the vampires he hunted were malicious, sly, and cunning, because once they were in the sights of The Colectiv, they were willing to do anything to get out of them. Emilia seemed to be that way, at least at first.

"I don't know what bullshit they feed you at that institution, but we're not all evil, you know," she argued.

"Are you talking about yourself or your brother?"

"I don't speak for Dante anymore," she spat.

"You didn't answer my question," he growled. "*Why* did you do it?"

Emilia cast a brief look at Eric and shrugged. "I couldn't let him die."

There was sincerity and a deep longing in her eyes. James didn't want to believe it.

"That simple, huh? Really?"

She scoffed, "Is it? 'Simple'? When you put your life on the line for your brother, is it simple? Or does it just go beyond reason, and you act purely on instinct?"

James squeezed the steering wheel, holding back just enough so it wouldn't break.

He wouldn't say it, but he knew, deep within his soul, precisely what she meant. It was that same instinct he had since he was a child. It was the one he acted on when he chose to help Eric three years ago, and it was the same one that had him in the situation he was in now. It *was* beyond all reason and not simple at all. He, out of everyone, should know that. "Simple" and "reasonable" weren't in his vocabulary for a long time.

Yet, for some reason, he was at war with himself again. He was faced with a truth that he couldn't wrap his head around. No, he *didn't* want to wrap his head around it because it would be like opening Pandora's box. He *shouldn't*.

"You really cared about him, didn't you?" he asked in surprise.

"Is that really so hard to believe?"

"I don't know. After what happened, you can't really blame me."

"Well, I did," she told him stiffly.

"Do you still care about him now?"

When she didn't answer, he looked over at her again. She averted her gaze and focused on the evening sky. He took her silence as a response, and it threatened to tear something within him.

What the fuck is it about love that makes people do the stupidest shit? How is it possibly worth the consequences? Why do you keep doing this to yourselves?

"You know you put his life in danger, right? And I don't mean that to be a dick. I mean that in the context of what we do and what *you* are."

"I know," she whispered.

"I made a promise a long time ago to do whatever it takes to protect E from danger. No matter what," he explained in a harsh tone, "and that includes you. And I don't know what other secrets you have up your sleeve, and I'm not going to pretend to know anything about your relationship with my brother, but if you really do care about him... I hope you can find it in your dead heart not to fuck him over again, because if you do... I'll take you out. Are we clear?"

He delivered his threat as fervently as he could, just above a whisper. When he was done talking, he looked the vampire dead in the eye. Emilia matched his intensity.

"Crystal," she replied.

There was more certainty in that threat, knowing it came from himself and not from someone else.

30

Fallen Angel

Eric

Call it defiance. Call it recklessness. Call it stupidity. Whatever it was, Eric knew what he had done when he chose to pursue a relationship with Emilia three years ago. [64] [65]

At that point, he had been away from The Colectiv for four years and was months away from getting his bachelor's degree in anthropology. With no more violent obligations, no more training, and no more punishments, he was living the "normal" life that he always wanted. His main focus was learning, getting his work done, and, above all else, having fun during his final year before graduate school. According to his counselor, he was a shoo-in for some of the best schools in the country due to his exemplary work and his cultural background (not including the vampire stuff). He had managed to

---

[64] Girl - Jim Sturgess
[65] Crazy - 2WEI

make a few friends and spent his days doing what he wanted without any expectations but his own. Sure, he was a workaholic, but it was on his terms. And nobody knew him as "Walker" or "Eric MacNamara," but as Eric or Eric Leone.

Of course, navigating life as a daywalker and an ex-hunter wasn't as easy as he thought it would be. Eric was lucky that he could go out in the daylight and that most regular foods didn't make him sick. In some cases, he simply made the excuse that he wasn't hungry, though it seemed to worry those around him since it often seemed like he never ate anything at all (little did they know that his brother smuggled blood bags into his dorm on his visits). However, none of that ever compared to the heavy psychological toll that The Colectiv left on him.

Eric became swiftly aware of the fact that his brain was wired differently, not just due to his biology, but his upbringing. Paranoia and hypervigilance weren't easy to turn off at will, not when they helped him survive for years. Loneliness, depression, anxiety, and nightmares plagued him, and since his past was so strange and convoluted, Eric realized that no living therapist would ever be qualified enough to help him. So, like many American college students, he resorted to distracting himself, whether it was by burying himself in his studies, drinking, smoking, having sex, or taking advantage of the fact that he couldn't die. He even discovered the bounds of his sexuality, letting his desires lead him to wherever or whoever he pleased.

If he ever needed a shoulder to lean on, James was always a call or a text away and didn't hesitate to pester him. His twin even requested more hunts in the States so he could visit Eric at school, and to his surprise, Michael granted it. And those days were some of Eric's favorite memories of that time—just him and his brother causing trouble in California. Not once did he exchange a word with the commander himself, even if the young daywalker often wondered if he may have been right.

Even if Eric had friends, there was a compulsive need to lie to protect himself. He lied about everything, whether directly or by omission—everything from his name to where he was from, who he was, or even his childhood. One wrong thing, one slip up, and it could mean unraveling his monstrous existence, and it created an invisible wall that separated him from everyone else. They may not have been aware of it, but he was. And he couldn't stop it. Not until Emilia came into the picture.

They met by pure fate while they were both in the same coastal town in Italy. Eric had been out at a club, having a drink at the bar with his other traveling friends, when he spotted her on the dance floor. Her beauty instantly captivated him.

Emilia looked young but striking in her looks, from her sleek black hair to her red dress, sharp makeup, and long, manicured nails. She was small but terrifying, and the way she moved mesmerized him. She reminded him of a siren or some kind of dark fey from a fantasy novel...and he liked it. He even found himself blushing when she looked his way, but he couldn't help but notice that there was something *strange* about her. Despite how lively and human she was, there was silence. In a room of heavy music and beating hearts, he could have sworn she had none. And he knew better than anyone else that there was only one thing in this world that could walk around without a pulse.

The first emotion that went through Eric was fear, but with an eerie quickness, that feeling morphed into intrigue. He debated talking to her, whether it was to confront her or not, he couldn't say, but in the end, she made the decision for him. He had turned away for a brief second and was commenting to his friend when he sensed her approach. There it was—the lack of a beating heart—and yet, when he turned around to look at her, any confrontational words died on his lips.

By all accounts, Eric should have fled from the situation. Doing otherwise went against everything he was taught and witnessed firsthand. He had killed a few vampires himself, and many of them had been terrifying and murderous beings who said and did the vilest things. However, at the time, Emilia struck him as none of that.

So he let her talk.

To Eric's dismay, Emilia was bright-faced, playful, and witty. She led the conversation at first and somehow showed genuine interest in his studies. And Eric didn't know what came over him, but he couldn't stop talking to her. Words tumbled out of his mouth like never before and the banter came effortlessly, especially as the night progressed. They ended up leaving the bar and walking down to the beach, where they talked some more, and the more they did, the more he saw something beneath the surface that drew him in further. She was like a precious gem—a diamond in the rough that he wanted to dig out. He never wanted the night to end.

It was then that he made a decision. He wasn't a hunter anymore, and he swore to never go back to The Colectiv. In fact, he hadn't abided by their laws for a long time, so why should he consider them now? After all, he liked this girl, and who knew how far it would actually go anyway? It didn't have to go anywhere at all. And some twisted part of Eric's brain that was fueled by rage and rebellion made him want to do it just to spite everything he ever knew.

One night wouldn't hurt, would it?

But then one night turned to two, three, four, and more... because if there was one thing that Eric MacNamara underestimated in all of this, it was his heart. He didn't expect to get so attached to Emilia the way he did. Even though he'd been in relationships of varying degrees, they fizzled out or didn't always end well, but even then, they didn't feel like *this*. He convinced himself that it would be a one-time thing, a dirty little secret, but the mere thought of Emilia became almost impossible for him to ignore, and the very next day, Eric went out looking for her again.

At first, Emilia urged him to stay away. She very clearly told him that he didn't know what he was getting himself into and that he should find himself a "nice girl" instead. However, with sheer stubbornness and naivety, Eric urged her to let him find out for himself. If Emilia had given him another hard "no" and made it clear that she didn't want him around, he would have left her alone without hesitation, but to his surprise, she didn't. Instead, she smiled and gave him her number, as well as when to meet her again. And Eric went back to Emilia evening after evening for almost his entire stay, and what started as infatuation turned into something more than he bargained for.

Knowing that she was a vampire, Eric's need for secrecy increased twofold. There was the inherent fear of being a daywalker, an abomination and being rejected for what he was, and then there was the fear of her finding out about his ties to The Colectiv. Primarily, the latter. After all, there was no one who vampires hated more than hunters, and as Eric's feelings for Emilia grew, there was nothing less that he wanted than for Emilia to be someone else who hated him.

[66]Like with all of his friends and past partners, Eric kept up the facade. He always told half-truths, like that he grew up in Queens, New York, and was raised by his uncle Michael after his mother passed away. He talked about his twin brother James, who had tattoos and liked to box and play the drums. The few truths he ever told were about school, his friends, and his interests. It made him feel horrible, but Emilia's secrecy was no better.

---

[66] The Liars Club - Coheed and Cambria

Emilia's vagueness about her own life brought Eric an equal amount of solace and deep-rooted frustration. Never had he wanted to know someone more and had them give him so little to work with. The few things she did tell him about herself, he remembered vividly, like her interest in movies, music, books, or museums, many of which they shared. He knew where she came from and her brother's name and had been told a vague story about her toxic parents being out of the picture.

It was all surface level, and neither of them came to know anything deep beneath the surface, but in the empty spaces, there was never any judgment. Perhaps they recognized something within each other that they knew was too fragile to touch, but they could read between the lines enough to never overstep. Perhaps, in a way, it was to a fault, but Emilia made Eric feel more alive than any book or blade ever could. She appealed to a certain part of him that he wasn't allowed to feel or express while under the commander's care and scrutiny. It was something he hadn't experienced since he was a child when his mother was alive and his father was a hero. It was unapologetic. It was simple yet impulsive, like a breath of fresh air after suffocating for nearly 22 years of his life. It was fire and passion. Even if it was brief, even if it was all a lie, it was enough to make him throw away every inhibition and keep lying to preserve it.

When Dante came along, it was the beginning of the end.

Emilia never gave too many details about her brother, and with hindsight, Eric understood why. The few things he knew about him were that he was older, only attracted to men, and was very overprotective. Years later, he knew what she had meant was that he was *possessive* and *controlling*.

At the time, Dante was supposed to be in Spain "doing business" when he spontaneously decided to pay his sister a visit. Not even Emilia expected it, which was pretty clear from her expression when he pulled up beside them in a fancy car as they walked down the street. Not knowing who he was, Eric became protective, but after reassurances and an explanation from Emilia, he dropped his guard a bit.

Up close, the resemblance was uncanny. Dante had the same straight black hair, facial structure, and sharp eyes as Emilia, but was masculine, and he was taller and tattooed. He wore a ruby-encrusted rosary, which was a larger version of the one that Emilia often wore around her neck. And just like his sister, Dante had no beating heart.

He introduced himself with a charismatic smile, but Eric caught the deviousness in his eyes and the hunter-like instincts that he thought he left behind seemed to come back in full swing. The daywalker had been soft and sweet with Emilia, but with Dante, it was as if his body knew there was a threat present. It was eerie how natural and immediate it happened. Hypermasculinity could've been to blame, but Emilia's change of demeanor in the face of her brother told Eric that something wasn't right.

She clammed up and was all at once on edge. Eric played it off and managed to hold his own until Emilia whisked him away. When he tried asking her about it, she waved him off and said it was "complicated." Eric liked to think he would've let it go if Dante hadn't made it impossible to do so.

From the moment they met, Emilia's brother made it his mission to weasel his way into their relationship. He'd conveniently appear at the places they'd be and interrogate Eric about his life, or even try to flirt with him as if to anger his sister. After years of no practice, Eric's training came in handy, but even when Emilia did her best to fend him off, it did nothing to keep the alarm bells from ringing in the boy's head. It was clear that Dante was bad news, and he wasn't going to stop until he got what he wanted. It pushed Eric to the edge.

With Dante in the mix, the situation with Emilia was starting to head into a downward spiral that Eric didn't like. The lies were making him sick and exhausted, and he knew that he had to confront Emilia before it was too late. He couldn't do it anymore.

So, *that night*, Eric went to Emilia's place to talk. In his mind, he was hoping—and damn near praying—that things would work out and that they could somehow start over. He thought that Emilia would understand. He *wanted* her to understand. And when he arrived, things seemed to be pointing in a hopeful direction. She made him coffee, and they talked like normal. He didn't want to ruin things by being his usual blabbering self, so he took things slow.

Before he could get the words out, his brother called him, and instead of telling him he was busy, he chose to go downstairs and take the call. The conversation was animated as usual, and Eric made sure to keep his voice down. James told him about a job he did and how he wanted to visit him since he was in town. Eric agreed to the idea but then told him he was busy and had to go. It wasn't until he hung up that a presence made itself known in the kitchen. [67]

He whirled around and called out to the shadows. "Who's there?"

The scent of a familiar cologne hit his nostrils, mixed with the smell of roses and cigarette smoke. Eric's heart sank just as a growl emanated from an emerging figure in the darkness. His irises glowed a pale blue.

Dante—the last person Eric wanted to see on this particular night. If he had known he'd take great lengths to lurk, he would've brought a weapon.

I'm such a fucking idiot.

It took no time for Eric to realize that he must have caught *every word* of his conversation with James because the vampire looked feral.

"A hunter?" Dante hissed. "I knew there was something off about you."

------

[67] The Prowler - Daniel Pemberton

Suddenly, Eric felt 11 years old again, and he was standing in the middle of the forest with a vampire before him. Except, this time, the vampire wasn't chained or gagged, and Michael wasn't around to finish the job. His veins went cold, and he raised his hands defensively, wishing that he had a gun or a sword right about then, but he left them all behind in Romania.

Eric tried reassuring him, but his words fell on deaf ears.

"Hey, listen, I'm not here to hurt anyone."

"I don't give a *fuck* what you have to say. I'm gonna make you pay for touching my sister, you piece of shit!"

Dante lunged at Eric and the daywalker dodged out of his way. From upstairs, Emilia shouted. Eric grabbed the nearest breakfast chair and hit Dante over the head with it, the wood breaking on impact. The vampire recovered and started striking and swiping at Eric with his hands and brute strength. The boy did his best to fight him, but Dante overpowered him. He took him down, flat on his back against the tiled floor. It knocked the wind out of him and a few of his ribs cracked. He tried freeing himself, but the young daywalker was out of practice and in the grasp of a pureblood vampire.

Dante got up onto one knee, his teeth bared, as he looked down his nose at Eric. He wrapped his hand around his throat, lifted him off the ground, and then slammed him against the floor once again. Eric groaned and choked in pain. At that point, Emilia was downstairs, screaming at her brother to leave him alone, but Dante wasted no time telling her the truth.

"Your boy is a hunter, Alé!" he shouted.

Emilia's face fell, the light instantly leaving her eyes. And when she looked at Eric, they were rimmed with red tears—bloody vampire tears.

"Is that true?" she whispered sharply. "Tell me it's not true!"

Eric couldn't lie anymore. He tried to explain, but no matter how he worded it, it never sounded right. It didn't matter that he wasn't in The Colectiv anymore. He was associated with them, and he had kept it from her. He lied just like she lied to him, and he let her know that too as his stupid heart shattered in that living room.

"Emilia," he choked out. "Emilia, please—"

"No. No, I trusted you! How could you?" she shouted.

"I trusted you too."

Her expression was a mixture of betrayal and disgust. His worst nightmare had come true.

"That was your first mistake," Dante said.

He then bared his fangs and sank his teeth at the base of Eric's neck. The boy cried out in pain as Emilia stood aside, looking numb as she did nothing to stop her brother.

Eric was used to pain. He could describe how the feeling of each kind of wound presented itself in his body by memory alone. All of it eventually healed and went away, but this one *burned*. This was different, and at the time, he didn't know why. His body reacted before his mind could process it, and his eyes glowed golden yellow as he writhed in agony.

Emilia gasped. Time seemed to freeze, and for a moment, even Dante stopped moving when he saw it. He pulled away, blood dripping down his face.

"What are you?" she asked.

"He's a half-breed," Dante spat.

His expression morphed from that of shock to a mixture of disdain and gratification.

"Look who's a dirty little liar," he sang. "Eric's got some demons. Or is that even your real name? My sister thought you were a real prince charming, but I knew better. No, you're a traitor and a *freak*. But look at you. It took nothing for me to take you down. Not only are you a freak, but you're *weak*. You might be a daywalker, but that human side's holding you down. What's the point of being a half-breed if you're not going to use your power, huh? If you're gonna be a hunter, you might as well make it a fair fight."

As the wound failed to heal itself and Eric continued to bleed out, he could feel himself drifting away.

He thought of his mom.

Is this what it felt like?

He was so powerless, that the only words that came out were, "I hope it was worth it."

After that, everything faded away.[68]

---

[68] I Started A Joke by Bee Gees

31

Old Friend

Emilia

Los Angeles, California—Present

Uneasiness crept into Emilia's soul as they drove past Los Angeles. The familiar towering buildings of downtown loomed to the right while they breezed down the highway, sparkling against the night sky. It was beautiful in its own right, yet being in its presence threatened to choke her with grief.

This was the city Emilia grew up in, the place she once called home, and where all her pain began. She abhorred it for such a long time in her youth, but now all she felt was sorrow. Despite how many years it had been, she found herself mourning her childhood, and most importantly, she mourned the girl she used to be, the one she had told Eric about. Was she ready to return and face that wretched place again?

No. She was headed somewhere with different demons, yet, somehow, Crimson Beach was a lesser evil in her mind.

"It's been almost 40 years since I've been here," she said softly.

She switched seats with Eric a while ago and was in the back once again. James was still at the wheel.

"You didn't come once just to visit?" he asked.

Emilia eyed him from the space between the door and his seat, catching a glimpse of his face. Their conversation from last night was still fresh in her mind, twisting at her insides.

"No. Bad memories," she replied.

He nodded in understanding. "Does it look different?"

She hummed, examining the skyline. "There are some new buildings, but otherwise, the same. At least from the outside."

He nodded again. Her eyes lingered on him despondently.

Emilia couldn't help but notice that Eric had been acting differently since Flagstaff. His usual brooding, steel exterior looked like it was giving way to quiet desolation, and she had a feeling that their talk by the pool had something to do with it. She hadn't expected to get such an exclusive, heart-wrenching view into his past, and surely Eric hadn't intended to open up to her at all, considering how secretive he was. Yet, without meaning to, she struck a chord in him like no other and unleashed a lifetime of skeletons he kept hidden in his closet. And knowing what she knew now, Emilia's heart ached for Eric MacNamara.

It had been so easy to loathe him for being a hunter or for all the deceit, but she understood something now that she didn't before— Eric's life *was* complicated.[69] She knew how Wade's death affected her and those around her, but nothing compared to the pain of the sons he

---

[69] i wish i hated you - Ariana Grande

left behind. To think, the whole time she knew him in Italy, he was bearing this weight. And she couldn't stop imagining two small 11-year-old boys being forced to endure such horrible things.

When Emilia became a vampire, she knew what she was getting herself into. It was her *choice*. She chose to lead a life of blood, violence, and immortality, and the things she committed were, for the most part, of her own volition. 22 years old was incredibly young, but *11*? And to have been born with vampire blood, with no choice? No wonder Eric said he was cursed. Emilia didn't know whether to cry for them or kill the man who did this.

Michael Iovaneau. The Silver Wolf.

All of a sudden, it made sense why Eric did what he did. It was the same reason she hid the truth about her own life. It was too painful to relive, and perhaps, just as she did, he wanted a chance at being someone else back then. He didn't want to be judged for something he left behind. Even Emilia didn't think talking about that part of her was worth the oxygen, yet when she shared a fraction of her past, Eric listened. He wasn't hostile or judgmental, and despite their heated argument, he accepted her apology and gave her his own. He returned the favor, and for the first time since seeing him again—no, for the first time *ever*—it was like they saw each other for who they really were. After three years, there was finally an understanding... So why did everything seem more difficult?[70]

This trip was a means for Emilia to save her brother. That had been her selfish intent, but gravity was pulling her back toward Eric MacNamara. Like inevitable magnetism. In past relationships, the more she knew about them, the less she liked them, but with Eric, the more she knew about him, the stronger her feelings became. It was

---

[70] BLUE - Billie Eilish

frustrating. And it didn't help that even when he was supposed to hate her, he still treated her better than most people she had ever met.

"He's not the same boy you met in Sorrento," Jean had said.

Perhaps he wasn't, but Emilia could see that, at his core, Eric was still Eric, in the dark and the light. Despite what she believed, it hadn't all been a complete lie. His heart was still there, but there was armor and barbed wire wrapped around it. And now that she'd gotten a good look inside, she didn't want to turn away.

"Where did you say your friend lived?" James asked suddenly, pulling her out of her thoughts.

She cleared her throat and said, "Right on the PCH, a little past Venice."

"And you're sure she'll be there?"

"Yeah, that's what she told me."

Earlier that day, Emilia sent Jaya an email to the most recently used account that Jean provided. The entire time leading up to it, writing it, and waiting for a response, she was restless. She half expected Jaya to blow her off or tell her she wanted nothing to do with her, but to her dismay, she received a positive answer. They caught up, and Emilia filled her in on as many details as possible. Though her friend was wary, she was open to the idea of the three of them stopping by.

While Emilia was excited to see her friend after decades of separation, she was unsure about the implications of involving her in all of this, especially since the main reason they parted ways was to keep Jaya safe from "The Hellhound's business. But Emilia didn't have any other plan otherwise, because, after everything, Jaya was the only one in Crimson Beach that she still trusted. Everyone else was questionable or scattered across the world. She needed to stall, and she needed to confirm Dante's location, which only Jaya could do.

"You said it's been 40 years?" Eric asked. "How can you be so sure she'll talk to us?"

"Yeah, were you planning on telling her what we are and who we work for, or...?" James added.

"That depends on you. Do you care if she knows?" Emilia said.

"If she's a rat, then yes."

She scoffed, "For Dante? Never. Like I said, she doesn't like him. And Jaya's always been good at keeping secrets. Although, I have a sneaking suspicion that there's a way to guarantee that."

"And what way is that?"

"By telling her *exactly* who you are."

However, in doing that, Emilia had to reveal another detail that she dreaded opening up about.

†††

Crimson Beach, California

Emilia's nerves did not abate as they neared her old beach home. Everything from the drive to the neighborhood to the Pacific Ocean itself was all too familiar, yet felt so much like a dream. After being away for so long, seeing it again was an out-of-body experience.

It hasn't changed one bit.

Her former home was a clean, cream-colored Spanish-style house. Like many homes on the PCH, it was narrow and stood three stories tall, but this one was especially beautiful. Right at the front, there was a driveway leading up to a garage.

"That one," she said, pointing across the console.

James pulled right in, and when he parked, both he and Eric looked up in awe.

"Nice."

"It's bigger on the inside," she told them with a grin. She then opened the door and hopped right out. "Come on, Jaya's waiting."

Emilia grabbed her purse and started making her way to the house, but stopped when she noticed the twins weren't following her. She heard the clinking of metal and the familiar click of a magazine. She looked over her shoulder and gaped in shock as they tucked weaponry into their holsters and hidden pockets.

She faced them and crossed her arms indignantly. "What did I say?"

"It's a precaution," Eric tried to reassure her.

"That is not a precaution. That is a threat," she argued.

"Emilia, let us do our job, and you can do yours," he said with a condescending smile.

"Whatever that is," James retorted.

Emilia groaned through gritted teeth. "Ay, te odio! Necio! Bruto!"
I hate you! Stubborn! Brute!

"I can understand you," Eric shot back.

"I *know*," she growled.

The vampire whirled around and continued up the driveway towards a gate that opened to some steps leading to the front door. She paused before going any further. All at once, it became so real and overwhelming. Memories of laughter, tears, screaming, and blood came rushing like waves.

She fled Crimson Beach decades ago, and now she was here, about to visit an old friend in hopes of finding a brother she swore she'd never see again. It was like walking into her dark past but as somebody else. She had thrown herself headfirst into this insane idea, and now she had to follow through. So much could go wrong and she wondered if she was way in over her head, if she could even get away with it, or if she even *should*. But it was too late to back down now.

"Something wrong?"

Emilia snapped out of her spiral and looked back to find Eric hovering right behind her. His warmth and familiar smell almost grounded her.

She shook her head and said, "Nothing. It's been a while. I didn't know if I'd ever come back here."

He nodded. She could tell he understood.

Together, all three of them approached the door, with Emilia in front.

"Let me do the talking first, alright?" she whispered to them.

"Fine."

"And be nice."

"No promises."

With a deep breath, Emilia knocked on the door three times. Jaya must have been waiting by the door because the lock clicked and it swung inward within seconds. All of a sudden, she was met with a pair of familiar, big brown eyes.

Emilia gasped.

[71]Jayashri Bhasin stood an inch or two taller than Emilia, with caramel brown skin and thick raven hair that cascaded to her waist in waves. She wore a chunky, knitted lavender sweater and beautiful gold earrings.

She was never afraid to wear color.

They stood there for a moment, staring at each other with wide eyes and decades of memories between them.

"Jaya," Emilia whispered.

---

[71] Rhiannon - Fleetwood Mac

"Took you long enough," she said, before throwing her arms around her.

Emilia froze for a few seconds, taken aback by the embrace. She expected much worse but found herself hugging her right back. They squeezed each other tight, afraid to let go. Jaya's hair tickled her face and smelled faintly of coconuts, which was also familiar. She had to hold back the urge to cry to avoid getting blood on her old friend's clothes. Jaya then pulled back and held Emilia's face in her hands, wiping away a stray tear that had fallen. Emilia rested her hands on her wrists, where golden bracelets clinked together.

There was one thought that kept repeating in her head:

"So much has happened."

"I know," Jaya laughed. She then dropped her hands and cast a wary glance over Emilia's shoulder. "Although some things I clearly know nothing about."

Emilia quickly wiped her face and pivoted to give her friend a proper view of the twins. They both stood tall and brooding, watching the interaction carefully.

"Boys, this is Jaya," she said, motioning to her friend, who nodded. She then gestured to the twins. "Jaya, this is Eric and James MacNamara."

They both gave her a curt nod and a short greeting. Jaya's doe-like eyes grew, bouncing back and forth between them as if she had just seen a ghost. Emilia didn't blame her because, in a way, seeing the twins *was* like seeing a ghost.

She turned to Emilia and said, "I almost didn't believe you when you told me."

"I know, it's a lot to process."

"Emilia, what did you do?" Jaya whispered, shaking her head.

"You mean, 'What did Dante do?'" Emilia corrected.

James spoke up then, saying, "I'm guessing you know who we are." Both he and Eric looked rather unfazed by Jaya's reaction.

She looked to Emilia as if for confirmation, and the vampire simply nodded. There was no escaping the truth.

"I know more than that," she told them. "I knew who your father was."

†††

They all gathered around the white marble-topped counter in Jaya's kitchen. Emilia took a gander around the first floor, which was a large space that also had the breakfast area and living room connected.

Though Jaya kept a few of the old pieces of furniture, for the most part, she made it all her own. There were whites, purples, teals, and yellows, much brighter than Emilia's aesthetic. Pieces of Jaya's South Asian culture made appearances all over the house with all kinds of design and decor. The fireplace was lit, and it smelled distinctly of jasmine, which gave the place a much warmer, homelier feel. Even the boys seemed to admire the look of the place, although they wouldn't say it out loud.

Upon entry, James asserted himself by sitting on a stool with his arms crossed and an intense expression. On the other hand, his twin stood by with his hands in his pockets, as if he were afraid to get too comfortable.

"Would you like something? Coffee? Tea? Water?" Jaya asked the room.

The twins kindly rejected her offer, rumbling their responses one after the other. Jaya eyed them hesitantly and raised her eyebrows at Emilia.

"I'll have some coffee, please," she said with a smile.

As Jaya busied herself with the coffee maker, Emilia looked over at Eric. He was wandering around, inspecting the details of the house and taking everything in like a museum exhibit.

Her friend leaned in and whispered, "Is he snooping, or...?"

Emilia shook her head. "No, he does that."

If there was anything that never changed, it was that Eric was an explorer at heart. He liked learning and observing, and it didn't matter what it was as long as he found it interesting, which he often did. He found a lot of things most people would consider "odd" to be intriguing. She remembered as much from when they were together.

When he was done meandering about, he stood idly by his twin's shoulder once again.

"You can sit down, you know," Emilia told him.

"The last time you introduced me to another vampire, he almost killed me, so no, thanks."

She rolled her eyes in exasperation. Jaya, however, stopped what she was doing and shot her a questioning look.

Emilia grimaced. "I'm guessing you don't know about that?"

"We haven't talked in at least 25 years. Keeping track of a vampire isn't exactly easy," she said. Her accent hugged her words as she spoke.

"Still, I thought the news would have traveled."

"No, it wouldn't," Eric said.

They both shot him looks of confusion, but he was nonchalant about it.

He continued, "The Colectiv does a pretty good job at covering things up, especially when it involves one of their own. As soon as they heard about what happened, they sent a team to deal with it. And I'm sure Michael and everyone else did their best to ensure that as few people knew about Sorrento as possible. Not unless, of course, the people involved decide to talk about it."

He gave Emilia a pointed look.

She raised her hands defensively. "I only ever told Jean about it, and Dante, well… I highly doubt he would talk about it, considering it's a sore subject for him, too."

"Maybe he should've kept his dirty hands to himself. Then it wouldn't be a subject at all," James muttered.

Jaya turned the coffee machine on and whirled around with a nervous smile.

"If we're going to do this, I'm going to need to hear your side of the story first."

"What about you?" James asked, furrowing his brow. "She said you'd know where Dante is, and you're the one who said you knew our dad."

"And I promise I will speak on that, but considering you're in my home on a spontaneous visit, I think I deserve some explanation," Jaya countered.

"I thought she explained what we're here for." He motioned to Emilia with his chin.

"An idea, yeah. You want to know where Dante is, a man whom I refuse to speak to, so excuse me for wanting a good reason why I should potentially do that again."

"Does *anybody* like him?" Eric inquired.

Emilia inclined her head and said, "You'd be surprised."

Dante preferred people who were about as like-minded as him and scared off anyone who wasn't, either on purpose or with his demeanor. He had friends, but they were as chaotic and shady as he was. Emilia wasn't sure if he managed to maintain those friendships even now.

"Well, we hate him about as much as you do, if not more," James stated with an icy smile. "The enemy of my enemy is my friend, right?"

Jaya furrowed her brow and crossed her arms, saying, "I'm not your friend, and I don't talk freely with hunters or anyone I don't know, for that matter."

"You knew our dad, though, didn't you?" Eric asked. "Doesn't that count for something?"

"Yeah, I knew Wade, but Wade wasn't a hunter, and you're not Wade," she said as assertively as a polite person could.

James scowled, and Emilia instantly dreaded what he was about to say. Even Eric looked at him like he was a bomb about to go off.

"You know, if I could kill that man again just to get you people to stop talking about him, I would," he seethed.

A strangled noise came out of Eric—a laugh that he tried covering up with a cough. Emilia shook her head. Jaya, however, was not amused, and clearly, neither was James.

"I'm not trying to be your fuckin' friend, alright?" he snapped. "All you people do is talk and waste our goddamn time. I've had to deal with not one, not two, but three vampires now, and I'm not allowed to kill any of you despite how fucking annoying you've all been. We just drove across the country for *five days* to find this motherfucker. Information is all we want. Not a heart-to-heart over coffee. We have places to be, so just tell us what we need to know."

James spoke all business in that threatening tone of his. There was something cold and authoritative about it, despite his language, and Emilia didn't like it. She followed the interaction, hanging back until Jaya needed her, but she was about ready to lunge. Eric, meanwhile, had his gaze trained on her as if expecting a repeat of when she tried strangling his brother to death. Luckily, Jaya spoke up before she could.

"Well, I'm sorry for the inconvenience, but I'm not going to let you intimidate me in my own home," Jaya said smoothly. "I've spent a very long life dealing with men like you who think they can say and do as they please with a few nasty words and some violence, and I've spent even longer learning how to be unaffected by them. One of those men is the same one you're seeking right now. You might be a hunter, and you're probably used to everything going your way, but acting like a child isn't going to help you here."

Emilia's jaw dropped.

Jaya wasn't an aggressive person by any means. As a vampire, she did what she had to do to survive but was otherwise shy and poised. Unfortunately, because she was so kind, many people tried taking advantage of that fact. Emilia jumped to her defense many times and even encouraged her to stand up for herself. When they parted ways, she often worried about her old friend, but it seemed that Jaya came into her own just fine. Somehow, she managed to keep her poise, kindness, and dignity in a way that Emilia wished *she* could.

Emilia swept her eyes over to James, who had an expression she never thought she'd see on his face. He blinked in shock, his face bright red as he leaned back in his chair. For once, he was at a loss for words, lacking a harsh comment of any sort. He fumed in complete silence, and it was a miracle he wasn't throwing knives at this point.

Eric eyed his twin charily before carefully approaching the counter. He leaned his hands against it and looked at Jaya with a level of amiability that was somewhere between authoritative and how he treated the waitress at the café. It seemed he was beginning to realize that his usual tactics weren't going to work this time.

"Take it easy, yeah? We're just doing our job. But if we tell you everything, will you tell us what we need to know?"

Jaya glanced at Emilia, asking for some kind of confirmation again. After all, the only person she trusted in that room was *her*.

Emilia nodded.

Her friend looked back at the hunter and said, "Yes, I will."

†††

Eric and Emilia gave Jaya a full rundown of their history, leading up to current events. Even though they left out a plethora of personal details, it didn't help the painful awkwardness of recounting it all in front of an audience. The whole time, Emilia refused to look him in the eye, but she could hear the discomfort in his voice and feel the tension heating the room.

When she was caught up, Jaya pointed between them. "So, the two of you were together?"

"Yes," Emilia confirmed.

"But now you're not because of what happened?"

"To put it lightly," Eric replied.

"But you're here now, so you can kill Dante?"

Emilia swallowed thickly at Jaya's growing disbelief.

"Yup," Eric rumbled.

"Em," she whispered, and Emilia knew what she wanted to say without having to voice it. She shook her head. Jaya looked at her and then at the boys. "Can you excuse us for a minute?"

Without waiting for a response, Jaya grabbed Emilia's hand and started tugging her towards the back of the house. The twins protested, of course.

"Wait, what?"

Jaya walked her to the sliding door that led to a patio and the beach beyond. She pulled it open and said, "A moment alone, or I give you nothing! You can watch us from inside!"

Just as Eric was on their heels, she slammed it shut in his face. Emilia's eyes connected with his through the glass, and he shot her a wild, questioning look. Emilia shrugged and smiled apologetically.

"We'll be right back!" she assured him.

"You get one minute," he threatened.

She gave him a curt nod as Jaya took her through the patio gate and onto the sandy beach. The cold winter breeze of the Pacific coast swept up her hair as they went into the night. Jaya didn't stop until they reached the place before the water met the sand. There, they were far enough away that the boys couldn't hear them past the harsh wind and crashing waves. The tourists were gone and most of the locals were either in their homes or too far away to notice anything.

Jaya tried pushing her hair out of her face and grabbed Emilia's hands in hers. There was a desperate look in her chocolate-brown eyes.

"Emilia, what are you doing?" she shouted.

Emilia shook her head, the weight of everything suddenly hitting her. "I don't know."

"I've seen you make some horrible decisions before. I've seen you at your lowest, but I also know that you are a good person, Emilia," she said, emphasizing her name like a scolding mother. "You're not seriously considering letting him, *him*, kill your brother?"

Already, Emilia was fighting back tears, her vision pink from the blood. She let go of one of Jaya's hands to cover her mouth and look away toward the ocean. Jaya turned her away from the house, so Emilia's back was to it. After holding back for so long, she could feel herself begin to break.[72]

---

[72] The Beach - Wolf Alice

"Listen, I am proud of you for standing up to Dante. I am. *Everyone* has fantasized about that day, but Em... Eric is a hunter! A daywalker! He's *Wade's son*! And Dante—"

"I know!" Emilia blurted out like a frustrated child, and then more gentle, "You don't think I know?"

The more time went on, the more painfully aware she was of those things.

"How is it possible that you fell for *him*, of all people?" Jaya asked in astonishment.

"The universe has it out for me, or Wade is haunting me from beyond the grave."

"And now you want me to help you, help *him*, get revenge?"

"No." Emilia shook her head again, more vigorously this time.

Jaya frowned. "What?"

"No. That's why I'm with him. I don't—I don't know what to do. I just know that I can't let him do it," she cried.

"Well, obviously not. Even if your brother did have it coming."

"No, Jaya." She squeezed her friend's hands, willing her to understand. "*I can't let Eric do it.*"

It was the first time she acknowledged those words out loud, even within herself. She couldn't let Eric kill Dante, not only because he was her brother, but because Eric would lose himself forever if he did. She knew what it was like to have Dante's words morph her perception of herself—to be convinced that the world had it out for you and that you were destined to be nothing but evil. Those same words catapulted Eric closer to a place he may not be able to come back from—a place he never wanted to be. It would be like selling his soul to the hunt and The Colectiv for the foreseeable future.

"Oh, God. You love him, don't you?" Jaya asked.

Emilia rolled her eyes. "That doesn't matter."

"It obviously does. Otherwise, you wouldn't be here. The only man you've ever risked your entire life for—in *your entire life*—is Dante. I know that firsthand."

Emilia stared at her with dismal eyes, unable to provide any argument as red tears cut through her face.

Yes. Yes, she did love him. From the day they met, it rooted itself in her, and being this close to him again only proved that. The fact that he was a hunter changed absolutely nothing. The fact that he wanted her brother dead didn't either.

I really am fucked in the head.

"I don't think I ever stopped," she admitted. Jaya's eyes softened. "I just need you to pretend to help him. Lie to him, stall, whatever you need to do."

Her friend looked unsure at first, but eventually she nodded in agreement. Something then caught her attention over Emilia's shoulder.

"He's coming."

Emilia straightened up and wiped her face with her sleeves. Eric approached within seconds and circled to look between them both.

"Time's up," he snapped, oozing impatience.

Immediately, he narrowed his gaze at Emilia. Despite how much she cleaned herself up, she no doubt still looked like she had been crying.

"It's been 40 years. We had an emotional reunion," she said through a stuffy nose.

"Right," he huffed. "I'm gonna need you both back inside before I start acting a little less friendly."

32

Branded

Eric

Eric stood with his arms folded, his scrutinizing gaze flitting between Jaya and Emilia, trying to catch any hint of what they talked about on the beach. It was important enough for Jaya to drag Emilia outside with such dire urgency, and when he went out there himself, there was blood on Emilia's face from her tears. She blamed it on the reunion, but Eric knew better than to believe that. The only reason he let it slide—for now—was because they had more pressing matters to get to.

They were all in the kitchen once again, hunters and vampires on opposite sides of the marble island. Jaya and Emilia had mugs in their hands as if they were about to have a normal conversation. James, however, had been dead quiet after what Jaya said to him. Eric didn't need twin telepathy to know that what she said struck a chord because, for the first time in his life, he closed his mouth instead of continuing to argue. If they were in a different setting, Eric would have talked to him privately, but he promised himself to do that when they weren't in the presence of purebloods.

"What do you want to know first?" Jaya asked. "Do you want to know about Dante, or...?"

"Dante first, please," Eric said.

As his brother said, they had traveled five days to find him, and Eric had waited three years before that. He was aching to know as much as possible, as soon as possible.

"Well, you just missed him," she told him.

Eric perked up. "He was here?"

She hesitated before saying, "He *was*. Last time I heard, he left to do business in Reno."

Any excitement and hope evaporated, and he let out a long, exasperated sigh. Eric ran his hands over his face. Beside him, James muttered curses.

"What is that? Another 8 hours?"

"Yeah."

So, fucking close.

"It's still closer than he could've been," Emilia contested. "I'm surprised he's not in Cancun right now."

"If you don't talk to him, how can you be sure?" Eric asked Jaya.

"I've learned through the grapevine that he's been around Crimson Beach. Friends of friends hear about him all the time. He has quite the presence that's hard to miss. When he's gone, it's no different."

Eric knew that from experience.

"What does he usually do when he's here?" James finally spoke up, his voice calmer than before.

Jaya turned her attention to him, but there was no malice or contempt in her eyes. If anything, she looked wary.

"He's usually seen at the local clubs, which is the case in any city, really. Popular clubs or casinos are a good place to look. Most cities, like Reno or even Vegas, attract vampires like bees to honey."

"I know the ins and outs enough, which should make looking for him easier," Emilia offered with a shrug.

Eric knew about secret vampire societies within and beneath major cities, so he wasn't surprised. It brought a sense of hope back into him.

"What kind of business does Dante do exactly?" he asked, narrowing his eyes.

"Dante's pretty ambitious," Emilia responded with a bitter smile. "Always has been since we were kids. Add it to the list of things he learned from our father. Back when we used to live here, he actually owned his own club, but it got closed down after everything."

The hunter raised his eyebrows in surprise. At first, he couldn't picture Dante as being an entrepreneur, but the more he thought about it, the more sense it made. If he was a businessman, then he must have had connections in many places, which meant someone else was bound to know his whereabouts. They just had to pull on the right thread.

Eric put his hands in his pockets. "Anything else?"

Jaya shrugged. "There are the local vampire gangs and distilleries you can look for both here and in Reno, but other than that, I wouldn't know."

"We can also check the missing person's cases and see if we find any weird connections," James added.

"Yeah," Eric nodded in agreement. "What about those friends you said knew about him?"

"They've only seen or heard of him in passing, but I can give you their information if you want," Jaya said.

"Please."

He let his eyes trail down as he skimmed through his brain to ensure he hadn't missed any vital details, but all the questions he had left over had nothing to do with Dante at all. It was a different personal matter.

"So...about Wade," he uttered casually.

Jaya's eyes flashed and her demeanor shifted into something more timid. Both she and Emilia shared a sidelong glance—something they had been doing throughout the entire night, and Eric didn't like it. It made him feel like they were hiding something.

"Why are you looking at her like that?" he demanded.

Jaya looked at him and said, "It's just... I knew your father because I knew Jean, and I knew Jean because of—"

"Because of me," Emilia finished for her.

Now, it was Eric's turn to share a glance with James, who was as confused as he was. They surveyed Emilia questioningly, and to spare them, she put the pieces together herself.

"I knew Wade too."

Eric's mouth fell open, his heart falling into his stomach.

James scoffed. "Wait, what?"

"You?" Eric blurted out. "*You* knew him?"

Emilia nodded, her eyes full of guilt and shame. Out of all the secrets she revealed to him in the past week, this hit Eric like nothing else. He should have seen it coming at this point. After all, she had 70 years' worth of secrets, and he was starting to see Jean's influence on her.

"This whole time?" he whispered sharply.

"Yes."

He never stopped to consider that maybe Emilia, his *ex*, had some kind of connection to his father, but now it was obvious. If Jean was his close friend, and he was the one who turned Emilia, then it was only a matter of time before they crossed paths. Suddenly, it didn't matter as much that Jaya or even Jean knew Wade because for Emilia to know him meant something vastly different to Eric. It boiled his blood.

"Personally? In passing? Did the two of you..." Even as he said it, the insinuation made him sick.

Emilia shook her head in disgust and waved her hands dramatically. "No! God, no. It was nothing like that. He made it pretty clear he wanted nothing to do with me, but that's beside the point. I knew him as a really good friend."

Eric all but collapsed with relief. Knowing that she and his father had never been together was, at the very least, one comfort in this baffling revelation.

"Jesus fucking Christ," James cursed under his breath and turned away, towards the living room.

"Why didn't you tell me?" Eric exacted, and then quickly added, "Why didn't you tell *us*?"

"I didn't know how!" she argued, raising her voice to his level. "It wasn't exactly on your list of questions during the interrogation, and I wasn't sure how smart it was to blurt it out, especially when you barely looked at me this entire trip as it is!"

"We talked," he hissed, alluding to their numerous conversations across the country. Even the coffee shop was a good opportunity. "There were plenty of chances."

"Well, I'm sorry. I didn't hide it on purpose or to be deceitful. I was just waiting for the right time," she said.

"Which would be when exactly?"

Emilia lifted her shoulders and then let them droop.

"I don't know," she answered in a small voice.

At the sight of her sheepish expression, Eric was struck with a pang of guilt that made him wince. He thought of the heartfelt look she gave him back in Arizona and averted his gaze to the marble-topped island, his cheeks feeling hot with a flush. It was all he could do to not audibly groan in frustration, except not at her—at himself.

Fuck. I'm such an asshole. She tells me she's happy I'm alive, and this is how I repay her? What the fuck is wrong with me? She didn't even do anything wrong.

He took a moment to still himself, and when he finally looked up at Emilia once again, he let his regret show, if only for a second, just for her. She must have caught it because her eyes softened.

"How did you know him?" he asked, less hostile now.

James came up behind him, ready for answers.

"It was a year or two after I got turned," Emilia explained. "He had been in Ireland for a few years because our government wasn't too happy with him."

James snorted. "Why?"

"Wade was very against the war in Vietnam. I think he got arrested at one of the rallies. It was a whole thing."

The corners of Eric's lips turned down, and he found himself harboring a little more respect for the man. It was rare when an immortal put their reputation on the line for a mortal cause.

She continued, "We used to live in this abandoned place called Hollydale. I was outside one day when, all of a sudden, Wade arrived with a bag slung over his shoulder. He was some random stranger with an Irish accent, fresh off a plane, with rebellion in his eyes. He was...uh...He was something else."

A soft smile played on her lips as she reminisced on an old memory. There was even a dreamy glint in her eyes.

Eric worked his jaw, seething.

"You said you had nothing to do with him," he bit out.

"Yeah, but I may have had a...teeny...*tiny*...crush on him."

"Tiny?" Jaya scoffed.

Emilia smacked her in the arm with the back of her hand. "Everyone had a crush on Wade, okay? It wasn't anything new. Even *you* had a crush on him," she shot back.

"Yeah, a fleeting crush."

"That's beside the point," Emilia said, rolling her eyes. "If you must know, I didn't just like him because of his looks. I liked him because he was...well... *Wade*."

"You say that like it means anything to us," Eric argued. "He died before we ever met him, remember? We don't know shit about him, and everything we learn is vague."

"Or straight fucked up," James added.

"He was passionate, funny, and kind, and he wasn't afraid to speak his mind no matter what anyone said. If he thought something was unjust, he would let everyone know, and if they didn't listen, he'd take matters into his own hands," Jaya said, drawing their attention towards her.

Eric recalled what Jean told them in Bucharest about the reason their father had Gabriel Iovaneau killed.

For Anya.

He had been so distracted the last few days that he had almost forgotten.

Was that him taking matters into his own hands?

"He could be a little blunt, yes, but in a way that came from the heart, and that meant something," she explained. "People respected him even when they wanted to punch him in the face. And he was probably one of the first men to treat me with kindness and respect."

"He didn't know it, but he changed a lot of lives. I know, because he changed mine," Emilia stated as Eric regarded her with watchful eyes. "I didn't know many good men until I met Wade. Everyone always wanted something from me, but he didn't. I hated it at the time, but he was right. I mean, he could be an asshole, and he never sugarcoated anything, but when he cared about you, it really meant something. You know?"

Weird.

The more they talked about his dead father, the less real everything seemed to Eric, because, for a long time, his biological father didn't seem real at all. He was a fantasy, one he'd given up on a long time ago. Michael refused to talk about him for obvious reasons, but even when Jean spoke of him, there was still an air of mystery. However, hearing such kind and tangible words... No one had talked about him that way since their mother died.

For 14 years, having the name "MacNamara" was like a brand across their skin. Everyone knew who it originally belonged to and the atrocities tied to it, and over the years, Eric came to detest it. He hated being seen as a "half-breed" and being associated with his murderous vampire father, who abandoned them. But even if he tried changing it to his mother's maiden name, it didn't matter because her name was tainted too. James and Eric were branded, and Eric hated himself for it. Being a MacNamara meant something bad, but now, for the first time, it meant something good in someone else's eyes. It was bitingly bittersweet.

Longing filled his lungs like water, threatening to suffocate Eric, and suddenly, everything sounded so far away. Yet again, he was made painfully aware of a void in his heart that could never be filled. It brought back a harrowing grief that latched on and clung to him since he was a child—a child who missed a father he'd never even met. Losing Wade was different from losing Anya.

How was it possible to mourn someone who was but an image in a locket? Someone who was only words out of someone else's mouth but never a part of his own memories? Someone who should have been there but wasn't and could never be? Eric shouldn't have been so affected, not after all this time, but ever since his breakdown last night, he felt strange. It was as if there was a dam holding everything within him, and now there was a crack in it.

He was feeling too much. [73]

Everyone around him kept conversing, their voices muffled, until his brother's voice pulled him from under the surface.

"E?"

James put his hand on Eric's shoulder and the boy blinked back to reality. He looked over, as if in slow motion, at his twin, who watched him with that familiar protective stare. It was then that Eric realized that Jaya and Emilia had stopped talking and were also looking at him with an equal amount of worry.

"You good?" James asked.

Eric put on a soft smile and nodded, patting his twin's hand. "Yeah. I'm good."

"We were just wondering," Emilia said, "do you know how Wade died?"

Eric furrowed his brow. "You mean you don't know?"

What Wade had done was such common knowledge among hunters that he never stopped to think about what the vampires knew or didn't know. He was surprised Jean never told her, but it seemed he kept secrets even from his adopted daughter.

"I know The Colectiv had something to do with it, but the 'why' has always been a mystery," she told him with a shrug. "Was it because he was with your mom? As far as I know, for vampires, that's not a punishable crime. At least not by death."

"That's because it's not," James replied. "He did something worse."

"What did he do?" Jaya asked.

---

[73]EVEN - Bad Omens

The twins glanced at each other, and Eric took the liberty of delivering the same news he learned when he was only 13 years old.

"Wade had the commander's older brother killed."

Emilia's jaw dropped, and Jaya's hand flew to her mouth.

"Michael? The Silver Wolf? *His* brother?" Emilia blurted out.

"Yeah."

"Do you know why?"

The twins made noises of uncertainty. Even they weren't thoroughly confident in the story Jean had told them. The vampire requested they not share it with anyone from The Colectiv, especially Michael, but Jaya and Emilia had no ties to either of them. Still, Eric kept it vague.

"Apparently, Gabriel, Michael's brother, tried messing with the person he cared about the most, and Wade snapped."

"Who?" she asked.

Eric hesitated, that protectiveness holding him back, before he said, "Anya."

Somehow, the fact hit him harder now than it did when Jean first told him. The idea of a person with that much power trying to cross a line with their mother made him livid. He could see that same rage on this brother's face too.

Did Michael know? He wondered.

Growing up, Eric scoured the estate's entire library for any source related to his father until there was nothing left, but any mention of him ended right before he met Anya. Everything else was surface-level information that everyone already knew. In fact, the section of history containing his parents' story, as well as James and Eric's birth, had yet to be written, assuming they planned to do it at all. Eric always found it strange that it was omitted, but when he asked Michael about it, he told him that it would be long before the history books were updated. It only frustrated him and broke his heart even more. Part of him had hoped to find some flaw or a lie that told him it was all wrong, but he never found it.

Not until now.

Not that it matters.

"And now he's dead," Eric muttered. [74]

He looked off with a severe expression that could cut glass.

"I'm sorry," Emilia whispered.

Eric's attention immediately went to her as soon as the words left her mouth. He looked her dead in those beautiful, brown eyes, and for once she didn't tear them away. All at once, it was just the two of them and no one else.

Memories of last night replayed in Eric's mind, and words she had uttered to James in secret echoed in a whisper. He overheard them when he was supposed to be sleeping, and even though it was only a fragment, it was enough.

"I couldn't let him die."

"That simple, huh? Really?"

"Is it? 'Simple'? When you put your life on the line for your brother, is it simple? Or does it just go beyond reason, and you act purely on instinct?"

"You really cared about him, didn't you?"

"Is that really so hard to believe?"

"I don't know. After what happened, you can't really blame me."

"Well, I did."

"Do you still care about him now?"

Silence.

Emilia didn't have to say anything else because Eric could already hear what lay in the words left unsaid. He knew. She had *shown* him that she still cared, with her apologies, her "I'm glad you're still alive,"

---

[74] Alien Blues - Vundabar

and the fact that she looked devastated at the thought of him dying. She watched him break. She witnessed him tear his own heart open and still looked him in the eyes when he could barely do that with his reflection.

Emilia couldn't fake that. She was never nice just to be nice.

How was he supposed to exist now, knowing that? Why was it easier to believe she despised him than it was to believe otherwise?

Doesn't she know what will happen? Don't I already know the consequences? [75]

All of a sudden, Eric couldn't breathe. It was too much to bear all at once—this conflict and yearning. He had a hunt to finish, and he couldn't do this right now.

"I need some air," he said, tearing his eyes away from her.

Eric turned around without another word, striding to the back of the house through the sliding door, and didn't stop walking until he reached the water's edge.

---

[75] Ascensionism - Sleep Token

33

Dead Man Walking

Wade

[76]It happened on a regular day.

Then again, every day was the same down in Charybdis.

He was in his dark, steel cell, a rectangular box with a mattress that no longer had a frame (he tried to kill the guards with it). A singular UV light shined from above, while the rest were shattered. A steel collar wrapped around his neck with silver-tipped spikes that dug into his skin. His hair fell past his shoulders in a matted mess, and his beard was no different. By all means, he should've been a frail shell of a man, but he managed to stand tall despite their attempts to weaken him.

That day, he was in the middle of doing pushups when he heard rustling outside his cell. He stopped and sat upright.

"Ey!" he called out.

---

[76] Wanted Dead Or Alive - Bon Jovi

No answer.

"Ey!" he shouted, walking up to the heavy door. "What day is it?"

Again, there was no answer.

He tried to keep track of time by counting shift changes, meals, and "outdoor" time, but it was hard to truly tell when he lived in a windowless prison beneath the sea. Now and then he'd give it a shot and ask the guards for the date. Sometimes one would answer, and other times they told him to stick it where the sun didn't shine. For all he knew, it could have been centuries, or it could have been five years, but from what he learned, it was more like two decades. Give or take.

"Give up already, MacNamara," the hunter shot back.

"You'll be long dead before I give up, you gobshite," Wade hissed.

He pushed himself away from the door and returned to his exercise. Then, a few moments later, there was a gasp followed by a thud...and then another. Wade paused and cocked his head to listen close. There was more quiet movement, quiet even to his vampire ears. There was labored breathing. Heartbeats slowed and then stopped. His eyes grew wider with each strange sound, until, suddenly, the latch on the window to his room clicked and slid open. A small rectangle of warm light was let in, making the vampire blink a few times. When his vision adjusted, a masked figure looked at him on the other side. They had no pulse. Wade stood up cautiously and dared to walk forward and lean in close. It was then that he saw a pair of dark eyes.

"Wade MacNamara," she said. Her voice was familiar.

"Yeah?"

"Do you know what day it is?"

"No, they wouldn't tell me."

"It's your release day."

†††

Tokyo, Japan—Many days later

Wade MacNamara stood under the water for a good while before finally coming out of the shower, and when he caught his reflection in the bathroom mirror, he couldn't help but jump a little. He hadn't seen his own face in over two decades. When he was rescued, his friends made it a point to poke fun at his appearance, and he took it in stride. But when he was alone for the first time in a long time—genuinely alone, with no guards or prisoners—he had to admit that he almost broke down.

It was easy to lose a sense of self and time in a place like Charybdis. It was easy to feel like the centuries were catching up to him, and like the almost 200 years he had lived were wearing away at his body and mind. He half-expected to see an old, decaying man staring back at him, but instead, there he was, 27 all over again. Still, his eyes said it all. He had half a mind to shave his head but decided against it because it reminded him of war too much. Now, he looked like some semblance of his old self again: brown curls that fell past his ears, porcelain skin, and blue eyes. Even his overgrown beard was reduced to stubble.

This was the same face of a man who came from nothing. This was the face of a man who survived. This was the face of a man who lost it all. And now, soon enough, this would be the face of a man who would get everything back.

Well...*almost* everything.

"I told you I would get you out someday, didn't I?" Jean told him over the phone. *"The time is now, Wade. They need you. They're in pretty deep, but I don't think they know who they're fighting for."*

My boys.

22 years. Nearly 22 years in a box away from his sons.

Wade never wanted any of this. He never wanted to live a life in hiding, apart from his blood, feeling like his heart had been ripped out and taken someplace he could never see. He fought tooth and nail to keep his family safe, and it got him exiled to a slow death.

He took them from me.

Wade MacNamara was many things. He knew what people said about him, vampires and hunters alike, good and bad. He was well aware of the image that his reputation painted of him, the rumors, and the truths. He's taken lives on and off the battlefield; he's stolen, hurt, cheated, and been reckless more times than he can count... but he knew *his* truth.

And he was going to make sure that the truth ate Mihail Andrei Iovaneau alive.

†††

[77]Wade Elias MacNamara was born on April 4th, 1837, in Kerry, Ireland. His mother was a woman named Maeve MacNamara, though he never came to know much more than that, because the second he was born, he was ripped away from her for having him out of wedlock. She was put into an asylum to wither and die, leaving the boy an orphan. As a result, Wade was alone in the world for the better part of his childhood, up until the age of 15, when he found a way to immigrate to the U.S.

With nothing to his name, he shacked up in the city of Boston, Massachusetts, with another teenager named Benny O'Malley, who became his first real best friend. And Benny and Wade survived by the skin of their teeth. They worked a lot of exhausting jobs in factories,

---

[77] Bohemian Rhapsody - Queen

coal mines, and even railroad construction. Wade hated those jobs, but poverty and discrimination left him with few options and often pushed him to turn to more questionable means of making fast money. Even so, it was very clear from the very beginning that he had an undying, unstoppable drive.

Like many other immigrants, Wade MacNamara moved to America for a better life, to attain something *more*. Stability, money, and acceptance, of course. He had his friends, his culture, and the Irish Community of Boston, but there was something else—something beyond himself—that he could never fully grasp. He didn't know if it was because he came from nothing and had no one that he *craved* to have something and *be* someone. It made him insatiable and rambunctious.

When he wasn't working, Wade liked to go out with his friends, cause trouble, and kiss pretty girls. And because he was a poor Irish boy, many of the other kids bullied him, so he frequently got into brawls. Being that he had a knack for it, Benny and his friends told him that he should try entering fights at the local bar to earn extra money. In Wade's mind, it was like killing two birds with one stone—he got to do something he enjoyed while also providing for himself and whatever future he dreamed of. With that, Wade quickly became the talk of the city, earning the reputation of a "street rat" in every way.

As passionate as he was, Wade MacNamara was, unfortunately, a man of tragedy. He lost his mother before he even knew her, he lost loved ones to British tyranny, and then he lost his best friend, Benny O'Malley, one autumn day. Benny, the boy who offered him a place to stay in that old shanty town, and worked with him every day. Benny, who watched him fight at the bar, and who he'd sneak out with to talk to pretty girls. And it was near that same shantytown that Benny was found stabbed and beaten to death in an alleyway. It was the first time

Wade cried, and because of the times, they couldn't even have a proper funeral. It only added to his already increasing anger towards the unfair world, and if it wasn't for Martha Murphy, Wade's neighbor and friend, he likely would have lost himself then.

Shortly after Benny's death, Martha Murphy formally introduced Wade to her granddaughter, Eliza. She was a nice Catholic girl and the daughter of a carpenter. They had seen each other in passing but barely spoke more than a few words. She was shy and reserved, but Wade thought she was incredibly kind and beautiful. Not to mention she could cook, sew, read, and play piano, which made her every mother's dream for their son. Wade didn't think that *he* was what any parent would want for their daughter, but Martha had grown rather fond of him despite his behavior. She wanted what was best for him and insisted that marrying her granddaughter would help clean up his act and alleviate their financial burdens.

"You're a good boy, Wade. But it's time for you to be a good *man*," she told him.

It wasn't that he didn't agree, but the boy was terrified. He had dreamed of having a family of his own, but he also didn't know if marrying under those circumstances could make him happy. Perhaps he expected too much. Maybe he was too much of a hopeless romantic, and he needed to stop craving *more*. So, despite his doubts, Wade chose to marry Eliza to find happiness. He stopped fighting at the bar, stopped causing trouble, and got a stable job working carpentry with Eliza's father.

The pair loved each other as well as they could, despite how hard it was to survive. Although they weren't wealthy, they were better off than before, even if the discrimination didn't quite abate. Wade tried his best to fit into the role of a loving husband while also being the man of the house. It was a completely new experience for him, seeing as he never had a father of his own to set an example, but Wade was always a very loving and caring person at his core, and the people around him knew that. No matter what, he was loyal to a fault, and he would never do anything to disrespect his wife's honor. As long as he was trying, she never judged him poorly, which was the least he could ask for.

Of course, things took a radical turn when Eliza became pregnant. It happened rather fast, as was expected, and nine months later she gave birth to a gorgeous baby girl named Daisy Aileen MacNamara. If Wade had any prior definition of "love at first sight," it went out the window, because as soon as he laid eyes on Daisy, he fell in love in an instant. He never knew it was possible to feel so much for someone that he had just met, and yet there he was, willing to risk it all. He'd move mountains and burn down cities if it meant keeping Daisy safe and giving her a good life. Daisy was his light, his newfound purpose, and she brought him closer to Eliza than ever before. They were happy, they were perfect, and they lived in bliss for 18 months.

Alas, there were certain invisible dangers that Wade could *not* protect his daughter from. Science was not what it is today, and it was a disease that took Daisy away when she was barely over a year old. Just as everything was looking up, Wade's world was turned upside down, and for the first time, he knew what it was like to feel like his heart had been torn out of his chest. The grief was insurmountable. No words could quite encompass the pain of losing a child. It was unnatural, and if he could trade places with her to give her another chance at a longer life, he would have. It was too much, so much so that the heartbreak took Eliza months later.

No one quite knew what to do with Wade MacNamara following the tragedies. Not the Murphy's, not his friends, no one. He lost a child and a wife, and even though he did his best to be a good man, his reputation preceded him. There were whispers in the halls from old religious crows outside the community, wondering whether it was a punishment or a curse he harbored. He often did a good job at ignoring them, but others dared say that at least he was attractive enough to find someone new. It enraged him so much that, amidst his grief, he punched a man in public for saying such things to his face.

As if women and children were replaceable items.

He had no remorse for what he had done.

The American Civil War was a godsend for a man consumed with grief and fury, and when the time came, Wade threw himself into the Union with no hesitation. It was for a cause he believed in, but there was a part of him that felt like he was ridding the world of the burden that he was—a bastard child left to die and fend for himself. He had nothing left to lose, and if the world wanted to kill him so badly, why not run headfirst into a battlefield and go down fighting? If they wanted him to be a man, why not become the most masculine thing there is: a soldier?[78]

So, a soldier Wade became, and a good one at that, and without anyone or anything holding him back, he finally had permission to fight. If it meant he could spare the lives of others, he allowed himself to be reckless and careless with his safety. Because if God wanted to kill him, then he would let him. And, perhaps, he would have...if Jean Beltremieux hadn't come into the picture.

Jean was a man from Louisiana, the son of former slaves, and he had joined the Union army as a medic. He was a black man in the 1860s, which spoke for itself. However, Wade, who didn't care what people said about *him*, stepped up to the plate. He had been on the receiving end of prejudice long enough to not let anything slide and

---

[78] Army Dreamers - Kate Bush

didn't hesitate to speak up for Jean when people thought they were being "funny."

"He's the only one around that can save you from dyin', so I suggest you shut the fuck up, or I'll speed up the process," he'd say.

More often than not, they'd shut their mouths because they knew he was right and no one wanted to make enemies with the Irishman.

He expected nothing in return from Jean, but to Wade's dismay, the medic took a liking to him. He said it was because Wade was direct, and he always knew what he was getting, and he found Jean to be very reliable and the type of person who could keep a secret to the grave. They were both playful and sarcastic, which drove others mad. Wade was the impulsive realist and Jean was the introspective optimist, they fueled each other's fire—instigator and problem solver alike. Nobody messed with Jean and Wade. But what Wade didn't know was that the person he called a friend had a secret that would change his life forever.

It became very apparent to everyone that Wade had a death wish, and it was only a matter of time before that wish came true. Despite his recklessness, he was a selfless man and cared about other people profoundly. So when they came across a burning house with people inside, he did not hesitate to run headfirst into the fire to save them. Confederate soldiers were amok, and he took a few of them down as his comrades yelled for him to stop, but their cries fell on deaf ears. All they could do was follow and cover him as he barreled through the flames. After what felt like an eternity later, Wade came back out with two victims in his arms before falling to the ground face down with severe burns and a bullet to the gut.

The other soldiers rushed him to Jean, who was in an abandoned house now used to treat the injured. At that point, Wade had already accepted his fate.

"Are they safe?" he asked weakly.

Jean applied pressure to his wound, his face full of panic.

"Yes. Yes, my friend, they are," he stammered.

"Good. Then my job here is done."

Wade's eyes fluttered shut.

Jean slapped him a few times, saying, "No, no, Wade. Stay with me."

"Was I a good man, Johnny boy?"

"Yes...and you still are. You still can be."

"No, there's nothing left for me, Johnny. Daisy's callin'."

After a moment of silence, Jean leaned in close to his face and whispered, "Listen to me. I can save you. I can help you. I can give you a second chance. You can leave this life and start over."

"What're you talkin' about?" Wade mumbled, his eyes closing again.

"Do you trust me?"

Silence.

"Wade!" Jean shook him until his eyes opened again. "Do you trust me?"

Wade looked his friend in the eyes seriously, his own becoming hazy as he started to lose feeling.

"You know I do," he told him.

Jean shut the door and then stood over him once more. All of a sudden, there were large fangs in his teeth and his eyes glowed. Wade was too light-headed to physically react, even as Jean bit his own wrist, drawing blood.

"What are you?" he whispered.

"Drink," Jean ordered, holding his wrist over his mouth. "Drink and you'll live."

Anyone else would have called the other soldiers at the sight of a vampire, but Wade was a man who lived his life believing that, unless a miracle happened, he wouldn't live long, and now that miracle was being offered to him by a trusted friend. So, with his last bit of strength, he drank Jean's blood. Not even a minute later, Wade succumbed to his wounds, everything went dark, and Jean publicly declared him dead.

Then, sometime past sunset, Wade came back to life...buried six feet underground. His wounds were healed, his heart stopped, and he had an indescribable *thirst*. He panicked, his survival instincts kicking in, and started digging himself out of the dirt with his bare hands. When he finally reached the surface, Jean was standing a few feet away, holding a shovel.

"What the hell did you do to me?" Wade shouted, choking up dirt.

"Trust me, you'll thank me later."

From that point forward, Wade MacNamara was a vampire, and with the freedom of immortality, he had all the time in the world to explore who he was and do things he never could have imagined. For a long time, he thought himself doomed to be the poor orphan boy, always struggling and never experiencing. He thought he'd die having lived a traditional life or on the battlefield, but now there was *more*. For once in his life, he had true power, and he was *allowed* to lean into the truer parts of himself and explore what was outside societal bounds. He swore to never operate under someone else's rules but his own, even if it went against the law—and Wade broke many. He and Jean both wreaked havoc, seeking retribution for their past selves, who had the world taken from them. They were inseparable, a force to be reckoned with as they made a name for themselves.

Years passed, then decades, then a century, but you don't live as long as Jean and Wade have and not see the worst of humanity. Dictator upon dictator, murder upon genocide—they witnessed the world crumble into ruin too many times to count. Wade thought it was only fair that he ran into the jaws of death, knowing he couldn't die, taking the brunt of it all. It was easy to get lost in war, one right after the other. If it wasn't the Civil War, then it was World War I, and if it wasn't World War II, then it was an Irish War. If he wasn't on the battlefield, then he was getting into trouble with the police, the mafia, or The Colectiv. But then war lost all meaning and the losses only multiplied. Both he and Jean stopped fueling such things and tried turning their focus on what mattered, but it was enough to make even an immortal vampire feel helpless.

At that time, Wade found solace in knowing that vampires couldn't procreate. It was one less loss, and besides, why would he ever want to put more children through the pain of this world? Why would he want to risk messing them up when he was already so messed up, to begin with? He never had a father of his own, so how could he expect to be a good one? He never had a real chance. It was a mercy that Wade MacNamara would never get to reproduce and pass on his agony ever again, but the universe had a wicked sense of humor because, in 1995, he met a woman named Anya Mészáros.[79]

He had been in Louisiana at the time, staying at Jean's estate. That day, he was at the local casino, playing at one of the poker tables, when a beautiful woman sat down next to him. Her dress was flattering, she had warm hazel eyes and dark wavy hair, but one particular detail he never forgot was the butterfly clips she wore.

She entered the game and engaged in banter with him. Not only was she gorgeous, but she was funny and clever, which had him hooked like a fish on a line. So, at the end of the game, Wade let her win and respectfully invited her to his room, which she accepted. It seemed innocent enough—until she pulled a gun on him. To think, he was

---

[79] Wicked Game - Chris Isaak

normally much more adept at spotting hunters, but it seemed that his better judgment was clouded by Anya's wit.

The Colectiv found my weakness: pretty women.

She took on a more authoritative tone and made some threats. She told him that she wasn't after him but someone else and needed information. In most other instances, Wade would have tried to get out of this situation, but Anya caught his attention. There was something light and airy about her, and unlike many members of The Colectiv, she didn't hold the same bitter prejudice against vampires that they usually did. She knew who she was after and why, and everyone else was only a problem if they became one. Wade admired that, so he cooperated and gave her what she wanted.

From that day on, Wade MacNamara kept a close eye on Anya Mészáros. Though he knew she didn't need or want his protection, he found himself silently assuming the role of her bodyguard. If she needed access somewhere or required extra muscle, he provided it. And even though Anya tried telling Wade to go away, it seemed she couldn't find it within herself to fully reject his help. There was always playfulness in her eyes, not disdain or even fear. If anything, she seemed amused by him, which, for Wade, was a breath of fresh air.

One day, she told him, "I've seen many kinds of men in power. There's nothing particularly horrifying about you."

It was without malice or condescension but stated as a fact.

For the first time in a long time, Wade felt seen, and all of a sudden, whatever intrigue he harbored for Anya became something else. There was a natural chemistry between them that he loved, and the more they talked, the more they seemed to naturally connect, and the more they connected, the harder it was for Wade to hide the fact that he was falling for her. Love was not a thing that he pursued anymore, but of course, somehow, he managed to find it with the last person he ever should have: a hunter.

Wade knew he was prone to impulsive decisions. He ran headfirst into danger many times, but when it came to Anya, he chose to be careful. Not just for himself, but for her. He admired and respected her too much to make any assumptions or put her life in danger because of his feelings. He thought it would be easier to let her go once she went back to Romania. Perhaps she'd forget about him and rank up or marry a human. So he held back, despite his emotions. However, this time, someone else decided for him...because not even a week after finishing her job, Anya appeared on his doorstep, ready to risk it all.[80]

---

[80] From Persephone - Kiki Rockwell

34

The Call from Inside the House

James

Crimson Beach, CA—Present

James followed his brother's form with a frown as he disappeared through the back door.

The memory of their father was an oppressive ghost that haunted them in their waking moments and directly impacted their lives. James didn't like to think about him at all and went out of his way to distance himself from the topic. "Out of sight, out of mind," he'd tell himself. He never knew the man, so he had no "real" reason to care, but now he was forced to feel things he hadn't felt since he was a kid, and he didn't like it. Still, he wondered why he wasn't reacting the same way Eric was.

Maybe he held onto that fantasy more than me. Even after all these years...

"Is he okay?" Jaya asked.

"Yeah, he just needs some time," he said.

This was supposed to be about E and Dante. How does Wade keep coming up?

Their father...a *good* man? Loved, adored, respected? How was that possible? As far as he knew, he was the bane of everyone's existence, including his own. James was supposed to hate him, or at least be over it, but all of this flipped what he knew right on its head.

He got out of his chair, intent on following his brother. "I'll be right back."

"Wait," Emilia stopped him. James frowned at her, and she said, "I have a better idea."

"Which is...?"

She turned to Jaya. "Hey, is the third floor still intact, or...?"

Her friend's face lit up and she nodded in excitement. "Oh, yeah. All of your stuff is still in there, plus a few things I've added over the years. I cleaned it recently, too."

A wide grin spread across Emilia's face. "Great."

She pushed her empty coffee cup away and walked around the counter toward the back of the house. James furrowed his brow and shook his head as he tracked her movement, understanding her intent.

"No, no, no, leave him alone. I doubt he wants to talk to *you* right now."

"Trust me," she argued.

"I don't!" he blurted out, but Emilia was already out the door and sliding it closed behind her.

James hissed and let out a long, exasperated sigh. He sat back on the stool and spun back around, muttering under his breath.

"She just does whatever the fuck she wants, doesn't she?"

Jaya giggled. "Yeah, but it's with good intentions. I don't think she takes kindly to men telling her what to do."

"I know. She's a pain in the ass."

He rested his elbows against the counter and toyed with the rings on his fingers. For a few seconds, it was quiet, but in the silence, James realized that it was just him and Jaya alone in the house.

He glanced at her as she peered down at her mug, and for some reason, James couldn't help but feel...*nervous*. Seeing her with her cable-knit sweater and her shy smile, he didn't think he had any reason to feel this way. Considering the types of people he dealt with regularly, she was the opposite of scary. Perhaps it was because they just met, perhaps it was her demeanor, or perhaps it was the fact that she had openly called him out earlier. Regardless, James didn't feel it often.

He expected Jaya to treat him with hostility or disdain after what she said, but instead, she was respectful. The hunter didn't know what to make of it. Many people spoke to him with unprompted contempt, and in those cases, he was always quick to defend himself, but this was different. For once, someone else's words impacted him enough that he had no immediate response to them.

Their eyes connected briefly, and Jaya looked about as anxious as he felt. Unable to contain himself, James spoke up, but she did it at the same time.

"So—"

"I'm—"

They stopped, their eyes flashing with surprise. Jaya started giggling and James cringed at himself.

"You go," he said.

"No, by all means, what were you going to say?"

"I..." He started hesitantly, trying to find words that weren't painful to say. Jaya watched him in anticipation as he struggled until he rolled his eyes and managed to say, "I know I can be...a *dick*...sometimes, and usually I like to think it's because people deserve it, but... I just wanna say that I'm *not* like Emilia's brother."

"Oh!" she exclaimed, her expression turning apologetic. "Oh no, I shouldn't have said that in the first place, or at least I didn't mean to compare you. You just...you know..."

"I was being a dick," he repeated with a nod.

"Abrasive, I would say, but I get that you were just trying to do your job," she said, nodding. "Sorry if I hurt you somehow."

James furrowed his brow in genuine surprise. She's *apologizing?*

"*Hurt me?* Nah," he said with a chuckle, "it takes a lot to hurt me. Trust me."

And my job is questionable these days.

He had never been so stressed to finish a hunt in his entire career. These things often came easy to him, but not this time.

Jaya hummed, eyeing him curiously as she sat up straight with her hands in her lap. James had never met anyone who was so... *pleasant* and *polite*. Normally, he didn't trust anyone so nice because, in his mind, they were usually hiding something, so he didn't know where to place her at the moment.

"You're worried about him," she said, referring to Eric.

James scoffed, "I mean, yeah, he's my brother. It's not every day that we're working closely with someone like *her* or you. I'm in a...really weird spot right now. I'm going against everything I know, and I... don't have a good feeling."

Jaya frowned. "Why?"

I mean, why wouldn't I?

He has to kill Emilia. He has to protect Eric. He has to lie to Eric. He has to lie to Michael. He has to become captain. He has to follow the rules. He has to follow his gut. He has to make sure Dante dies.

Juxtapositions left and right.

"It's just a gut feeling. Probably paranoia," he said lowly.

"Well, you clearly care a lot about your brother," Jaya said softly. "I'm sure you're also good at what you do. As long as you stay together, everything will be okay."

I don't know...

There was a crunching of sand underfoot and shuffling before the sliding door opened, letting in the breeze and sound of the ocean for a moment. James twisted around, and to his surprise, his twin was following Emilia close behind, albeit looking pretty vexed.

"We're going upstairs," she said.

"Alright," Jaya answered warily.

As Eric passed by, James took his arm and gave him a questioning look. Eric raised his eyebrows, his eyes looking tired.

"You good?" he asked.

His twin nodded. "I will be. You?"

"Yeah," James said with a shrug. "You gonna be okay up there?"

Eric snorted. "I think you should be asking *her* that," he said, patting the front of his jacket over where his pistol was hidden.

He walked out of James' grasp, and the lieutenant's frown deepened as his brother ascended the stairs.

"If you take too long, I'm coming up there!" he called out.

"Yeah, yeah," Emilia sang.

James rolled his eyes and crossed his arms in his seat. The bad feeling worsened.

"What's even up there anyway?" he asked Jaya.

"Nothing you should be concerned about, I promise. It's an old library Emilia put together when she used to live here, amongst other things," she explained.

"Oh, the nerd's gonna love that one."

For some reason, he couldn't help but feel a twinge of bitterness towards Emilia at that moment. It seemed that she knew his brother better than he expected, and he didn't know if his feelings were rooted in jealousy or overprotectiveness. All he knew was that he could hear Michael's words echoing louder and louder with the passing days.

"The last thing we need is for something to happen like it did with your mom."

And if it did, what the fuck *do you want me to do about it? Stop him? Turn him in? Kill her?*

He already had an answer for the last one. *But...*

James despised Emilia when he thought she wanted Eric dead, and now he was supposed to hate her for caring about him? He was supposed to kill her when she saved his brother's life? Nothing makes sense to him right now.

Nothing's happened yet. Yet.

"Are you okay?" Jaya's soft voice cut through his battling thoughts.

The hunter was almost surprised by her question. He wasn't used to overthinking this much. He was often so sure.

"Why did she do what she did?" he inquired, desperate for answers.

The vampire frowned. "You mean 'The Hellhound'?"

"Yeah."

There was a part of James that wasn't just asking for Emilia but for himself. One of the things hunters were taught early on was that conventional morality had to be thrown out the window. Hunters had to learn to live with the things they did and make peace with the possibility that some of them would sooner end up in purgatory than the pearly gates up above. Their deaths were destined to be violent or however karma might have it. And when Emilia herself accused the twins of their murders back in New York, it only made James even more aware of such things.

"We don't kill for the same reasons," Eric had said.

Perhaps he was right, but these last few days, with the increasing weight of everything, James was forced to take a brief pause. If Emilia could do what she did for his brother and at the same time have done horrible things, then what did that mean? He never liked to dwell on whether he was good or bad. It wasn't part of the job.

"Emilia sees the good in people. And she loves hard—harder than most," Jaya explained. "Personally, I would never do what she did. Then again, she's always been braver than I. Even when she's scared, she runs into the flames, and I can't really say the same. And you can think what you want about her, but… at the end of the day, she was hurt. And she wanted the same people who did horrible things to her—to her brother, to me, or to anyone else—to hurt even more.

"But she also wanted to help," she continued with a shrug. "That's the thing about Emilia. She's willing to pour her entire heart and soul into the people she cares about, no matter the cost. You could be battered and broken and come from the depths of hell, but once Emilia sees the light in you, she'll do everything in her power to make sure you see it too. It was how she found me all those years ago."

James clung to every word but was careful not to pry. To his surprise, he didn't have to ask anything at all because Jaya didn't seem to have anything to hide.

"Let's just say I was stuck in a very horrible marriage. I lived in constant fear, and I didn't know what to do or how to defend myself. But Emilia saw me when no one else did. She saw my bruises and the look in my eyes, and she gave me a choice, an opportunity to be free… so I took it."

There was no shame in Jaya's voice or expression. It was clear she didn't regret her decision to become a vampire and leave her horrible life behind. James never had a choice in whether he wanted to be a daywalker—he was just born that way. It was all he knew. So, he figured that to choose such a life, you had to come from an incredibly dark past, and it was the one viable means of escape. The fact that Emilia had been her savior once again made his respect for her go up even more, much to his chagrin.

Is that what she does? Save *people? It* wasn't *a one-time thing? She doesn't do this for her own benefit. She just does it because she wants to. Why?*

Other than Eric, he didn't know many people like that in his life. If he looked back further, his mother was like that too. But James wasn't sure if he could say the same about himself. Especially not right now.

A voice in the back of his mind asked: *Emilia had a reason for killing... what's yours?*

Because...

There was no answer.

James took a long look at the vampire before him. They just met, but his first impression was that she was a warm, colorful woman with a lot of class—unlike him. She was more on the introverted side compared to Emilia but was very independent and took care of herself all these years. However, thinking about a time when she lived a waking nightmare made him feel a sense of injustice. He knew that a lot of people, himself included, were simply destined for violence and hardship, but he didn't think it was fair when people like Jaya faced such things. Trying to figure out how she remained so kind despite being a vampire was like trying to shove a square peg into a circular hole.

He found himself speaking before his mind could catch up.

"Hey, uh..... *sorry*...for being an asshole earlier."

The word tasted wrong in his mouth, and Jaya looked about as stunned by his apology as James was.

She smirked at him and said, "It's okay. I accept your apology."

"Just don't tell anyone I said that, especially Emilia," he added quickly.

She laughed. Her eyes sparkled under the warm kitchen light, and for a moment, James felt a faint flutter in his heart. He covered it up by clearing his throat.

"Don't worry, James. Your secret is safe with me. Eric is lucky to have you."

His face softened, and guilt hit him like a bullet to the chest. Such a short and sweet statement, yet so impactful.

The moment was sorely interrupted by the sound and feeling of James' phone going off. The suddenness startled him, and he cursed when he dug it out of his pocket and saw the name on the screen.

Michael.

"Aww fuck."

"Is everything okay?" Jaya asked with concern.

"It's my handler," he derided, getting up from his seat. Upon seeing her bewildered expression, he added, "It's my boss. I need to take this. I'll be right back."

"W-wait!"

He turned back around to see Jaya staring at him with big doe eyes full of fear, her hands clutching her chest.

"You're not going to tell them where you are, are you? Or do they already know?" she asked.

James opened and closed his mouth a few times, unsure of what to say, but the look on her face made him shake his head.

"Don't worry about it."

†††

The lieutenant took his turn standing on the dark sandy beach with his heart pounding in his chest.

"Hey, Mike," he said coolly.

"Hey, Jimmy. For a moment there, I thought you weren't gonna pick up. I was about to send the cavalry," the commander joked.

"Sorry, I just got out of the shower. It's been a long fucking day," he lied with a casual chuckle.

"Hey, uh...are you and E in LA yet?" James couldn't help but notice the urgency in Michael's voice.

"Yeah, we got here a while ago. The last drive took nine hours."

"Jesus, I don't miss trips like that."

"It's not easy. I almost lost my fucking mind."

Then, with an air of authority, Michael asked, "Is the task complete?"

James worked his jaw as he stared hard into the water, trying not to think about the fact that Eric and Emilia were currently upstairs, *alone*. He kept his answers short to not slip up.

"Yeah. Yeah, it's done," he responded.

"She didn't give you any trouble, did she?"

"Nothing out of the ordinary."

"Did you burn the remains?"

"Before I left, yeah," James said, his mouth twisting uncomfortably.

"Did, uh...did E suspect anything?"

Not yet.

"I'm pretty sure if he did, he would've said something by now. As far as I can tell, he doesn't know shit. I don't think he'll miss her, either." James winced, not believing his own words.

"Damn..." Michael uttered with what sounded like awe, "I gotta hand it to you, Jimmy...you really are good."

The daywalker scoffed, "Whoever said I wasn't?"

"So, what are your plans? Are the two of you going out tonight?"

"Nah, we're too exhausted to do anything crazy. I'm pretty sure E hasn't slept this entire trip, so I'm hoping he finally gets some sleep, but...tomorrow we're gonna start looking for leads."

"Yeah, it's better to save your energy for what's to come."

"Yeah."

There was a moment of stillness. It wasn't long, but the anticipation killed him and set James on edge. He watched the waves tumble onto the sand, the cold breeze nipping at his skin and messing with his hair. He pushed it out of the way in annoyance.

"Are you guys at the beach?" Michael asked.

James closed his eyes, his heart dropping into his stomach as he cursed himself. He didn't think it would have been so obvious, but he should have known the commander was sharp. He still tried to maintain control and stayed quick with his words.

"No, that's, uh, that's just the TV. Some surfer movie is on."

"Surfer movie? Which one are you talking about?"

"The one with Keanu Reeves, I think," he said from the top of his head.

"Ah, 'Point Break'. What part are you on?"

James hesitated, considering he had seen that movie *once* in passing as a child. "Uh, I don't know. I wasn't actually paying attention. E's pretty into it, though."

He moved away from the water to reduce the obvious sound.

This conversation was becoming painful, too painful, and he wanted it to end. All of a sudden, he was a teenager again, lying to Michael about something he did, afraid to get in trouble. He was ordinarily so good at keeping himself in check, but the circumstances were getting to him.

"Right," the commander huffed, but then got serious. "Well... I'm glad you two are getting far. We'll talk about your promotion when you get back, alright?"

James perked up at that, suddenly overcome with excitement. Could it be? Was there still hope after all?

"Yeah, yeah, of course."

"I'll let you two get back to it, but... Jimmy?"

"Yeah?"

Michael let a pressing second pass before telling him, "Don't do anything you'll *regret*, okay?"

James furrowed his brow. He thought he was imagining it, but he swore it sounded like a veiled threat.

He looked off toward Jaya's house and said, "Okay... I won't."

"I'm proud of you." The words sounded empty.

"Yeah. Talk to you later, Mike," the daywalker replied before ending the call.

James stared down at the phone in his hands in crushing bewilderment.

"Don't do anything you'll regret."

What the fuck was that supposed to mean?

Michael had never said such words to him before, at least not unprompted or with such ominousness. But then he remembered something that Michael told him back in his office.

"...the more you rise, the more secrets you need to keep. You need to keep your cards hidden and always be one step ahead of your enemy and those around you."

His eyes widened as paranoia and fear crept into his bones. He spun around and started scanning the area for anyone who could be watching. He went up and down the sand, looked up onto rooftops, and even went out to the road and scanned the cliffs. He expanded his senses, honing in on them, but there was nothing—nothing was out of the ordinary at all.

He's not here. Nobody's here. You would've sensed them by now. You're just paranoid. It's all in your head.

Yet he returned to the sand, unable to shake the deep terror within him.

Something wasn't right.[81]

---

[81] Know Your Enemy - Green Day

35

The Face of the Silver Wolf

Wade

[82]The Iovaneau's ruled the Transylvanian estate, which, in the 90s, was still run by Commander Constantin Iovaneau. And Constantin had two sons named Gabriel and Michael. Wade wasn't well versed in the history and politics of their family, but from what he knew, Gabriel was Constantin's heir, and Michael was an afterthought. But it also happened that Michael was Anya's childhood best friend.

Michael trained with the Mészáros family in America until he was an adult, so their families knew each other well. Anya always spoke of their friendship with fondness, but while Anya saw him as a brother, he wanted something more. In fact, he proposed to her more than once. Of course, she rejected him, but Michael took it in stride, perhaps thinking that she'd change her mind down the line. However, what he

---

[82] War Pigs - Black Sabbath

didn't know was that the reason she turned him down was because of Wade.

At the time, Wade's biggest problem wasn't with Michael at all. He was wary about his intentions with Anya, and though it sparked a bit of innocent jealousy, Michael, at the very least, respected her. His brother, however, did not. The vampire didn't know Gabriel Iovaneau personally, but from what Anya told him, he was an arrogant, spoiled young man who wasn't as smart as he thought he was. He may have been a good hunter, but he abused his power more often than not, and it was that behavior that got him killed.

The first thing Wade remembered was being at his apartment in Bucharest when, all of a sudden, there was incessant banging on his door. When he opened it, Anya was standing on the other side with a bruise and tears streaming down her cheeks. Wade had seen her with cuts and bruises before, but the look on her face told him this wasn't a hunting injury. In her shaken and agitated state, Anya told him that earlier that evening, when she was alone in the training room, Gabriel put his hands on her. When she rejected him and pushed him away, he got violent. Unfortunately for him, Anya was a good fighter, so it didn't get very far before she took him down long enough to run.

As she told him this story, Wade saw red and had half a mind to walk into the estate to kill Gabriel Iovaneau with his bare hands, but Anya talked him down and pleaded for him to stay with her. She told him that Gabriel would be too proud to talk about what happened and that wouldn't be a problem for the next few days anyway, because he'd be on a hunting trip in the mountains. Wade listened to her, held her, and comforted her, making a mental note of this detail for the future.

Then, a few days later, up in the snowy mountains of Romania, Gabriel Iovaneau was mauled to death by a vampire on Wade MacNamara's orders. Michael, who had been with him, was spared and managed to fight his way out of the fray. It earned him the title of The Silver Wolf of Romania and put him next in line to be Commander of The Colectiv.

Anya found out the same day she told Wade that she was pregnant. There was a shouting match and fighting over what he had done before she blurted it out. Then everything went quiet and time seemed to slow as Wade started to spiral. He gave up on the idea of being a father over a hundred years ago, and the possibility never crossed his mind. Vampires, for the most part, were infertile, and daywalkers were a biological rarity, an urban legend, so at first, he doubted Anya. He thought perhaps she was wrong or that the baby belonged to someone else, but she assured him that wasn't the case. In the end, he had no reason not to trust her.

Wade was going to be a father. *Again.*

It was forbidden—beyond that—so Wade gave her the option to get rid of it. He'd get her to a reliable clinic if she wanted, but Anya refused. After what happened with Gabriel, she cared more about her future with Wade than The Colectiv, and she wanted to keep this baby. She knew the implications and was willing to do anything, despite the consequences, and by God, Wade wouldn't have loved her so much if she didn't.

So Wade and Anya resolved right then and there that they were doing this together.[83] He, a wanted man, used every resource he had to flee with his pregnant wife and unborn child. They backpacked around Europe, living off the grid as Anya's belly grew over time. They even got married in secret, exchanging vows only to each other. For a while, his wife was even reluctant to risk going to the doctor, but for her and the baby's safety, Wade was adamant about it. And it was

---

[83] ANYWHERE BUT HERE - PVRIS

because of Wade's vehemence that they found out they were having *twins*.

He wasn't a religious man by any means, but all Wade could think when he found out was: *I lost one child, and God gave me two.* And he was going to do everything in his power to not lose them this time.

Eventually, he and Anya found a place to hide in Ireland, which the Iovaneau's had no jurisdiction under. Anya went into early labor, and contrary to all the hearsay, Wade was present for the birth of his sons. The entire time, he feared for their lives. The last time he had a child was in the 1800s, and he hadn't been allowed in the same room, only ever hearing Eliza's cries from the hallway. This time, Wade got to be there as the midwife pulled them out one by one—James and then Eric. He held them in his own two hands—two bundles of joy that filled his heart with so much love it could burst. He cried his eyes out when he brought them home.

James Danior and Eric Django MacNamara.

Despite his previous fears, Wade found comfort in knowing that they carried his blood and that not even the invisible could touch them this time.

For three years, they lived in blissful seclusion. Wade got to live with Anya and watch their boys grow, walk, and learn to talk. They were a handful, natural-born troublemakers, and incredibly clever, but it was nothing he couldn't carry. Anya no doubt had her work cut out for her, but her love was overabundant and she never hesitated to spare a single drop. Of course, when they started exhibiting vampire qualities, Wade took it upon himself to fulfill their needs when she couldn't. It was a team effort, and despite living in caution and secrecy, they were happy for those first three years.

When The Colectiv found them, it was Michael who showed up, but if Anya thought her childhood friend would take mercy on her, then she was sorely mistaken. Michael was allowed to run an entire army when he otherwise wouldn't have, and now that he had power, ruthless cunning took over. Not only did Wade have his brother killed, but even worse, Wade was the reason his beloved best friend was in this mess and not by his side. It made him so spiteful that he and his team went to Ireland without warning or jurisdiction. But the Iovaneau's never cared about the laws of others.

In some twisted version of mercy, Michael sent a letter in the mail addressed to Wade himself:

I can't save her from my father's wrath, but I can save her from you. You have a choice, MacNamara. You stay with them, and I'll do my worst, or you let her go, and I'll take it from here.

This was the difference between Michael and Wade. Wade was willing to burn the world down to *protect* the people he loved, and Michael was willing to burn the world down to *own* it—Anya's world included. And Wade wasn't the type to stand down, but when you're a man who has lost so many people and your whole family is on the line, difficult decisions have to be made.

So, to save them from himself and the clutches of The Colectiv, he chose to separate from Anya and his children. With the help of Jean and a few other vampire connections, he put them on a cargo plane to the U.S. with promises to see them again. The boys cried and Anya demanded that he come with her, but he couldn't risk it. It broke his heart beyond repair, but he promised to write and call and send money and told his wife that he'd find a way to take down Michael Iovaneau so they could be together again. Until then, he needed them safe.

That was the last time he ever saw them.

When the vampire left the airport and went back to his small home one last time, The Silver Wolf and his secret army of hunters were already waiting for him. Wade had expected it, yet, in a blind rage, he was ready to barrel through them. He lashed out and managed to take some of them down, but at a certain point, it didn't matter anymore. No matter how hard he fought, he was outnumbered, and Wade MacNamara was swiftly taken down.

He was sure that was it. He lost his family and was about to lose his head, just like he wanted to all those years ago. Instead, he was shipped off to the Black Sea to continue his suffering in a steel box, underwater, away from the rest of the world. As torture and leverage come to find out, to keep Jean Beltremieux in line.

When Anya passed away, Michael was the one who delivered the news—the executioner of his heart. Anya—his savior, his wife—had been sick and died less than a year later. Wade almost didn't believe him at first, but the man didn't strike him as someone who could feign such grief, and it broke him. It broke him apart and with nothing but his pain and his dark cell, he was left with no other choice but to feel everything. There was no war, no drug, no distraction to take it away. He thought of the boys and how they were all alone, two daywalkers without a parent to take care of them.

But then, like the final nail in his coffin, Michael said, "And don't worry about the twins. They're well taken care of."

The insinuation was clear.

Wade screamed at him, but it did nothing. Wade MacNamara could do *nothing* but rot in his cell for 20 years.

He didn't know how he lasted so long in a place like Charybdis. He had seen plenty of other prisoners go insane and wither away in less time, but somehow Wade made it this far. Perhaps it was because, in the back of his mind, he was always thinking of his family. He thought of Eric, James, Jean, and especially Anya and what she would've wanted. The hope that the rest of them were still alive kept him going. After all, Wade came from nothing, and when you took everything away from someone who was used to losing, there was no telling what they would do in the aftermath.

You think you can take me down? You think punishing me will make me better? You think you can teach me a lesson? Well... I'm going to show you how I've gotten so much worse.

†††

Tokyo, Japan—The Devil's Basement

[84]The lights over the fighting cage painted the room crimson.

Wade stared down at his opponent. His glowing eyes were set in a predatory gaze above the black mask covering half of his bloody face. His hair was a mess around his head, and his bare chest heaved as he paused before his next move. The other vampire who was much bulkier than him, bared his fangs in a snarl, his own eyes glowing with the same intensity. Around them, the audience watched with anticipation.

His opponent lunged and swung for his head. With quick reflexes, Wade ducked out of the way, and then he hit him in the ribs and the face in succession. His bones cracked from the impact, and he stumbled sideways slightly before righting himself again. The vampire threw a low kick to Wade's legs, aiming to sweep them out from under him. However, Wade was too quick, and he jumped over his leg with ease and punched him in the nose.

Here in the Devil's Basement, where the dead put their immortality to the test, there were no holds barred. Fighters used every weapon in their arsenal: fists, elbows, legs, and knees. The only thing

---

[84] Other Side - MIYAVI

that wasn't allowed were their teeth. It was veiled in anonymity, which was perfect for someone who didn't want to be found by the wrong people. Fighters submitted a name of their choice and got queued up with the next available person of their stature. It gave rich vampires some entertainment, and it gave others a chance to earn money. In an immortal sense, it wasn't illegal, but it was a secret to anyone who wasn't looking for it. It was a harmless hobby, for the most part, and one that Wade partook in during his last visit to the country. As soon as he returned, he wasted no time in finding it again to let off some steam and get back into shape.

The fighters went back and forth, breaking bones and drawing blood from each other. Though the other vampire was good, Wade was better. He always was. He was fast, impulsive, and ruthless. He moved like a jackrabbit in the ring, with the ability to get close and dodge hits. But even if he practiced different fighting styles for over a century, at the end of the day, his roots came from the streets, and the last 20 years have made him a little more feral.

Wade lunged forward to drive his shoulder into his opponent's waist, grab his legs, and take him down. They both fell to the floor, and Wade maneuvered into position to grab his arm, wrap his legs across his chest, and pull him into an arm bar. He bucked his hips upward and then, with zero hesitation, broke the other vampire's elbow with a crack. The man cried out in pain as the crowd cheered. With the other man's guard down, Wade sat up, took his opponent's head in his hands, and snapped his neck. He went limp, and Wade let his body fall to the floor.

With that, the fight was officially over.

"Santos takes the win!" the announcer exclaimed over the speakers in Japanese.

Wade, Elias Santos, got to his feet and raised his arms in the air as the crowd went wild once more. He smirked devilishly beneath his mask, but the pride he felt did not outweigh the true rage that lay underneath.

When he was in the locker room, unraveling his hands, all covered in blood, Wade received a phone call. He barely glanced at the caller ID because only one person had his number.

"Yo, Johnny."

"Hey, Wade. I have some interesting news you're gonna wanna hear about your boys."

Wade straightened up and dropped his voice to a whisper. "What now? What happened?"

"Some*one* happened. Nothing bad...*yet*...but you're not gonna like it."

He furrowed his brow. "What d'ya mean? Who're you talking about?"

"It's Emilia," Jean said carefully. "The boys interrogated her about Dante, and somehow she ended up tagging along with them."

Wade's eyes widened.

"What?" he blurted out.

"I know."

He rolled his eyes and groaned, pinching the bridge of his nose.

Out of all the people.

Emilia was Jean's protégé and was all but like a daughter to him. Wade considered her a good friend many decades ago, back when she was on a rampage with her brother, Dante. But now that Jean caught him up, he also knew about her tryst with his son, Eric. Wade had more of a personal problem with Dante regarding that, but Emilia was not a saint either. He cared about her, but she had her issues.

"What does she want with him?" he demanded.

"She claims that she wants to save Dante and that she has unfinished business with Eric."

"So, she's meddling?"

"Seems like it."

"Of course she is."

Wade knew how relentless Emilia could be when some wild idea got into her head, but it was different when he dragged his family into this.

He rested his elbows on his knees and looked down at the locker room floor.

"A pureblood vampire taggin' along with two hunters," he muttered.

"And one of those hunters was in love with her. Sound familiar?"

"Too familiar."

He and Anya had chosen their fates long ago, but he never expected his own family to repeat it.

What a wicked twist of fate. What a curse.

"Does The Colectiv know about this?" Wade asked.

"I think if they did, we would know."

Wade chuckled darkly and said, "Michael's a sneaky bastard. He's always one step ahead, and with my escape, no doubt driving him up the wall? Yeah, I don't fuckin' trust him. She's gonna get 'em fuckin' killed!"

Wade growled in frustration and pushed himself off the bench. He started pacing up and down the row of lockers.

"Hey, easy, Wade—"

"Jean, please! She doesn't know what the fuck she's doing!" he shouted.

"Then we act fast," Jean offered.

Wade stopped moving and looked off in confusion.

"What do you mean?" he asked.

"It's the perfect opportunity. With Emilia in the mix...something's bound to happen, especially if Michael has a say in it."

As he picked up what Jean was putting down, Wade's lips spread into an excited grin.

"Permission to fuck shit up, Johnny?"

"Permission granted."

Wade refused to be at the mercy of a cruel king any longer—a wolf in sheep's clothing.

The sole reason he was in Japan was because Michael had no jurisdiction here. After what he did in Ireland, he was banned from the country indefinitely, so the Japanese vampire hunters knew better than to trust him. It made it the perfect place to lie low and recalibrate after being imprisoned. However, Jean and Wade had a plan—a plan they never thought they'd have to execute, but if there was ever a perfect cause for a war, it was this one.[85]

---

[85] And So It Went - The Pretty Reckless

36

I Don't Want to Set the World on Fire

Emilia

Crimson Beach, CA—Present

Emilia could see Eric standing far down the sand, where she and Jaya had been earlier, staring out onto the western horizon. She slowly and carefully made her way toward him, and he sighed in frustration.

"Go away," he muttered without looking at her.

"I just wanted to make sure you were okay," she told him.

Emilia stood beside him but maintained a safe distance.

He scoffed, "I'm about as okay as I'll ever be. Stop worrying about me. I'm fine."

"You don't seem fine."

"That's not for you to care about."

Why not?

Eric kept his gaze forward, but Emilia could see a storm in his hazel eyes. He was holding his emotions at bay, just like he always fought hard to do.

She didn't think mentioning Wade would affect him so much. She didn't intend to hurt him by doing so. The anger was expected, but not this. Part of her felt guilty, but the other was confused.

Had he really not known anything about him? Did no one tell him?

Of course, they didn't. She shouldn't have expected The Colectiv to paint a pretty picture of any vampire, especially Wade.

But what about Anya? Did she die before she had a real chance?

"He would've adored you, Eric," she told him in earnest. "Wade would've adored both of you. There wasn't anything in his life that he didn't put his entire soul into. And I'm sure he loved your mom the same way. He would've loved you *so much*."

Eric closed his eyes, and his lips quivered. A lump formed in Emilia's throat, seeing him like this. Last night, after his downpour of emotions, he played it off like it was no big deal, but it almost seemed harder for him now. She found herself wanting to hold him and tell him that everything was going to be okay. It was the same urge she had yesterday by the pool.

She crossed her arms, resisting that feeling.

[86]"That's the problem," he choked out. He opened his eyes and glared down at the sand. "All these people got to meet him, live with him, and love him...except *us*. His own kids. Sometimes I swear I can remember him. Bits and pieces, but I can't tell what's real and what's not. I used to fantasize for a long time about how different my life would have been if he had been alive. If *he* raised us, and not..."

---

[86] The Ghost of You - My Chemical Romance

He trailed off, not daring to say the name out loud. When he spoke again, his voice was a harsh whisper.

"Maybe it would've been easier. I don't know...but when I think about it now, I just get...*angry*. It doesn't seem fair."

A single salty tear fell down his cheek, and he angrily wiped it away. Tears of her own prickled in Emilia's eyes.

Rather than continuing to resist, she took a cautious step towards him, as if approaching a scared animal, and put a hand on his arm in a comforting gesture. Eric's head snapped to look at their hand and then at her, except this time he didn't pull away. Instead, there was a softness in his eyes and a deep yearning that Emilia hadn't seen in years. It made her breath hitch.

Before he could run away, she asked, "Can I show you something?"

He furrowed his brow. "Show me what?"

"Something to take your mind off things. It has nothing to do with Wade, Dante, or anything else. It's just...a collection of sorts."

"A *collection*?"

"Yeah. It's something I...*curated*...over the years," she smirked. "It's upstairs, and it'll only take a minute. I just thought you'd enjoy it more than...*this*."

She finally let her hand drop and clasped it behind her back, still feeling his warmth on her fingertips.

Eric eyed her skeptically before rolling his eyes and saying, "Fine. Make it quick."

Emilia grinned and waved for him to follow.

James and Jaya were still at the kitchen counter when they were back inside the house, much to Emilia's dismay. Even more surprising was the fact that they were having a conversation. About what she couldn't imagine. She let them know where they were going, ignoring

James' threats as she led Eric up the stairs toward the third floor, passing by more of Jaya's personalized decor. At the end of a short hallway, Emilia stopped outside a chamber to the left. It was then that her nerves kicked in.

Emilia hadn't seen what lay inside in 40 years, and it was one of the most personal pieces of her soul. The only people who got a glimpse were Jean, Jaya, and—at a certain point—Wade. Dante, however, never even knew about it. At a certain point in time, she fantasized about showing it to Eric, but after what happened, she didn't think the day would ever become a reality.

"What's in here exactly?" Eric asked.

"It's an old library. You'll see. I haven't been here since I left."

"And you're showing it to me...*why*?"

Emilia looked over her shoulder at him, his curious eyes taking her in.

She shrugged. "I feel like you'd appreciate what's in here. Think of it as my least gruesome secret and a way to make up for not telling you about Wade."

He looked even more bewildered now. "Okay..."

With a nod, Emilia opened the door. She walked in first but stepped aside to let Eric get a full view, and she watched him as his cold demeanor fell away and his eyes widened.

His jaw dropped and he scoffed, "Holy shit."

It was exactly as Emilia remembered it.

This room made the rest of the house look like a minimalist dream, as it was filled to the ceiling with *everything*. It was roughly the same size as the entire first floor, but with a higher ceiling, and was divided into different areas for different purposes. Half of the chamber had giant bookcases set into the walls, filled with an overabundance of literature. Glass cases sat in various parts of the room with more books, paintings, and other memorabilia. There were areas dedicated to comic books, music, maps, and even old pictures. There were sculptures and framed art pieces from throughout the 20th century. The furniture was certified vintage, as was the sitting area in the center for talking and reading. Except for some new additions from Jaya, it was as if Emilia had never left at all.

Eric was utterly speechless. Emilia hadn't seen him look this giddy and enthusiastic in years, and she found herself smiling from ear to ear just being in his presence. It sweetened her nostalgia instead of souring it.

"Do I—Where do I—Can I?" He stuttered, unable to form sentences.

She giggled. "Yeah, you can look."

"Okay, fuck. I'll, uh... I'll go this way."

Eric headed towards the far-left wall, and Emilia followed close behind. In a way, she needed the tour herself after being away for so long. This place once belonged to a girl far beyond herself, and returning felt like she was reconnecting with her somehow.

In the first section they came upon, there was a large sepia map high above. Below it, a map of Mexico was next to a vibrant Huichol yarn painting of a hummingbird. There was a glass case with artifacts like statues made of black clay, painted dishes with intricate designs, and animal figurines adorned with colorful beads. All were items she acquired on trips to her mother country.

Eric leaned in and admired everything with keen eyes.

"Have you ever been?" she asked.

"Once for school," he replied. "It was one of my favorite trips."

Emilia smirked. "Would you ever go again?"

He nodded. "If I ever had the chance, yeah."

The next area had shelves full of records, cassette tapes, and CDs. Below that, there was a console with a record player on top and a stereo from the 80s underneath. Eric sifted through the collection, seeming surprised to find the wide array of genres that Emilia possessed. She had anything from disco to rock music to hip-hop to Latin.

"Are these all originals?" he asked in wonder.

"Most of them, yeah. I always tried buying them once they came out. As you can see from this room, I'm a big fan of collecting," she said with a sweeping motion of her hands. "I had an ex-boyfriend who once called me a hoarder."

Let's just say that he's lucky to be alive.

Eric clicked his tongue in annoyance and said, "Fuck that guy. This is great."

The fact that he was defending her took Emilia by surprise. It warmed her heart, and she stared at him fondly, though he was too preoccupied to notice.

"I should probably put some music on," she said suddenly. "Any requests?"

"Your selection is so vast that I wouldn't be able to make up my mind, to be honest."

She snorted. "This isn't even everything I own, but... I think I know what I'm in the mood for."

Emilia looked up at the shelves, and without having to think too hard, she pulled out a record. She held it out for Eric to see, showing him a vinyl from the 1930s by a band called The Ink Spots. It was in decent condition considering its age.

"Jean gave me this one," she told him as she placed it on the record player.

[87]The Ink Spots played in the background as Eric continued to explore Emilia's library. She let him roam free, while he let her explain everything with zero complaints. He listened attentively, absorbing the information, as he always did. It brought her immense joy that her idea to bring him here worked, and it made her even happier to know that this part of him that she had loved so dearly was not lost. It was like they were back in Sorrento, just two people in love and enjoying each other's company, unaware of what the future held, except this time, Emilia was finally sharing pieces of herself instead of hiding.

They had just finished talking about the art on the walls when Eric started pursuing through the many binders of comics on the shelves. Some of the most precious issues were even hung up in frames.

"I didn't know you were into this stuff," he mused.

"Yeah, I was always kind of a nerd," she chuckled nervously. "It was hard not to be when I was always locked up in my room with nothing else to do but read, watch TV, and listen to music. They were all I had back then."

"Yeah, I know the feeling. Stuff like this was my escape back at the estate, and even back when we moved around a lot. I got caught stealing a few comics once. Mom wasn't too happy about it."

A laugh bubbled in Emilia's throat. "Of all the things for you to steal, of course, it was that."

"Hey, desperate times. I'm pretty sure I still owe money at the library too," he admitted with a giggle.

She rolled her eyes playfully but ended up laughing along with him. They locked eyes with each other and lingered there for a moment until the tension silenced them. It was brief, but it was enough to throw Emilia a little off balance, and she swore she heard him falter

---

[87] I Don't Want To Set The World On Fire - The Ink Spots

too. She had to clear her throat and eagerly moved him along towards the literature section, which made up the majority of the room.

They stopped at some display cases first, where Emilia kept the oldest copies that needed to be protected. Some were in different languages, but others were recognizable, like Mary Shelley's *Frankenstein*, Bram Stoker's *Dracula*, and *The Works of Edgar Allan Poe*. They were editions that were published well before Emilia was even born, and Eric was flabbergasted.

"Woah, what the fuck? How did you get *these*?"

"They were gifts from Jean and some other friends of mine who are way older than me," she explained. "They're all in Europe now, but they know how much I like to read and how much I have a thing for horror."

"That's really fucking cool," he said with an enthusiastic grin.

Emilia bit back a smile. "You're probably the only person to ever say that in 70 years, so thank you."

Eric turned his focus on the massive bookcases, his eyes scanning the numerous covers and titles. Here, Emilia had gathered an array of genres, from fiction to biographies to poetry to modern Shakespeare plays. They weren't as old as the ones in the glass displays and were editions that she deemed safe enough to hold and read.

When he came upon books on mythology, symbolism, and vampire lore, he scoffed, "Funny. I've read all of these."

Emilia rolled her eyes. "Of course you have."

"The Colectiv doesn't exactly carry Game of Thrones or graphic novels."

"Why would they?" she derided in annoyance.

What did they have other than traumatic experiences?

"Why do you even have these?" he asked, motioning to the shelf. "They're not even factually correct. It's all speculation and myths written by people who don't know anything about vampires."

"Not everyone is a walking encyclopedia, Eric," Emilia argued. "I thought it would help me understand myself better. After I got turned, I mean. Plus, I thought it was kind of ironic for a vampire to own books about vampires."

Eric shook his head, and his mirthful smile made Emilia's dead heart flutter. He instinctively reached for a book, but then stopped halfway and scratched the back of his neck.

She giggled at his nervousness. "You can touch them, you know."

"You know, these are probably worth thousands," he told her.

"Yeah, but I don't keep them for the money."

"Then why do you?"

The vampire shrugged. She walked towards the center of the room and swept her arms around as she said to him, "Because, Eric... life is for *living*. Music is for listening. Books are for reading. I'm not the type of collector who just *stares* at what I have. I *use it*. If I die, I would rather that historians or archaeologists see how much everything was loved. *That's* history to me."

When her eyes found his again, he was watching her with a deep, peculiar stare. She couldn't quite put words to the emotion in his eyes, but it nearly made her legs buckle beneath her. It took her a second to find her voice again.

"What?"

Eric tore his eyes away from her, shaking his head. "Nothing."

Feeling like her chest may implode, she turned around and walked towards the velvet seating area. Emilia sat down and curled up on the loveseat, ignoring the feeling.

"Well, that's my collection," she said, taking a gander around the room. "Maybe I *am* a hoarder."

Eric slowly but surely followed her lead and sat on the opposite end of the small couch.

"I don't see anything wrong with it. Like you said, it's history," he said casually.

A smile tugged at her lips. "Yeah, it is."

Emilia glanced over at him as he leaned back with his arm resting against the back of the loveseat. For once, Eric looked more relaxed, and it settled something in her. The eclipse on his neck peaked out from the collar of his jacket, and she couldn't help but sneak glances at it or the sharp lines of his face and jaw. For some reason, the more time they spent in this space with no one else around, the more nervous she became.

"Did you like it?" she asked in a softer tone.

"Yeah. Yeah, this place is great," he answered with a nod. "I, uh... I didn't know what I was expecting, but it is like your own personal museum in here."

That wonder was still present in his eyes and his voice as he continued to marvel at it all.

"It is, yeah," she affirmed. "I just never have the heart to throw anything away, especially stuff that means so much to me. I'm lucky Jaya feels at least somewhat the same way. I'll have to repay her for that."

"Yeah."

In the quiet that followed, the tension in the air hung differently. It was like their time in Sorrento, yet nothing like it at all. They were in a bubble of their own making, frozen in time, and all their troubles and obligations were far away and put on hold. But there was still a gap between them, a distance neither of them was willing to cross. It was agonizing, and Emilia found herself talking just to relieve it.

"I hope you got what you wanted," she said.

Eric frowned. "What do you mean?"

"Answers, I guess," she replied with a shrug.

"About?"

"Me."

Eric studied her carefully, working his jaw. Emilia tried holding his intense gaze until she couldn't anymore. Instead, she glanced down at her hands and started fidgeting with them. All at once, she was 22 again, too afraid to mess things up.

She was never one to be apprehensive around men. It was quite the opposite, but Eric was different. He always had been. He didn't make her feel small, but he did make her feel vulnerable and bare, especially now that she'd shown him parts of herself that not many people got to see. She felt like a gaping wound. After everything, Emilia just wanted him to see her.

"I did."

Her head snapped up, startled by his answer and Eric's expression was soft as he faced her. For the first time in three years, she swore that she could melt right then and there. She didn't think he was doing it on purpose, but even if she was terrified, she dared to be bold.

"Was it what you hoped it would be?" she whispered.

Eric opened his mouth but hesitated to speak. He winced and looked away from her as if his answer was too painful to say.

"I don't know if I should answer that."

"Why not?"

"Because... it'll just..." He trailed off and sighed in frustration.

Emilia knew the answer without him having to say it because she had been silently warring with it for days—*years*.

"It'll complicate things," she finished for him.

Without looking at her, Eric gave Emilia the smallest, nearly imperceptible nod, and his heart lurched. It was enough for her—enough to set off a spark that she hadn't felt in a long time. She bore her eyes into the side of his face, willing him to look at her.

What if we just stopped fighting? What if we stopped warring?

"I should go," he said abruptly and got up to his feet.

Emilia put her hand on his arm to detain him. "Eric, wait!"

He looked at her questioningly, but he didn't pull away, didn't yell, and didn't fight. Instead, he sat back down, at the edge of his seat. Emilia faced him in full and started inching towards him ever so slightly. His breath hitched, but again, he didn't back away. No, instead he kept his eyes laser-focused on her face, piercing and full of fire. The vampire stayed where she was—not too close, but not too far.

"What are you doing, Emilia?" he uttered. There was no hostility in his voice.

Instead of using words, she raised her hand and delicately pushed a piece of Eric's hair aside. His eyes fluttered and when she brushed her fingers against his cheek, he closed them and leaned into her touch with a sigh. Emilia let out an exhalation of her own at the feeling of his warm skin against the palm of her hand. She leaned forward and rested her forehead against his. He furrowed his brow, his lips shaking as they both stayed that way for a moment. It was small and intimate, yet enough to make her feel emotions of such high intensity that threatened to make her break down.

Eric put his callused hand over hers and pulled it away gently as he opened his eyes.

"We can't do this," he whispered.

"Why not?"

Emilia yearned to touch him, to be close to him like they were before, and she could tell that Eric wanted it too. She looked between his eyes and his lips and then back up again. Eric's throat bobbed as he swallowed hard, shaking his head. His stuttering heart betrayed him.

"Because *I* can't. I can't do this with you, especially now," he chuckled nervously, trying to push away from her.

"Why?" she demanded. "You still want me, don't you?"

[88]It was undeniable now. She could see it, clear as day, those deep, lovesick eyes that made her want to dive in. It was the same way he looked at her before, and it was the same way he looked at her earlier in the kitchen. She never thought he'd ever look at her like that again—like he could love her—but for the first time in a long time, hope was running rampant in her soul.

As Emilia stared into his beautiful face, Eric's pupils were blown out, his eyes looking darker as she inched even closer. His hot breath fanned over her face and his heart pounded with reckless abandon.

"Emilia..."

"If I'm wrong, just say it," she snapped, her brown eyes indignant. She threw caution to the wind. "Tell me you don't want me, and I'll leave. I'll disappear forever and you'll never see me again. I promise. Because I still want you. And I don't know if—"

"No," he said, shaking his head.

"'No' what, Eric?" she growled.

All of a sudden, he took Emilia's face in his hands, putting her to a halt. She froze as he looked her dead in the eyes, full of fervor.

"No, I will never say that Emilia, because it's not true," he told her, his voice shaking. "I want you so bad it physically pains me. You drive me absolutely fucking insane. You've driven me insane since the day

---

[88] Habibi - Tamino

we met. You make me question everything I am, and I hate it. I *hate it*. You ruin everything. You ruin me. But the crazy thing is…" He laughed before saying, "I would let you keep doing it. *I would let you*."

[89]Eric crashed his lips into hers, driving his point forward. Emilia gasped against his mouth and melded into him. Her fingers searched for something to hold onto—his jacket, his shoulders, and then his hair. Eric grabbed her waist and pressed her against him. Emilia pushed herself onto her knees, leaning even further into him, until he grabbed her thighs and pulled her onto his lap so that she straddled him. His hot lips devoured hers with hunger, his tongue making its way into her mouth as he held her firmly. It took everything in her not to moan out loud.

Emilia had forgotten how good it was to be touched by him like this—to be *desired* by him. It was like an all-consuming flame, and she longed to burn with him. Three years apart suddenly seemed eternal, and now they were like two atoms colliding to create an explosive reaction. She could tell how much he had been holding back by the way he kissed and touched her with desperation.

Aching for more of him, Emilia pushed Eric's hunting jacket away from his shoulders, and he shrugged it off, tossing it aside. She took off her shirt, leaving her in her bra and jeans. His mouth fell open at the sight of her.

"Oh shit."

Eric cupped the back of her neck and pulled her in for another kiss. His other hand started kneading at her breast as his lips traveled to her jaw and neck. The feeling of his calloused hands on her bare skin sent heat to her core. Emilia clung to his arms, anchoring herself to him as

---

[89]THE DEATH OF PEACE OF MIND - Bad Omens

her eyes fluttered shut. She reveled in it, nearly drowning in it, and a soft moan escaped her lips.

"Eric."

His motions slowed and he started to pull away, looking up at her in a daze with blushed cheeks and swollen lips. Drunk on the moment, Emilia reached between them to unbuckle his belt, but Eric grabbed her wrists before she could go any further.

"No. Wait. Stop."

Emilia frowned. "What?"

Eric's shoulders went rigid and he started shaking his head. He leaned away from Emilia as his eyes grew in fear. The passion left his eyes, now overcome with shock. It was as if he had been in a trance and had now suddenly woken up.

"What's wrong?" she asked with genuine concern.

"What the fuck am I doing?" he muttered.

Eric let go of her wrists and started getting up, carefully pushing Emilia back onto the loveseat. She watched as he walked off and stopped a few feet away with his hands in his hair. She quickly put on her shirt and stood up on wobbly legs, reaching for him.

"Eric, it's okay!"

"No, it's not!" he snapped, drawing away from her touch.

Emilia's face fell, his change of tone and demeanor was like a knife to the heart. Eric grabbed his jacket and shrugged it on as he started walking towards the door. She couldn't bear it.

"Eric, stop! Please!"

He froze, his muscles tense beneath his clothes, but he refused to look at her. The fortress was back up again.

"Don't," he whispered sharply.

"Please, don't shut me out again," she pleaded, on the verge of tears. "I know you like to pretend like nothing's wrong and like you feel nothing, but I see through that. I know the Eric I fell in love with is still in there—"

"He's dead," he hissed.

"Shut up! You're a goddamn liar!" she barked. "Didn't you see what happened just now? Didn't you hear what I said? What *you* said? Why do you keep doing this?"

Eric whirled around and shouted, "Because I'm terrified, Emilia!"

The vampire clammed her mouth shut in stunned silence.

[90]"I know how this ends," he continued. "I told you that I'm cursed. And I made promises to myself, to Jimmy, and Michael, and I can't—"

He groaned lowly, running his hands over his face in irritation.

"I promised myself this wouldn't happen."

"Eric, things are different now," Emilia stressed. "*We're* different now, and maybe that's a good thing. I never meant to hurt you. I never meant to be the reason you wanted revenge. I'm sorry. I'm sorry that I let it happen."

To her dismay, Eric gave her a strange look.

"You weren't the sole reason I wanted revenge, Emilia. I don't think I could ever bring myself to get any sort of revenge on you, no matter how hard I tried. I told you I didn't hate you, and I meant it. I wanted to blame you. I thought I could, but after these last few days, I realized that I could never hate you the way I should."

His breath came out shaky and with a bittersweet smile, he said, "You are everything that I have ever dreamed of." He motioned to the entire room and then to her. "*Everything*. Do you know how painful that is? It's why I have to stay away from you...because you scare the

---

[90] Dead Man - David Kushner

shit out of me. You bring out something that I have to kill, and I'm strong enough to take on your brother, but not you."[91]

Eric's voice broke amidst his unfiltered passion. Emilia stared at him in astonishment, her world now tinted with pink and red. A single red tear rolled down her cheek.

"You think that part of you deserves to die?" she asked.

Eric clenched his jaw, falling silent.

Emilia knew what it was like to want to shield the more vulnerable parts of herself from the world. She did so to survive, but she couldn't remember ever feeling the need to get rid of them completely. If anything, she leaned into her emotions more as a vampire *because* she wasn't allowed to as a child. Even if it had brought her pain, it was something she would never erase, but it seemed that Eric, much like her own brother, took the other route.

"What is it with you, men?" she muttered. "Why are you all kind until it no longer benefits you? Why do you all turn cold? What's so wrong with being soft and loving sometimes? What's wrong with *love*?" she demanded, louder now.

"Sometimes it's the only way to survive in the world we live in," Eric answered somberly.

"I would argue otherwise."

Look at Jaya. Look at Jean or Misha. Or look at Wade and what he *did in the name of love.*

"I told you... My world is different from yours, Emilia. Our kind of love is hunted down. I can't let that happen to you," he told her.[92]

Emilia bit her lip as more bloody tears cascaded down her face. Even Eric's eyes looked red-rimmed once again.

---

[91] THE LONELIEST - Måneskin
[92] Wounds - Tris Mikal

"So, you're protecting me? Is that it?" she asked bitterly.

"Baby, believe me when I say that I will only get you killed. I'm bound by blood and a higher, ungodly power. I chose to accept what I am. I chose to be a killer, and because of that, it means I'll only get you hurt, and I don't want that."

"Don't you dare say that! You are *not* a killer, Eric MacNamara!" Emilia shouted as she raised a scolding finger. "You're more than that. You're more than just a daywalker, a hunter, or Wade's son. You're *Eric*. That part of you doesn't deserve to die. You could never hurt me."

She strode towards him, extending a hand to touch him, but Eric caught it before she could do so. Emilia looked up at him through rose-colored vision and was surprised when he didn't let her go.

"But The Colectiv can," he replied.

Emilia groaned angrily and tried pushing herself away from him, but Eric refused to loosen his grip despite her struggle. He intertwined their fingers together and held them against his chest.

"Em, you need to understand," he implored. "I lost both of my parents because of this. I don't know what I would do if something happened to you because of me. I *can't* let that happen. Please!"

Emilia whimpered.

It was the most desperate she had ever heard him, and the sad part was that she understood why. He was willing to sacrifice himself and his fate to keep her safe. He was willing to give up what they could have together just so she could live. She understood, but she didn't want to.

It filled Emilia with so much unbridled emotion that more tears streamed down her face. She became feral and enraged. Emilia wrenched herself away from Eric and pushed him hard, over and over, screaming in between each shove.

"You honorable bastard. Why do you have to be so goddamn perfect all the goddamn time? Why can't you just treat me like shit and leave like the rest of them? Why can't you just hate me and get on with it? Why did it have to be *you*?"

It would be so much easier if it wasn't you.

When she went to shove him again, Eric took her by the shoulders and wrapped his arms tight around her. She tried fighting him, but he held her firmly against him until she stopped struggling and went limp in his arms. Emilia then sobbed in his embrace, clutching onto him as he held her to his chest. Blood poured out of her eyes and onto his clothes, but Eric didn't seem to care at all.

Somehow, this was more painful than getting her heart broken by someone who treated her poorly. To find someone who was perfect in every way, that she felt safe with, and that she loved, only to not be able to have them, was ten times more soul-crushing. It was death in and of itself.[93]

Eric rested his chin on the top of Emilia's head, his hand stroking her hair gently. It did well to soothe her, even if it was for a few moments.

"I never wanted to be that way with you," he whispered.

Emilia sniffled and asked, "What do you mean?"

"Like them. Cold. An asshole. A monster," he explained. "It's what I was avoiding. But I'm starting to think maybe it's for the best."

Eric pulled away and kissed the center of Emilia's forehead, the act soft and tender. He then put his hands on her shoulders as if to get a look at her. He wiped away the blood from her cheeks with his fingers and let his touch linger against her skin. Emilia leaned into it.

---

[93] All I Wanted - Paramore

All of a sudden, his eyes darkened, and with a cold-hearted tone that she heard many times before, he uttered his next words:

"Emilia... I'm going to find your brother. I'm going to find him, and I'm going to kill him with my bare hands, just like I promised I would. And there's nothing you can do to stop me."

The words hit like lightning. Emilia's face contorted with pain as her heart immediately shattered. She sobbed once again and slid out of Eric's grasp, falling to her knees on the floor. She braced herself on the cold ground as drops of crimson fell onto the wood.

Eric lingered for a moment, and although she couldn't see his face, she could hear the pain in his voice when he spoke.

"I'm so sorry."

37

Shattered Glass

Emilia

"What's going on up here? Why is there blood on your clothes?" Jaya asked at the door.

"We have to go," Eric said, evading the question.

"'Go'? Go where? Eric?"

There was no response except for the sound of his quick and heavy footsteps moving down the stairs. Lighter footfalls approached Emilia, and then hands fell on her shoulders as Jaya got down on the floor beside her.

"Emilia? Emilia, what happened?"

It was difficult to find the words amid her agony. Emilia's shoulders shook under Jaya's touch from her heaving sobs. When she didn't answer, her friend embraced her in her arms and consoled her until Emilia found the voice to speak.

"He's gonna kill him. He's gonna go through with it."

"Emilia, you knew this was bound to happen."

"I know...but I... I thought..."

I thought he would change his mind. I thought he would choose me. How stupid.

She squeezed her eyes shut in a mixture of embarrassment and shame.

What Emilia had expected was a miracle, an outlandish fantasy, but she knew where Eric was coming from, and that was the curse of it all. It wasn't easy for him to break away from The Colectiv and his obligations to the organization that raised him, especially with the immense power they wielded. And Emilia knew all too well what that was like.

"He's trying to protect me," she whimpered. She drew away from Jaya to look up into her eyes. "After everything, that's what he's thinking of. And I'm—"

I'm plotting against him.

No, we've been plotting against each other this whole time. One of us was just more upfront about it. Two different worlds, two different reasons for killing. It doesn't matter how much we want each other because the circumstances are against us.

"I'm going to kill your brother."

Not before I stop you.

Emilia had no choice but to continue with her original plan.

The cogs turned in her mind. Eric said that he had to go, which meant he was no doubt going after Dante as soon as possible. After all, he had a lead, or at least that's what he thought.

"Emilia, you need to get up," Jaya said.

Emilia snapped back to reality and let her friend pull her to her feet. She then leaned in close to Jaya and whispered so low that no other immortal ears could hear.

"Is Dante actually in Reno?"

Jaya shook her head. "No. He came back from Reno a few days ago. He's here, in Crimson Beach."

Emilia gasped, "Right now?"

"Right now," she confirmed. "He opened up a club called 'The Tiger's Eye' downtown, right on the promenade. If he's not there, then he's at Hollydale."

That didn't surprise Emilia at all. The old club had been his passion, after all. Regardless, it meant that it was just a matter of time before the twins found out that what Jaya told them was a lie.

"Do you have a car or some way for me to get out of here?" Emilia asked suddenly.

Jaya gave her an odd look. "What are you thinking?"

"I'm thinking I need to get to Dante before they do. They'll scour the city before they leave. They won't be satisfied until they do."

"Are you sure about this?"

"I've never been more sure of anything."

After a moment of hesitation, her friend smirked. "I have something better than a car."

"Like what?"

"Wade's bike," Jaya said with a playful shrug.

Emilia's jaw dropped. "How did you—?"

"He left it behind before he disappeared. Said he'd come back for it, but..."

Emilia nodded understanding. "Where are the keys?"

"In the garage, on the wall."

"Okay. I'll get cleaned up. You go down there and distract them, so I can escape," she explained quickly to not waste any more time.

"You know they're gonna go after you," Jaya warned.

"I know, but I have to try."

38

Bloody Knuckles

Eric

Eric bounded down two flights of stairs, his heart hammering in his ribs. The fight to hold back tears was harrowing, and his chest ached with a hellfire of his own making. It broke him to say such cruel words to Emilia when she had poured her heart out to him, like a sledgehammer to porcelain. The look in her eyes, the tears running down her face, and the way she collapsed to the floor before him... It was the most violent thing he had ever done in his entire life.[94]

It took everything in him not to comfort her, to take it all back, but he couldn't. He knew he couldn't. Eric meant what he said about keeping her out of harm's way. He'd been so preoccupied with having her at arm's length out of selfish anger, but this was different. This was the very thing he had feared three years ago—the reason for his secrets.

---

[94] Near - Bilmuri

Eric's fate was chosen for him the moment he was born, and he put himself in this mess. He chose to right his wrongs, and now the only direction for him was forward. If he couldn't spare himself, he could at least spare her—at the cost of her brother. And maybe if he got her to truly hate him in the end, it might somehow make the future easier.

When he made it to the first floor, James was coming in through the back. He had his phone in his hand and, for some reason, looked agitated, but when he locked eyes with Eric, his expression shifted, his gaze focusing on the blood on his hands and clothes.

"What the fuck happened?"

"It's not mine," Eric said as he peeled off his jacket and tossed it aside.

He went to the sink and started scrubbing his hands thoroughly with soap. He could still feel Emilia's gentle hand caressing his cheek, her lips against his own, the weight of her, and the feel of her skin beneath his fingertips. No one had touched him so tenderly or *passionately* in years. Not like that. It had been so easy to give in. He *wanted* to give in—to let go and let her devour him. In those moments, it was the freest he had ever felt in a long time. His pulse fluttered at the memory, but he tried to steel himself.

"Okay, then whose is it?" James demanded.

"It's not what you think," Eric assured him.

"Okay, then what is it? You're looking pretty shaken up right now, and being a vague asshole isn't helping."

Eric shut the faucet and dried his hands as he looked at his brother seriously.

"I'll explain in the car."

"The car?" James blurted out. "Where are we going?"

"We're gonna find Dante."

"*Now?*"

"Now."

"What about Emilia? Don't we technically still need her?"

Eric's face went grim. "No. She's not coming."

His twin frowned. Eric could see in his eyes that he had a million questions and didn't know where to start.

"What? That's it? This is the end of the line, just like that?"

"Yeah, it is," Eric argued. "I thought you would've been happy about it, considering how much you hate her."

"I mean, yeah, but..." James took on a serious and protective tone. "Dude, are you sure about this? Are you sure we're ready to do this right now?"

Eric threw him a strange look. This was the last reaction he expected from his brother, but before he could argue, the sound of footsteps drew their attention away. He listened in anticipation, expecting Emilia to come down the stairs with more confrontation. Instead, it was Jaya who appeared.

"What did you do to her?" she demanded.

"I did what I had to do," he replied coldly.

"You left her crying in a pool of her own blood. Have you no heart?"

"Not for a long time."

He looked at James, who was as bewildered as ever, and motioned with his head for him to follow. Eric grabbed his jacket and started making his way to the door. Jaya, however, raced down the steps and planted herself between the twins and their exit.

Eric sighed in annoyance but tried speaking evenly. "Get out of the way, Jaya."

She crossed her arms. "Where do you think you're going? Are you just going to leave her here? After she came all this way for *you*?"

"We didn't ask her to do that. She said she'd help us find Dante, and she's gotten us this far. This is where we part ways."

Eric tried going around her, but Jaya followed his movement and blocked his way.

He hissed, "Jaya—"

"Hey, come on," James spoke up, somehow being the nice one in the situation, "we don't wanna hurt you."

"Then don't," she shot back.

Eric glowered at her, his patience already wearing thin and becoming tempestuous. Jaya met his cold gaze with a brave, unrelenting stance, but he could sense her nerves underneath. His hunter instincts began to take over, and any part of him that operated out of kindness was dwindling.

There was the sound of quick and heavy footfalls once again. All three of their heads snapped to attention, following the sound with their eyes. Again, Eric expected Emilia to come running to the first floor, his heart stuttering, but the sound suddenly stopped. A door opened and slammed shut, and the garage opened with a creaking whir.

His eyes widened in realization. "Shit!"

He pushed past Jaya, who finally let him by, and bolted out the front door. He sprinted down the steps as he heard the harsh roar of an engine and dashed out the gate, towards the driveway. At that exact moment, Emilia flew right past him on the back of a white motorcycle. She raced north, up the highway.

"No!" he shouted.

The daywalker ran at maximum speed, trying to chase her down with his own two legs, but he didn't get very far before he found it useless. He pulled out his gun and tried aiming it at her, but she was already too far away for him to get a good shot. Just like that, Emilia was an indiscernible dot in the distance.

Eric let his gun fall to his side and groaned, "Fuck!"

With terror and fury burning in his veins, he whirled around, marching back up toward the house. James was halfway out the driveway, his arms out in question, and a knife in his hand.

"What the fuck just happened?"

"Emilia's gone," Eric seethed.

"What?"

Eric brushed past him, his focus intent on Jaya, who was standing by the gate. Emilia's friend stiffened as he approached her with what may very well be murderous intent. He towered over her, the gun still at his side.

"Where is she going?" he rumbled.

Jaya was silent, arms crossed in a protective stance, but he could see that she was trying hard not to shake. He snapped.

"Where. Is. She. Going?" he yelled, waving the pistol in her face.

The vampire gasped, stumbling back a little. James grabbed Eric's shoulder and wrenched him back a few feet.

"Yo, easy," he chided, placing himself between them.

Eric pulled away from his touch, puzzled by his twin's response.

"*You're* defending her? You of all people should know what it means for Emilia to get away!"

"I do! But you need to calm the fuck down, E! We're not gonna find her like this!"

Eric sneered at him. "Don't tell me to fucking calm down."

He shook his head. The entire scene from earlier replayed in his head. His own words came back to haunt him, and he panicked, his body shaking.

"You don't understand. She wouldn't just leave. Not just like that. Not unless it was somewhere important. She *knew*…"

The hunter trailed off as an epiphany sparked and then burned within him. His words tumbled out without thought, but once they were in the air, it was obvious. Where could Emilia possibly be going after everything that's happened and in such a hurry? He doubted it was on a flight back to New York. She could be going to Reno. Unless...[95]

He looked over his brother's shoulder at Jaya.

"Dante's not in Reno, is he?"

She gazed at him tentatively before whispering, "If she can't save you, then she can try to save him."

Eric grimaced. "Jimmy, get in the car. We're going downtown."

---

[95] She Knows - J. Cole (ft. Amber Coffman)

39

Cry, Little Sister

Dante

Crimson Beach, CA—Hollydale Asylum

[96]Three men lay tangled up together amidst velvet sheets beneath a canopy made of jewel-toned fabric. It was a messy kind of regal and a juxtaposition with the decades-old paint that was peeling away, though most of it was covered up with posters of musicians and rock bands from across the ages.

Sitting at the edge of the bed was a fourth man. Dante.

He wore nothing but the blood coating his skin, lighting a cigarette in his red hands. He took a long drag and let the smoke billow from his lips. He sat there in the quiet darkness, ruminating until the cigarette ran out, which was his cue to get up and do something more productive.

---

[96] Cry Little Sister - Gerard McMann

Like looking hot and causing trouble.

He got himself squeaky clean, because he did pay someone for running water (nobody human, of course), and returned to his companions, who were now fully awake. He lit some candles and pulled open the black-out curtains to let the moonlight filter through the slatted windows. He then went over to a record player sitting on a stand and picked out a Led Zeppelin vinyl from the stack. A huge, cat-like smile split across his face at the sound of beloved nostalgia.[97]

The vampire proceeded to blow-dry and style his thick black hair in front of a full-length mirror. When he was done, he let the towel around his waist fall to the ground and went to the racks of clothes hanging on display next to a dresser. He pursued through it all with careful hands, pulling out a long-sleeved button-up patterned with purple, black, and cream-colored stripes, as well as a pair of black pants. From the line of shoes below the rack, he grabbed a pair of chic black ankle boots. He bopped his head to the music as he tucked his shirt into his pants, leaving a few buttons undone, just how he liked. It gave a glimpse of a chest tattoo of marigolds surrounding a heart with swords in it. He also put on a smattering of gold rings, as well as a ruby-encrusted rosary with a cross as big as the palm of his hand.

Dante hadn't believed in God or religion in decades. After his upbringing, he made an active decision to shed that belief, so now the cross was merely a pretty piece of jewelry to him. If anything, he wore it as a symbol of power. As a vampire, it did nothing to him, and the fact that not even God could touch him filled him with a sense of victory. He used to share one just like it with his sister, but he didn't like to think about that anymore.

---

[97] Black Dog - Led Zeppelin

In the reflection of the mirror, he took himself in with a smirk of satisfaction and then made eye contact with Matthew, one of his companions who was watching him from the edge of the bed. He was slender with blonde hair and baby-blue eyes. Dante raised and dropped his eyebrows in a playful motion. Taking it as an invitation, Matthew walked toward him and tried circling his arms around his torso. But before he could touch him, Dante grabbed his wrists.

"Easy. I just put this on. Save it for later," he hissed.

Matthew clicked his tongue in annoyance and sat back down. "Don't you get tired of looking at yourself in the mirror?" he asked.

Dante scoffed, "If I don't think I'm hot, then who will?"

"Everybody knows you're hot, Danny. There's no need to be vain about it."

Dante scowled, the use of the nickname setting off his anger. He snapped his head toward Matthew and pointed a threatening finger at him.

"Hey," he growled, "don't call me that. You don't get to call me that."

Matthew raised his hands defensively. "Sorry, my mistake."

"And I don't care what anyone else thinks."

Dante strode over to him and aggressively took Matthew's chin in his hand. The young vampire didn't even fight him.

He was beautiful, a fresh vampire in his late 20s, but Matthew had an almost angelic look in his eyes compared to the others. Ironically, Dante liked it. And with the way he looked at him with pleading eyes...He'd save his thoughts on that for later.

"You shouldn't either," Dante added, before planting a big kiss on Matthew's lips and then shoving his face away.

†††

Back in the 1970s, when Dante and his sister were just turned, they were brought to an abandoned mental hospital called Hollydale. It was on the edge of town, hidden in a patch of woods, and there was an abandoned subway tunnel that led right to it from the beach. It was large, creepy, and empty, which was ideal for any vampire looking for a safe haven, and it wasn't long before the Bernal siblings started calling it home.

Back in the day, one of the ways Dante made money was through a club he opened up called The Inferno. He thought it was clever since his name was Dante, like Dante's *Inferno*, but also because the song "Disco Inferno" had been a big hit. It was his dream to open up a club for as long as he could remember, and he managed to do it with some stolen money and a loan from an old vampire he was friends with. Unfortunately, The Colectiv ran them out of Crimson Beach, the club was forced to shut down, and now the property was used for something else.

[98]However, now Dante successfully made his return, decades later. California had always been his home, and following his separation from Emilia, it seemed fair to come back. The hunters weren't after him anymore, and he always revered it with more fondness than his sister ever did. And this time, he'd be the one making the calls. In fact, he decided to start fresh and opened up a new club called The Tiger's Eye.

The clan was smaller now and mostly consisted of Dante and his boys, but having a source of income was always a great idea. Seeing as they were chained to the nightlife, clubbing and partying were normalities in vampire culture. If they were well fed, their energy could

---

[98] Back On '74 - Jungle

be double that of humans, and clubs were one of the best places to scout out potential victims to feed on. Not to mention, the Crimson Beach promenade was a cesspool for all kinds of lost souls doing dark business, including Dante himself.

He wasn't exactly subtle as he arrived with his pack in a glossy black Jaguar with music blaring. He parked behind the club, and they traveled through the alleyway toward the front entrance of the building, instantly drawing people's attention. After all, a group of mysterious, good-looking twenty-something-year-old men was hard to miss. And it gave Dante a sense of gratification every time. Some part of him even dared someone to say the wrong thing to his face.

The bouncer at the door to the club was a vampire named Vinny. Without question, he let them all into the building, which was already vibrating from the music coming within, and as always, The Tiger's Eye was alive. It was a living, breathing body of technicolor and beating hearts. The bass from the speakers reverberated in Dante's chest, making him grin as purple lights dappled across his skin. He loved it when it was full like this. The smell of humanity—and vampires— filled the place with sweat, alcohol, and blood. It was a place for chaos and freedom, whether you were alive or dead.

Before doing anything else, he went to the bar where Angie, the bartender, was. She was a vampire, like all the employees at The Tiger's Eye, because Dante didn't care for humans, and he trusted them even less. Vampires knew to keep their mouths shut about any non-human activity, and they kept an eye out for anything suspicious. With Angie, he talked about business, such as the shipments of alcohol and supplies, as well as the money they made that week.

As much as Dante liked to have fun, The Tiger's Eye was his baby, and he wanted to make sure everything ran smoothly. Not only did he have to worry about the "normal" stuff like human liquor, food, replacements for glassware, clean-up, and such, but he also had to think about the immortal side of things. Considering vampires couldn't consume most human liquids or foods without imploding, Dante had to provide for himself and his people.

Most alcohol did nothing or made them unbearably sick, so centuries ago, vampires started making their own from certain digestible plants and flowers. Rosewater, ironically, when fermented and distilled enough, had effects much like tequila. There was also whiskey made out of barley and monkshood, as well as special kinds of gin and rum (because what was an immortal nightlife without intoxication?).

When it came to blood consumption, Dante asked to spill none in his building, or they would suffer the consequences. They could've gotten away with that 50 years ago, but not today. If anyone needed a quick fix, he would send them to a backroom and give them a blood pack or two for a price. Or if they wanted some in their drink, all they had to do was ask. Discretion was the key when living amongst humans. Code words were *everything*.

When the business talk was over, Dante went up to his usual spot in the VIP area. Matthew and the rest of his boys were up there, talking, kissing, and laughing. He ordered himself some rosewater and sipped the flowery liquid. The whole time, he scanned the club, always keeping an eye out for trouble or any potential victims. Last night he had blood from his storage, but tonight he wanted something fresh.

He wasn't too particular about the victims he chose. Whoever looked alone or easy to manipulate was who he went for. He could be a bit careless, but he didn't always bleed them dry. He tended to lean towards people who wouldn't be missed, which by his standards usually meant the shadier ones. He didn't like having those people in his club, but at least in Dante's hands, they'd be dealt with. He didn't mind bleeding *them* dry. However, they didn't taste very nice, so he tried not to pick them too often. Even if it was risky, he liked treating himself more often than not. Sometimes, if he was bored or inclined enough to, he'd turn someone that he found intriguing. For *fun*.

His eyes caught on a broad-shouldered man with black hair and glasses. He was standing awkwardly against a pillar, holding a drink in his hands. Dante's lips curled into a devious grin.

He took off his coat and sauntered around the dance floor, his eyes flashing in the neon lights. As he approached, the man's pulse quickened, and he looked nervous.

Dante sidled up next to him. "Hey, pretty boy. Wanna dance?"

†††

Later in the night, Dante's victim sat paralyzed halfway on his lap on the upholstered couch. His lips were on his neck, sucking the blood from the bite he had nipped into his skin. He lapped up the sweet taste—its effects like a drug. He kept a firm grip on his waist and his head to steady him. Just like every other time, the vampire venom would keep him in a fog, and he wouldn't remember anything when he regained consciousness. *When*, not *if*, because Dante was feeling generous today.

When he had enough, he let him fall gently against the back of the couch, and the vampire sank into a corner like a cat. His glowing eyes turned back to brown, and his fangs retracted, but his face and neck were covered in blood, doing nothing to hide what he truly was. His mates were sitting on other chairs and couches before him, drinking from victims of their own.

They were in a part of Hollydale that used to be an old theater but was now a barren room with an empty stage and missing seats. They

447

did their best to redecorate with couches, tables, tapestries, and trash bins for fire, but Dante was no interior designer. The place looked decrepit compared to the old days, but he didn't mind. Not at the moment.

"I'm gonna get a drink," he muttered.

He pushed himself off the couch and walked over to a table to pour himself a large glass of liquor. He drank it in one go and winced as it burned on the way down. When he went to get a refill, he froze, staring at the glass goblet in his hands.

Emilia, his dear little sister, had gotten a set of these goblets years ago and gave them to him as a gift. Dante found them in a box when he came back, but he hadn't dared to touch them. He realized that one of the boys must have taken the liberty of cleaning them and putting them on the cart without thought.

The sudden reminder of her was like a punch to the gut, and it sent him back to that painful day, three years ago.

†††

Sorrento, Italy—3 years ago

The furniture of Emilia's rented apartment was strewn across the living room. Broken glass littered the floor, crunching beneath Dante's feet, and a pool of dried blood stained the tiled floor like a black hole.

The last thing he remembered was wanting to tear Eric to shreds before his sister attacked him and snapped his neck. She left him unconscious on the ground, and before he knew it, he awoke to find the apartment empty and Eric's body disappeared. At that point, his sister had been gone for God knows how long, and he heavily debated going after her until she came storming back in a fury.

"You!" she shouted and shoved him hard in the chest. "Do you have any idea what you've done?"

Tears stained her face, and her hands were covered in blood.

"Where is he?" Dante demanded.

"He's gone!" Emilia pushed him again. "You killed him, you motherfucker! He was mine, and you killed him!"

"Hey! I saved you!" he shouted, fending her off. "That guy was a hunter, Alé. He was a half-breed too. Don't you think that's too much of a coincidence? That out of all the people in the world, he found *you*? *Us*?"

New bloody tears streaked down Emilia's clothes.

She shook her head, saying, "I refuse to believe that. You don't know him!"

He scoffed, "Oh, and you do? Clearly not, considering what just fucking happened. He's a daywalker. I'm sure he'll be fine."

"You didn't see what I did. He was dying, Danny. You did something to him."

Dante groaned in annoyance, "Y que te importa, eh?" *What do you care?* "You were just as pissed off as I was until you fucking lunged at me. You were ready to let him die! I thought we were on the same side! You should've let me rip his head off."

"Don't you fucking say that," she hissed.

"Y dices que a mí me gusta la mala vida. Qué suerte tienes, la pura verdad."

And you say I like the bad life. What luck you have.

"Ay, ya cállate, Danny!"

They glared at each other, neither of them backing down. Dante eventually rolled his eyes and shrugged in exasperation.

"What do you want me to say, huh? 'I'm sorry'? Because I'm not. I don't give a shit what happens to people like him, and neither should you."

"Newsflash, Danny, not everything revolves around what *you* think, okay?"

"Maybe not, but it would probably be good for you to stay away from men for a while. You picked a real winner this time. You got worse taste than me."

Emilia was quiet for a moment before she said, "You're right. I should."

He smiled and gestured with his hands. "See? How hard was that?"

"And that includes you."

Dante did a double take and nearly choked on his own spit. He fixed his little sister with a bewildered look.

"What did you say?"

"Ya estoy harta, Danny," she told him. "I'm done. I'm done with all of it. With you and me and all the bullshit. I'm done."

"You don't know what you're fucking talking about," he said, shaking his head.

"For once, I think I do!"

"All of this over some *guy* you had a fling with?"

"He's not 'some guy'!" she bellowed. Her lips trembled as did her voice. "His name was Eric, and I... *loved* him. It was *real*. It wasn't a 'fling,' Danny... and you took him from me before I had the chance to even think. He may have hurt me by lying, but you have broken me beyond repair. Everyone was right. I should've listened to them."

Dante scowled. Tears stung in his eyes, but he turned to rage instead.

"Of course you'd listen to them instead of me," he muttered.

"Your word is not the end all be all! You are not the only one who gets to be right!"

"Yeah, but we're family, Alé!" he shouted. "You're supposed to take my side!"

"Oh, like *you* take *my* side?"

"I take care of you, okay? I protect you."

Emilia scoffed, "To what end? I take care of myself just fine, Danny. You? You've changed. You're an image. A name. A title. A statue or a scarecrow to ward off stupid pests because you look and act scary and because you're a *man*, but that's all you are—an image. We both know it's not real."

Her words struck him and cut so deeply that he was left floundering. She had never said such things to him before and suddenly he couldn't control his words.

"I've killed for you, Alé!" he yelled with an extreme motion of his hands. "Provided for you! I kept you safe! I give you everything! I put up with people just for you! I let you have your stupid little romances with men who don't deserve you! And I even saved you from a hunter! Because I love you!"

His little sister went dead quiet, her eyes as big as saucers. Dante didn't understand why she was looking at him this way or why his words didn't seem to get through to her.

"I didn't know loving me was such a burden to you, Danny," she said somberly. "I never asked you to do any of that. If I could give it back to you, I would."

"Then what the fuck do you want? It feels like nothing I do is ever good enough for you. It's like you don't even love me anymore. You said you loved him. You can love all these other people, but not me?"

Emilia balled her hands into fists and screamed in frustration, "That's the problem, Danny! I do! I do love you! I love you so much that I was willing to let you get away with everything! And it would be so much easier if I didn't, but I do! Because this whole time, I didn't want you to *tolerate* who I am! I didn't want your control! I just wanted you to be my brother!" [99]

The room was all at once so cavernous that Dante swore he could hear an echo of their words. Crimson drops fell from Emilia's eyes onto the tiled floor, but all Dante could do was stand there. A single red tear streamed down his cheek—not in anger but in genuine sorrow. He rarely felt true sorrow. This was more painful than getting a bullet in the gut. Dante and Emilia had gotten into plenty of arguments throughout their lives, but none were even close to this.

You're all I have.

"Wow," he said out loud, "I didn't know you felt that way, Alé."

She sighed, "Danny—"

"No, no, ya," he waved her words away and wiped away the stray tear. "You wanna leave? You want us to go our separate ways? You can't stand who I am? Fine. Have it your way."

No... I'm all I have.

He moved towards the door, stopping by her ear to say, "Pudrete," before walking out of her life forever.

†††

Crimson Beach, CA

Dante looked down at the glass cup with distaste.

And for what?

For what, huh?

---

[99] One Day The Only Butterflies Left Will Be In Your Chest As You March Towards Your Death - Bring Me The Horizon & Amy Lee

The emotions within him were so severe and complicated that they triggered mania, and instead of focusing on the hurt of her betrayal or even his faults, Dante chose to feel rage.

He threw the glass goblet against the wall with so much force that it shattered on impact. He then whooped like a howling animal as the glass rained down and turned to the room with fire in his eyes. Everyone watched him with wary expressions, but Dante had his gaze set on Anthony, another one of his lovers and marched towards him. He took his face in his hand and kissed him ferociously. He pushed his tongue into his mouth and let himself get a taste of him and the blood of his victim. Anthony moaned and Dante let himself get lost in the sounds, the taste of him, and nothing else.

40

A Silent Choice

James

Crimson Beach, CA—Present

James double-checked the magazines of his pistols as Eric bounded up the highway at full speed, following Emilia's path. He put them back in and pulled back the chamber before sliding them into the holsters against his chest. He then eyed his twin cagily, who was as wrathful as ever. James was amazed that he wasn't burning a hole through the windshield with the fire in his eyes. Not even he was spared from that murderous look tonight.

It was obvious that something happened with Emilia. He saw it in his demeanor the moment he came down the stairs and could hear how agitated he was. Even then, Eric tried convincing James that he didn't care about what happened to her, but as soon as she was gone, a switch flipped, and it seemed like he would tear the world apart.

"You shoot her on sight," Eric said. "You don't have to kill her, but keep her away from Dante...and from me."

"Look at you giving orders," James teased bitterly.

Eric had given a command or two before, but never to his brother. Not only did James outrank him, but their relationship was never like that. Something clearly changed. Though he wasn't going to fight him on it, it was still unnerving.

"Jimmy..."

"I know. I'm not a fucking idiot, E," James argued. "Although I sure do feel like one right now. What the fuck is going on? What happened up there?"

His twin worked his jaw as he came ominously quiet. James stared at him, on the edge of his seat.

"E..." Again, his brother said nothing, and James was left to assume the worst. "Did... Did the two of you—"

"No," Eric blurted out, shaking his head, but then backtracked. "I mean—well, no, no, we didn't, but—"

"Did you or did you not?"

"We kissed. That was it."

James leaned back against the headrest with a long, aggravated sigh. "Fuck my life."

There it was. Michael's warning comes to life. It was just what he needed after that bizarre phone call.

"That was it," his brother stressed.

James already knew he wasn't painting the full picture.

"Okay, but that couldn't have been the only thing that happened because Jaya said you left her crying in a pool of her own blood. How do you go from kissing to that?"

Eric winced as a painful memory seemed to flash before his eyes. James wished that twin telepathy could somehow show him what he was seeing. Considering the literal blood that had been on his hands, he could tell it had been intense.

"Don't worry about it," Eric told him. "Nothing is going on between us. I made sure of it."

James furrowed his brow, his concern only shifting. "What did you do?"

"I broke her heart. That's what I did."

"What the hell did you say?"

His twin shrugged drearily before answering, "The truth. That it's forbidden, and that we'd only get killed… and that I was gonna kill her brother regardless of our feelings."

James scoffed and stared at him in astonishment. He knew he shouldn't have felt bad for Emilia, but James couldn't remember the last time he had said anything as cruel. He made a lot of threats, and he could break people apart in many ways, but it was different. He knew Eric's tactics were different from his, but he *had* loved Emilia, hadn't he? He'd be bold enough to say that perhaps he still did.

"Jesus Christ, E."

"What?" Eric asked defensively.

"Nothing, I just…"

"I'm doing what I'm supposed to do, aren't I? Keep emotions out. Do what I need to do to complete the mission. Never make things personal. Don't have ties with vampires. Blah, blah, blah. I'm *protecting* us," he argued.

"Yeah, but…you're scaring me a little. Look who's sounding like Mike now."

James' body lurched forward as Eric all of a sudden hit the brakes. He groaned as he crashed against the seatbelt and then snapped back against the seat. James threw him a look of disbelief, but Eric was already glaring at him full of rage.

"What the fuck did you just say?"

"I said you're starting to sound like Michael," he repeated with more vigor.

Eric said it to him when they were on the road, and James didn't blame him for it, but his twin wasn't perfect either. There was a reason Michael was the commander. He was cold and calculating on top of having good physicality, and he had a way of getting things done no matter the cost. James grew up alongside him enough to witness the way he made decisions or gave orders. He learned a lot from him, and for a long time, he thought the reason they got along was due to their similarities, but he was starting to wonder if the reason Eric butted heads with him so often was because *they* were similar.

"Don't fucking say that," Eric hissed.

"Yeah, well, considering you've hated the guy your entire life, I thought you should know!" James spat.

His twin stared at him long and hard before continuing to drive. A few cars honked at them, but they paid them no mind.

It was then that Eric whispered, "That's easy for you to say."

James gave him an odd look. "What? What's that supposed to mean?"

"I mean, it's easy for you to say because you weren't there."

The lieutenant scoffed, "We grew up together, E. Of course, I was there."

"Not all of it."

"Okay, then spit it out."

His brother went off, "While you were off learning something new or going on hunts with everyone else, I was stuck with Michael. I didn't advance fast enough for his liking, so he had to resort to other tactics. He treated me differently than you, Jimmy. He always has, even now. He was more comfortable *saying* certain things. With you, it was *easy*. He didn't have to worry about you because you were good at what he wanted you to do. Even when you got into trouble, it was different. He just always made sure you weren't around for it all."

Eric didn't shout or speak with aggression as he explained this. If anything, he sounded tired or resigned, but James could still hear the wrath in his voice. Even if it wasn't directed at him.

"Some things are bound to rub off, I guess," he added grimly.

James vividly remembered how hard Michael was on Eric. He had done everything in his power to defend him or to take those punishments with him, but he couldn't always be there. Most of the time, it was out of his control, but he never stopped to think about what happened behind the scenes. Eric didn't tell him the finer details, so he didn't come to know the true scale of how much Michael ruined him.

It filled him with guilt.

"Why didn't you tell me?" he asked.

Eric shrugged. "I don't know. I didn't wanna rain on your parade, I guess. Michael said I'd mess with your progress and that I shouldn't depend on you anyway."

James let out a low, irritated growl. *That* was news to him.

"No, he fucking didn't," he uttered in disbelief.

"Yeah, he fucking did."

Yeah, he fucking did.

After all, he said something similar to James before they left for this job.

"This is how things are gonna be moving forward."

He had been all for completing Michael's task for the sake of making it to Captain, but that ick was starting to come back, and the idea was becoming less enticing. Something like that had never crossed his mind before, not about any hunt, and if he was honest, he wasn't sure if he was allowed to.

Wait a minute.

When the fuck did I start caring about what I'm allowed to fucking do? When did this become such a fucking problem?

James crossed his arms and stared out the window seriously.

The twins weren't very good at expressing their emotions very often, keeping them like secrets. James had trust issues since childhood, but becoming a hunter made them worse. He just never thought that The Colectiv would create such a wedge between him and his brother, especially when he had fought so hard to avoid it.

We were never supposed to keep secrets from each other. This isn't what Mom would've wanted.

James was overcome with the sudden urge to tell his brother everything. He wanted to tell him about the promotion and Michael's deal. He didn't want to keep it in anymore, and maybe if he told him, they could figure things out together.

But there was so little time.

They approached the downtown promenade and parked on the backstreet. Throngs of people filled the sidewalk, eager to get to the beach or whatever bar they were intent on going to. Even from within the car, James could smell the salty sea air and the scent of tequila and sunscreen.

Eric stared off, his mind transported somewhere else.

"Hey," James called to him softly. His brother glanced over at him, an eyebrow raised. "Starting tomorrow, no more lies. Got it?"

Eric nodded. "No more lies."

"Fuck what Michael said. I don't wanna hear any fucking excuses," James told him.

Something started to piece together in his mind, just like it did back in that hospital three years ago.

His brother smirked. "Aye, aye, Captain."

James rolled his eyes and got out of the car, but he wasn't so sure if he should get used to that title anymore.[100]

---

[100] Animals - Architects

41

The Inferno

Emilia

Meanwhile...

Emilia raced up the PCH on the back of Wade's white Ducati. It was a few decades old, but it was already getting her downtown faster than a car would. He also left behind an old helmet, which was a little big on her, but it served its purpose. She hadn't been on a motorcycle in years, but muscle memory took the wheel. Wade taught her how to drive one after she practically begged him to, and it was a skill she'd be eternally grateful for.

He'd kill me if he knew what I was about to do.

The route to the Crimson Beach promenade was all too familiar to Emilia, and she arrived in record time. She parked the bike in an alleyway next to a line of motorcycles, half expecting to see a familiar vehicle on the way, but didn't recognize any. After pulling off her helmet, she all but ran to The Tiger's Eye in heels and all. Luckily, the club wasn't hard to spot with the purple neon sign hanging out front. A tall bouncer stood outside, guarding the door. From what she could sense, he was a vampire, but not one she knew. He stared at her skeptically as she approached.

"I.D., please," he muttered in a deep voice.

She smiled. "I forgot mine at home."

"No I.D., no club."

Emilia pouted, her voice oozing sweetness, "I thought pretty girls were supposed to get in for free."

"Not if the pretty girl is underage. The boss is pretty adamant about it."

Emilia raised her eyebrows. "Well, I'm flattered that you think I look underage, but I have seen Mick Jagger perform in his prime, so..."

The bouncer narrowed his eyes. "Who are you?"

"My name's Emilia. I was actually hoping to talk to your boss, Dante."

"And why would he want to talk to you?"

"I'm surprised you don't see the resemblance. I'm his sister," she said.

"Dante never said he had a sister."

Emilia scoffed, feeling mildly hurt. "He doesn't talk about me, does he? Figures. Well, if you don't know me...then maybe you know Jean Beltremieux and Wade MacNamara. We used to run around these parts back in the day *with* Dante. The name Hollydale might ring a bell."

The mention of their names seemed to spark genuine interest in him, and now that she had him, Emilia made sure her next words were swift.

"I don't have much time. I know he owns this club, so I need to go in there and speak to him. Urgently. Like, life or death."

"Well, sorry, but he's not here. He left a while ago."

She narrowed her eyes suspiciously. "Are you lying?"

"No," he said with a stoic expression.

"Do you know where he is?"

"The asylum, I'm guessing."

She nodded and started backing away towards where she came from. "Thank you!"

Emilia ran back to the alleyway and hopped back on the white Ducati. She zipped up her jacket, pulled on the helmet, and let the bike come to life with a rumble beneath her. But just as she was about to pull out onto the street, she was met face-to-face with her pursuers.

Goddamn, he's fucking fast.

Down the street, Eric was walking away from the Jeep, with James in tow. He locked eyes on her and even though he couldn't see her face, he immediately recognized her.

"Emilia!"

Shit.

Instead of going out the way she came, the vampire made the clever decision to take a narrow U-turn and drive the bike straight toward the promenade. Eric's cries fell behind her as she maneuvered past a line of metal posts that were wide enough for the motorcycle to fit between. She then turned the corner to head east. The civilians screamed and yelled as she whizzed by, not expecting her on a path made for pedestrians, but Emilia needed a shortcut, and she needed to lose the hunters fast.

†††

Hollydale Asylum

She hid Wade's bike and helmet in an overgrown lot behind a large tree. The building that was once there was now a pile of crumbling brick and graffiti, so no one important would find it anytime soon. Emilia then walked a short path until she came across a cracked road. Looming before her on the other side was the back of a giant compound with abandoned buildings. They stood behind a tall fence with a giant red sign that read, NO TRESPASSING.

Hollydale Mental Hospital—yet another piece of Emilia's past that she hasn't seen in decades. She was overcome with heavy melancholy just looking at it and vividly remembered many nights spent in its decrepit rooms and hallways—the place she once called home. A lot of blood and tears were shed within its walls, but she could never ignore the good memories she still looked at with fondness.

With a glance around, Emilia walked up to the fence and climbed it with little to no effort. The chain link rattled with the movement, and at the top, she threw her legs over the other side and let herself fall to the ground, knees bent. She proceeded to walk at a brisk pace past the old buildings holding dormitories. She needn't waste time exploring because she already knew exactly where her brother would be.

The theater.

The entire walk there, her anxious mind raced with memories of her last interaction with Dante. It was one of the most difficult and heartbreaking things she had ever endured, and she wasn't entirely certain if she healed from it yet. There were so many things that had been said, and there was no telling where Dante's head was after three years. Of course, by no means was Emilia *scared* of her brother. She just didn't think she'd be seeing him again so soon.

I'm not here to make amends. I need to do this. I came this far. It's for his own good.

She almost scoffed at herself.

I sound like Eric. Maybe he wasn't wrong about that.

As she approached the large building on the other side of the lot, she could hear the indistinct sounds of voices, music, and laughter. Through the broken windows, she could even smell sickly sweet blood. With every ounce of boldness in her body, Emilia walked up to the doors and pulled them open with a click. The sound echoed through the giant room, which was a much louder cacophony of stimuli on the inside.

Vampires sat on couches, their mouths stained with blood, while some drank earthy liquor. Fires burned in old barrels, lighting up the room with a warm glow. Loud rock music boomed through some speakers. Tapestries hung from the ceiling, and posters were plastered all over the walls. It was a messier and more chaotic version of what Emilia knew it to be, and it was clear that it lacked a feminine touch.

The second she walked in, everyone stopped what they were doing and feasted their eyes on her. A lot of them were men of different ages, but most of them physically looked closer to Dante's. The vampires that weren't gathered around the center sat at a distance or on the old stage that was once used for shows. Emilia scanned their faces, but her brother was nowhere to be found.

"Who the fuck are you?" someone said.

Others whispered variations of the same question. Emilia stood her ground, unafraid, despite entering a lion's den by herself. She stepped further within, towards the edge of the main sitting area.

"Where's Dante?" she asked.

"Aquí, Alé."

Here, Alé.

Emilia let out a tiny gasp. It was a nickname only *he* called her—a shortened version of an old name that belonged to a dead girl, and by his tone alone, it was like he knew she was coming. Everyone around her looked up, following the sound of his voice, but Emilia didn't need their indication to know. She twisted around and followed their line of sight.

There, staring right back at her from the second-story gallery, was her older brother, smirking at her with devilish mirth. His brown eyes looked amber in the firelight, and his thick black hair—just like hers—stuck up in that unkempt way he liked. A thick chain dangled from his neck, swaying back and forth as he leaned forward.

"Danny," she answered in kind, the Spanish accent rolling off her tongue.

"You found me."

Emilia hummed, "It wasn't very hard."

"I didn't think you'd ever come back. Did you miss me?"

She rolled her eyes. "Hardly."

Dante chuckled darkly. He then climbed up onto the balcony, towering over everyone, and then suddenly, he stepped forward and let himself fall. He landed before Emilia, knees bent, and then brought himself to full size like it was nothing.

Dramatic.

He stalked over to her in slow steps until they were about a foot or two apart and looked down his nose at her.

Dante was a head taller than Emilia, and even when they were teenagers, he loomed over her. At her eye level, she got a good look at the familiar rosary he always wore—the one that once matched hers. It glistened against the shiny material of his black satin shirt. The skin around his lips was stained red. The look he gave her could have brought anyone to their knees, but not her. Emilia refused to cower in fear and perhaps that's why Dante did it on purpose. He liked to tease her, annoy her, and challenge her. Even now, with so much pain and so many unspoken words between them, the tension was clear.

He broke that tension with a sigh and leaned forward to kiss her on the cheek. Emilia returned the greeting, though no embrace or warmth followed.

"Dónde está tu collar?" he asked.

Where's your necklace?

"Por ahi, en una caja," *in a box somewhere*, "I got bored of wearing it."

In reality, it was in the purse she left at Jaya's house.

Dante huffed indignantly and took a few steps back, giving her room to breathe.

"Vinny told me you were coming," he said.

"I assume Vinny is the bouncer."

"Yeah." Dante regarded her almost distastefully with his hands in his pockets and asked, "What are you doing here?"

There was nothing friendly or loving about his tone.

"Danny, we need to talk," Emilia said urgently.

Emilia managed to lose the boys, but they were relentless. She knew as much.

He scoffed, "About what? You did plenty of talking last time. If it's about that, then save your breath. Unless, of course, you're here to apologize."

Dante gave her a smug smile as if he had said something clever. Emilia, however, was completely taken off guard by his wild assumption, so much so that an involuntary cackle came out of her. Somehow, it made the stress over the reunion dissipate. Emilia may have been blind to or lenient about most of the things he did in the past, but now that she had distanced herself from him long enough, everything seemed crystal clear. It solidified the choice she made, like cement.[101]

---

[101] Happier Than Ever - Billie Eilish

"Apologize? Me?" she exclaimed.

Dante scowled. "Are you fucking laughing at me?"

"Yeah, because you're ridiculous. Thank you for reminding me that you still haven't changed, but no, I'm not here to apologize. I came here to save your ass."

"From what, exactly?"

Emilia spoke more gravely now, "You're in danger, Danny. You need to run. *Now*. Get out of Crimson Beach. *We* need to leave immediately."

She didn't even care if there were other vampires present, because this information benefited them too.

To her dismay, it was Dante's turn to laugh.

"'We'? What the fuck are you talking about? There is no 'we' anymore, Alé. You made that pretty clear."

"Your selective hearing is astounding," she said with a roll of her eyes. "I'm trying to tell you that The Colectiv is after you, you idiot!"

Dante put a hand on his chest and blurted out, "Me? What the fuck did I do?"

What haven't *you done, Daniel?*

"It's Eric. Remember him?"

Her brother's eyes flashed for a split second. Emilia couldn't tell if it was recognition or fear.

"Your boyfriend from Italy?" He asked with distaste.

"Yes."

"What about him?"

"He's a hunter now. For real, this time. And he's coming after you for what you did to him."

Dante's jaw dropped in a mixture of amusement and disbelief. He chuckled for a good while before speaking again.

"You're fucking with me, right? That little bitch?"

"That 'little bitch' is Wade's son, you asshole," she barked.

"I know who he is," he hissed.

Emilia raised her eyebrows at that.

If Dante knew Eric was Wade's son, then the fear Emilia saw in his eyes was real. She wondered how he came to find out and wished she had been there to see his reaction. After all, the only person that her brother was ever truly scared of, was Wade MacNamara himself. It was pure dumb luck that Emilia fell for Eric, but it was damn near comical that Dante had almost managed to kill his *son*.

"Well, then you should know exactly what that means," Emilia continued. "If you don't leave, he *will* kill you."

"And how do you even know that? Who told you?" Emilia hesitated, and her brother's glare deepened. "Alé...?"

"Who cares, Danny? Trust me," she stressed, her patience wearing away. "We need to go. He could be here any minute. I tried to lose him, but you don't know him. He—He's changed..."

Dante's eyes grew in realization. "You've been talking to him again? And you lead him *here*?"

Emilia resisted the urge to shriek in aggravation. Instead, she marched up to him and shouted, "Will you listen to me? Jesus fucking Christ! I tried to stop him. He was going to come after you, whether I had anything to do with it or not. He found me to get to *you*! He chained me to a fucking chair! I'm lucky I'm still alive!"

"And *you led him here*!" he shouted in her face.

The double doors banged open. Within a fraction of a second, two gunshots echoed through the theater. The first bullet hit Dante in the chest, sending him falling backward, and the second pierced Emilia's shoulder. She cried out and crumbled to her knees as the entire area burned with white-hot pain. There was a pop, followed by a sizzling sound, and a faint mist began to fill the room. The smell made Emilia's heart drop into her stomach before it started to take effect.

Roses.

The vampires in the room started coughing and screaming, already scattering out of the building. Dante and Emilia were left behind, unable to move due to their injuries. Emilia tried covering her nose and mouth, but her eyes were already starting to burn, blood filling her vision. Dante was coughing on the floor beside her, crimson dripping down his nose.

There were heavy footsteps, and then Emilia felt the barrel of a gun against the back of her head. With a bloody glare, she looked over her shoulder to witness James towering over her. At his side was Eric, his eyes forward, heading straight towards Dante. [102]

---

[102] Hayloft II - Mother Mother

42

The Cruel Prince

Eric

Hollydale. That's what she had called it back at Jaya's house. Eric didn't know if Emilia meant to let that piece of information slip, but it came in handy when they lost her downtown. One Google search later, and the abandoned mental hospital wasn't that hard to find. According to "eyewitness reports," the place was overrun with paranormal activity. Eric just hoped those people never had to testify in court.

The scent of roses filled the room. It was a pleasant smell to the twins, but toxic enough to clear the abandoned theater of any unwanted vampires and debilitate whom they were really here for. Eric didn't waste a single second to put a bullet in Dante and now that the time had arrived, the last thing Eric MacNamara was going to do was hesitate.[103]

The daywalker strode over to him with his sword strapped to his back, fueled by wrath and adrenaline. He didn't even look at Emilia, who was wounded on the floor and coughing up blood. He was too enraged to even acknowledge her at that moment. She had deceived him yet again, and he had trusted her *again*, except this time it was truly his mistake.

Was this her plan all along? Of course, it was.

He didn't want to think about it.

"Eric, stop. You don't have to do this," she pleaded, trying to make her way toward him.

"Jimmy, please," he said coldly.

Behind him, James fired another silver bullet. Emilia cried out in anguish, her efforts put to a stop. Despite how hard he tried to hide it, Eric grimaced.

He approached Dante, who was on his hands and knees, also coughing up his insides. When he looked up, Eric kicked him in the face, forcing him down. The vampire's hands flew to the area with a groan as he fell backward. The hunter put his boot down on his torso to keep him there as the mist dissipated. Dante's noises of pain then turned into maniacal laughter.

"You try anything, and I'll start cutting shit off," Eric hissed.

"Fuck you," the vampire choked out.

Eric let his eyes glow dramatically, just as they had that night—the golden eyes of a daywalker. His fangs itched to come out, aching for blood.

"Remember me?" he asked.

---

103 Drama Queen - iamjakehill

Dante gawked at him with a mixture of awe and fear, which satisfied Eric. Yet, despite the pain and the fact that he was choking on his blood, the vampire had to poke fun.

"I'm a little old, so my memory isn't that great. What's your name again?"

The hunter smirked, his gaze dark. "Let me jog your memory."

With a swift movement, he took out a dagger, crouched down, and plunged it right in between Dante's neck and his shoulder on his left side. The vampire let out a guttural scream and writhed beneath him, but Eric kept a solid hold on him beneath his boot. Behind him, he could hear whimpering.

"Jesus Fucking Christ!" Dante cursed, chuckling through the agony.

Eric hovered there, leaving the dagger in Dante's body while he pointed his gun at him. Using his free hand, he pulled back the collar of his shirt to reveal the scar in the same spot where he had bitten him a long time ago. Dante blinked a few times, panting as he took in what Eric was showing him, in shock.

"Remember now?" he growled.

"How?" Emilia's brother asked in disbelief. "I thought you were a daywalker. Don't daywalkers heal?"

"Turns out some wounds can't heal, but you don't need to know the science behind that." Eric pulled his shirt collar back up and told him, "I've carried this with me every day, everywhere I go. And I'll carry it with me long after you're gone."

"Eric, stop it!" Emilia shouted, her voice cracking from the pain.

"Emilia, don't make me put a bullet in your head," James muttered.

"Fuck you, James!"

Eric rolled his eyes and sighed. Dante's eyes flitted past his shoulder.

"So that's your twin, huh? I heard there were two of you, but I almost didn't believe it."

"Better believe it now, motherfucker. You're lucky it's not me having to deal with you," James seethed.

Dante's head rolled over, his movements and demeanor lazy as he looked back at Eric. The effects of the rosewater and the silver were getting to him.

"All this for me? I gotta say, that's awfully romantic of you," he drawled with a grin.

Eric pushed the silver blade even further into him, and Dante tried biting back a groan.

"We've been over this. I'm not into narcissists," the daywalker said dryly.

"I didn't believe my sister when she tried telling me you were coming. You were always an annoying little shit. I couldn't imagine you having the balls to kill someone, but I guess I was wrong. You really do have it in you. Congratulations."

"That's your problem, isn't it? You underestimate everyone who isn't like you."

Dante leaned as close to Eric as he could with the blade at his neck. "And yet here you are...a killer just like the rest of us."

The hunter bared his teeth, fangs, and all. His face was hot with fury.

"I am nothing like you," he hissed.

Eric grabbed the hilt of his mother's dagger and pulled it out of Dante's collarbone with no mercy. Blood splattered on his face as the vampire cursed. The hunter then pushed himself to his feet. He carefully withdrew the pistol and dagger and reached behind him, his fingers wrapping around the hilt of his sword. He unsheathed it with a metal scratch and twirled it before gripping it with both hands.

Emilia wept in silence, and Eric tried not to let it break his heart as he prepared himself for what he was about to do—something he had done many times before.

"Close your eyes, Emilia," he said, to spare her.

Dante shouted, "No, Alejandra, mira! Mira lo que tu príncipe está haciendo!"

Look at what your prince is doing.

Alejandra. The name fluttered for a brief moment in Eric's mind.

Dante lay there, seemingly prepared to accept his fate as he bled out, his skin taking on a violet hue.

"Any last words... *Danny*?" Eric asked.

The vampire snickered like a hyena.

"Yeah, I've got some." He pushed himself to his elbows and looked Eric in the eyes before saying, "Say hi to your daddy for me."

Eric faltered, his cold gaze falling. "What did you just say?"

"I said, tell Wade I said, 'Hi'." Dante repeated more enunciation.

Any thoughts of murder or revenge left Eric MacNamara's mind for a long, pressing moment upon hearing his father's name from Dante's mouth. It wasn't just that he mentioned him, but the *way* he said it.

He pointed the sword at his throat. "What the fuck are you talking about? Wade's dead."

Dante sighed, "You know, you were supposed to kill me after that. Now, I just spoke too much."

Eric kicked Dante in the side, forcing him to roll over on his stomach with a grunt. The hunter crouched down and grabbed him by his hair, forcing him upwards. He held the broadside of his sword against his throat menacingly, and the vampire hissed.

"*What do you know about Wade?*" Eric demanded.

Dante winced, choking out the words, "He's... alive."

It was as if the wind had been knocked out of Eric's lungs. He couldn't believe what he was hearing. It was impossible. His father was dead. Everybody knew that. It was all anyone ever told him to this very day, but now the man he swore to kill was telling him otherwise?

"You're lying," he growled.

"Unfortunately... I'm not."

"Then, you better talk fast before you start losing pieces."

Eric let him go but kept his sword pointed at him. With a groan, Dante rolled over and sat up, clutching his neck. He glared at the hunter but spoke to save his life.

"Apparently some of the distilleries got raided by your people a few days ago. The old whiskey factories. It was a bitch because we didn't get anything in our last shipment, and we had to start rationing everything so they'd keep their eyes off us. A vampire buddy of mine said there was a break-out in Charybdis, and they were looking for the man that escaped."

"Michael told me about that," James said. "He said he was handling it, but he didn't say how or who it was."

Eric finally looked over his shoulder at his twin, and he looked about as stunned as he did.

"Well," Dante chuckled, "word started spreading around pretty fast, and apparently the man that escaped was none other than old Wade MacNamara himself."

Eric could hear his heartbeat pounding in his ears. He gripped the sword tight to keep his hands from shaking.

His father, *alive*? Eric couldn't believe it.

He shook his head. "No. No, there has to be some kind of mistake. Wade is dead. If he was in Charybdis this whole time, we would've known."

The vampire shrugged, hunching over in pain. He said, "Honey, I'm just the messenger."

Eric whirled around to look at James, who looked as if he had just seen a ghost. His brother slowly lowered the gun that was pointed at Emilia's head, who also looked shocked by the news.

"Did you know about this?" Eric demanded.

Emilia shook her head vigorously, wiping at the blood on her face.

"No, *no*, I swear. I thought Wade was dead. Jean told me he was dead." She stumbled to her feet and tried limping toward her brother. "How is he not dead, Danny?" she shrilled.

"I don't know!" he shouted, getting up to his knees. "I'm just repeating what I heard. I thought he was dead too."

"What the fuck is going on?" James whispered.

"Wait, you guys said that if The Colectiv didn't want anyone to know their business, they covered it up, right?" Emilia said, drawing their attention to her. "James knowing about the break-out makes sense, but why does everyone else know?"

Eric locked eyes with his brother and worked out the puzzle at the same time that he did. It could've been that The Colectiv was spreading more lies, but it didn't make sense for them to perpetuate such a false rumor. They hated Wade. *Michael* hated Wade. The last thing they wanted was for people to think he was alive. And the fact that the commander didn't already tell James *who* had broken out was a cause for skepticism.

"Someone outside The Colectiv is trying to get ahead of them."

Even though Eric said it, even though it meant that his father could very well be out there, it was all too much. He could see that same storm of emotions in his brother's eyes. There were years' worth of questions that all amounted to lies. Confusion, grief, and anger.

"Who told you he was dead?" Emilia asked.

Eric looked at her now fully, for the first time. Her face was stained red and streaked with tears. He wasn't even angry at her anymore. No, his anger was for someone else.

At the same time, he and James answered, "Michael."

Eric didn't know if things were starting to add up or if they were making less sense.

The main doors to the theater cracked open. Eric took out his gun, and both he and James instinctively pointed their weapons toward them. However, to everyone's dismay, it was Jaya who stood by the entrance with a black shawl around her head. Her eyes were wide with panic. The boys immediately lowered their guns.

"Holy shit," James cursed under his breath.

She scanned everyone's face and the state of the entire room. Her gaze caught on Dante, still alive, but she didn't address it. Emilia limped toward her.

"Jaya? I told you to stay at the house. What are you doin—"

Jaya held her finger to her lips and shushed her. Emilia stopped in her tracks and fell into silent bewilderment. She then looked at the twins and spoke in a hushed whisper.

"Did you guys, by any chance, call some of your hunter friends?"

Eric frowned and shook his head, "No."

"It's just supposed to be you two?"

"Yeah," James uttered, "why?"

"Because I just saw some coming this way. They're on the lot."

43

The Tower

"What?" they all blurted out.

Eric could sense them now, a team of them scattered about and making their way toward them.

He shot James an accusatory look. "Did you know about this?"

"No, of course not. I talked to Mike earlier today, and he didn't..." James wavered, his face falling.

Eric's concern worsened.

"Jimmy...?"

His brother started shaking his head, saying, "E... I didn't... I didn't think he'd—"

From outside, someone shouted, "There's music! In here!"

Shit.

The doors flew open once again. With no hesitation, Eric grabbed Emilia and maneuvered her behind him protectively. She sputtered but didn't fight or protest. Jaya scurried into a corner, and Dante staggered to his feet, trying to dig a bullet out of his chest.

Eric expected Michael and his pack to filter in and assume their position, but to his disappointment, Caleb Lochmann, his second lieutenant, arrived in his stead. He was by himself while the rest of the hunters lingered outside, no doubt awaiting his order. Now that he wasn't distracted, Eric could sense at least 15 of them, which wasn't a normal amount for the average hunting party.

Who are they here for?

Caleb lumbered before them with his arms crossed, a smirk playing on his face as he looked around the room. Eric scowled at his arrogant demeanor.

"Buna băieţi," he drawled. *Hello, boys.*

"Caleb," Eric bit out.

"What the fuck are you doing here?" James snapped.

The hunter grinned. "Nice to see you too, Lieutenant."

"What are you doing here, Caleb?" Eric reiterated hotly. "This is *our* job. Michael knew that. He's known that for years."

"Yeah, but he thought you could use some help."

Eric scoffed, "Help? *Us?* From *you?* We didn't ask for the cavalry. Some of us don't need it."

"Yeah, well, the boss seems to think otherwise," he said with a shrug. "Things have been a little hectic on his end and he wanted to make sure someone kept an eye on his boys. He had a feeling that you weren't being entirely honest with him, which I now see why, considering you're hanging out with not one, but," he pointed at Jaya, Dante, and Emilia, respectively, "Three vampires... in Crimson Beach."

"What does it even matter? We work with vampires all the time. They're our informants."

"Yeah, but you and your family have a history of getting a little too friendly with vampires." He looked over Eric's shoulder at Emilia and said, "Isn't that right?"

Eric clenched his jaw and squeezed the sword in his hand.

"She's our informant," he repeated through his teeth.

Caleb snorted, "Isn't that what Anya said 25 years ago?"

Eric's reaction was instinctual. He lunged forward with a growl, but Emilia pulled him back by his sleeve. However, James beat him to it. He grabbed the collar of Caleb's jacket and punched him square in the gut. The hunter doubled over with a groan, clutching his stomach. Eric stared at his brother, surprised but with pride.

"Keep her name out of your fucking mouth," James hissed.

The second lieutenant chuckled as he straightened up. Eric could make out the faint voice of someone speaking over the communications device in his ear, asking if he was alright.

"No, no, everything's fine," Caleb assured. He then raised his eyebrows at James. "You should be careful, Lieutenant, because when I'm done, I'm gonna outrank you."

James' eyes flashed and Eric furrowed his brow. It was obvious he was talking about the promotion.

"No fucking way they'd make you captain," Eric spat.

"After the stunt, Jimmy pulled? I think they might."

He cast an odd glance at his brother, but James was busy staring daggers at Caleb.

"You shut the fuck up before I kill you," he growled.

"Jimmy, what's he talking about?" Eric asked.

Caleb's face lit up, completely ignoring James' threats. "Oh, you don't know, do you? Of course, you don't. I'm sure Michael didn't want him to tell you, considering your ties to all of this."

Eric's stomach slowly dropped at the insinuation because it was obvious he was missing something vital—something that his *brother* kept from him. He looked over at James again, but still, his twin refused to look at him. He didn't even defend himself. No, he just continued to stare at the other hunter with murderous intent. It made things even worse.

"Jimmy... *What is he talking about?*" he half-begged.

James gripped the gun in his hand so hard that his knuckles went pale.

His voice wavered as he said, "I was gonna tell you after all of this was over. I *wanted* to tell you..."

"Tell me *what?*" Eric demanded, losing patience.

Caleb answered the question for him, "Jimmy was supposed to get promoted to captain... in exchange... for *her* head." He pointed past his shoulder, towards Emilia.

The blood drained from Eric's face, his skin going cold. He glanced back at Emilia, who shared the same stunned expression. He then looked back at Caleb before settling his gaze on James. It was then that his brother dared to look back, his expression riddled with guilt. All Eric could do was stand frozen, completely speechless.

He expected the secrets and the lies, but not from his brother. Not James. And not something like this.

A promotion in exchange for Emilia's life. Of all people, James knew what she meant to him. He knew what Eric had done three years ago and helped save him from The Colectiv's potential wrath. They made a deal with Jean. They had an agreement to keep things between themselves and to hide certain things from Michael, but it seemed to be the other way around. This shock and betrayal cut deeper than anything else he had ever experienced in his life.

Funny. Every time I think I hit the bottom, I reach a new low.[104]

"You…"

"E—" James began.

"When did he give you the order?" Eric exacted, cutting him off.

"Before we left."

"And you were gonna tell me—what—when she was already dead? If at all?"

"That *was* the plan. It's what Mike wanted me to do."

Eric groaned.

"What Mike—" He paused to chuckle angrily and then continued, his voice growing louder with every question. "So… this whole time… you were working behind my back? That's why you went along with everything? That's why you've been acting weird? You were *selling out*?"

"I wasn't selling out, E! You knew I wanted this! You knew this was coming!" James argued.

"Yeah, but I didn't think this would be the price. I didn't think—" *I didn't think it would be* her.

"I didn't think so either!" his brother shot back.

"But you still agreed!"

His twin nodded. "Yeah, I did. Because she's a fucking Hellhound, E! That's all I knew! What else was I supposed to do?"

"You were supposed to stick to your word! Like we always do!" Eric shouted, and then, in a broken voice, he said, "But just like everyone else, you're a goddamn liar."

He turned away and took a deep breath, swallowing past a lump in his throat.

Michael lied, Jean lied, Emilia lied, and now… James?

---

[104] In The End - Linkin Park

Do they all think I'm stupid? Am I a fucking idiot? Do I just know nothing at all? Am I just that easy?

Caleb spoke up then, interrupting their argument, "Funny, I think Jimmy's having a hard time sticking to his word these days."

Eric turned back around to give him a confused look. The older hunter shrugged.

"That's part of the reason I'm here. Your brother choked. Emilia was supposed to be dead days ago, but he lied. He couldn't do it."

Caleb threw a condescending look at James. Once again, Eric was taken aback.

"What?"

"I didn't choke," James growled.

"She's still alive, so I'd say that means James MacNamara finally choked."

Eric's anger from his brother's betrayal dissolved little by little, and when they locked eyes, his twin looked close to tears.

"I was going to tell you."

Not only had James lied to Eric, but he lied to Michael too. Unfortunately, for him, the commander had his way of finding things out. There was no way James could have predicted that he'd pull something like this. He had eyes on them from all directions, and it took them this long to see how far he would go.

The familiar sound of scraping metal made him snap his focus to Caleb, who was now holding a greatsword in his hands.

"Don't worry, *Walker*. I'll finish the job for you," he said.

With casual arrogance, the man made a beeline for Emilia, intent on barreling through Eric to get to her... but the daywalker would have none of it.

Before Caleb could get too close, Eric stepped forward and blocked the hunter's path.

"Step aside, corporal," he ordered, his emerald eyes sharp.

"No," Eric rumbled.

Caleb scoffed, "What did you say?"

"You heard me. I said, *no*."

Fury crackled beneath Eric's skin, shaking his every limb as he eyed the human with a lethal glare.

He had dreaded since he fell for Emilia because he knew exactly what these people were capable of. It was both comical and astounding how right he had been. It was why he lied back then, and it was why he pushed Emilia away now. Perhaps he thought that, by doing so, they could've been safe. Perhaps if he played the system while simultaneously burying his feelings deep into the ground, it would all work out, but Michael Iovaneau didn't just want to bury them; he wanted them uprooted and destroyed.

[105]Of course, *of course*, this was *his* doing. Of course, he tried turning his brother against him. Of course, he had him tracked. Of course, he sent Caleb to finish the job. Because no matter how many years it's been, Michael was afraid of what Eric and James might become if he weren't there.

But Michael *wasn't* here.

"If you touch her, I'll kill you," he threatened.[106]

He heard the soft click of James' gun like he was preparing himself for what was to come. Eric twirled his sword tauntingly, the blade catching Caleb's eye for a brief second.

"What are you gonna do, *Walker*? You already have one foot in the grave. Stop playing with fire."

---

[105] What It Cost - Bad Omens
[106] A Match Into Water - Pierce The Veil

Everything suddenly came into focus. This world was never meant for someone like him, not the one The Colectiv made. He knew that since he was a child, yet he tried forcing himself to believe that he could exist in a place that put him through hell. It was a hell that threatened to kill him from the inside out. It did the same to his parents, and it was doing the same to him and his brother. And now... it threatened to take the last person he cared about most.

"It's MacNamara," Eric corrected him, "and I'm taking matters into my own hands."

Without another ounce of hesitation, he lunged at Caleb with his sword. With fast reflexes, the other man raised his blade and parried it with a metal clang just in time. Gasps echoed all around the room.

"E!"

"Eric!"

Their cries fell on deaf ears as Eric entered a sword fight with Michael's second lieutenant. Caleb was good and he was strong. He was the best of The Colectiv's humans, after all, but Eric was a daywalker—a daywalker with a lot of rage and excellent sword-fighting skills.

He shouted, "Emilia, get out of here!"

"No, not without you!"

He kicked Caleb square in the chest, sending him flying backward.

Eric groaned low in his throat and looked over his shoulder at her. "Emilia, *go!*"

In the short moment that he was distracted, Caleb recovered, took out his pistol, and immediately aimed it right at her. With a sharp inhale, Eric barreled towards him, but by the time he knocked him down, the gun was already fired. They fell into a tangle of bodies, struggling until Jaya screamed.

"Emilia!"

Eric rolled away from Caleb and looked up. To his horror, Emilia was unconscious on the floor with Jaya cradling her bloody head. She wasn't dead, but seeing her like that was enough for Eric to lose his mind.

He glared at Caleb, who pointed his gun at him next. Eric dodged, but the gunshot that followed came from somewhere else, and the bullet shot right through Caleb's hand. He cried out, and the gun clattered to his feet. Another bullet was fired, and it lodged itself into his shoulder.

They snapped their attention towards James, who had a scowl and a smoking gun raised. Caleb tried lunging toward him with his sword, but Eric jumped in his way and parried him once again. They glared at each other from across the blades as Eric's eyes glowed like two fiery suns.

The second lieutenant looked down at him, and at someone who wasn't present, he said, "On my order."

"There's not gonna be an order," Eric hissed.

Something possessed Eric MacNamara, and from that point forward, everything happened in slow motion. He pushed Caleb's sword to the side, drew his blade back, and with a resounding cry, drove it forward, piercing it right through him. The hunter's bones cracked as the sharp metal ripped through his body, and he choked out a strangled gasp. Then, with all his strength, Eric pulled the sword back out with a yell, and Caleb fell to the floor. His weapon clattered out of his hand, his heart no longer beating.

[107]Eric stood motionless for a long time afterward, still clutching the sword. Blood covered his face and hands. His breathing was ragged, and an unsettling numbness seeped into his bones. He was like he was

---

[107] Wonderland - The Word Alive

underwater again, deep in the abyss, and not entirely present. There was noise in the background and panicked voices, but they sounded far away. Heavy footsteps approached him. He felt a hand on his shoulder and then...

"E! E, look at me!"

Eric's gaze trailed up to meet James' eyes at the sound of his muffled voice. They were wide and full of terror. He had never seen him so scared. Eric said nothing.

"E, we need to get out of here," James implored. "You need to take Emilia and go as far away as you can. Caleb's army is outside, and I'm sure they've realized by now what's happened. I barricaded the door, but they're bound to get in. I don't know how many there are, but I think I can hold them off."

That snapped Eric back to reality, the sound suddenly rushing back.

"Hold them off? What about you? Aren't you coming with me?" he asked, shaking his head.

"No. Not right now. Not if you want her to survive, and not if you want to lessen the chances of the two of us getting captured. Never mind Charybdis, E, you'll both die."

Eric's expression went grim as he glanced at Caleb's dead body. "I'm—I'm sorry, Jimmy. I just... I never wanted to drag you into this. I don't know what happened. I didn't... I didn't mean to—"

"Hey, listen to me." James grabbed both his shoulders and looked at him fondly. "That was the coolest, craziest shit I've ever seen. If anyone should be sorry, it's me. I fucked up, E. I didn't want to lie to you, but... he was right. I choked. I couldn't go through with it."

"You didn't choke," Eric told him. "You did the right thing."

James' eyes softened. "Yeah, but I have a lot to make up for. I know what I have to do."

"Jimmy, don't say that... I can't just leave you here. I'm not gonna let you do this alone!"

[108]"You have to!" his brother shouted. "He gets us both, then he gets all of us. Me, you, Emilia, and dad. I know how his mind works, E. He can't win the game if he doesn't have all the pieces. It's better if you run right now. We can regroup and meet back at Jaya's place. But if I'm not there before the sun rises, you fucking go. You hear me?"

Eric clenched his jaw, fighting back tears. He was right. Even if it tore him apart, he knew he was.

"Fine...okay."

James gave him a sad smile. "I said I'd follow you into the depths of hell, you asshole. This is it. Now go! That's an order!"

Eric instantly snapped into action. He put away his sword and ran over to Emilia, briefly locking eyes with Jaya before hoisting Emilia into his arms. The sight of her made his heart constrict in a painful twist. There was blood running down the side of her face and even if she was still alive, it filled him with guilt and shame.

I'm sorry, he thought for the millionth time.

Never again.

Eric could hear the hunters outside trying to break down the door. He looked around and realized that someone was missing.

"Where's Dante?"

"He fled a while ago, while the two of you were fighting," Jaya said.

"The bastard probably ran. Figures."

He doesn't matter now.

Despite how much his need for revenge had consumed him for years, it suddenly became irrelevant.

---

[108] Tangled In The Great Escape - Pierce The Veil (ft. Jason Butler)

There were gunshots and then glass breaking. Eric shielded his and Emilia's faces as fragments rained down, and when he looked over his shoulder, hunters were coming down from ropes.

"Shit," he cursed.

James went to Jaya and said, "Get them out of here."

"What about you? What are you gonna do?" she exclaimed as they started to move.

He took out his sword, twirled it, and said, "Getting my revenge."

With his gun in the other hand, James kicked over a barrel of fire. The flames spilled out and started eating away at everything they touched. Without another word, he went into the crossfire. Eric had no chance to process when shots started firing from every direction and Jaya forcefully tugged him away from the fray.

"Come on, I know another way out!"

They went towards the stage, to the back, through a small labyrinth, until they reached a door that led outside. Eric followed Jaya around the many abandoned buildings on the lot with Emilia in his arms. His sword clattered against his back, sweat beating down his face. Eventually, Jaya pointed towards the edge of a high fence.

"The road's just up there, and so is my car," she whispered.

She stepped into the moonlight, and he followed her towards it, but they suddenly heard footsteps and then,

"Hey!"

"Go, go, go!"

There was gunfire, and bullets flew by them. They dodged what they could, but as they reached the chain link, one of them lodged itself in Eric's shoulder blade. He groaned and stumbled, almost dropping Emilia as stars filled his vision, but managed to regain himself.

"Are you okay?" Jaya asked.

"Yeah, I'll be fine," he answered through gritted teeth.

At a glance, the fence looked like a dreadful climb for his situation, until Jaya lifted a piece of it, revealing a hole big enough to crouch through. She ushered him on, and Eric managed to squeeze himself and Emilia through. When he was on the other side, he eyed the hunter, who had another one following closely behind.

"Come on, Jaya, let's go!" Eric shouted.

She gave him a grim look and shook her head. "They'll just catch up. I'll buy you some time. Here."

Jaya threw her car keys through the hole, and Eric managed to catch them in one hand. He looked down at them and then at her in bewilderment.

"What? Are you joking?"

"Eric, take them and go!" she scolded.

Eric slowly backed away from the fence, watching as she rushed both hunters with her bare hands. He turned away, resisting the urge to charge back in there as weapons were fired. Jaya's cries followed. At that moment, he did as he was told and used his remaining stamina to sprint off down the street.

†††

Eric's body shook with adrenaline, and his hands were still covered in blood. He chose to take a detour through some winding hills, and at the very least nobody seemed to be following him.

He cast a glance at the rearview mirror to see Emilia still unconscious in the backseat. Until he took the silver bullets out of her wounds, she wouldn't be able to heal properly enough to wake up, which is why he needed to get her back to Jaya's as soon as possible. That's where his brother told him to meet him, and that's where he would go.

In the middle of his drive, the sound of Eric's phone going off nearly made him jump out of his skin. He fished it out of his duffle bag with one hand, his heart beating with anticipation. For a moment, he thought it would be James calling to tell him that he had made it out alive, but to his sheer disappointment, it was not.

As soon as he saw it was *him*, Eric pulled the car off the empty road and parked on the shoulder before answering the call.

"You," he bit out.

"E, where the hell are you?" Michael demanded.

"Like I'd fucking tell you after everything."

"E, they told me what you did. There's no denying it. They heard everything, and they saw you running away from the scene. You did some irreversible damage, kid. You took a man's life, one of our own. If you keep running, I won't be able to pull you out of this one."

Eric scoffed, "And if I let you, then what, huh? At best, you'll put me in a cell. At worst, I'll lose my head, and to be honest, I think the latter is better considering the first one wouldn't be any different from living with you."

Michael went deathly quiet for a moment but maintained calm when he said, "E, you need to take it easy. I warned you about this."

"No, I don't think I will," Eric snapped, and then suddenly, he was shouting. "I never wanted any of this! I never wanted to be like you![109] I *told you* time and time again, but you never listened. You told me this was the only way, and for a second I believed you...just like when we were kids. But now I know that you're just a lying piece of shit."

The commander sighed, "Is this about the deal I made with Jimmy?"

---

[109] Numb - Linkin Park

"Yeah, there's that, and there's also our father. Wade," the daywalker growled. "He's alive, isn't he? You had him locked up this whole time?"

Even now, he was still in disbelief. The commander evaded the question.

"Who told you that?" he asked.

"Ironically enough, Dante did. He gave more to me in five minutes than you did in 14 years. I've learned more about Wade in the last *two weeks* than I ever did from you."

"E, you forget that Dante is a psychopath—a killer. You know what he did, right? What he and that girl you care about so much did?"

So, it seemed that plenty of people in The Colectiv did know the identity of "The Hellhound," and Michael was at the top of the list.

"Don't bring her into this," Eric hissed.

"She's a wanted criminal, which means you're aiding and abetting her cause."

"There are plenty of vampires and humans who have killed just as many, if not more, people than her - people who kill innocents. You don't go around hunting all of *them*."

"But we sure do try."

"How long have you known that it was her? Because if Caleb was ready to kill her for it, and you sent Jimmy after her..."

The commander huffed. "I've known since Italy, E."

"Italy?" Eric exclaimed.

"Yeah. When you told Jimmy the story about what happened— about your girlfriend and her brother... I knew it had to be them. Down to the descriptions you gave."

"Three years," the boy whispered in shock, connecting the dots as he stared out the windshield. "You knew I was going after Dante. Was it just part of your plan? To get me back to The Colectiv and use me to track both of them down?"

"I didn't 'use' you, E," Michael contested.

"You took advantage, then. It doesn't matter what words you choose, because it's still the same."

The commander groaned, "Yes, I may have taken advantage, but only because I believed that you would go through with it. I thought you were finally being the hunter I knew you to be and that you'd take him out just like you said."

"What changed your mind? Because sending Caleb after us isn't really a sign of good faith, is it? Was it the breach?"

"You know, I never doubted your hatred for Dante. I was worried about your feelings for the girl," Michael explained. "I knew it was inevitable that you'd see her again, and I was worried that, when it came down to it, you wouldn't be able to take her out. I figured, 'Why not kill two birds with one stone by having Jimmy deal with her?' He was tagging along anyway. But then...well..."

He made a noise of disappointment, which angered Eric more.

"So that's why you ordered Jimmy to kill her? Her head in exchange for a promotion? Is that your sick and twisted way of making sure you have us both in line?"

If James had gone through with it, Michael would have had an obedient and ruthless captain, and if Eric killed Dante and no longer had Emilia in the picture, then he'd have nothing to distract him from rising himself.

"I ordered him to do his *job*, and you both lied to my goddamn face. I thought we had an agreement to communicate, and you *lied*," Michael snapped. "But when Jimmy started clamming up, I knew something was wrong. After the breach, I sent Caleb to California until I knew what was going on. Then Jimmy slipped up the last time

I called him, and I knew exactly where you two were. Crimson Beach has been pretty quiet for decades, and I knew it couldn't be a coincidence that you'd be there. I directed Caleb in that direction, and he spotted you chasing after that girl—the girl Jimmy said he had dealt with already. Before I knew it, Caleb was dead... by *your* blade."

The memory of it all made Eric's blood boil all over again.

"He deserved it," he muttered.

"You murdered him, E."

"I've murdered plenty of people for you before. It's what you *taught* me to do. What difference does it make?"

"The difference is that Caleb was part of The Colectiv! Part of your family!" Michael shouted.

"Family?" Eric bellowed incredulously. He had to resist the urge to laugh. "Not once has anyone in that shithole ever felt like family to me. All those people ever did was make me feel worthless—like a freak—and you were no different. I was never good enough for you, but you just couldn't let up, could you? Even now, you have to be right. Jimmy and I were just your little science experiments. You told us we were supposed to be *heroes*, so tell me...why the *fuck* do I feel like the villain?"[110]

"E—"

Eric didn't let him interrupt his long-overdue, explosive tirade.

"Family doesn't put each other through what you put me through. Do you know why I hid in that library? To get away from you. Do you know why I left Romania? It was to get away from *you*! All of you! Caleb was never my family. *Anya* was family. Jimmy is family, and I know because, despite everything, he turned his back on you too. And Wade..."

---

[110] Like A Villain - Bad Omens

Eric choked on the name and had to stop. He wiped away a tear before gathering himself to repeat the one question that Michael refused to answer.

"*Did you put him in Charybdis, yes or no?*"

The commander hesitated before finally replying, "Yes...I did."

"Why did you lie?" Eric demanded in frustration.

"To protect you," Michael argued.

"From what?"

"From him!"

"Why? Because from what I've learned, he's not dangerous. If anything, you just wanted to keep us from going off and finding him. That's the other reason you sent Caleb, right? You have no fucking idea where he is."

Eric could almost feel Michael's cold anger through the phone. It was in the silence where it was most palpable. He had never known his mentor to be at such a loss for words, but it seemed that Eric managed to back him into a corner, and he refused to let up. He was done keeping his mouth shut.

"Do you know why he killed Gabriel? Do you know what he did to our mom? Or are you going to cover that up too?" he spat.

That was enough to set Michael off, and any ounce of professional fatherliness left him.

"Listen here, you little shit. Let me honor you with a piece of truth since you love it so much, because here's something the rest of The Colectiv won't say. My brother? Yeah, he was a piece of shit. He was a fucking idiot, and I'm glad he's dead. But that still doesn't change what Wade did," he hissed.

There he is.

Eric raised his eyebrows in surprise. There was something in Michael's voice that told him there was something deeper to this story than he was letting on.

"What was that about making things personal?"

Michael's chuckle rumbled through the speaker. "E, I don't know where you are, but Jimmy is getting dragged back to Romania as we speak."

Eric's expression fell. "What?"

"He did a lot more damage than you did, but they managed to take him out, and now there's a cell waiting for him when he arrives."

Eric closed his eyes and bared his teeth in anguish.

We were supposed to meet back at Jaya's. He was supposed to make it out. I should've stayed back with him.

"The Black Sea?" He whispered.

"Not yet."

Though he was happy that his brother wasn't dead, the thought of him in chains was an image that made him lose his mind. There were worse things than death, and he had a feeling James was in for hell.

"You fucking bastard. If you touch him—"

"Easy, I don't plan on killing him if that's what you're getting at. I won't have to, not if you get your ass back here and turn that girl in. Bonus points if you can find her brother."

"You're threatening Jimmy's life for this?" Eric whispered in disbelief. "You know I've always hated you, but Jimmy looked up to you, you know. He almost took that fucking deal for you. You're a real piece of shit."

"I am well past needing to be liked, E. You don't get to where I am without making some tough choices. I'm sure he'll see that eventually."

"Bullshit. They're still shitty choices that you made. You might be at the top, but I know what you are."

Michael whistled lowly. Again, Eric could almost feel that dangerous, steel-like anger from afar.

"I'm sending the hounds after you. Let's see what *you* decide before they catch up."

Without another word, the commander hung up, leaving Eric in silence. With a shuddering breath, he let the phone drop into his lap. He gripped the steering wheel with both hands and looked out at the road for a few seconds in total numbness. Then, unable to contain himself any longer, Eric inhaled before letting out a long, feral scream. He screamed and screamed until his voice gave out, and he couldn't anymore. It took everything in him not to break the car apart.[111]

When he was done, Eric got out of the vehicle, taking his phone with him. He went to the edge of a downhill slope leading to a patch of trees below and crushed the phone with his bare hand until the screen cracked and went black. The glass cut into his skin, drawing blood. He threw the shattered pieces down the hill, went back to the car, and proceeded to drive off to safety.

---

[111] Your Blood - Nothing But Thieves

44

The World on Fire

Emilia

"If you touch her, I'll kill you."

That's what Eric had said.

It was so quick to come out of his mouth. It wasn't even a question. Then, all of a sudden, he was mercilessly attacking the other hunter with his sword. It was like something out of a movie, and Emilia would've admired it if she wasn't so terrified for him.

He told her to go. She wanted to stay. And the last thing she remembered was the sound of a gunshot.

It repeated in the back of Emilia's mind—Eric shouting and the gun firing—and the sound jolted her awake. Her eyes snapped open, and she fell into a coughing fit, forcing her to sit up. A headache pounded on the side of her skull—an uncomfortable, familiar sensation. As she came to full consciousness, she noticed the room she was in was quiet and devoid of light. She was on something soft, like a warm bed, but it juxtaposed with the stickiness on her skin and the smell of blood and metal tickling her nose. She wasn't in Hollydale anymore; that much was clear.

She recalled the final scene she witnessed before blacking out.

That bastard shot me.

She gasped. *Eric.*

Emilia fell into a panic when, suddenly, there was a sound by the bed. Her attention snapped in that direction, her vision swimming as she still recovered.

"Who's there?"

There was a slow, steady heartbeat coming from a dark figure, and she recognized who it was before he even spoke.

"It's just me," Eric whispered. His voice sounded broken.

Emilia reached for the lamp on the nightstand and turned it on, setting the room alight (they were in Jaya's house, based on the wallpaper). Her eyes briefly caught on a hand towel on the stand with four silver bullets covered in blood next to a pair of pliers. Two were from when James shot her, the third was from Caleb, and the fourth she didn't know. But it seemed Eric had taken them out himself. When she glanced over and got a good look at him, her breath caught in her throat.

Eric looked about as broken as he sounded. He sat slouched in a chair by the bed and was holding his sword with the tip pointing down into the carpet. The silver eclipse glistened on the crossbar, and blood muddied the handle. In fact, there was blood everywhere—on his hands, his clothes, and his face too. She could've sworn he hadn't looked that way before.

Something terrible has happened. She could see it in his eyes.

Emilia crawled to the edge of the bed, eyes wide, as she spoke softly, "Eric... Eric, what happened?"

He stayed silent, simply staring off with an empty expression. Streaks of tears cut through the blood splatter on his cheeks.

"Eric?" she repeated a little louder.

His eyes connected with hers, but they were devoid of light. His lack of an answer struck a deep fear in her. Emilia sat at the edge of the bed, facing him fully. She reached out and took his hand in both of hers, willing him to speak.

"Baby, please," she pleaded. The pet name seemed to pull him out of his tormented mind so he could look her in the eyes. "You're scaring me. What happened? Where's James? Where's Jaya? What happened to that hunter? Did you...did you—"

"I killed him," he admitted.

Emilia craned her head back. "Killed...killed who? Caleb?"

"Yes."

"W... Why?"

"He was gonna kill you. There wasn't a doubt in my mind. And when he shot you, I just..." Eric sighed and worked his jaw as the memory passed over him. "I lost it. I put my sword through him like it was nothing."

Her lips fell open in disbelief. She squeezed Eric's hand, and he squeezed right back as he bore his hazel eyes into her own. Despite his anguish, there was also a softness when he looked at her.

"What does that say about me?" he asked.

She shrugged. "It depends on why you did it."

"To save you," he answered immediately.[112]

Emilia's brow furrowed, and tears stung in her eyes. She shook her head at him.

"You didn't have to do that," she whispered.

"Yes, I did."

"You killed one of your people for *me*?"

"I had to," he repeated more sternly.

---

[112] Demolition Lovers - My Chemical Romance

"No, Eric!" she cried, jumping to her feet. "What does this mean for you? You said your fate was chosen. You told me—"

"I told you that I couldn't let you get hurt," he blurted out. Then he said softly, "I made a promise. I just thought I was protecting you by shutting you out. I thought it would keep something like this from happening by killing Dante, but...it didn't."

Emilia straightened up at the mention of her brother. He hadn't even crossed her mind this entire time, despite how far she traveled to save him. He disappeared from the asylum before she had a chance to stop him.

"Do you know where he is?" she asked.

"No, he ran off."

Emilia rolled her eyes. "Of course he did."

Dante could've died in a ditch somewhere, been caught by a hunter, or even gotten out Scott-free. Regardless, she wouldn't know, but for once, she truly didn't care. It was freeing.

"What about James?"

The last thing she remembered was their heated argument over the fact that James was sent to kill her and Eric knew nothing about it. Considering how close they were, she didn't think they could fight in such a way, and it pained her to watch it unfold.

To her dismay, Eric looked away, pulling away from her touch. Emilia frowned as she noticed his eyes began to water.

"He stayed behind to fend them off," he said. "We were supposed to meet back here, but then... he got captured. Jaya too."

Emilia gasped, her hands flying to her mouth.

"James MacNamara choked," the hunter had said. If by "choking," he meant choosing his love for his brother over an order. Emilia and James didn't see eye to eye, but she respected him and knew there was a heart underneath that tough exterior.

"No," she whimpered. "They're—they're not dead, are they?"

"Jaya, I don't know. Jimmy's still alive. Michael won't kill him because he can use him as leverage."

"Leverage for what?"

"To get me back. To get you," he said, giving her a serious look.

"Me?" she blurted out.

"Yeah, he knows who you are. You *and* Dante. That's why Caleb tried to kill you. It's why he ordered Jimmy to kill you too. If I turn you in, then, maybe, *maybe*, he'll set him free."

Realizing the gravity of the situation, Emilia shook her head frantically and took Eric's face in her hands. Red tears flooded the edges of her vision and she spoke with urgency.

"Eric, listen to me. Just turn me in. Get James back. F-find Wade. I'm the reason you're in this mess, and I can't—I can't let this happen to you because of me. Don't make this any harder on yourself."

Eric scoffed, "What? No."

"What?"

"No," he repeated firmly.

She rested her hands on his shoulders. "Don't you want your brother back?"

"It doesn't work that way, Em," he stressed. "I turn you in, Jimmy doesn't die, and what then? I go back to The Colectiv again? We're supposed to live like nothing happened and let them cover it up? That's not gonna happen. *They're* not gonna let that happen. Not with my dad out there now, apparently. It's not gonna *free* us. It's going to tighten our chains and make things worse than they already are. The cat's out of the fucking bag. It's too late for that. And turning you in would mean that it was all for nothing. Jimmy sacrificing himself would be for *nothing*."

Despite the fury in his voice, Eric gazed at Emilia tenderly as he brushed his fingers against her cheek.

"It's not your fault. I don't blame you for anything. This was bound to happen with or without you," he said. "From the moment I was born or even before, I don't know. But I already made my choice, and I'm not going to take it back. I can't. I'm not just doing this for you. I'm doing this for me. For Jimmy. For my mom. I'm not playing Michael's games anymore. I've broken my back doing things for him for half of my life, only for him to fuck me over. I'm done."

Emilia rested her hand over his. It was hard not to take the blame for what transpired, but she resonated with his words all too well, even if the context was different. She admired his resilience and determination—*loved it*—even if she wished it wasn't necessary. Even if she wished she could fix it all.

"So...what are we gonna do?"

A small smirk pulled at his lips as he said, "We run. For now."

Emilia nodded. It was the only answer now.

"I know a thing or two about that."

"Me too."

"Together?" she asked apprehensively.

"*Together*...unless you've got some other place to be."

A giggle bubbled in Emilia's throat. "After today, I don't think you're getting rid of me anytime soon."

Eric's smile deepened. He took her hand and kissed the back of it. "Good."

Despite the terror and the dread, there was a sense of safety in knowing that Emilia would be with Eric and that he would be with her. A good companion was a rare thing to find, she knew. After all, she had done plenty of running in her life.

They stared at each other for a long time in silence, though she was sure his thoughts were racing as much as hers. Eric's breathing faltered. He looked like he was mulling over something.

"There's still one more secret I need to tell you before we go," he said suddenly.

Emilia frowned, feeling uneasy all of a sudden. "Oh God. What is it?"

"Nothing horrible, but..." Eric hesitated before telling her, "I lied to you back in New York, during the interrogation."

She snorted. "Which time?"

From what she recalled, a lot of words were exchanged.

"When you asked if I knew you were a vampire, I told you that I didn't, but that was a lie. I did know you were a vampire, and I didn't tell you," he admitted. "It wasn't because of some sick ploy, I just... I knew the whole time, and I was too scared to say anything."

Emilia's expression dropped. "What? Why didn't you tell me?"

"I lied back then to protect myself and you. I lied the other day because I didn't want you to know why I stayed."

"And why did you stay?"

"Because I fell in love with you," he said simply.[113]

Emilia's dead heart swelled, not just because of the words but because of how quick he was with his response. It was the fastest he had ever admitted to something this whole time. No hesitation and no sarcasm. She didn't even have to say it first.

"I still do," Eric continued in a broken yet gentle voice. The whole time, he looked at her with those lovesick eyes. "I still love you, Emilia. I never would've turned you in."

Suddenly, she was transported to a different time on a beach on the other side of the world—a little bubble that she shared with a sweet boy she loved. She held back a lot then, but she had no need now. She allowed herself to be overwhelmed with love and devotion.

"I love you too," she said in a small, wavering voice.

---

[113] Let Me Be The One - Elias

With a shaky breath, she threw herself into his arms. He accepted her embrace, letting her curl into his lap as the sword clattered out of his hand onto the floor. He wrapped his arms around her and held on tight as if he were afraid to let go, and she did the same. Emilia closed her eyes, focusing on his warmth, his breathing, and the sound of his still-beating heart. Then, after a few moments, Eric's shoulders shook as he proceeded to cry. Emilia hugged him tighter and held his face against her chest as he proceeded to mourn his life.[114]

---

[114] Goodbye - Ramsey

Epilogue

Wade

Crimson Beach, CA—48 hours later

The sun dipped low on the horizon, painting Wade's skin in gold as he looked up at the familiar Spanish-style house, duffle bag in hand. It's been decades since he stepped foot in this city, let alone this driveway—since before the boys were even born and before he met Anya. It was Emilia's secret home away from Hollydale and was later handed down to Jaya. Wade came upon it by chance. He didn't visit frequently, but he knew it was a safe house from prying eyes, which was what he needed.

He walked the path to the front door and knocked three times. At this time of day, he expected Jaya to be home, so he awaited a response or any sign of life, but to his dismay, there was nothing.

Wade frowned and knocked again, this time saying, "Jaya? It's me... Wade."

He risked name-dropping, knowing that there was probably no one else of importance around and hoping that it would make her more inclined to answer. However, again, there was nothing. No footsteps, no voices, nothing. He rang the doorbell. Nothing. It wasn't like her to not answer. It made him wonder if she still lived here at all.

No... Jean said she was here. He said Emilia was heading this way.

Wade looked around the potted plants and searched under the mat until he found a spare key. It was a wild guess, but he was right. He used it to unlock the door and pushed it open, but lingered in the doorway hesitantly. He hadn't sensed anyone around, but he could never be too careful.

He called out again, "Jaya?"

Silence.

He walked inside, put his bag down, and closed the door behind him. The house was dark and quiet, but he could tell someone had been there before. It smelled like jasmine, coconuts, and coffee, but beyond that, he also smelled blood, gunpowder, and cologne.

Oh, no...

He crouched down and reached into his duffle. From it, he took out a golden 1911 pistol—something he had specially made. He pulled back the chamber and inspected every inch of the house for his friend or any potential threat.[115]

At a glance, nothing seemed *too* out of the ordinary. Dishes were in the sink, and the coffee maker had been used within the last day or so...but blood bags were missing from the fridge—all *of them*. And when he checked the garage, it was empty.

What the fuck? Didn't I leave my bike here?

Jaya's car was missing too, and based on the state of the house, whoever took them left recently.

Wade proceeded upstairs, where there were more obvious signs of something having gone awry. The alarm on his face only worsened.

---

[115] Hayloft - Mother Mother

There were traces of blood on one of the guest beds, on an armchair, and even on the floor. In the bathroom trash, there was a dirty towel with four silver bullets and some pliers left on the sink. Closets and drawers had been rifled through, but the last thing he found, which gave him a clear answer, was in the laundry basket in the main bedroom.

Inside was a pile of bloody clothes. Wade reached in, and the first thing he took out was a leather jacket, but it wasn't just any jacket. It was the kind that hunters wore, with a lining on the inside to differentiate themselves, and this one had a pattern of wolves.

Wade gripped it firmly as the answer dawned on him.

The boys. At least one of the boys was here. Emilia too, most likely.
And for some reason...they had to run.[116]

---

[116] Blood (End Credits) - My Chemical Romance

Acknowledgments

I created Eric and James when I was in middle school, which were some of the worst years of my life. At the time, I was in the thick of being obsessed with Supernatural, Twilight, and a book called The Summoning by Kelley Armstrong. All three of those pieces of media altered my brain chemistry and inspired me to write something similar. Of course, being 12/13, I basically copied the tropes and plot, while somehow melding them into something my teenage brain didn't quite understand the depth of. For years, I found myself starting and stopping the twins' story, until about 2020, in the middle of the pandemic, I had an epiphany while watching the 1987 film, The Lost Boys. Again, it was the start of some of the worst years of my—and many others'—life. From there to the summer of 2022, with the help of intense therapy, I was able to finally understand the depth of my characters and finished the first true draft of Daywalkers. It's deeply personal and went through so many drafts and hands before landing here, but I'm glad I finally made it.

I don't really know how acknowledgement pages go, so I'm going to use this as a glorified dedication page.

To start, I'd like to thank my very first therapist, who not only helped me deal with my life but who helped me understand these characters by helping me understand myself first.

I'd like to thank my little brother, Ollie, who has always been my biggest supporter no matter what, even when I burst into his room to ramble about my insane ideas. And my mom for always supporting my art, no matter how dark it is.

To Maria Alcantara, the first and only literary agent who truly believed in Daywalkers from the beginning. Even though the universe turned our lives upside down and things didn't work out the way we wanted, you stuck by my side as a friend, and I am forever grateful.

Without you, I wouldn't have had the guts to self-publish on my own.

To my friends and anyone who had a chance to read Daywalkers before it was published – thank you! Sam, thank you for telling me that Eric was annoying in that very first draft. It only made me work to make him hotter and cooler. I can't believe you're all still here.

To the girlies who read my fanfiction and loved it so much that it made me want to write original content! And to the ones who write fanfiction who are too scared to write original content: do it!!

I'd also like to acknowledge the writers and storytellers who have inspired me and continue to inspire me to this day: Hayao Miyazaki, Guillermo Del Toro, Victoria Aveyard and Suzanne Collins. You make me unafraid of the stories I want to tell and to go in the direction my heart leads me.

Lastly, I'd like to thank myself. Somehow, we're still alive, by sheer force of will.

I love you all,
Emilia

Turn the page for a sneak peek of the next installment of the

SONS OF THE ECLIPSE DUOLOGY

BY EMILIA MONDRAGON

1
The World in Ashes

Ireland—20 years ago

He had been deep in his slumber when the creaking of the bedroom door awakened him. There was the sound of whispered shushing intermingled with small and quick heartbeats, and one slow but steady. The smell of chocolate and sea salt hit Wade's nose. He bit back a smile but stayed stock still, listening intently as two bodies shuffled closer to the bed. Tiny voices counted down, but before they could finish, Wade sprang up with a playful roar, beating them at their own game.

The two little boys screamed before falling into a fit of giggles. Wade grabbed the nearest toddler—Eric—and pulled him into his arms to plant kisses all over his face.

"Dad!" he squealed.

By the door, there was soft laughter, like a beautiful song.

"We were trying to scare you!" James exclaimed.

Wade looked over at the other boy, who seemed mildly disappointed and couldn't help but chuckle.

"I know, but you gotta be sneakier than that. C'mere you little devil."

James threw himself onto the bed, and Wade held the twins in each arm, giving them kisses until they squirmed their way free.

The twins' hair was getting longer with each passing day, their curls twisting at the ends. They were still quite small and had many years to grow into their features, yet Wade and Anya couldn't help but frequently comment on who they looked like. They had her eyes, but they had his brows. When they smiled they looked more like her, but they had his judgmental gaze that Anya found hilarious. In the end, they were still hard to tell apart, which is why Anya made them bracelets out of string with their initials on them.

What they looked like didn't truly matter because it was their personalities that kept them on their toes. Every day was something new to learn and explore about these little humans that they brought into the world. Even Wade, an old man twice over, was relearning everything he ever knew and seeing the world with fresh eyes. It had been over a century since he felt anything close, and in a way, that was also why their innocence and wonder both frightened and emboldened him.

"Mommy says it's time to wake up," Eric said.

"Did she?"

Wade then turned his attention towards the door, where his wife leaned against the frame with her arms crossed and a smile on her face. She was dressed casually for the summer, with her dark, curly hair held up in a clip, some of it falling against her face. Her hazel eyes were like a warm fire enveloping them with her love.

"It's sunset, Mr. MacNamara, and the boys are very eager to spend time with you."

"I wanted to show you a cool rock I found!" James blurted out.

"And I got books about trains at the library!" Eric said.

They were at that age where they had strong, coherent thoughts but were still learning how to properly string sentences together, which was both surprising and amusing. Wade and Anya spent half of the time deciphering what they were saying like a puzzle.

"And I would love nothing more than to see everything you've collected, but before all of that...don't you think mommy should join us here in bed for a cuddle?" Wade asked with a smirk.

He gave Anya a sidelong glance, and she narrowed her eyes at him as the boys pleaded for her to join them.

"How could I ever say no to my boys?" she asked.

The twins cheered as Anya lay down beside them. Wade put his arm around her and looked into her eyes, taking in her entrancing before kissing her. It filled him with a fire that was more invigorating than coffee or liquor.

"Good evening, Mrs. MacNamara," he said with an exaggerated Transylvanian accent.

Anya snorted, but returned in kind, "Good evening."

Eric and James, however, made noises of disgust and proceeded to wedge themselves in between their two parents, with one twin against Anya's chest and the other against Wade's. They both giggled, holding their children tight as they looked at each other from across the bed.

This was how most nights started in the MacNamara household. While being a vampire made things a little less conventional, Wade and Anya managed to establish a dynamic and schedule that worked well for everyone. She made sure that the kids had their breakfast and sunshine while the sun was out until sunset came and the boys yanked Wade out of bed for the evening to take his "shift." In between that, they soaked up every single second of the time they had together, even if it meant losing a few winks of sleep on either side. It was the happiest Wade had ever been in his life. His heart hadn't felt so full – *overflown* – with love and happiness in over a century. It filled the cracks within him like gold to porcelain to have his wife and children here in his arms day in and day out.

"Did you sleep okay?" she asked.

"I did. Did you have a good day with the boys?"

"We went to the library!" Eric chipped in.

"We went to the library," Anya reiterated with a nod. "We also went to the park and got some ice cream. After that, we went to the post office."

Wade's face lit up. "Did anything come in? Did Johnny send anything?"

"He did. He sent another care package. More books and some toy swords that light up and make noise."

Wade rolled his eyes. "Greaaaat. That won't be a headache at all."

"We were being pirates, Dad! You should be a pirate too!" James said.

"It would be my dream, Jimmy boy," Wade answered with a grin, kissing him on the head.

When he turned back to his wife, her expression suddenly darkened, and her heart began to stutter. She looked between his eyes warily, as if she had something to say. He furrowed his brow as alarm bells went off in his mind.

He stroked her cheek gently. "What is it, love?"

"Wade…" The use of his name in such a serious tone put him on edge.

He sat up on his elbow. "What? What is it?"

"A letter came in the mail," she told him. "It was addressed to you."

"From who?"

"I haven't opened it yet, and it doesn't say on the envelope… but it's addressed to *you*. Your full, legal name."

They had only been using code names for the last few years. All of their close friends and family knew that.

As the boys played among themselves, Anya's eyes began to water, and Wade's heart sank into his stomach. It could only mean one thing.

"Wade, I think I know whose handwriting it is," she whispered. "I think he found us."

†††

Crimson Beach, CA—Present

Wade walked down the damp and dark tunnels running beneath Crimson Beach with a sword strapped to his back. It was a familiar tunnel, one he had used many times before when he lived in the city, but only one of many he had used in his lifetime. Being a vampire meant living a life in secrecy, and secret tunnels were simply one way of doing just that. The older the city, the more hidden corridors and passageways there were, but places with subway systems were a modern favorite. If worse came to worst, then the sewers were used, but that was for the more desperate.

He followed the train tracks, gravel crunching beneath his feet with the clatter of the approaching train not that far behind him. He continued until the tracks split off, and one of them ended by a hole in the wall just large enough for someone to fit through. Just as the screeching of the metal subway approached, Wade disappeared into the shadows. From there, he continued through another tunnel until he eventually came upon a door in the cement wall, which he was happy to find was unlocked. Inside was a small square room about two feet all around, with a metal ladder going up. Without hesitation, Wade made his ascent.

At the top was a circular manhole cover, however, just as he reached to open it, the sound of nearby voices made him freeze.

"No, we didn't find anything else. Looks like they cleared out pretty quick."

It was a feminine voice with an accent that sounded eastern European. The second voice, however, sounded far away, as if through a speaker.

"As I expected. E knows better than to stick around for very long. They're probably on the road as we speak."

Wade's eyes widened at the very recognizable voice of Commander Michael Iovaneau. He'd know it anywhere.

"We questioned the ones that were left over, but they were just lackeys. They didn't know anything about what was going on, so we took them out," the woman said.

"It's fine. We got what we need for now."

"With all due respect, sir, why are you keeping him alive? He killed our men, both him and his brother."

"Because Jimmy is valuable. He's the only one who can tell us where Eric and the Hellhound are. But if he doesn't talk... then I'm sure we can squeeze something out of Emilia's friend."

A sickening wave of dread washed over Wade at that moment. He had to resist the urge to scream and clenched his jaw so hard it was amazing his teeth didn't break. It took everything in him not to go up there and kill that hunter or to talk to Michael himself. Instead, he gripped the ladder until his knuckles turned white, the only way to keep himself from going underwater again.

Eric and Emilia were gone. James and Jaya were captured.

How?

"Fall back and regroup. I already put the word out that we have two vampires on the run. Wait for my call," Michael ordered.

"Yes, sir."

The hunter ended the call and walked off to speak to someone farther down, her boots echoing against the pavement. Wade listened intently at the top of the ladder until he heard them get into a car and drive away. He waited and waited until it was certain there was no one left, and then slowly, he lifted the manhole cover and pushed it aside. He poked his head out and took a sweeping look around. When he was sure there was nothing, he pulled himself out into the cool air of the winter's night and followed the labyrinthine pathways of Hollydale.

The entire lot was one of many homes to Wade, with each building like a ghost with their peeling walls, cracked windows, and cobwebs. It was by no means the prettiest place he had stayed in, but all things considered, it wasn't the worst. He'd slept anywhere from a cave in a desert to a palace in Spain, yet Hollydale held a lot more emotional weight than he expected. Especially now that he was in the face of it again. The 1970s were the best and worst of times for a lot of people, Wade included.

The further in he walked, the more signs of life he could sense—blood, roses, and... smoke.

As soon as the theater came into view, all memories and nostalgia were put to a halt, and Wade stopped dead in his tracks. Rather, what *remained* of the theater.

"Holy shit."

The familiar building that he once knew so well was now half burned to the ground and surrounded by caution tape.

"What did you do?" he asked aloud, as if his boys could hear him.

Wade approached the scorched building and its doors that were burned at the edges, the doorknob now half-melted. He carefully

stepped under the yellow tape and pushed inside to find a sad
representation of an old life.

It was the skeleton of the theater in which he had spent many
nights and years in a post-war world as a lost and empty man who
had forfeited all purpose. Time, people, places—they come and go.
As a vampire, he knew this all too well, but at his core, Wade was a
sentimental man. In fact, most immortals secretly were, they simply
hoarded pieces of history in their homes instead of dealing with
their emotions. As an orphan, such things were a little more
complicated to Wade, and he was more meticulous with what he
became attached to and stored away. Jean was better at doing that
for him, and so was Anya. Yet, as he stood before the remains of
the abandoned building, something deep inside of him couldn't help
but feel a tiny sliver of grief over it.

It was a scene of destruction.

Everything was covered in ash like the first snowfall in winter.
The ceiling was completely caved in, burying most of the seating
area in burnt wood, plaster, and glass. He could see what remained
of a few couches, pieces of charred tapestries on the remaining
walls, and the stage, which was now a blackened mess. It sent a chill
up Wade's spine, as it reminded him a little too much of war and the
fire that took his life.

If what he heard was right, then Eric and James had killed a few
members of The Colectiv before running (or trying). Why? He
didn't know. Although considering Emilia was involved, he had a
feeling he knew the reason a little too well.

Wade MacNamara felt no sympathy for the militarized band of
monster hunters, aside from the very few exceptions. After all, it
was because of them that he had his family ripped away and was
sentenced to death in an underwater prison. It was because of them
that he never got to say goodbye to his wife before her death and
knew little to nothing about the boys he loved with all of his soul.
Even so, he felt he knew enough—whether from experience or
Jean's own words—and if they set the world ablaze, there had to be

a reason. And if Michael Iovaneau was involved, then the culprit was clear. Whatever the case, guilty or not, Wade was intent on getting them back no matter what it took. Eric and Emilia were still out there, and he needed to find them first.

He explored the decay, tentative to watch his step as he looked for anything of significance in the remains, when all of a sudden, a flash of red caught his eye. Wade furrowed his brow, thinking it was a trick of the light until he saw a red glint in the debris once more. He crouched down and moved things aside only to find, at the bottom of it all, a ruby-encrusted rosary that he had seen decades ago.

No way.

Wade picked it up, the chain now broken, and stared down at it thoughtfully.

Wasn't E supposed to kill you?

The more he thought about it, the more he realized that the one person Michael and the hunter failed to mention was Dante. The Colectiv knew everyone else's whereabouts, whether they were captured, killed, or fled, but not him. And Dante was no lowly vampire with little to no reputation; no, he was a Hellhound just like his sister, which made him valuable. Michael made that very clear. So, if he was out of The Colectiv's clutches for now, then maybe, if Wade found him, he could be of some value to *him*.

"Where did you go, you fucker?" he whispered.

Wade straightened up, and with the cross in hand, he took out his phone to make a call.

"Wade?" Jean answered.

"Johnny, get your ass over here. We've got a situation on our hands."

About the Author

Emilia Mondragón a California-born daughter of Mexican immigrants. She is a disabled, bisexual goth girl with a love for fantasy and horror and has been writing stories for as long as she can remember. Emilia spent most of her adult life pursuing creative endeavors such as directing, screenwriting, acting, singing, and is a crafty person at heart. However, it was in late 2020, after watching The Lost Boys too many times, that she decided to write a story that eventually became her debut novel that you now known as, Daywalkers. You can find her on Instagram, TikTok, and Threads as emiliathevampire.